PRAISE FOR KATE MORETTI

The Vanishing Year

"A woman's perilous past and her affluent present converge in Kate Moretti's latest jaw-dropping thriller. Replete with unsavory characters, buried secrets, and a bounty of unexpected twists and turns, *The Vanishing Year* is a stunner. A perfectly compulsive read that's impossible to put down."
—Mary Kubica, *New York Times* bestselling author of *Don't You Cry*

"*The Vanishing Year* is a chilling, powerful tale of nerve-shattering suspense. Kate Moretti pieces together a stunning, up-all-night thriller with a throat-gripping twist that will leave the reader reeling."
—Heather Gudenkauf, *New York Times* bestselling author of *Missing Pieces*

"Great pacing and true surprises make this an exciting read. Fans of twisted thrillers featuring complex female characters will devour Moretti's latest."
—*Kirkus Reviews* (starred review)

"Moretti maintains a fast pace . . . chillingly satisfying."
—*Publishers Weekly*

"Fans of S. J. Watson, Lisa Unger, and Sophie Hannah will enjoy this fast-paced psychological suspense novel."
—*Booklist*

The Blackbird Season

"A powerful story about a missing girl and an accused suspect that takes a haunting look into the characters and relationships you think you know. *The Blackbird Season* explores the fine line between guilt and innocence, truth and perception, the moments that break people apart—and those that bring them together. Riveting and insightful, this is a book that lingers long after you turn the final page."

—Megan Miranda, *New York Times* bestselling author of
All the Missing Girls

"This cautionary tale keeps the reader guessing to the end."

—*Publishers Weekly*

"The tale's suspenseful core should catch and hold most readers, especially *Gone Girl* fans."

—*Booklist*

"Kate Moretti's insightful, starkly human mystery about a girl they call 'witch' has that sit-down, gotta-cry eloquence readers long for. Mean-girl alliances and small-town loyalties collapse in unison on the day the blackbirds fall. This story will hold you tight to its pages well past your bedtime. *The Blackbird Season* is Moretti's best yet."

—Lisa Turner, Edgar Award–finalist author of
The Gone Dead Train and *Devil Sent the Rain*

"*The Blackbird Season* pulls off a very difficult thing: it's nail biting and thought provoking all at once. It's rare that a book can make you turn pages like your life depends on it but also give you food for thought because the characters are so perfectly drawn. A stunning achievement from an extremely talented writer."

—Gilly Macmillan, *New York Times* bestselling author of
What She Knew

"Moretti spins a tale of suspicion, deceit, and dreams that die as suddenly as a flock of starlings falling from the sky. A thrilling morality tale of the highest order, *The Blackbird Season* will make you question the lines between right and wrong, victim and criminal, and the unknowable intentions that form our innocence and guilt."

—Mindy Mejia, author of *Everything You Want Me to Be*

"A skillful blend of family drama and domestic suspense . . . it kept me turning the pages and was resolved to my satisfaction at the end. Highly recommended."

—Eileen Goudge, *New York Times* bestselling author of *Garden of Lies*

"Moretti begins *The Blackbird Season* with a sinister premise—a cloud of birds falls from the sky on the same day a teenage girl people call 'the witch' goes missing. A spellbinding tale of long-held secrets and small-town scandal, *The Blackbird Season* is one of those stories that sneaks up on you, each chapter building steadily to an ending that will haunt you long after you turn the last page."

—Kimberly Belle, bestselling author of *The Marriage Lie*

In Her Bones

"Morbid . . . Moretti pulls some tricky tricks when she sends Edie on the run, where she slips in and out of some neat disguises and suffers just enough to satisfy the most judgmental reader."

—*New York Times* book review

"Heightened language takes *In Her Bones* to a higher level than the standard thriller. Readers will enjoy this book for the suspense and plot twists but love it for the skill and mastery Moretti has for her craft."

—*New York Journal of Books*

"Captivating . . . Fans of twisty psychological thrillers will find plenty to like."

—*Publishers Weekly*

"Kate Moretti is incredibly talented! *In Her Bones* is at once chilling and compelling, frightening and insightful—and truly, madly, deeply satisfying. You'll gasp at every twist, and you'll turn these hauntingly sinister pages as fast as you can."

—Hank Phillippi Ryan, nationally bestselling author of *Trust Me*

"Kate Moretti's *In Her Bones* is a suspenseful, whirling spiral of mysteries within mysteries, plot twists you won't see coming, and characters linked by deadly fates that stretch across the years. Moretti's prose is crisp and masterful, her people rich and real. Don't miss this haunting, wild thrill ride."

—David Bell, author of *Somebody's Daughter*

"Reading *In Her Bones* is like watching a true-crime documentary . . . And you seriously won't be able to put it down."

—HelloGiggles

"A masterfully crafted, multilayered novel . . . Kate Moretti manages to cover all the angles, making the story deep and dynamic . . . *In Her Bones* is complex, honest, and heartbreaking. It is much more than merely a mystery and is well worth reading."

—Bookreporter

"Sensational—a stunning psychological thriller that kept me riveted from the first page to the last. A dark and compelling exploration of what it's like to grow up with someone who just may be the worst mother in the world, Moretti's chilling and insightful novel answers the question: If your mother is a serial killer and you're obsessed with her victims, what does that make you?"

—Karen Dionne, internationally bestselling author of *T he Marsh King's Daughter*

"Suspense at its best: a chilling voice, an unlikely heroine, a haunting story. *In Her Bones* is Kate Moretti at the top of her game."

—Jessica Strawser, author of *Not That I Could Tell*

"We dived headfirst into *In Her Bones*, its riveting twists and turns keeping us up well past our bedtime. Moretti has meticulously crafted this gripping mystery, which begs the question: Is it possible to escape our own fate? Another stellar contribution to the suspense genre."

—Liz Fenton and Lisa Steinke, authors of *The Good Widow*

GIRLS OF
BRACKENHILL

OTHER TITLES BY KATE MORETTI

Thought I Knew You

Binds That Tie

While You Were Gone (a *Thought I Knew You* novella)

The Vanishing Year

The Blackbird Season

GIRLS OF
BRACKENHILL

KATE
MORETTI

Text copyright © 2020 by Kate Moretti
All rights reserved.

No part of this book may be reproduced, or stored in a retrieval system, or transmitted in any form or by any means, electronic, mechanical, photocopying, recording, or otherwise, without express written permission of the publisher.

Published by Thomas & Mercer, Seattle

www.apub.com

Amazon, the Amazon logo, and Thomas & Mercer are trademarks of Amazon.com, Inc., or its affiliates.

ISBN-13: 9781542000086
ISBN-10: 1542000084

Cover design by Christopher Lin

Printed in the United States of America

To Lily and Abby, who almost died to help me research this book. I'll admit it wasn't my finest parenting moment, but really, you're fine. And I hope we have many, many more adventures together.

CHAPTER ONE

September 2, 2001

I didn't mean to kill the girl.

I found her skulking around the woods, hiding behind trees, darting behind the shed.

Hey, *I called. Dizzy with panic when I saw who it was. I waved the shovel in her direction. I'd been turning over the compost.*

I said, You aren't supposed to be here.

My voice wasn't nearly as strong as I'd hoped. I'd hoped to frighten her away. I sounded meek, terrified.

Oh, that's right. I'm human garbage, *she spat.* I came to give you something!

She had a folded envelope, shoved it roughly into the pocket of my jacket.

It gave me a shock, really, that she would put her hands on me. Such defiance for someone so young. But then, she wasn't that young anymore. How old was she? Sixteen? Seventeen? She'd be striking out on her own soon. Too pretty for Rockwell, not quite pretty enough for the city.

No human is garbage, *I said. I tried to reason with her; truly I did. She carried so much anger inside her. Some people were just born angry.*

She said hateful things: You never cared for me. You treated me like I was nothing.

None of that was true, of course.

After everything I'd done for her. How could she be so hateful? I'd done so much for her. I'd tried more than anyone. Even after.

Well, not after—I'll be the first to admit that. But who would?

It's time to go home, *I yelled, and I was ashamed at how my voice shook. I was afraid of her.*

I tried to hurry her along, despite the swell of adrenaline, so consuming that my vision blurred. I tried to breathe through the anger.

She wouldn't leave me alone. She rushed at me, a wild thing, hair a tangled sight.

I wasn't proud of the fact that my heart had hardened. I wasn't proud that I'd run out of love for this lost girl.

I took the brunt of all her problems, you see? That night was a culmination of all the things that had ever happened to her, and I was in the wrong place at the wrong time.

She yelled and ranted: You never forgave me. No one did. I was ruined.

I stood there and took it all, shoulders squared, legs solid. Absorbing her hate and her hurt and her words. Until.

Say something. Anything! *She begged me to talk.*

But I didn't reply to any of it. Felt the mounting, growing rage deep in my gut. An anger I'd never known. A helplessness I couldn't fathom.

You know what? I did it, *she whispered right in my ear.*

The rage overwhelmed me, and I closed my eyes and swung and felt the shovel in my hand connect with her skull, and she fell to the dirt, and oh God, there was a lot of blood, but it pulsed out onto the wet leaves, absorbed by the earth, and I watched her tremble and sputter out her last breath in a matter of seconds.

I didn't mean to kill her.

But after it happened, I wasn't sorry.

Not for a long, long time.

2

CHAPTER TWO

Now

August 15, 2019

The call came in shortly before midnight, as they mostly did. Huck slept like he was dead, but the buzzing phone gradually woke Hannah, first becoming part of a recurring dream. Hannah held a garden shovel; she was digging a hole, the dirt sifting over the metal, a feeling of dread deep in her chest, her shoulders aching. The smell of something rotting, soil and death, leaves and worms. Then, suddenly, the spade was a cell phone.

"Hannah Maloney?" the voice on the other end asked, soft and clipped.

"Yes. Hello." She woke instantly, the number unfamiliar, a 607 exchange: New York. And she knew it all right away, like a vision. (Except not truly; she always had to clarify, if only to herself.) She nodded, her legs swinging over the side of the bed, before the voice on the other end even said the words: *car accident.*

She shook Huck awake. "We have to go. I have to go." They didn't have a polite relationship. They had a bathroom-door-wide-open-while-reading-the-obituaries-aloud relationship. Huck felt, at times, like an appendage: firmly attached, essential. It was natural for her to wake him at the first hint of disaster. It was equally natural for him to assimilate, even while half-asleep.

The woman on the phone said, "You were listed in her phone as 'in case of emergency.'"

At the same time Hannah said, "I know."

Hannah thought, *What about Stuart? Is he alive?*

She asked the woman on the phone about Aunt Fae's husband.

A beat of silence, the faint rustle of paperwork before she came back on the line. "There was only one person in the car, dear. Your aunt Fae."

"I'll be there as soon as I can." Hannah's voice, to her own ears, sounded breathless, like she'd run miles. Her brain ticked through a frantic to-do list. The phone to her ear, she looked for her sneakers under the bed, then in the closet. She motioned to Huck to get up, and he nodded.

Rink, their Irish setter, stood alert at the panic in her voice. She patted his head, then stopped moving. "Does Uncle Stuart know? Does her husband know?" She imagined Uncle Stuart, what she'd seen in movies of people dying of cancer: gaunt figures under bedsheets in dark rooms. Raspy breathing. She'd heard from her mother, a year and a half ago, that the cancer had spread. She assumed he was still alive, assumed she'd be informed if he wasn't. But who would have informed her? Her mother was dead, and Aunt Fae hadn't spoken to Hannah since she was fifteen.

She imagined Uncle Stuart waking in the morning, no breakfast, no Fae, confused and hungry.

"We will send an officer to the house," the woman said. "Is there a caretaker who has keys?"

"No. Fae is the caretaker. There's a nurse who comes daily for meds. Or at least there used to be. I don't know what time, though." Hannah stuffed jeans and T-shirts into a bag. Huck was just standing up and flicked on a bedside lamp. She sat down, light headed. Too much, too fast.

"How long will it take you to get here?" The woman's voice had softened, become kindly.

"I'm in Virginia." She'd never driven to Rockwell from her new town. *Their* new town, as Huck gently reminded her every day. They were a "they" now. She stopped, took a few breaths. She wasn't alone anymore. If you were lucky, fiancés were built-in assistants, therapists, and financial advisers all rolled into one. Hannah was lucky.

She did the math: three hours from Pennsylvania, plus three more.

"About six hours, I'd guess." The woman on the other end beat her to it. A pause. "You should leave now, dear."

Hannah realized she'd misjudged everything, hadn't asked the right question, the only question: "Is Fae going to die?" She had assumed it wasn't serious. She'd thought a broken leg, an arm, a concussion, maybe unconsciousness. "A car accident" could mean myriad things.

There was a beat where the woman didn't speak, and Hannah felt the silence down to her bones, the chill instant, the phone still in her white-knuckled grip, and Huck, without speaking, placed a palm flat between her shoulder blades, rubbing gently. His hand moved up to her shoulder, and she gripped it there. In the dim light her engagement ring winked.

"You should leave soon."

CHAPTER THREE

The Ghost Girls of Brackenhill are an urban legend.

Brackenhill was the name of a castle on top of a mountain deep in the woods in the Catskill Mountains. It was built in the 1800s by a wealthy Scottish immigrant named Douglass Taylor as a summer lodge. He built the castle originally for his wife, who was committed to a sanatorium shortly after the birth of her only child. Taylor himself then died young, and their daughter, Merril, inherited the land and the Taylor fortune. She married and lived in happy seclusion for years until she, too, was committed to a sanatorium shortly after the birth of her fourth son. Brackenhill was passed down from generation to generation in a family riddled with mental illness.

It has been said that over ten girls went missing on Brackenhill grounds over the course of 150 years. Some were children living in the castle; some were residents of the village below. Brackenhill stole the sanity of women and the bodies of children. The children, ranging in age from seven to eighteen, have never been found. Some people think they're all buried on the expansive grounds. Sometimes, especially when it rains (and no one knows why), you can hear their laughter as they play.

CHAPTER FOUR

Now

Grover M. Hermann Hospital was a half hour south of Rockwell, New York. Huck steered Hannah's car into the brightly lit parking lot just before dawn on Friday morning. Huck, the saint, had driven the full six hours, letting Hannah doze in the passenger seat, violating Road Trip Rule #7: absolutely no sleeping. But those rules had been made for beach trips and summer getaways, not middle-of-the-night emergency trips to visit long-lost—and gravely injured—relatives.

Hannah's mother, Trina, had passed away a year and a half ago. Huck and Hannah had been new, and he'd met and charmed her only once. He tried to come with Hannah to the funeral, make the arrangements, see the house she grew up in. That sad little box house in Plymouth, Pennsylvania. She'd stopped him. She hadn't needed him then. She wasn't even sure that she'd cried. "You're so strong," he told her then. Proud of her, like strength was an accomplishment, something to strive for. It never occurred to him to question where it had come from.

But this felt different. Heavier. They were *engaged*. It hadn't even been a question this time: Huck was here. The thought made her hands clench. There was so much he didn't know. Would he think she was strong this time? Unlikely.

Hannah sat up, smacked her mouth. She dug around for a piece of gum and a dog treat. Rink slept soundly in the back, sighing softly, legs kicking at a dream. She turned around and tucked the treat between his nose and his front paws. He woke long enough to eat it and drifted back off.

Hannah's eyes burned, reminding her that her car sleep had been spotty at best. She dialed work and left a voice mail for her director. "I should be back on Monday; there's been a family emergency." She thought of her boss, Patrice, a severe, private woman who would scoff at the excuse. It was a hot, sunny Friday. Surely Hannah had just taken off for a long weekend with that "hunky fiancé," as Patrice called Huck.

Hannah was in charge of brochures: ad copy and placement of pictures of happy couples frolicking on beaches. She loved the idea of making life look wonderful and glossy. But still, she had the odd habit of trying to imagine her life like the pictures on a brochure: *perfect boyfriend, pristine apartment, small yet loyal circle of friends laughing around a campfire.*

"Hannah?" Huck's hand on her knee. She jerked her leg away and regretted it. She was jumpy, too little sleep, too much energy charging through her veins.

Hannah reached out and gripped Huck's hand. It was calloused, even in the summer—especially in the summer—because of his job as a landscape designer (*the gardener*, she sometimes called him, sexy and silly).

Huck knew almost nothing of Aunt Fae and Uncle Stuart, aside from their names. He'd never met them. He didn't know much about her childhood, and he knew nothing of the castle. He knew her mother had died. He knew very little of the summer of 2002. He knew she had an older sister who'd died when she was young, but not why or how. Well, no one knew how, Hannah supposed. He knew that she and her sister had spent summers at her aunt's house in New York, but surely he imagined something normal: a cabin, a ranch, a colonial.

Hannah knew so much about Huck's life before her: his idyllic childhood, his four brothers, parents who swelled with pride for their children and love for each other. His whole childhood had felt like a slap. Even after meeting the whole brood, she'd glossed over her own childhood with a broad, shiny brush. Huck's family was loud, raucous, ribbing each other at holidays. His mom sat at the head of the table, cheeks flushed. His parents lived less than an hour from them in Virginia. Somehow Hannah still managed to find plenty of excuses to beg off visits.

Besides, they'd only gotten engaged three short weeks ago. They hadn't progressed past the showing-off-the-ring stage of engagement. The word *wedding* had barely been uttered. They had time, Hannah reasoned. They should be *enjoying* this time. Not mucking it up with heavy pasts and childhood traumas.

Would she have told him about Brackenhill eventually? Of course. Maybe. She'd rarely given it a thought in seventeen years. Except for the nights she woke up sweating, crying, the faint outline of a dream tugging at her subconscious. Her hands clenched until they cramped, a deep ache across her shoulders. A heavy refrain, the memory of a sound. *Click, click, thump, thump.* Once and only once Huck had found her standing in the living room naked, her clothes strewed on the floor. Hannah didn't remember it, but Huck had told her she had clawed at the hardwood, crying.

Later, when she woke up and he recounted the story, he'd laughed. "Like you were digging something up. It was bizarre." At the time, she pretended to laugh with him as her heart raced. He hadn't noticed. Sometimes Hannah thought what she loved most about Huck was his obliviousness. His willingness to not look too deeply.

They'd met at a brewery in the next town over. Before Hannah worked in marketing for a PR firm, she'd tended bar in the evenings while she job hunted. Huck had come in with his rowdy friends, him in jeans and a T-shirt, them in suit shirts and loosened ties. His fingernails with their blackened crescent moons had struck her as odd among all the manicures. Bartenders noticed hands. The first words she spoke to him were "You don't fit in," and he'd grinned at her, thrown an extra ten on the bar top. Before he left, he slid his business card under the tip, scrawled *neither do you* on the back.

"Are you okay?" he finally asked, the silence in the car wearing thin. He'd been more patient with her than required, but Hannah suspected this trip would try him. Huck hated messes, despised melodrama.

And now he was about to get his trial by fire and perhaps more answers than he'd ever wanted. Hannah wondered if he'd be there at the end of it. Would he stay if he knew the whole truth? That last summer, her sister, Wyatt. The knot in her stomach tightened, and she stopped, swallowed back the panic in her throat.

She'd worked so hard to relegate her childhood, her sister, and her aunt and uncle to the background of her life. She never examined her childhood in direct light, only in periphery—dreams where Julia was still alive, racing her back through the forest, the sunlight blinking between the leaves. And now they were going back. Her shiny new life, handsome fiancé, everything she'd ever wanted.

She wanted to go home.

"I'm fine," Hannah answered quickly and pushed open the car door. "I haven't seen her in seventeen years. I'm fine."

It was still cool, the sun barely cresting the horizon. They rolled a window partway down for Rink, who paced in the back seat, excited, whining. Huck let him out briefly to go to the bathroom, the leash taut as he sniffed around bushes on the hospital lawn.

"I'll come back if we're in there too long," Huck assured her when they locked the car door. He took care of things. He was the task man of their little team, always. What was Hannah? The compliant one, the go-along girl. *Girl with big ideas*, he sometimes called her, his eyes crinkling at the corners.

She walked into the hospital a good ten feet in front of Huck (briefly reminded of Josh tagging along behind Julia all those summers ago), but she couldn't have articulated why. Inside, she was directed by the administration desk to a family-crisis center. The room was small, a few couches and a chair. A round coffee table and a sideboard with a Keurig. She touched nothing and did not sit. When a woman entered and introduced herself as a crisis counselor, Hannah didn't flinch. Huck tried to touch her again, a gentle palm against the small of her back, but she moved slightly out of his reach, so his hand was left dangling in midair.

"I'm Claire McKinney." The woman was older than Hannah, probably only by a few years, but her hair was streaked with gray. She took Hannah's cue and also did not sit but instead held Hannah's arm with both hands and spoke succinctly but kindly. "I'm afraid your aunt has passed away."

Hannah felt the punch in her lungs, heard the whoosh of air before realizing it was her own breath. Willed her brain to focus on the woman's words.

Claire McKinney told Hannah about the crash, the car moving too fast down the winding road, away from the castle, hitting a slick patch from recent rain, and pitching over the guardrail and into the ravine. Someone had come along and seen the lights in the car, the coiled smoke from the hood, and called 911, but Aunt Fae's internal injuries were too serious. The rescue effort had been a bit of an undertaking. (Hannah remembered the steepness of that ravine on Valley Road, having flown away from the castle in a speeding car herself.) They were sorry, of course, but would Hannah be able to identify the body? No other family member was listed. (They were all dead now, see?) All Hannah could say was, "Absolutely, of course, anything for Aunt Fae." Claire McKinney pushed an eight-by-ten photograph across the table—Hannah couldn't recall sitting down—but she turned it over without thought and wished she had taken a moment to prepare herself.

The photo was a close-up of her aunt's face, black and white. In a split second she saw the deep grooves in her aunt's forehead between her eyebrows, the shadowy wells under her eyes, a light but familiar birthmark in the curious shape of a butterfly on her temple that had darkened in death. Or maybe it was just that her coloring had gone gray, almost white as bone. There was thick stitching around the crown of her head, a leathery incision devoid of blood. She'd been wiped clean.

"That's her," Hannah said, feeling like she was in a movie or a detective show and grateful she wasn't standing inside a sterile morgue the way it was portrayed on television. She tried to arrange her face into something like sadness, as she imagined she was supposed to feel. Or maybe shock. Huck watched her carefully. She could tell he was trying to comfort her, that comfort was the normal, everyday reaction in this situation. That she should want his support. Later, maybe he'd tell her, *You're so strong*, and she'd be pleased at that.

It was over that quickly, and they were back out in Hannah's car before Huck even had to check on Rink. There was an air of formality about the whole thing. Claire McKinney's compassion had been an act, part of her job, nothing more or less.

Hannah held a business card for a funeral home where Aunt Fae would be prepared for arrangements—which meant a viewing and a funeral, or perhaps a cremation. She supposed she should have known what her aunt's wishes were, that the hospital would assume that as next of kin she'd spoken to her aunt during the past seventeen years.

She'd call the funeral parlor in the morning. But it was morning, wasn't it? The clock blinked 6:52. They'd been in the hospital for less than an hour, too little time for her life to be entirely changed. And yet lives were upended all the time in minutes and seconds, not hours. Hannah knew that. Also, it felt too dramatic: her life would not be changed. She'd do whatever she'd come to do and go home, back to Virginia, her career, planning the wedding.

She'd escaped Brackenhill once. She could do it again.

"What can I do?" Huck asked, and Hannah recognized the despair in his voice. Huck hated helplessness. He was an action person, a problem-solver. He admired this trait in her more than anything else: she was always fine. He'd complained of ex-girlfriends: needy, calling and texting at all hours. Her independence, even when it frustrated him, was attractive.

"Nothing," Hannah said, and it was true. She didn't need anything from him, maybe never had. This time she almost asked him for one thing: *Drive me home.* He would have in a heartbeat. But she knew she had to head farther north, past Rockwell on the only road in, the switchback road her aunt had taken out. To her once-beloved uncle, who lay quietly dying. It fell to her to tell him about his wife.

Hannah let Huck drive, the car winding around steep curves, her arm gripping the handle at the window, white knuckled and breathless, the fear starting as a steady thrum in her legs, a jittery helplessness. From the back seat even Rink whined as Huck punched the gas, the car stuttering up the steep incline. At the top, the first of the stone turrets came into view, and the car slowed as Huck's foot faltered.

For the first time in seventeen years, it was time to go back to the castle.

CHAPTER FIVE

Then

The castle sat high on a hill, shrouded by towering oaks and pines in Rockwell, a town in the Catskill Mountains. It had a name: Brackenhill. At the time Hannah thought it belonged in a fairy tale, which made sense because it was named after a castle in England. Before summers in Rockwell, she hadn't known houses could have names at all.

Hannah and Julia were driven up in the old Buick, their mother's left arm out the window. She brought it in only to light one cigarette off the other, balancing the wheel with her knee. The fingers on her right hand held the cigarette while simultaneously tapping along to the radio, the ash flying. The Buick's vinyl seats stuck to Hannah's thighs. Her mother parked at the end of the driveway, and the girls clambered up the gravel drive, wriggling with anticipation, dragging suitcases on wheels that caught on the stones.

Before they became part-time residents of Brackenhill, the sisters had not known the castle existed. They'd never been there, never visited their aunt and uncle. Their mother had said the drive was too far; her sister was unkind, she'd said. Then suddenly, one summer, for no obvious reason, everything had changed. Their mother had announced she couldn't work at night, sleep during the day, and trust that they would behave themselves all summer. Julia, newly thirteen, had been caught sneaking a neighbor boy into her bedroom. Their mother, strangely pious when it suited her, had taken to praying about Julia's virtue until she'd somehow stumbled on an elegant solution: the girls would spend the summer with her sister in the Catskills.

That was Hannah's first glimpse of the castle, and of Aunt Fae and Uncle Stuart, hands gripped together at the gate, mouths set in a line.

Aunt Fae was Mom's sister, and Mom spoke of her only in the pejorative, her tone lilting a bit, dragging out the -*ae*, mocking her in a way Hannah and her sister didn't understand. *Oh, you know Fae,* she'd say, but in truth they didn't. Not really. She and her husband had come to visit a handful of times in their lives. If asked, they'd have to concentrate to come up with their aunt's and uncle's names.

They knew Aunt Fae was more rounded in the middle than Mom, who was bony and flat. After that first summer they knew Fae would hug them in a way Mom never did. They knew Uncle Stuart would bop the crowns of their heads with a soft closed fist and a little pop of his tongue. They knew their aunt and uncle would laugh sometimes, shockingly, from the back of their throats, in a way their mother and stepfather did not. Yet Aunt Fae's eyes were always a bit rheumy, like she'd just finished crying.

But that first summer of 1998, all they knew was they got to live in a castle for almost three months. The castle was a square, with turrets at each corner and a courtyard at the center, bursting with flowers and arbors, stone walkways. It smelled like peonies and honeysuckle, the whole expanse of garden exploding with reds, yellows, pinks; deep-orange lilies; sedum and daisies; tall splashes of lupine and irises. Deep-green vines fingered their way up the stone walls, wrapped around lancet windows, their Gothic arches softened in the midday sun.

Hannah took a room in the turret, the round expanse of windows looking out into that courtyard. She saw it all for the first time, flinging open the windows to smell the lavender, freesia. She hoped she'd never go home again, back to the powder-blue-and-white bedroom, the stale silence of her mother's absence, and felt disloyal. Julia took the room next to hers, down the hall (what a long hall! Built for cartwheels!), but eyed Hannah's exuberance enviously, a thirteen-year-old who wanted desperately to be a teenager and still a child at the same time. They discovered a door between their rooms—technically two doors, with a small space between them. Julia would sometimes leave Hannah notes or tiny gifts in that little space. At least, in the beginning.

Hannah squealed with delight at her first view of the woods, trees and trees as far as she could see from her bedroom window—"A thousand acres in all," Aunt Fae told her proudly—imagining hours of lost time, exploring, finding brooks, salamanders, tree hideouts, secret passageways. Nothing but her imagination, stretched far and wide, and her best friend, Julia. The Beaverkill River ran below Valley Road to the west, shallow and burbling in the dry July heat. The girls could hear it from the castle, an always-welcoming music box, mixed with the sounds of the birds, the silence of the mountains, and the smell of pine and something earthy and rotting.

Hannah discovered that if she lay in the right place, right in the center of the courtyard between the honeysuckle and the roses, next to the fountain, she could see all four turrets at once in periphery, their towers poking at the listing clouds, the blue above her like a song, and she'd never known happiness like that, a bubble in her chest about to burst, gasping like she couldn't catch her breath. Even years later, Hannah couldn't remember a better kind of peace.

Julia once asked about the history of the house, who had lived there, had it been a queen and king? Aunt Fae laughed and told her, "No one important, just us." They'd inherited it, Fae told them. Which Hannah understood to mean it had been given to them, but by whom? Why? Any further questions were always met with vague responses, *hmm-hmmm*s and *oh, just family*, until the girls got bored and wandered away.

The grounds were wild in appearance but cared for, vines and ground cover creeping over everything. Trimmed daily by Stuart with his shears as he whistled a lilting tune, something unknown to Hannah but melancholy, ripe with sadness to match the hoods of her uncle's eyes. All the adults in her life seemed so *sad*, even if only when they thought no one was watching them. Her mother was a frequent crier, and her stepfather, Wes, was given to bouts of anger, particularly when drunk. She'd never known an adult in her life to display actual joy.

But the house! She counted thirty-three rooms: ballrooms and sitting rooms and winding staircases (more than one!) and servants' quarters and empty bedrooms, closed off and drafty even in the belly of summer. She thrilled at imagining ancient horrors hidden behind the doors, even after Fae insisted it was simply easier to close them up than to clean them.

"Then why are they locked?" Hannah persisted, following behind Fae as she cleaned and puttered up and down the hallways, driving her aunt crazy.

"Because I don't want you girls making a mess. There's no reason. Some of them don't even have furniture! It's expensive to keep up a home this size." Fae shooed Hannah outside, the conversation over.

Hannah had goose bumps in certain corners of the castle, some hallways that were colder than others.

Each year they learned more about the woods: her trees and creek beds, her trails, her vines and crumbling stone walls, her bugs, bees, birds, the chirps and calls the soundtrack to their wild days, alone and exploring. At least until the year Uncle Stuart bought them bikes and Hannah and Julia rode to town and found other teenagers, and the spell of their childhood, it seemed to Hannah, had been broken.

And that summer, the summer of the broken spell, when they left their castle and let others in—*let evil in,* as Hannah thought later, so dramatic—was the beginning of the end. The summer of lost chances and faded hope. Brackenhill, she would imagine later, was always frozen in that one moment, the first summer when Hannah had lain in the courtyard and watched the clouds, the points of the towers prodding the sky, breaking it open to rain on her face, matting her clothes to her body, filling her mouth and her eyes, mixing with her tears.

In the end, Hannah would return home alone, and never come back to Brackenhill.

CHAPTER SIX

Now

Rockwell Mountain Road was two narrow lanes with sharp curves, flanked by a steep ravine and the Beaverkill to the west and an imposing vertical wall of shale and slate—the tumbled face of Rockwell Mountain—to the east. As Huck drove, Hannah studied the guardrail, looking for signs that a car had blown through. A mile from town she found the breach—a post had been violently uprooted, the wood splintered. Instinctively Huck punched the brake, and the car jerked and slowed. Hannah couldn't see over the side, down to the bottom of the ravine. Was the car still there? How long had Aunt Fae lain there, bleeding and in pain, before she'd been helped? *On impact,* she remembered. Hannah turned her head away from the ravine, toward Huck, and he reached out to grasp her fingertips.

"Turn on Castle Drive at the top of the hill," Hannah said.

"Inventive." Huck squeezed her fingertips and gave her a half smile. Hannah tried to form her lips into what would pass as a smile but found she couldn't. The thrum of dread pulsed in her ears, her chest.

The gate at the end of the road was swung wide, the driveway looming in front of them like an open mouth, the stone archway like large yellowed teeth. Huck inched the car forward, and Hannah held her breath as the tower points came into view.

Hannah's heart lodged in her throat. She hadn't been to Brackenhill since a week after Julia disappeared. Her clearest memory of the end of that summer was the house receding in the rear window of the Buick as the car sped down the driveway. She remembered Aunt Fae holding a handkerchief over her face. Uncle Stuart's left hand raised, unmoving, his face gaunt and stricken.

Her stepfather had steered the car with one hand and rested the other on the empty front seat. Trina, her mother, hadn't made the trip to retrieve Hannah, and for the rest of the summer she rarely left her bedroom. It was after Julia vanished that her isolated piety turned full-blown zealous. Julia had been *hers*. A special mother-daughter bond that Hannah used to study, try to understand. Hannah and Trina had never been close. Hannah was too exuberant, too much. Everything Hannah did seemed to exhaust Trina, particularly after Julia left.

Hannah's mother took to carrying rosaries with her everywhere, her lips always moving, her fingers rolling the black beads in small circles around the pads of her thumbs.

Now, in the early-morning light, the castle looked ethereal, a black shadow lit pink from behind. Only as they edged closer could Hannah see its age: Crumbling stone and missing mortar, sagging flashing along the roofline and dangling slate shingles. Window ledges with peeling paint in various shades of white, tan, even green, like Aunt Fae had run out of one color and just used whatever she'd found in the basement.

The basement. Hannah closed her eyes, her nose and mouth filled with the smell of rot, whether real or imagined, she couldn't say. The maze of small rooms connected with no discernible pattern by a series of arched doorways. They'd played hide-and-seek there, convinced the rooms shifted, the house accommodating their wild imaginations. They'd tried to tell Aunt Fae once. A labyrinth in the basement that seemed intent on trapping them, keeping them hostage. Fae had laughed, waved her hand around in a circle, dismissive. "Everyone tells stories about this house; don't feed them," she'd warned. But the rooms had moved. As a child, Hannah was certain of it.

"Holy shit, Hannah," Huck whispered next to her. "I had no idea."

Of course he didn't. He didn't know about any of it. Hannah felt a burst of impatience with him, a quick bolt of frustration at his inability to keep up. She didn't want to explain Brackenhill, her aunt and uncle, her family, her sister. More than not wanting to—she *couldn't*.

Hannah approached the building to search for the key. She heard Huck's sharp intake of breath next to her as she led them through a stone archway and into the courtyard. Aunt Fae had kept up the garden: green and full, bursting with color, pinks and blues. Even in the hot August months, when perennials would be wilting, Fae's garden looked lush as spring. Dappled with birdhouses and fountains.

Hannah found the cobalt-blue flowerpot in the corner and lifted it; the brass key glinted in the sunlight. Brackenhill never changed.

Inside it smelled like a memory: damp and sweet, musty carpets and layers of perfume. Aunt Fae's banana bread. Peeling paint along the concrete walls. Dust trapped in fluted moldings. The ceilings were uneven—barely above Huck's head in some areas, looming over fifteen feet high in others. Their voices echoed. Rink ran in a circle, barked, the sound ricocheting off the stone walls.

"Hannah." Huck stopped. The question unspoken. He touched her elbow. His eyebrows pinched as he searched her face. There was never a moment when Hannah looked at his face, his gray-blue eyes sometimes dark and brooding, sometimes bright with love, and didn't feel the gentle tug of something wonderfully sweet. Love. Desire. Admiration. Even now, in this castle, her heart a trapped bird inside her rib cage, her breath sour in her mouth, she loved him. He deserved some kind of explanation, of course.

"This house," she said, her voice wobbly and unsure to her own ears. She began again. Squared her shoulders, stood up straighter. "For five years, we came here every summer, my sister and I. From the time

I was eleven to the time I was fifteen. My stepfather was a drunk. My mother was incapable. Brackenhill was . . . our sanctuary. But something happened to my sister here, and that was the end of it. I was fifteen. Julia was seventeen. She was acting so strangely that summer . . ." Her voice trailed off, her thoughts winding back to that August: Julia's bed empty, the sheets cool, the tug of jealousy in Hannah's core, the girl with the long red hair. What was her name? Evie? Ellie. The new feeling of a boy, the first boy, the weight and smell of him (his name she'd not forget, and she still woke up with it full in her mouth—*Wyatt*). Wondering if it had all started, or ended, because of a teenage boy who was loved by two girls who happened to be sisters.

"She left one day and never came back," Hannah finished. "We fought, she left, and I never saw her again."

"Did she run away?" Huck asked, his voice hoarse, his eyes wide. "Have you looked for her? Now, with the internet?"

"No. They found her purse in the river. She was declared dead years ago." Hannah touched her forehead, felt the sweat beading there. Heard her breaths coming fast and tried to regulate herself.

"I don't understand. What happened to her?" Huck pressed.

"We don't know. It's still an open murder case, but without a body . . ." It was a cold, clinical dissection, she knew. "Everyone suspected them. The town turned on Aunt Fae and Uncle Stuart. I was never invited back." Not that she would have come. "It was a forbidden topic with my mother. We rarely spoke about Julia. I had to force myself to just . . . move on."

"What do you think?" Huck asked, his voice quietly insistent but also incredulous. His face still. Hannah tried to read him and failed. How strange it must be to be told information of this magnitude so late in the game.

"I think she ran away."

She'd never said it so definitively, out loud, before. She'd thought it plenty of times. Especially in the beginning. When Hannah first left home, got accepted to Dickinson, a private liberal arts college in the middle of nowhere, Pennsylvania. When her college roommates would ask her basic questions about her family, why her mother never came to parents' weekend. She'd say she was an only child. But she'd lie in bed at night and let her mind wander wildly. She'd try to force herself down one thought path, then another. From the obvious (Julia had been killed by a stranger in the woods and thrown in the river) to the probable (Julia had run away from Brackenhill because of some secret Hannah never understood) to the downright ridiculous (Julia was in witness protection).

Senior year of college, she found herself blurting it out one late night while studying: *I had a sister who ran away.* Her roommate at the time became singularly focused, perhaps even obsessed, and they spent a few nights scouring Google for signs of Julia Maloney (and all her incarnations: *J. Maloney, Julie Maloney, Julia Lorraine Maloney*). Somewhere between college and adulthood, Hannah had accepted that version as truth.

She didn't utter the *second* part, the unformed thought: *She'll come back.* She'd said it once, to her mother, years ago. They'd been fighting—no memory of what about—and Hannah spat it out, suddenly, almost violently. "Julia will come back for me." Her mother had raged, "Julia is dead! Dead, Hannah." She threw a pot that had been in her hand, dish soap flying, and it left a divot in the linoleum where it landed. Later in her room, Hannah tried out the word: "Dead." Felt the heaviness of it on her tongue, the finality of it. It never felt true. As an adult, she crafted elaborate fantasies about her sister returning, their reunion, a tearful homecoming, a long dinner and a shared bottle of wine and her sister—returned to her! She'd had friendships, of course, but nothing as close as a sister. Someone to know you down to your bones, every halting sigh familiar. Someone to exchange a look with that said, *I know.* At a joke, a shop window, a drunken man in a crowded bar. It was the unspoken things that felt the most powerful. Hannah had lost that. Sometimes she didn't even realize how much she missed it until she saw it pass between two other women. Sisters, mothers, neighbors.

It never occurred to her to question specifically why Julia had run away. That night, knotted tightly in her chest like a closed fist.

Hannah should not have shut Huck out. But that wasn't quite right; it was never about Huck at all but rather what Hannah felt willing to say aloud. Her family had rarely said important things out loud, aside from Trina's one "dead" proclamation. Her mother rarely mentioned Aunt Fae after that summer. Her mother's most frequent emotion was fatigue—too tired to talk about Julia, Fae, Brackenhill. Too exhausted by Hannah's presence, her relentless need to be fed, clothed, driven. Talking was a bridge too far.

Hannah never learned how to talk about Julia. She knew, instinctively, that she should, at least to Huck. And yet the words would never come. It was too easy to push it all aside, ask instead, *What do you want to do for dinner? How was your meeting? Did you stop at the dry cleaner?* It was easy to be distracted by daily details of life and easier still to never say a word about a past that seemed irrelevant. Immaterial to the life she was carving out for herself. In those moments she could convince herself she was a strong, independent woman. Overcoming a childhood trauma.

And the one thing she never told anyone—not the police, her mother, Wyatt, Huck. Julia had come back that night. It had been close to dawn. Hannah remembered seeing the brushstroke of pink out the window. When she tried to put a fine point on that memory, anchor it with details (What exactly had Julia said?), she found it too fuzzy. Incomplete. Then she wondered if it had really happened. She doubted her own memories of that summer at every turn.

She couldn't have said whether it was the fighting with Julia, the hazy excitement with Wyatt, the feeling of something on the horizon—something big and life changing for all of them. But Hannah had been plagued with insomnia that whole last summer. Sleepwalking all over the castle. So much of those last few weeks passed in a fever dream. What had been real?

Her sister had stood poised between their bedrooms, her hand on the doorjamb. "Hannah, please," she'd whispered. She'd been streaked with dirt, her face pale in the moonlight, like she'd been crying. It was all Hannah remembered, the simple two-word plea, and then her sister was gone. It could have been anything.

Earlier that night Julia had said, "We are in danger here," her voice a rush, her hair wild. Begged Hannah to come with her, but Hannah flatly refused, all her trust in her sister broken. They'd been to a fish fry picnic in town. Julia had kissed *her Wyatt*, and Hannah had screamed, pushed her. The fight had gotten ugly—but still, not terminal.

Hannah vaguely remembered her own anger, how she'd known that nothing good ever came from running out of the house in the middle of the night. Especially this house, teetering high on the edge of a cliff, pressed against the wind, the Beaverkill River swollen and rushing below. What had Julia said?

"We can go to the police. I have proof, okay? Come with me. We have to leave."

Leave! Absolutely not. Hannah would not be made to leave. Brackenhill was hers, and sometimes it felt like she was the only one who knew all the house's secrets and loved her anyway.

And then the reckless pulse of fury in Hannah's chest as Julia turned, clicked the door shut. She had no idea what her sister was talking about, and she was tired of caring so much about one person. All her emotions invested so heavily in someone who seemed to care so little in return. The anger flooded back, the images of her sister kissing a boy, his red hair curled in her fingertips, her lips against his cheek.

She almost, *almost*, opened the door again that night. Her hand was on the knob. She heard her sister on the other side. "I hope you understand."

Hannah waited until she heard silence at the door between their bedrooms. Then she inched open the door to the hallway. She listened carefully to whispering on the stairs and the patter of quiet footsteps.

Let her go, she told herself. *She's a bitch anyway.*

CHAPTER SEVEN

Now

Hannah ascended the curved concrete staircase, Huck following closely at her heels, his breath warm on the back of her neck in the chill of the stale castle air. From somewhere in the distance, in another room, a fan whirred. The clunk of a wooden door being blown shut.

"I thought you said your uncle was bedridden?" Huck asked, startling at the distant slam.

"He is. That's just Brackenhill." It had become so normal to Hannah, the muted groans and moans of a fortress standing against the whipping wind high on a hilltop. When she was younger, the night sounds had been soothed away by Aunt Fae's honeyed voice, and the things that had happened at night had become dreams in her memory. During the day the castle was benign, even charming. Whimsical, with its loose pieces clattering against the outside stone. Through the telescope of age, everything else seemed like the conjuring of an imaginative child.

Stuart and Fae's room was the last door on the first hallway from the parlor staircase. There were three staircases, four hallways, and ten bedrooms, two in each of the north and south halls, three in each of the east and west hallways. Each room that extended to a corner held a turret.

Most were closed up, locked even. Fae and Stuart's was the largest, with the only attached bathroom, a later addition, Hannah assumed.

The door to Stuart's room was ajar, and Hannah pushed the door fully open. Huck hovered in the doorway.

The room was unchanged. Hannah, for a moment, felt a vertiginous déjà vu: Fae ambling out of the en suite bathroom and, upon seeing Hannah, pressing her hands together, rings clicking, and giving her a big smile. Her long, colorful caftan flowing around her. The sound of her voice echoing in Hannah's ears.

A large four-poster bed took up the center of the room, pushed against the far wall. The canopy Hannah remembered from childhood had been removed, leaving only the wooden posts. Flanking the bed were intricately carved armoires with large ball feet, reaching almost to the ceiling. The amber wood glowed in the beam of a night-light. The red brocade curtains were drawn, so although the early-morning light had begun to illuminate other parts of the castle, Stuart's room remained dark.

Stuart lay in bed, his eyes closed, just as she'd imagined him: thin and frail, the sound of a pump drowning out his labored breathing. An IV pole next to him held a bag of fluid, plastic tubing connecting to his left arm. An oxygen tank sat on the opposite side, emanating a quiet hiss.

She spoke quietly. "Uncle Stuart, it's me, Hannah."

He didn't move or flutter his eyes. His face was gaunt, his hair wispy. He was only sixty-two, but he looked ninety. His mouth hung open inside the oxygen mask, and she could see the scrim of white stubble beneath the green elastic. Hannah reached out and placed her hand on his shoulder. She was shocked by the bumps and knobs of bone protruding under the skin. A small blue plastic box on the IV pole displayed numbers: *70, 90, 65.* Pulse and blood pressure. Both abnormally low.

Hannah wondered what she would do if the machines started beeping right then. Would she attempt CPR? Did she even remember CPR? It had been years since she'd been trained—the summer after Julia had disappeared, she'd lifeguarded at the community pool. She could vaguely recall the steps: chest compressions, followed by two breaths. Or was it four?

Hannah tried to feel something: remorse, revulsion, fear. She pressed her hand farther into her uncle's shoulder, willing him to wake up, open one eye, but he did not.

A folding chair sat in the corner, and she pulled it up to the bed. Bent her head close to his ear. He smelled sharp, medicinal.

"Uncle Stuart," she whispered again. "It's Hannah. Aunt Fae was in a car accident." Hannah slid her fingertips underneath his palm. His hand was cold but dry. "Squeeze my hand if you can hear me." Nothing.

She looked at Huck and lifted her shoulders. *What do I do?*

He shook his head, held his palm up. After crossing the room, he touched Hannah's back, his hand warm. She leaned into it for the first time since they'd arrived in Rockwell. His touch felt welcoming. Comforting. Hannah felt her throat constrict. There was so much he didn't know, couldn't know, about her life here. So much she couldn't tell him, even if she'd wanted to.

She had to get them both out of here as soon as possible. Their relationship had felt so perfect. Pristine in its bubble. And now Brackenhill would leave its smudgy fingerprints all over everything.

In the distance, down the hall, or in another part of the castle entirely, Hannah heard it: the soft opening of one door, the closing of another.

Creak, click.

CHAPTER EIGHT

Then

2001

"Do you think Mom would let us live here?" Hannah asked.

"You mean go to school? In Rockwell?" Julia was lying on a double inner tube, pale-pink toenails kicking up a quiet plume of water against the side of the pool. She wore a red polka-dot bikini and a large straw hat she'd found in one of the bedrooms. The pool was in the backyard through a barrel vault from the courtyard. It was old, square, with faint moss along the edges and a spray of weeds shooting up through a jagged crack in the deck. The water, though, was warm and clear, reflecting the faded blue swirls stamped into the concrete below. "Could you imagine this place in the snow? Aunt Fae said once they didn't leave the house for almost a month. We'd lose our minds." They'd only been into town a handful of times. The road leading down the mountain was treacherous in good weather, the switchbacks sending Mom into a tizzy every June and August, cursing as the Buick rattled against the narrow gravelly shoulder.

Hannah tipped her face up to the sky. The sun beat down, hot and bright for the first time in a week. The castle was a glorious place to spend a summer. Until it rained for seven days straight. "I think I'd like it. It would be cozy."

Julia's face was turned away, her eyes closed, her voice whispery. "This place is a lot of things, but cozy isn't one of them."

That, at least, was the truth. It was magical. Beautiful. Eerie. Looming.

"Hannah, do you ever see anything here?"

"Anything like what?"

"I don't know. This place isn't . . ." Julia's voice trailed off, her eyes staring at some distant point. "It isn't what it used to be. I feel like I've started to *feel* something bad here."

"I don't care how bad it feels; it's still better than Plymouth." Hannah shook her head. Her sister was so dramatic. Sometimes Hannah thought Julia did it for attention, always talking about auras and energy, her voice floaty. Even back home, sometimes Julia would talk about spirits and *seeing things*, a vague reference with her hand waving. It made their mother impatient, even frustrated.

She thought of their house back in Plymouth, Pennsylvania, squat on the dusty road, two bedrooms, one bathroom, no air-conditioning. The roof that leaked, the sound of water dripping into hallway pots any night it rained. Mom driving the rattling Buick into Wilkes-Barre, where she worked at PJ Whelihan's next to the mall. Wes asleep on the sofa, the stink of him as he exhaled. Like BO and cigarettes, which he wasn't supposed to smoke anymore on account of his COPD. The way he swept all the butts into a coffee can, which he emptied into the toilet before Mom came in the door. She'd caught him once, and the fight had lasted long into the night. "If you lose your disability, we're sunk. You know that, right?" Mom's voice had been panicky. Her mother never panicked. She never yelled, screamed, slapped. Her voice was always measured, pleasant.

The girls had never known their real dad. He'd left Mom with a colicky infant and tantruming toddler and the long-held belief that when things got tough, people left, as well as the refrain of her childhood: *It's all just too much, Hannah.* The lesson that lasted, long after Mom died: *Don't ask too much of anyone.*

Wes was all they ever knew of a father. They lived in his house and had for as long as Hannah could remember. Hannah hated Wes, and sometimes she found herself wishing he'd drive himself drunk off a bridge. She tried to tell Julia once, who looked shocked by the confession. She wanted to ask her sister if Wes did to Julia what he did to Hannah. She couldn't bring herself to do it.

The first time it had happened, he was drunk, smelling like beer and piss. Mom was working, and Julia had taken to locking her room at night, but Hannah only wondered why later. Before that night she thought it had been about privacy. Or maybe she'd been sneaking a boy in. After that night she wondered, Did it happen to Julia too?

She was asleep when she felt the bed move, his hand on her thigh and then higher. She woke up fast, like being doused with cold water, his fingertips icy on her bare skin. She felt frozen, unable to speak, hardly able to breathe.

He thinks I'm Mom, was her thought that first night. A drunken misstep. The wrong door, a stumbling, dreamlike delusion.

But then it happened again. And again. Sometimes months between, sometimes only days. She never knew when she'd hear the telltale creak of her old bedroom door, the one loose floorboard that clattered. She always smelled him before she opened her eyes.

Sometimes she never opened her eyes at all.

He never spoke to her. Never said her name. Just his hands, cold, on her thighs, her stomach. Later, when she got breasts, he would touch them, pinch her nipple.

All she ever heard was the sound of his breathing, the feel of hot air against her neck as she pretended to sleep. He didn't seem to care if she stayed curled away from him, staring at the wall, willing it to be over. Pretending to be asleep.

She swore to herself that she'd tell.

Next time.

If he did more than touch.

He never did more than touch.

She never told.

She asked her mother, later and more than once, *Why do you love Wes?* Her adoration of him always felt like a mystery—some secret Hannah would be let in on later, when she was older and could magically understand love. He was repulsive to her, even before that first night in her room. His eyes were mean, his teeth yellowed, his skin sallow and gray. Hannah had found a picture a long time ago: Mom in a simple white dress, Wes actually handsome in a tux. She and Julia, chubby preschoolers, clinging to Mom's legs, the skirt puddling around them. Everyone had been smiling.

Her mother closed her eyes, tilted her head toward the ceiling, sighing. *He wasn't always like this. He's sick, you know?* Or sometimes she'd just say, out of nowhere, *We need him. He gets a check from the government. We get to live here because of him.*

And sometimes, *I stay for you. For both of you.* She'd find her mother sometimes in the kitchen alone, clutching a plastic tumbler of wine, crying. Hannah never interrupted her, never let her know she saw.

If her mother left him, where would they live? Sometimes when they drove, Hannah would study the streets from the back seat. Every house looked lived in. It was possible there wasn't anywhere for them to go. No houses left. She knew people lived on the street—her mother had called them homeless. That would be their family.

If her mother could stay for Hannah and Julia, Hannah could keep quiet for her mother.

Hannah wanted desperately to ask her sister: *Does he come into your room too?* But she never did. She was always afraid Julia would go through the roof. Her sister was unpredictable—wild mouthed and untamed. She'd never be able to take the words back, and if she told and they ended up homeless, then what? It was like shaking a bottle of soda and popping the cap off. Who knew what would get caught in the fray? Besides, Hannah was happiest when Julia was happiest.

The next summer her mother drove them to Brackenhill for the first time. At the time she simply said, "I work too much. You're alone all day here. That's not a summer vacation." Only later she wondered if her mother had known the whole time.

After that first summer at Brackenhill, her fate was sealed. She knew she'd never breathe a word. She'd had three months of magic and exploring and woods and her sister. The smell of the river. The feel of the water. Fresh-baked banana bread and peas straight from the garden. Music and laughter and games and jokes. Faerie houses and hidden trails. Flowers and sunshine and swimming pools. An uncle who taught her about trees and animals and plants and nature. An aunt who taught her how to bake, cook, even clean. The enchantment of a castle. Her room in the turret. And Julia, her best friend, even seemed lighter, happy and free, and they'd never had so much fun in their whole lives. If Hannah told, what if her mother took it all away? What if her sister, thirteen then, had to get a summer job? Brackenhill would be over. No. She'd hold her breath through a hundred nights of drunken fumbling, cold hands, hot beer breath, if it meant she could come back.

Floating in the pool now, Hannah thought of her friends at home, Tracy and Beth, how she should be mad that she was missing a real summer. Her first teenage summer of boys and freedom and biking around town. The community pool. She wondered if Pete Reston would be there, a lock of blond hair falling into his eyes, his mouth turned up into a smirk, like he was always teasing her, and his smell like watermelon candy. And Tracy and Beth had been fighting almost constantly, Hannah stuck in the middle.

Hannah thought of Julia's best friend, Miranda Pike. The gaggle of popular girls Julia and Miranda had slipped into: lip gloss and long hair in a cloud of perfume and pink. Her sister's new boyfriend, Josh

Fink, cute and nice. Dimples on both cheeks when he lightly punched Hannah on the arm. And the way he said her name, *Hah-nnah*, so that it sounded older and like she was one of them, not the pestering younger sister. When Mom worked nights and Julia walked Josh right past Wes in the living room and into Julia's bedroom, locking the door, Josh still grinned at her, even as he followed her sister around like a dog.

"Do you miss the Fink?" Hannah asked.

"No." Julia sighed, her fingers skimming the water, picking up a leaf and twirling it.

"Why? Did you break up?"

"Who would break up with Josh Fink?" Julia laughed, but it sounded forced. She adjusted her hat and kicked against the side of the pool, and the tube propelled away.

"Then what?" Hannah pressed. Julia had always felt like her equal, her very best friend, but this year had somehow spun away from them. Lost, somehow, in ways Hannah couldn't figure out. Her sister, previously so fresh faced, open. And now? It was like Hannah couldn't get a good look at her. Every time she tried, Julia turned around, closed her eyes, bent her head. She was pulling away, even before Brackenhill, and Hannah felt desperate to keep hold of her.

Julia sighed again. So much sighing, which was also new. "Hannah, drop it. I'm fine. I'm just . . . bored here, I guess." But her eyes were closed, her fingertips tapping the hollow of her throat.

"Don't you miss him?" Hannah couldn't imagine choosing to leave Josh Fink. What if he found someone else over the summer? Julia seemed unconcerned.

"No." She pulled the hat over her face, propped her head against the raft's handle. Her voice was muffled from the straw when she said, "Do you think we could ride our bikes into town?"

"Town? Why?" They'd never really done that. Aunt Fae wouldn't allow it. The shoulder was too narrow, the road too winding, the cars too fast.

"I told you. I'm bored. We know everything about this place. It never changes."

Bored of me? Hannah wondered but didn't ask. "That's not true. Remember the place in the corner? By the embankment? It was in the ground, like a storm shelter. We found it last year but never got the lock off before we had to go home. That was our project this summer. Remember?"

Julia muttered a *hmm-mmm*, meant to indicate that she was tired. Tired of questions, exploring.

It had been an odd little door, built into the side of a small incline and covered with debris and leaves. They'd asked Uncle Stuart about it, and he'd only squinted his eyes, twisted his mouth, before shaking his head. No, there wasn't a key. "Probably a root cellar," he'd said. Hannah had thought about that little door all winter, and now Julia just wanted to forget it!

Hannah slid through the opening of her raft, her legs slick with lotion, her toes barely grazing the bottom. She held her breath and sank down, opened her eyes, the water dappled with sunlight, her long dark hair billowing around her. She sat, the sandpaper concrete against her thighs, her lungs aching, her eyes beginning to prick with starbursts. She watched her sister's silhouette against the sun, floating aimlessly and undisturbed.

When she finally propelled herself upward and broke the water's surface with a gasp, Julia didn't even flinch. Hannah pulled herself up on the side of the pool, toweled off, and went inside. She showered and changed into shorts and a tank top and wandered into the arboretum, a room filled with windows like an enclosed porch with a vaulted glass roof. Her favorite room in the castle, warm, even hot—everyone always complained it was hot, but Hannah thought the sun-filled room felt like a haven. She was dozing lazily, sleepily, on the chaise with a book when she heard a prolonged scream. At first, she thought it was an animal, something getting hunted in the surrounding forest, and only after a moment did she make out Uncle Stuart's name and realize it was Julia.

Julia!

Hannah raced through the halls, out the back door, and onto the pool deck, reaching it the same time as Uncle Stuart, who'd come running from the garden, gripping a spade in his fist like a weapon.

Julia had pulled her legs onto her raft, the hat floating ten feet away. She gestured wildly, helplessly, toward Uncle Stuart, who gaped at the pool, stunned.

The pool, glittery and blue only an hour ago, had turned rust red. In the bright-white midday sun, if Hannah didn't know it was impossible, she would have thought it was filled with blood.

CHAPTER NINE

Now

Hannah found the hospice nurse standing in the back hall, blinking. She'd come in the side door, near the driveway, scaring all of them.

"Is Fae here?" the woman asked, and it occurred to Hannah that telling people their loved ones had died was exhausting. Was the nurse a loved one? Maybe. She was at Brackenhill every day. The same woman for over a year, she'd heard.

"I'm Hannah." She extended her hand, and the nurse shook it. "Please come in." Which felt stilted and unnecessary. The woman was likely more at home here than Hannah.

"I'm Alice." She was tall with a wiry build—so thin she appeared gaunt. Her hair was pulled tight against her head, and she wore plain gray scrubs. She gave off an air of no nonsense, something that in regular circumstances Hannah would appreciate, as she always valued efficiency. Nature's cruel joke, then, that she'd ended up engaged to Huck, whose internal time clock had two speeds: cautious and careful. But Alice, she vibrated nervous energy. Hannah immediately liked her, but without a clear understanding why.

In the living room Hannah motioned to the chair, and it occurred to her that was Uncle Stuart's old leather La-Z-Boy. Alice sat and stared at her expectantly. Hannah took a seat across from her on a deep-green velvet sofa with worn patches on the armrests and ornate claw feet. Fae's taste in decorating ran more bohemian than regal, and this living room reflected both the older furnishings inherited with the house and Fae's tendencies toward plants and natural fibers. The eclectic combination lent itself to comfort and familiarity, even when Hannah hardly remembered any of it. The room was large, spacious to the point of echoing, and too late Hannah realized she and Alice were awkwardly far apart.

"I'm so sorry to tell you this, but there's been an accident." Hannah took in a steadying breath, and Alice nodded, a look of realization crossing her face. Hannah continued, "Fae died in a car accident last night."

Alice's mouth parted, her eyes widening in shock. "What happened?"

"Valley Road happened. That, and she was likely speeding. We don't know why, or where she was going. I'm sure the police might touch base with you, considering you saw her every day."

Alice's eyes teared up, and she glanced around the room. Hannah had no idea what the nature of their relationship had been—had they been friends? Had they operated as an employer and employee? Had Fae been cool or warm to her? Had she made Alice tea in the afternoons as she'd done for Hannah and Julia?

"I'm sorry," Hannah repeated, and Alice dipped her chin, her ponytail falling over her cheek.

"What about Stuart?" Alice finally asked.

"He still needs you. In fact, I'm not sure what role Fae played in his care, but we may need more of you for a bit, if you can manage it, and then I'd like to find him placement."

"Placement?" Alice repeated. "As in a home?"

"Yes. I can't stay and care for him. I have a job in Virginia. I . . ." She let her voice trail off.

Alice was visibly shaken, her hands smoothing her hair in a nervous tic and her eye twitching. Hannah knew she seemed cold. She couldn't seem to say the socially acceptable words and felt a strange temporary amnesia: What were the words she should be saying? Fae and Stuart were strangers to her now. After Julia had disappeared, they'd faded into the woodwork of Hannah's life, relegated to a dusty, sepia-toned past. She found out brief updates from her mother: Stuart's cancer was in remission, and then it was back. Her mother's contact with them was sporadic and informational. Then again, her mother's relationship with everyone but God became transactional.

In the rare moments that Hannah had let herself remember the castle, Julia, Fae, and Stuart, she wasn't entirely sure it had happened. After all, it had been a total of five summers from the time she was eleven to fifteen. Cumulatively, it was fifteen months. A little more than a year of her life, peppered throughout her early teens, when so much of that time would have passed in an adolescent fever dream anyway.

But those summers had happened, and Julia was gone forever. The truth was laid bare in her mother. After Julia disappeared, Trina shrank her entire life down to the head of a pin, rarely leaving the house. She'd lived the rest of her life on state disability, depressed and anxious, mostly hermitic, except for Sundays, which were for church—a new development.

Wes, tired of Trina's depression, lasted two years before he split. Trina bought out the house using an insurance policy she'd taken out on Julia when she was a baby. Trina died of congestive heart failure in the winter of early 2018 at only fifty-eight, likely exacerbated by anorexia over the course of a decade. The few times Hannah had visited, her mother's refrigerator had been nearly empty. Hannah had grocery shopped, filling the shelves with fruits and vegetables, meats, potatoes. Trina, seemingly more frail with every visit, had merely shaken her head. "I'll never eat all that," she'd said, and Hannah had asked her, "What do you eat?"

"Mostly eggs. Sometimes yogurt or granola."

"What about carrots or broccoli?"

"I can't be bothered to cook." Trina waved her hand at Hannah. "It's all such a fuss."

Hannah had heard that phrase her entire life, *it's all such a fuss*, about everything from school activities to sports to Brackenhill. Even Julia's disappearance had seemed too exhausting to fully focus on. Trina was predictable in her complacency, in her desire for routine.

When Julia left, it was like Hannah's heart shut off. She couldn't find the empathy or patience for her mother's insularity. She came home when she had to, once because Huck seemed to disapprove of her nonchalance toward her mother's health (he'd chided her—only twice, but it had stuck because he never, *ever* did that), and she worried that he'd think less of her, that he'd think her cold and unfeeling. But what was expected of her? When Julia left, Trina retreated into herself. Like she only had one daughter worth giving her full self to, and it wasn't the one who had stayed.

What Hannah struggled to explain to Huck was that Trina had left her first. She was merely following her mother's lead.

Trina's funeral had been short and sparsely attended. She'd become active in the church before she died, but it was a small congregation. Hannah performed the funeral tasks, picking out the casket, the burial plot. She paid for it with another life insurance policy, significantly smaller than the one Trina had for her children, and Hannah could never quite figure out what that said, if anything, about her mother.

"Are you okay?" Alice asked.

Hannah's attention snapped back to the present. "Yes. I'm fine." And then, "Are you?"

"I'll be okay. It's a shock, of course. Does Stuart know?"

"I've told him," Hannah offered helplessly, her hands splayed.

"He likely doesn't hear or understand you." Alice sighed, wiping the tears from under her eyes with a tissue she'd fetched from her handbag. "He should have been admitted to hospice a long time ago. Fae was insistent that she care for him. And she did a wonderful job! Never missed an afternoon PT. Now I'm not sure what will happen. We may have to hire someone. There are occupational and physical therapists who will come in, of course."

"Hospice, you think?" Hannah mulled this over. "How long does he have?"

"Could be days or weeks or months. It's so hard to say. He stopped eating a few months ago and has a feeding tube. We thought that would be the thing."

Hannah again tried to feel something—sadness, grief—and came up blank. She remembered the Stuart of her childhood, quiet and sometimes silly. Pulling quarters out of her ears or standing to her right and tapping her left shoulder just to watch her turn one way, then the other while she giggled and he feigned surprise. She remembered Stuart down the embankment behind the castle, by the Beaverkill, showing her how to fly-fish and, later, clean the fish they'd caught, but first he'd made her admire the beauty of an eighteen-inch rainbow trout, its mouth pulsing with the last gasps of life. She remembered how it had tasted, fresh and delicate, and Stuart, who rarely said anything, had swelled with pride, telling her, "Nothing tastes better than food you catch or grow yourself." She remembered thinking then that this was how a father should be. How would she have known? Her own father was a ghost, her stepfather a drunk.

Hannah should be mourning the loss of the two most influential people in her life.

So why did she feel so empty?

CHAPTER TEN

Now

On the second day Alice stayed four hours, until noon. Hannah and Huck ate breakfast in the kitchen, out of Alice's way, Rink curled at Hannah's feet. He'd barely left Hannah's side since they'd arrived, whining when he was let out, barking at dust motes in the air, pacing their bedroom at night. It had been a long few days for everyone.

They sat at the long stainless steel worktop obviously intended for food prep for stately dinners. Hannah could tell by the wear, the scratches in the steel, that Fae and Stuart had regularly eaten there. She tried to envision them actively living in the castle, alone, and failed to conjure an image. When she and Julia had visited, they had dined every night at an ornate fourteen-seat mahogany table. Her shoulders pushed against tall-backed chairs, and she moved her bare toes against the rough wool of their Persian rug. There weren't many rules, and in fact, they'd been permitted to run wild, hiding behind the heavy brocade drapes, sending a folded square of paper—a football, they'd called it—down the length of the table, and cheering when the game piece traversed the distance. They were never hushed, never told to quiet down. Dinners were freewheeling. Aunt Fae always looking vaguely alarmed by the mayhem but Uncle Stuart chuckling, if never laughing outright. Hannah had the sensation of being the entertainment, like working to make them laugh was payment for the summers they were gifted. Aunt Fae was never overly effusive, but Hannah could tell when they delighted her. A laugh would burble out, and then her eyes would go wide, surprised by an unexpected drop of happiness.

But now the castle stayed eerily silent.

Huck had gone into town the day before for some provisions: his yogurt and granola, apples, almonds. Huck, the creature of habit, both infuriating and endearing. He'd asked her what she wanted, and she'd snorted. "Whatever they have. It won't be much." Rockwell was not one to follow trends, particularly those of the organic, grass-fed, gluten-free variety.

"I could hardly sleep last night," Huck said, spooning yogurt into a bowl.

"Really?" Hannah had fallen asleep quickly, overtaken by exhaustion, and woken in the same position as she'd fallen asleep. Huck generally did too. They'd slept in Hannah's old room; it looked the same, smelled the same. Deep-red carpeting. Heavy red drapes. Grand European furniture. Hannah had yet to open the door between bedrooms, to take in Julia's old room: the bright blue against Hannah's dark red. She couldn't bring herself to turn the knob, knowing her eyes would cast downward at the narrow transition between the doors for a note, a pretty, heart-shaped rock ground smooth by the river, or another gift Julia would sometimes leave her. Hannah had never returned the kindness—a regret.

"Didn't you hear all those noises? We're used to neighborhoods, I guess, not the forest and . . . well, this crazy place." He shrugged and ate a spoonful of granola. "But seriously, you didn't hear it?"

Hannah shook her head. "It's the doors," she said finally. She'd heard it for five summers, particularly in the black of night: creak, click. Aunt Fae had always told her it was the wind. She'd believed her, and after a while she'd stopped hearing it.

Huck stared at her. "You're not serious."

"Castles are drafty, uninsulated, you know." Hannah felt stupid, hearing her own words.

"You think there's a wind strong enough coming through a stone wall to close and open oak doors from the 1800s? Some of them have iron hardware," Huck said. "This place is freaky, Han. I don't know how you stayed here as a kid. I would have been on the first bus home."

"Not when *home* was worse than here," Hannah snipped, then adjusted her tone. Huck could be judgmental, quick to chastise others' decisions and bad choices, although she'd never felt it directed at her until now. He had a happy, boisterous family, loud and loving. Brackenhill was all she had. "It's fine. There's nothing to worry about, I promise you."

He stood up, rinsed his bowl, carefully dried it, and returned it to the cabinet. "I'm not worried, necessarily. It's a beautiful place. But you don't *feel* that?" He waved his hand around, implying something was in the air.

"Do you believe in that stuff? Everyone always told us, Julia and me, this place was haunted. Julia believed it. She had *experiences*. But she was a hormonal teenager." She swirled her cereal and sighed. "I didn't. Not really."

It wasn't entirely true. She'd felt *something*: a pressure, a draft, the feeling of someone watching her, a quick huff of air on the back of her neck, making the hair on her arms stand up. Even the idea of the basement—the shifting rooms, the pervasive smell of death, the echo of her own panicked breathing—felt like a distant childhood delusion. The pool, turned glittery red, had been a copper reaction to the chlorine, of course. Everything that had happened had an explanation, firmly planted in reality, offered up by Aunt Fae or Uncle Stuart and happily gobbled down by Hannah.

Until, of course, Julia had left.

Huck sat, attentive, and she realized it might have been the first time she'd talked freely about Julia. Being here, in this place, in the summer, was disorienting. She tried to remember being in *this room* with her sister. She tried to remember Julia's laugh and couldn't grab hold of it.

Huck stood and kissed her forehead, and she leaned against him, for a moment absorbing his calm, his heft. Sometimes she felt like they were diametrically opposed, and she didn't know if that balanced them or set them off kilter. He, so measured and governed by routine, careful and sure, offset by Hannah, her insides in a perpetual swirl.

Huck left to walk the woods, take Rink outside to run. The dog had been cooped up first in the car, then in the castle because he'd refused to leave Hannah's side once they'd let him in. Huck had adopted Rink before Hannah, from a friend—one of the financial men from the bar the night they'd met—who'd married a man with an allergy. Rink was an Irish setter but mixed with something—golden, maybe? His snout was shorter, his coat a shimmery gold instead of deep copper, but long. Rink had the energy of a puppy, even now at eight years old.

Hannah watched them walk away, Huck's long-legged lope across the flat expanse of green, past the pool, still covered in August, the black plastic collecting debris and leaves. Rink broke into a run, and Huck jogged after him; Hannah could hear his laugh echoing back to her, and she felt swollen with something, puffed up and weepy. His goodness permeated everything around her and always left Hannah feeling guilty, bereft, as though she were undeserving.

She straightened up the kitchen and thought about what to do next. She had to wait for Aunt Fae's body to be released to the funeral home, and then she could schedule services. Autopsy might take a few days, she'd been told. She'd have to call Fae and Stuart's lawyer, see about getting access to money to pay for everything. Fae and Stuart weren't religious, so Hannah assumed she'd want to be cremated, but she wanted to be sure. The *business* of death was consuming, but it kept her from questioning her mourning. She couldn't focus on her emotions, or lack thereof, because she had so much *to do*. It was convenient.

The front bell chimed—a deep, tonal echo throughout the house. Hannah stood to answer the door right as Alice appeared in the kitchen doorway, hesitant and on the verge of tears.

"Alice! What's wrong?"

"Nothing. Nothing!" She wiped her eyes. "I just . . . it's so strange now. I miss her. Stuart knows something's amiss. He's out of sorts."

"Why? What is he doing?" Hannah couldn't imagine what "out of sorts" meant for a semiconscious man.

"He's moaning. I upped his morphine drip, but I don't think it's pain. I . . . I know what pain looks like on him. He's trying to talk. He's upset."

Hannah was at a loss. The door chimed again. She held her finger up to Alice. "Please don't leave. Let me just see who this is, okay?"

Alice nodded, and Hannah walked quickly across the living room, through the sitting room, down the hall, and into the foyer. The foyer was grand, stretching all the way to the peak of the roof. Sconces dotted the walls, and an imposing crystal chandelier hung from the ceiling. The room was all deep-colored woods, forest greens, and blues, and it looked as regal as anything Hannah had ever seen. She'd forgotten about the foyer; it was so rarely used.

She opened heavy double doors that moaned under their own weight.

She felt, in an instant, light headed and breathless. Standing on the stone steps was a man she hadn't seen since he was a boy. Since the night, seventeen years ago, that had altered both their lives. She knew her face registered the same shock she saw in his. He wore jeans and a blazer, his reddish-brown hair curling into his eyes, which widened at the unexpected sight of her.

"Hannah." His voice was the same as it had been when he was eighteen: throaty but kind. Hannah closed her eyes and, for a moment, could hear him all over again: *Please, don't leave.* When she opened them, he hadn't moved. In his hand, he held a badge.

Wyatt McCarran.

CHAPTER ELEVEN

Then

June 2001

When Julia first suggested they ride their new bikes down Valley Road, Hannah had to admit she was skeptical. The road down was treacherous, and what could be so great about the small, dumpy street that was Rockwell? They'd been there with Aunt Fae, food shopping or running errands (or once visiting Aunt Fae's kooky friend Jinny Fekete, who smelled like smoke and oil). But they'd never gone alone. They hadn't needed to! They had each other, the forest, the river, the gardens, the castle. Why did they need to now?

Julia packed a backpack with sunscreen and towels, a book and sunglasses, and declared she was going with or without her sister.

"There's a pool here." Hannah wanted her sister all to herself. She wanted last summer all over again. She wanted to find the little door in the side of the hill. There had been a small winding creek that had a mouth at the Beaverkill a half mile through the woods. They were going to look at maps and figure it out.

A trip to the public pool wasn't in the plans.

Julia laughed. "When it's not turning blood red?" She hadn't gone swimming since that day, despite Hannah's pestering.

"It was a rust reaction, Jules. It's not gross. Stuart had it cleaned up in a day." Hannah tried to remember what Uncle Stuart had told them. "It was from copper, I think? He treated the pool that morning. Vacuumed out the sediment. It was an easy fix."

"I don't care. It looked like a crime scene. He has an excuse for everything that happens around here. They both do, and it's not right. I'm going a little nuts at the thought of another summer. Okay?" Julia stopped throwing stuff into her bag and faced Hannah. "This place is just freaking me out."

"Why, though?" Hannah felt the weirdness, too, but it never scared her exactly. Nothing truly bad had ever happened. She just knew she never felt *alone*, even in her room at night. "It's not new. It's just . . . Brackenhill."

"Everything feels different this year. Something's happened." Julia sighed and shook her head. She started to speak and thought better of it. "I just . . . it doesn't give you the creeps? We could be murdered, and no one would ever know. We're so isolated."

"Who would murder us?" Hannah threw her hands in the air. The whole conversation was infuriating! Honestly. They lived in a fairy tale three months a year, and Julia wanted to throw it all away for what? Drama. They both had that at home in spades.

"Please, Han? Please?" Julia placed her hands on Hannah's shoulders. "Look, I just want something different, okay? We'll come back and do all the things I know you want to. Just you and me. It'll be like old times. But wouldn't it be fun to find other people our age? We could have friends. *A summer crew.* Who knows? Maybe there's a cute guy hiding down in Rockwell."

Julia had gone boy crazy sometime in the last year. Josh Fink was always hanging around, and Hannah watched her sister flirt with everyone from lifeguards at the Y to the grocery baggers. Frankly, it was gross.

"Aunt Fae will kill us, you know." It was a last-ditch effort, but Julia just shot her a look and shrugged.

"Then we won't tell her."

Fine. They'd go.

At the pool, Julia shucked her jean shorts and T-shirt to reveal a black ruffled bikini Hannah had never seen before, showing off a new deep well of cleavage that Julia was always adjusting, scrutinizing. Hannah wore her two-year-old racer-back Speedo and spent half the day pulling it out of her bottom.

Julia spread the towel on the grass and adjusted her sunglasses. She leaned back on her elbows and crossed her ankles. Her oily skin glistened in the sunlight.

"Don't you want SPF?" Hannah asked her, but Julia didn't bother to answer. "Is this what we're going to do? Lie here? Like . . . old ladies?"

Julia dug into the bag, produced a ten-dollar bill, and handed it to Hannah.

"Where'd you get this?" Hannah took it, eyeing her sister suspiciously.

Julia shrugged. "Aunt Fae's purse. She won't miss it. Now go get a soda or something, okay? You're driving me crazy."

Hannah ambled across the grass toward the snack pavilion and took her place in line. She surveyed the crowd: teenagers and small children being chased by harried parents. Girls lounging like Julia, skin plump and sparkling in the midday sun. Huddled groups of girls being eyed by a line of four boys. One of them laughed and tossed a blue playground ball in their direction. The girl squealed and batted the ball back, but it rolled and came to rest at Hannah's feet. Gingerly, she kicked it with her toe until it rolled back down the hill.

"Hiya, can I help you?"

She was next. She surveyed the board above her head. "Um, can I get a Coke and an order of fries?"

"Sure. Pepsi okay?" The boy behind the counter had reddish-brown curly hair and an impish smile.

"Yeah, that's fine." Hannah didn't smile back. She moved to the side and let the boy take other orders. After a few moments, the wooden screen door on the side swung open, and the boy emerged holding a paper boat filled with fries and a fountain soda.

"Here ya go!" He was cheerier than he should have been. He was working at the hottest place at the pool, for God's sake. He held the boat out to her, and as she brought her hand up to retrieve it, her fingertips brushed his hand. A weird little jolt zinged up her arm, and the boy suddenly let go. Fries scattered at her feet. She managed to hold on to the soda but jumped back, the liquid sloshing out all over the front of her old red bathing suit.

"Oh, what the hell, I'm so sorry." The boy bent down to pick up the paper bowl and runaway fries. Hannah knelt beside him. "You know, it's not the first time I've done that. Not even the first time this week." He gave her a funny smile, half-raised on his left side, and she realized suddenly that he was older. Sixteen or seventeen, maybe? But still.

"You'd think they'd fire you," Hannah grumbled but grinned back, teasing. She could flirt too. *Take that, Julia.*

"Nah, not too many people want to work the fryers on the hottest days of the year with a pool only feet away. Besides, then they'd have to give me a job as a lifeguard." He pointed to his arm, pale and freckled. "Everyone would go blind. The place would go out of business."

"Oooor else they could just, I don't know, fire you for good?" They were both still kneeling, teasing.

"Nah, my dad's the owner," the boy said, standing up. He dusted off his shorts and raised the boat of dirty fries in her direction. "Take a seat. I'll be right back, okay?" Hannah sat at one of ten wooden picnic tables under the pavilion.

He returned five minutes later with a new, hot order of fries and a Popsicle for her trouble. He parked next to her, straddling the bench.

"Can someone really own the public pool?" Hannah asked, unwrapping the ice cream first and taking a bite. Creamsicle was her favorite. How did he know?

"Sure. I think a lot of them are owned. It's a business like anything else." He paused and plucked a fry from her plate. "I'm Wyatt, by the way."

"Hi, Wyatt, I'm Hannah." She swatted at his hand. "So first you spill my food; now you steal it?"

"I told you about my dad, right? I do anything I want around here." He nudged her with his elbow and laughed. "So listen: I know everyone in Rockwell, and I don't know you. What's the deal with that?"

"Everyone? I doubt that."

"No, it's true. There are only about two thousand people in this town. I'm related to half of them. But I've never seen you before, and I gotta be honest—people don't just move to Rockwell. It's not . . . a highly desirable place to live." His voice had an edge of bitterness, but it could have been Hannah's imagination.

"I'm staying with my aunt and uncle at the top of the hill. My sister and I come every summer, actually." She picked imaginary dirt from her fries and kept her head low, avoiding Wyatt's gaze. His intensity made her nervous, which was rare. People never made her nervous.

"You mean Brackenhill?" Wyatt's eyes widened. Hannah realized they weren't brown, as she'd originally thought, but brown flecked with green.

"Yep, that's it." She nodded.

"You live at Brackenhill?" Wyatt asked again, his voice edging higher. He sounded excited.

"Yes. Why? Is that bad?" Hannah started to feel weary. This was why she didn't want to come here, meet people, deal with their hang-ups. She knew she and Julia would be a curiosity and that interest would be a distraction. She wanted to go back home, up the hill, like Julia had promised her they could.

"No. It's amazing. I love that place. Would you ever let me see it?" He leaned closer to her. He smelled like sunscreen and something boyish, laundry left in the washer. "Is it haunted?"

Hannah paused. "Maybe?" She watched his mouth and wanted to touch it, run a fingertip along his bottom lip. She'd never just looked at a boy before and wanted to kiss him.

"Maybe what? It's haunted, or you'd let me see it?" Wyatt's leg bounced up and down, vibrating the bench. "Do you live with the witch?"

"She's not a witch. She's my aunt," Hannah snapped. Aunt Fae had made comments about the things people said. How people didn't understand her life, her and Uncle Stuart's choices. But Hannah had never heard anyone directly call her aunt names before.

"Well, whatever, are they as weird as everyone says? She almost never comes down off that mountain. Once she was in Norton's—the store on the corner—and I swear everyone talked about it for days after." His eyes glittered, and he gave her a crooked smile. She studied his face, close to hers, and could see the outline of light-brown stubble along his freckled cheeks. He was definitely older, but by how much? He had the confidence of a popular boy, a class clown, someone who would never normally have paid her any attention. She softened.

Hannah wasn't ugly, but she knew she wasn't beautiful like Julia. In the right light she might be pretty. Sometimes. She had wavy dark hair and blue eyes. Long lashes and a slightly too-large nose with a bump that only she seemed to notice. Her eyes were maybe a bit too close together and her chin a bit too pointy, but these were self-criticisms. She was, she supposed, average. Even though she flew under the radar, boys were scared of her. Her tongue was too sharp, her wit too quick. Things she thought were funny came out mean by mistake. She'd never cared until now.

"So which was it? Maybe it's haunted, or maybe you'd let me see it?" Wyatt leaned toward her, his breath sweet like mint gum and cool against her cheek.

"I don't know. Both?" Hannah stood, her head spinning. "I have to go. But . . . I'll be back tomorrow. Are you working?" She didn't know if that was true, if they'd come back.

Wyatt reached out and touched her arm, almost spilling her food a second time. "I'll be looking for you, Hannah-Banana," he teased.

"How original. No one has ever called me that before." Hannah tapped into the smart-ass corner of her brain again.

Wyatt didn't flinch. He didn't seem to mind her edge. And that, if nothing else, rattled her. She wanted to ask him how old he was but didn't dare. His hand rested on her forearm; he still grinned at her in a way that made her whole insides feel as slippery as butter.

Hannah made her way back to her sister's towel, where Julia stood with a group of four girls clustered in a circle, and felt a stab of something nasty. Julia got what she'd wanted: new friends, other teenagers, *summer crew*. A bright redhead was talking, gesturing dramatically with her hands, and the whole group laughed. She pulled her hair off her neck, twisted it into a bun, and let it unspool against her back. She was the center, this girl. The only girl whose name Hannah knew so far: Ellie. She turned, spotted Hannah, gave her a wicked smile.

It was fine. As Hannah licked salt from her fingertip, she felt like she, too, had a secret.

CHAPTER TWELVE

Now

"Hannah," Wyatt said again. And smiled—all teeth and dimples—and for the love of God, he looked exactly the same.

"Wyatt." She hoped she sounded composed or at least less ruffled than she felt. "You're a cop now?"

When Hannah had left Rockwell, she'd left. She hadn't looked back; she hadn't kept in touch. It was like Brackenhill had never happened. It was like her sister had never existed. Within two years her stepfather had been gone and her mother had been a shell and Aunt Fae and Uncle Stuart had just vanished into thin air, like Julia. She'd finished high school, moved away from Plymouth, and shut off that part of her life, her whole childhood, as easily as one licked an envelope shut. She'd pressed her fingers against the glue, held all the memories, the smells, the sounds, wonderful and awful and unthinkable, shut tight in a sealed place inside her heart.

And now he was here, standing in front of her, acting as though their parting had been normal.

"I'm a cop, yes." He exhaled. "I wasn't expecting you. I don't know who I thought would be here, but I assumed Fae had other relatives."

"No. There's no one. Just me." Hannah squared her shoulders and forced herself to meet his eyes, hold them, until he looked away.

He eyed the grand tympanum above him, then the foyer beyond her, until he settled his gaze back on Hannah.

She felt her pulse in her throat, and Hannah held the door wide. "Come in, please."

Behind Wyatt, another man stood, hands in pockets.

"Hello, Hannah," he said, and it took a moment before it registered.

"Hello, Reggie," Hannah said, formal and stiff. Reggie Plume looked the same. Didn't anyone age around here? Was the Beaverkill a fountain of youth?

"We're partners now," Wyatt explained, and Hannah barked a laugh. Rockwell stayed the same. Everything stayed exactly the same.

Inside, Hannah remembered Alice, whom she'd left crying. She led Wyatt and Reggie through the foyer, the hall, and the sitting room and into the grand dining room. Behind her, she heard Wyatt mutter, "Jesus." As far as she knew, he had never been to Brackenhill in the daytime. Only at night and only once. But it had been a very long time.

She motioned toward the dining table for the men to sit. "Do you want a cup of tea? Coffee?"

"No thanks, Hannah." Wyatt cleared his throat, and she wished he'd stop saying her name. It sent a current through her every single time, a single pulse of electricity up her spine. Reggie stood behind him, silent, taking it all in. He'd never been to Brackenhill. She could see his mind working, his eyes darting around the jumbled furnishings that at first glance seemed opulent.

"I just have to ask you some questions, okay?" Wyatt asked gently.

"About what?" Hannah said.

"Fae Webster's car accident." Wyatt cleared his throat again. "It's mostly a routine investigation, but there are some . . . inconsistencies."

"What does that mean?" Hannah asked.

"Let's just sit down," Reggie said, his voice still smooth. Lilting. Meant to be calming, but something about it set Hannah on edge.

"You're not in a uniform," Hannah said to Wyatt, stupidly, and wanted to pull the words back immediately.

"No. I'm a detective. I cover the whole county, but it's not that populated, so it's fine." Wyatt pulled out a chair and seated himself to the right of the table head.

"Okay, let me get Alice."

"Alice?" Reggie asked and cocked his head to the side. Wyatt withdrew a small recorder from his interior pocket.

"She's the hospice nurse but probably Fae's closest friend." Hannah had no idea if this was true. She should have known who her aunt's friends were, shouldn't she? She was suddenly aware of how odd her time after Brackenhill would seem to others. The complete excommunication, Fae's silence. It could read like anger, and Hannah didn't want to reinforce the notion that Fae was responsible for Julia's disappearance.

There had been a fair amount of suspicion thrown on Aunt Fae and Uncle Stuart at the time, or at least that was what her mother had said. "Everyone thinks they did it" had been her exact words, but Hannah could never be sure who "they" were in either case. Had it been the police or just town gossip? She remembered asking her mother, "Well, did they?" Maybe to get a rise out of her, something besides that listless presence, the relentless clucking of her tongue at every little thing that went wrong (dropped plate, spilled water glass, missing daughter).

Her mother had fixed her with a stare, uncomprehending, eyes narrowed. Finally, she'd said, "Of course not." But she'd said it softly, whispered, as though trying to convince herself. Hannah had taken pity on her, told her, "Ma, she ran away. I saw her leave. She'll be back. She and Fae had a fight." But there had been nothing on the bus station cameras. No cash missing from Aunt Fae or Uncle Stuart, and certainly no credit cards missing. Where would she have gone with no money at all? Her mother had mouthed the word *fight* before wandering listlessly back to her bedroom, her head shaking.

It was shocking how many people simply vanished into thin air. No body, no indication of a purposeful disappearance, little evidence of foul play. Their cases remained open, files gathering dust on the desks of grizzled detectives, or perhaps passed on to rookies years later. Or even more common, relegated to cardboard boxes in station basements. Scant bags of evidence jumbled in with other bags of evidence until all that was left was rumor and suspicion and diner chatter that, in the absence of a newspaper headline, became fact.

Alice sat opposite Wyatt—did Hannah have to call him Detective McCarran?—and Hannah took the seat between them at the head of the enormous dining table. Reggie rested his back against the wall, a spectator. Hannah wondered if Wyatt always took the lead on their cases—was he the senior? She couldn't remember who was the older of the two when they had been boys, always together.

The dining chairs were throne style, high-backed and ornately carved walnut, with red leather seats, and Wyatt had studied them before sitting down.

"It was all inherited," Hannah needlessly explained. "Fae would have lived in a box. All she needed was her garden." She felt compelled to paint her in this light: wonderful, warm, simple. She *had* been those things when Hannah was fifteen, but as she kept reminding herself, she had no idea who Fae had become once Hannah had left.

"She *was* very humble." Alice jumped in, her eyes tearing again.

Wyatt clicked a button on the recorder and opened a notebook. He asked the basic questions: names, ages, relationship to victim. *Victim.* The word sat in Hannah's mouth like sour milk.

"Married?" Wyatt was looking at Hannah, unblinking. His expression remained unchanged. Hannah wondered if the question was truly standard.

"Engaged," Hannah nearly whispered, and next to her, Alice said, "Yes."

"When was the last time either of you saw Fae Webster?"

Alice said, "Two days ago."

Hannah paused and then said, "2002."

Wyatt finally reacted, snapping his head up and holding Hannah's gaze. "Really?" He seemed to not believe her.

It was amazing how much he looked the same: same freckled skin, reddish-brown hair, but with a hint of graying around the temples— and what was it about gray that made men sexier? His hands, as he wrote, looked like his eighteen-year-old hands. She didn't chastise herself for noticing his lack of wedding ring, but she should have. And just like that, a man she wouldn't let herself think about for seventeen years was insistently, steadfastly *here*, to occupy her thoughts for the next however many days until she could get back home, with Huck—Huck! For a moment she'd forgotten about him—and Rink and her life, her real life. Her simple, predictable *real* life.

"Really," she finally said.

Alice stood, and Wyatt and Hannah looked up, the spell broken.

"I have to go to my next appointment, if that's all? Maybe we could continue this later?" She was brusque, done with both of them. "They're expecting me"—she checked her watch—"a half hour ago."

From the back, through the kitchen, Hannah heard her name being called, and Huck burst through the door, filling the space with his presence and his smell and his bulk—broad shoulders and a slight outward curve to his belly, only a little, large hands and a thick neck and all the things that had made her feel small, dainty, loved, now seeming crude and boorish, which was ridiculous; Hannah *knew* this. But next to Wyatt, whose eyes were widening in surprise, his mouth open like the fish they'd caught in the Beaverkill, Huck looked like a caricature of a giant. Rink ran behind him, barking and growling.

Huck stopped short at the sight of Alice and Wyatt and said, "Hi there, I didn't know we had company."

Wyatt stood, too, crossed the room and extended his hand. "I'm Detective McCarran, just doing some basic follow-up to Mrs. Webster's car accident. I'm sorry for your loss."

"I'm Detective Plume." Reggie and Huck shook hands, and Huck's gaze shifted to both men and back to Hannah.

Hannah realized that he cupped something in his left hand. "What's that?" She pointed.

"Right. So look what Rink dug up." He held up a stick. "I was down by the river, and he came running out from somewhere with this. He couldn't have been gone for more than a minute. It was the damnedest thing . . ."

Huck held it out between his thumb and index finger. It was, at first glance, a curved piece of wood, jagged in the center and symmetrically bowed on either end. One half was chipped, with a long crack extending from the center to the left side; the other half was smooth. It was off white where Rink had carried it in his mouth but caked in dirt. Hannah said, "That looks like a—"

"Bone of some sort. Right?"

The floor shifted under Hannah's feet. The room blurred, then focused.

Huck couldn't have understood; he simply didn't know enough. Hannah found herself staring at Wyatt, waiting for him to answer her unasked question. Huck continued, oblivious to the change in the room, the energy crackling between them all. "It is, don't you think?"

Wyatt held out his hand—"May I?"—and Huck handed it to him. Wyatt turned it over and looked at Hannah. The implication was unmistakable, and Hannah sank back onto the chair. What kind of bone? A dog? A deer? Was it human?

Alice hovered in the doorway between the dining room and kitchen, ready to leave the way she'd come in, late, impatient.

"It's a jawbone. These were teeth." Wyatt ran the pad of his index finger along the jagged center, and Hannah could see an incomplete set of molars. There were wells where the missing teeth would have been. Wyatt reached into his pocket and extracted a miniflashlight. He turned it on and aimed it at the bone, inverting it to look at the underside, a sharp bow, the ends flared like wings.

Both Wyatt and Reggie had been hunters at one time. Hannah didn't have a reason to believe they'd stopped. They, if anyone, would know bones.

Reggie said quietly, "It's definitely human."

Hannah felt herself go cold, her lungs constricting, a sharp blade of pain.

Julia.

CHAPTER THIRTEEN

Now

Wyatt dropped the bone into an evidence bag he retrieved from his car.

"If it's human, and I think it is," he warned, "I'll be back with a warrant, an excavation and crime scene team. We'll have to run some tests first."

"Do you really need a warrant? Can't I just consent to a search?" Hannah wanted this over with as quickly as possible.

"You don't own the property. You can't consent to anything." Reggie's voice was sharp and—it could have been Hannah's imagination—gloating.

Hannah rubbed her hand across her forehead, the events of the past few days catching up to her. Alice hung out a moment longer, caught in limbo, unsure what to do next, how to handle the bone discovery. Before she left, she whispered furtively, "Do you think the rest of it's back there?" And Hannah's face must have looked stricken, because Huck ran interference, walked Alice to her car.

Hannah had assumed Alice didn't know the story, but of course, people talked. She imagined Alice, upon taking the job years ago, learning of the castle's sordid history. She wondered if she'd been worried, scared? Perhaps she didn't know that Hannah was the missing girl's sister.

After everyone had gone, Hannah was instantly exhausted, her eyes drooping before she even reached her bedroom. Huck followed behind her, up the stone stairs, down the hall, and into the room they'd slept in the night before. It had been her room as a child, and it felt like second nature to take it back now. He dimmed the lights, closed the brocade drapes, and lay next to her.

"What do I do if it's her?" Hannah whispered and felt Huck's hand reach for hers in the dark. "What do I do if it's not?"

Who else would be buried in Brackenhill? It could be anyone, Hannah reasoned. The property was almost two hundred years old. In fact, it seemed unlikely that the skeleton would be Julia at all.

But what if it was?

She pressed herself into the space between his chin and chest, his arm curled around her waist.

"Tell me about her," Huck said softly and stroked her hair, winding it around his index finger.

It was like saying, *Tell me about the ocean.* Vast and consuming, stormy, complicated. How did you describe where it began and ended? Not knowing where to begin wasn't a good reason to never begin at all.

"There's so much, and still so little. She could be thoughtful and kind and funny. She could also be dismissive and cruel and cold. She was my best friend—for much of my childhood, my only friend. When we were small, my mother would never drive us anywhere, so while other kids got to know each other through playing and sports, I was home. Later, we had friends from school, but even then, we had to find rides places. I was with Julia more than I wasn't." Hannah closed her eyes, the smell of Julia hitting her memory: sweet and light and fruity, like gum and lipstick. Her voice drifted. "She was a writer. A lot of people didn't know that. She scribbled in journals and loved pencil more than pen—so she could erase, make it perfect. She was a perfectionist. Everything in her room had a place; it had order. If it didn't have a home, she threw it away. Nothing was sentimental. She didn't get attached to things, she said." So different from Hannah, whose spaces were always stormy—belongings strewed about, papers buried under clothing, subway tickets from vacations long over, small programs from museums, pamphlets from a whale watch she hadn't even gone on. She tried to be tidy; it never worked. "She hated being alone. She was always looking for people, searching for something else, something better than what she had. She was an extrovert. She was *funny*. Always poking fun at people in a way that others called charming."

"Like you," Huck said, kindly. Too kind, really. Hannah's humor ran more cutting, often called more bitchy than funny.

"No, people loved her. They tolerated me to get to her. Julia was everything *more* than me: prettier, funnier, kinder. I wanted to be just like her." Hannah let out a short laugh, and Huck pulled her tight. Meant for comfort, but something about their newfound confidence made her heart quicken; she felt a pull down low in her belly, and she coiled a leg around his.

In the dark, Hannah's mouth found the hollow of Huck's throat, and he held her. He tasted of salt and skin, and she felt his sharp intake of breath. Her body moved to his, melted against him, and he whispered against her hair, her neck, "I love you, Hannah," and she knew that he meant it. And that now, someday soon, he'd want to know all of her, the parts she'd kept secret: Wyatt. Julia and Aunt Fae and Trina. Wes. She'd never told anyone about her stepfather, not even Julia. She couldn't imagine telling anyone now; it felt like it had all happened in another lifetime, to another person.

And still predominant, the circling uncertainty: Would Huck have loved her more had he never come to Brackenhill? Had he never seen with his own eyes the complications of her childhood, of her family? And what if he had never known the secrets of the castle, the ways in which this visit would change her, change *them*, because surely it would if it hadn't already done so. She tried to push away this feeling—that this was an ending for them, not a beginning—and found she couldn't.

And maybe it was a necessary end: the end of false happiness. To be married, you had to be real. True. Complicated. Messy.

When they shed their clothes, Hannah had the disorienting feeling that she wasn't in bed with Huck but with Wyatt. She remembered the first time, her first time ever, in Wyatt's bed in his dad's house, with the shades drawn in the middle of the day. She remembered the way he'd smelled—musky and woodsy—the way he'd moved, carefully, fervently, how fast it had been over. And the second time, that same day, hours later, when she'd climbed on top of him, clinging, desperate.

And now Huck whispering that he loved her as he climaxed. She felt the shame in that, thinking of another man during sex. Wyatt showing up at the front door had done a number on her.

She refocused on Huck, on his smile, a glint of something both loving and mischievous in his eyes. "I want to know all of you, Hannah," he whispered. She let herself be pulled under, away from the castle, Uncle Stuart, the accident, the bone, to a place where nothing mattered, where her sister was alive and they were all happy and she could lie in the garden and see all four turrets in periphery and the sun beat down and she loved a man who loved her back.

CHAPTER FOURTEEN

Now

Hannah found Huck in the kitchen later, preparing a sandwich for dinner. She felt disoriented, hardly believing that Rink had found the jawbone this morning. That it was still the same day, even the same week.

A purple sky was a thin streak through the kitchen window. Twilight at Brackenhill. She remembered it. The smell of Aunt Fae in the kitchen, the house settling in for the night, the heavy anticipation as they'd prepared for the evening, Uncle Stuart washing his hands—long trails of dirt swirling in the porcelain sink. In late summer, the air felt pregnant with rain.

Still, even in the night, Brackenhill hadn't scared Hannah. The pool, the basement—these things were thrilling. Terrifying in an exhilarating way. Hannah had never felt in danger. Julia would tremble at each creak and groan, but Hannah had blown it off, hardly noticed it. She'd accepted it when Aunt Fae had attributed the strangeness to the house's age, its size, the wind, the mountain air.

Hannah slid onto a stool at the kitchen island. When Huck turned, he held out two plates, two sandwiches. He smiled at her, a dimple in his left cheek, and Hannah said, "Thank you."

"You must have needed the nap. You've been asleep almost two hours. You never nap," he teased her.

"It's so weird. I don't think I've been sleeping well here. I mean, when I wake up, it seems like I was knocked out, but I don't feel *rested*." Hannah took a bite, pressed her lips with a folded paper towel. The food tasted like dust. "That doesn't make sense, I guess."

She'd forgotten that she hadn't slept well as a child. In Plymouth she'd always been listening for the creak of her bedroom door—something else Huck knew nothing about. Here, at Brackenhill, she used to sleep fitfully. Waking up all over the house, sometimes in the middle of tasks: making a sandwich or once, dangerously, starting a fire in the fireplace. The sleepwalking had only happened during the summer at Brackenhill. That last summer had been particularly bad, with episodes nearly every other night. Hannah had tried to tell Julia, but her sister had blown her off, acted like she was imagining things or like it hadn't happened.

In Virginia, as an adult, she'd slept so soundly and peacefully she'd forgotten about her childhood insomnia entirely.

"What did Wyatt mean about Fae's accident being irregular?" Hannah picked a line of crust off her sandwich. At the thought of eating it, her stomach churned, and she put it back on her plate.

"I think car accidents typically have a standard investigation, even when it's only one car. Try not to read too much into it. At least, not yet." Huck was so practical, steady. "You should eat, Han."

"I just . . . can't. What if it's Julia? What if it's not? What if someone ran Aunt Fae off the road? Why?" Hannah pushed her plate away. "Even the idea of eating is just . . . blech."

"What if instead . . ." Huck's voice caught, and he stopped. Then he took a deep breath, started over. "What if you gave me a tour?"

"A tour." Hannah repeated it dumbly and looked around the kitchen. Trying to see the house, the castle, through Huck's eyes. The wide old stove, the small square porcelain tile floor, the stainless steel worktop of the island. The hanging pots in the corner, near the back door. The outside had always been more impressive than the inside.

They stood, and he took her hand, as if trying to understand all the new things about his fiancée, this new place, a new piece of her history slotted into place, while simultaneously assuring her that he was there for her: a shoulder to cry on, to lean on.

Hannah could see his need, which should have been endearing. She preferred him when he was just *there*, rather than continually inserting himself. She didn't need him to save her. This wasn't fair—of course it wasn't. They'd made love; he'd made her a sandwich. She could give him a tour. It was so little to ask of her. And yet Hannah was overwhelmed. At the same time, she was sure he didn't want the full tour—all the ugly secrets and truths of Brackenhill. Of her.

Hannah started in the kitchen, tonelessly gesturing. It was the one room he was familiar with. As she warmed up, she started to remember.

In the living room: Uncle Stuart playing old records for her. Artie Shaw, Glenn Miller, the pop and crackle of a forty-five on the turntable (she'd never even seen records before Brackenhill) while Uncle Stuart and Aunt Fae showed the girls how to jitterbug, music and dancing well before their time, but Uncle Stuart had always absorbed musical decades until they were part of him: his marrow infused with everything from Tommy Dorsey and Benny Goodman to Elvis to the Rolling Stones and Ozzy Osbourne.

In the front hall, the chandelier glittering in the moonlight, and the tall windows stretched floor to ceiling on either side of the door, wavy leaded glass playing tricks on the mind. The woods beyond the drive, black in the deepening night. Aunt Fae on a tall ladder, cleaning the crystal, and Hannah watching, mesmerized, as it glittered and reflected rainbows of light onto the ceiling, walls, floor. Then, quickly, a scream. The ladder teetering. Uncle Stuart, seemingly out of nowhere, catching Fae as she fell, both of them landing in a heap. Hannah, stunned, never fully understanding what had happened, just that Fae would have been badly injured if not for Uncle Stuart. The incident cementing the idea that Uncle Stuart would always, whether he was there or not, come to save them.

Hannah told Huck these stories as they walked. He took her hand, his arm slipped around her waist. He gazed at her with wonder, as if this made her seem like a wholly new, exciting person—a whole life's worth of experiences he'd never known existed. It was a shame how exhausting she found it.

"You've never said anything about any of this," he said more than once.

Hannah could barely explain it. "I didn't remember much. I feel like . . ." Her voice drifted as she pushed open the heavy double doors into the library. The library—one of her favorite rooms. Ceiling-high bookshelves. Ladders on each wall. Rich red velvet couches that you could sink into. Lose hours of the day in. "I feel like Brackenhill was always a dream. It was this place of safety." She couldn't tell him more without telling him about Wes, and something inside her resisted that. Halted, like a screeching car. "The days after my sister . . . ran away. I don't remember them at all."

She'd never said that out loud before.

She never talked about the morning after: Aunt Fae calling for Julia, up and down the halls. The frantic call to the police and then a man in their kitchen who looked remarkably like Reggie, and she'd had the realization that he was Reggie's father. A distinct memory of studying his face—his skin peach and ruddy with a smooth sheen, like a doll. He'd smiled at her and said something in a sugary voice—she didn't remember what. In retrospect, it was odd her mother never asked. Never said, *Tell me every detail.* Instead, Wes retrieved Hannah. Hannah told her mother Julia had left, she'd seen her leave and tried to stop her but couldn't, and her mother went to sleep and never woke up again. Lived the rest of her life half-awake.

Hannah, on the other hand, was left with two memories: *Hannah, please,* her sister's dirty hand on the doorjamb, her face white. And the police officer with the shiny skin, speaking as though through water.

And then? Nothing.

A blank expanse of nothingness where her sister should have been. What had happened in those four days? She couldn't seem to remember. And then watching the shrinking castle out the back window of the Buick, memories slipping from her mind like a slow leak of water.

She'd been questioned at some point, and she told the truth: she and her sister had fought, and her sister had run away. She didn't tell them Julia had returned, dirty and pleading. She wasn't sure if it was real. She'd had so many nightmares, sleepwalking episodes, and half-awake delusions that summer.

There had been flashes of Brackenhill in her life, even when she actively tried to avoid it: A Beatles song would bring with it the clarity of Uncle Stuart's hands in a clay pot, a glare of concentration on his face. The smell of fresh basil would conjure Aunt Fae chopping chiffonade for a salad. But if she tried to invoke the days after Julia left, the blank nothingness would return.

The police questioned her. Her mother pleaded, quietly, desperately. She used to close her eyes at night, willing her mind to bring forth the days after Julia left. She had other snatches of memory: Aunt Fae crying, frantic, calling into the forest. Uncle Stuart, pale and stooped, coming in from outside and shaking the rain off his shoulders, eyes closed as he shook his head. Hannah didn't remember if she herself had ever looked for her sister. Scoured the woods, their hiding spots, the trails, the river.

Then, months later, Julia's purse was found on the riverbank downstream, a small denim backpack of a purse that she'd always carried. It held her license and a waterlogged lipstick, the zipper still closed. It still hadn't been enough for the police to charge anyone. That was when the rumors in town had started. Fae was unhinged. Fae had been driven insane by

Brackenhill. Fae had killed Julia in her sleep, for reasons unknown. What else could have happened? When her mother had told her that, years later, Hannah had laughed. The whole idea was preposterous.

Upstairs, she skipped Julia's room entirely. Instead, her hand settled on the doorknob between Stuart's room and her own and found it locked. It had always been locked, she remembered.

"I don't have keys, but I'm sure they're somewhere," Hannah offered softly, the crystal knob still tight in her hand. Huck shrugged, asking only if the locked rooms were empty. Hannah had never known. She'd only asked about them once, never tried to pry open the doors.

"Julia knew, though." Hannah closed her eyes, tried to remember how she knew that. Her sister had said it once: "I know what's in one of the locked rooms." Hannah hadn't wanted to hear it. It was in that last summer of madness, Julia suspicious at every locked door, every whisper between their aunt and uncle. It had made Hannah crazy.

Back in the kitchen she stopped talking, the silence settling around them like a fog. The night had fallen, and the kitchen had grown dark, the only light emanating from the muted glow of the pendant above the sink.

Huck reached out his hand, cupping the steel knob on the basement door. "What's down here?"

Her chest swelled instantly with fear, anticipation, excitement. The feeling preceding actual memory.

The labyrinth. Julia. The feeling of childhood, fleeting, magical, dangerous. What if she took Huck, descended the steps, and found a mundane set of rooms, immobile, perhaps odd or strange but not extraordinary in any way? What then? It seemed, at once, crushing and terrifying. She felt protective of the memory then. That afternoon with Julia, when reality had seemed to slip, when they'd both found magic at the same time and felt united in their excitement and shared terror.

She said the only thing she could that felt true. "We don't go down to the basement anymore."

CHAPTER FIFTEEN

Then

June 1999

The door that led to the basement was in the kitchen. Aunt Fae and Uncle Stuart didn't care if they played down there. The cement walls were painted white; the floor was packed dirt. It seemed unremarkable as far as basements went. The first few rooms held cardboard boxes stuffed to the gills with picture frames and old notebooks, cookbooks, smaller boxes. Things they didn't know what to do with. Seemed a lot like their basement at home.

The rooms in the basement were small, about the size of a large closet. But the thing that made it interesting was that there were just so many of them. Like little horizontal blocks stacked sideways, connected in a multitude of ways so that each room might have two or three doors in it. Which made no sense—why not just have one large room? Or even, like upstairs, one hallway with storage rooms on either side?

"Who would build a basement like this?" Hannah asked. She was so close to Julia that when Julia stopped, Hannah would bump into her back. She could hear her sister's huffs of frustration every time she gave her a "flat tire" by stepping on the heel of her sneaker.

They were trying to get to the "end" because they never had before. They'd push through two, maybe three doors before doubling back, squealing in terror. What was at the end of all the little rooms? They had no idea. What if no one knew? Hannah had wondered. What if no one had ever made it all the way through? Julia told her that was dumb, it was probably just a regular old cement wall, but the point was, *Who knows?*

At the foot of the basement steps, you could only turn left. To the right was a solid white wall. From there you could enter a succession of three sequential rooms, each with doors at both ends and one on the right or left wall. In the past, they'd split up and tried to find each other again.

They hadn't yet gotten past the three sequential rooms because they hadn't been lit. They would have had to bring a flashlight and more courage than either was prepared to muster. The second room of the three had four doors—four!—and if they each exited through the sides, they'd meet up in room three.

But the strangest thing: once they'd walked back to room two from room three, only to find the room now had two doors instead of four. The doors were all old, wooden, and paneled, with strangely fanciful door handles: some crystal, some shiny metal, some old, painted. Like they'd been installed at different times, different centuries maybe.

"Unless we screwed it up, right?" asked Julia, who was fourteen and, Hannah loathed to admit, smarter.

"We didn't screw it up," Hannah insisted and walked them back to the steps, to the starting point, again. Room one, room two (four doors), exit either side, meet in room three, and walk back to two. Two doors instead of four. It was difficult to envision what rooms existed beyond the walls of the small room they were in. But still, not impossible. They were smart children; everyone told them that.

"Let's just go straight through until we can't go straight anymore and see what happens," Julia suggested, and so Hannah followed her sister. They pushed through one door, then another, doors alternately on the right and straight ahead, until it felt like they were going in circles. Hannah's job was to count.

1, 2, 3, 4, 5, 6, 7 . . . dead end, back to 6, 8.

"I fouled up the count," Hannah said finally. Were they in room nine or ten?

Julia huffed at her, and they retraced their steps back to the beginning, to the staircase that led them upstairs to the library hallway.

"I have an idea!" Julia exclaimed and bounded up the steps, only to return a moment later with a stack of index cards and a marker. "I'll hold the flashlight; you just number the cards and leave them in the room. When we come to the dead end, just call it whatever number and move on to the next number, okay?"

Julia really was the brighter one. So smart.

Hannah began again with counting, this time with *documentation* (a word Mr. Fare, her sixth-grade science teacher, had spent so much time on this year—she felt proud of using it over the summer). She wrote carefully, as her mother was always yelling at her for sloppy handwriting.

1, 2, 3, 4, 5, 6, 7 . . . dead end, back to 6, 8.

Hannah pushed open the door on the far side of eight. Not the door they'd come through (six).

There was a card on the floor. Room five.

Not possible—they hadn't gone in a circle.

"What the hell." Julia let a rare curse fly out. They retraced their steps. Eight, six, and then three, four, one, two. Then the stairwell. It was all out of order. Either the cards had moved—stuck on their sneakers, maybe?—or the rooms had.

"I don't understand what's happening." Hannah stomped a foot, dirt billowing below her sneaker. It made no sense. They collected all the cards and started over.

"This time, we won't go backward. Only forward, okay?" Julia instructed. "We'll get to the end and see what happens."

Hannah renumbered the cards up to thirty and then ordered them so all she had to do was drop them. They started off again. *1, 2, 3, 4, 5, 6, 7 . . . dead end.* The air had begun to smell like must and something foul and felt still, cooler, like they'd been descending downward, except they hadn't. She didn't think so, anyway. Everything *felt* the same level. *Back to 6, 8, 9, 10, 11, 12 . . . dead end, back to 11, 13.*

Thirteen was a quarter the size of the other rooms, barely enough space for both girls, and Hannah could feel Julia's hot breath on her neck. The door shut behind them, and Hannah screamed. She could reach out, past her sister, with both hands and touch cool concrete in all directions. The flashlight dimmed and flickered, and Julia caught her breath, which was starting to come in funny starts and stops anyway.

"Back out, Hannah," Julia ordered, her voice pitched and wobbly with panic. The room felt like a coffin, and Hannah thought of a documentary about being buried alive she had seen on television once—how they used to attach bells to the outside of coffins. People could pull a string, and a gravedigger would come dig them out if the bell rang. She shuddered, and suddenly it was hard for her to breathe too. Hannah's breath came in panicked gasps, and she started to cry.

Julia grabbed her arm. "You can be scared, but don't you ever show it. You're a rock, you hear me?"

Hannah turned, the doorknob right at her back. She tried to push, then pull; the doorknob wouldn't give.

The door was locked.

CHAPTER SIXTEEN

Now

She woke at three.

Huck snored gently next to her, facedown, his arms under his pillow. The room was hot; the castle was not air-conditioned, and by August it could get insufferable. A breeze lifted the curtains, and Hannah had the sense of being watched. She sat up, eyes scanning the room. Everything looked as she remembered it: white chenille coverlet with long ivory fringe, deep-walnut four-poster bed with oversize armoires on either side of the room. The floor was heart pine—variable-width planks with square nails. The doorway was vaulted, and the heavy wooden door swung open, soundless.

In the doorway stood Uncle Stuart. Alert, awake, dressed in the way Hannah remembered him: khaki pants and a deep-green bush shirt, with Velcro pockets and sleeves rolled up to his forearms. He motioned to Hannah, *Come here,* his smile reaching his eyes. His hair gray, salt and pepper, not white. His face lined but not gaunt.

She stood and followed him down the hall, down the stone steps, and into the foyer. He moved with the grace of a healthy fifty-year-old man. He didn't speak. She followed him through the kitchen and out the side door, into the courtyard. She double stepped to keep up, through the garden, down the stone path. Hannah walked quickly, her feet bare, her nightgown snagging on branches and sticks clinging to her hair. Stuart led her past the pool and to the edge of the forest to the path that led to the embankment and then the Beaverkill. He navigated the embankment deftly in his well-worn hiking boots, descending the way he'd shown her when they were small—sideways, long step, short step. She followed him barefoot and yet felt no pain.

The forest was dark, but she could see Uncle Stuart's hair, bright in the moonlight.

"Uncle Stuart," Hannah said, not sure what was real. Was this a dream? She tried to wake up.

He turned and smiled again, his eyes crinkling and the laugh lines deepening around his mouth. She felt a sting in the back of her throat and wondered if she'd finally, *finally* cry.

Slowly, he lifted his index finger to his lips, hushing her. With his other hand he pointed to the riverbank. The river was low; it hadn't rained in three weeks.

On the sandy hill stood a girl. Her hair long and shining, blonde curls in ringlets, wild around her pale face. Even from this distance Hannah knew her eyes would be blue, her mouth shaped like a heart, her nose rod straight, without Hannah's characteristic ridge. When Hannah stood in front of her, she could barely breathe.

"Julia," Hannah said, her voice husky. She looked seventeen. She wanted to fling her arms around her sister but knew now it must be a dream. "You're dead," Hannah said, trying to wake herself up. She'd read that you couldn't dream and feel pain. She pressed her toe into a pointed rock, felt the sharp sting.

Julia reached out, touched her hand, and tugged her gently into the river. The water in this stretch was pooling, slow and lazy. Rapids were upstream and down, but here, behind the castle, had always been meant for swimming.

Hannah felt the lump in her throat, larger now: What she wouldn't give for the dream to be real. For Julia to be here with her. She squeezed her hand; Julia squeezed back. Touched her cheek. Her fingertips felt warm, substantive, alive.

Hannah turned Julia's hands over and saw the dried blood, her fingertips raw, her palms shredded.

"Julia!" she exclaimed, but Julia gently pulled her hands away, a finger to her lips.

"Hannah, please," she said, and Hannah felt the tingle of memory. Her sister's dirt-streaked face, her hand on the white doorway, her mouth open, pleading.

Julia waded into the water, her dress, a pale-yellow bathing suit cover-up, billowing up around her. A laugh burbled out, and Hannah finally remembered her laugh, the thing she'd been trying to remember for what seemed like a year. Julia was her old self again, not the tightly coiled version of herself from that last summer. Not the secretive, angry, bitter sister. She kicked off the bottom of the shallow riverbed, the water spraying Hannah, and Hannah touched her cheek.

"It's time for you to go now." Julia stood in front of Hannah, somber, her hands on Hannah's shoulders. She pointed into the distance, and Hannah turned to see Uncle Stuart lingering on the embankment, waving her in. Julia leaned in, kissed her sister's forehead, and whispered, "Find the green door."

"What does that mean?" Hannah asked, her mind racing. What green door? There weren't any green doors in the castle. "Julia! What does that mean?"

Julia just pointed to Uncle Stuart and shooed Hannah with her hands. She smiled, waded back into the river, lay back, her hair floating around her. Hannah turned to see Uncle Stuart, arms waving frantically now, and glanced back at the river. Julia was gone.

Hannah followed Uncle Stuart back up the embankment, up the path, back to the pool, through the courtyard garden, in through the kitchen door. She followed him down the hall, through the foyer, up the concrete winding stairs to the second floor, down the hallway meant for cartwheels, to the turret room, her room. He opened her bedroom door, and she paused, gazed up at him, grateful and happy to be given the gift of her sister, even if only in a dream. Grateful for a few minutes with her dying uncle the way she remembered him: loving, robust, protective. Uncle Stuart kissed her forehead, bopped the crown of her head with a gentle closed fist, and she smiled. He turned and shuffled down the hall, back to his room.

Hannah crawled into bed, curled into the curve of Huck's body, his steady breathing lulling her back to sleep in seconds. As she drifted, she wondered, What was real?

In the morning, Hannah woke to the smell of fresh coffee and a cool swath of sheet where Huck should have been. She checked her phone on the bedside table. It was ten o'clock, later than she'd slept in years. She had an appointment with Uncle Stuart and Aunt Fae's estate lawyer today at noon.

Hannah tossed back the bedspread and quickly but quietly eased open the door. She crept down the hall and around the corner. The door to Uncle Stuart's room was cracked, and Hannah nudged it, peering inside. Alice would be coming soon, if she hadn't already. The steady hiss of a breathing tube, the click of the pulse-ox machine. She eased the door shut and padded back to the bathroom in her hallway. Hannah ran the water for the shower while sending Huck thought vibes to bring her a cup of coffee. In their house back in Virginia, she could have simply called down the steps. Not so much in the castle.

The dream was just a dream, then. Of course it was, right? What else would it be? She felt silly. She had wondered quickly if Stuart had died in the night, the dream his way of saying goodbye. She'd heard stories about that. It sounded nice, actually. Hannah had never had the opportunity. Maybe that was what the dream was about: a goodbye from Julia, seventeen years later.

She stripped off her nightgown and was stepping into the shower when she noticed her feet. She sat, hard, on the bathroom tile and looked at the bottoms, the heels, one and then the other. Caked in dirt and scratched, not deep but surface cuts, painless, thin streaks of blood from heel to ankle.

Like she'd been walking in the woods barefoot.

CHAPTER SEVENTEEN

Now

Two days after Rink found the jawbone in the woods, Wyatt knocked on the front door with a warrant, as promised. Alone this time, for which Hannah was grateful. Hannah had never understood Reggie Plume, then or now, and he always seemed to demand something of her, something unsaid and primal. Hannah knew, or could sense, even as a young teen that what lay beneath his smooth exterior was not a good person, as if at a cellular level he was put together wrong.

Wyatt brought an excavation crew and a forensic team and talked amiably to Huck, who led his team back to the spot in the woods where Rink found the jawbone. Hannah watched the two men stride across the courtyard from her bedroom window: Huck towering a foot above Wyatt, Wyatt motioning with his hands and speaking with muted purpose. Hannah felt the swirl of emotion in the pit of her stomach: fear of what they'd find in the woods, years and layers of earth being turned over and unburied, secrets exposed—amid a rush of love for Huck, who had only risen to each occasion since he'd been here with the grace and humility she'd come to expect, and an uneasy longing to know the person Wyatt had become, the man he'd grown into. Wondering how different he was from the boy she had known.

After that first day at the pool, Hannah and Julia had ridden into town every day, parked their bikes outside the diner, chained them to a light post, and walked with bathing suits, towels, and beach bags to the pool (Wyatt's pool, as Hannah had come to think of it). Julia dropped her stuff in a heap and wandered off to find her friends, leaving Hannah to set up.

Hannah felt bereft at her sister's sudden disinterest in her but also a building excitement at her own secret budding friendship with the redheaded boy in the refreshment stand. Her sister and her newfound friends wouldn't touch french fries with a ten-foot pole, so it was easy to keep their meetings clandestine. She hadn't pinpointed why she thought Julia would disapprove; Hannah just knew that she would. He *was* older, seventeen, she'd learned. But their friendship was so weightless, easy. The age gap felt like nothing. Julia wouldn't treat it like nothing—she treated *everything* like *something*, especially when it came to Hannah. Even when Hannah had brought home a D on an algebra test, it wasn't their mother who pitched a fit; it was Julia, ranting around her room. "A D! Do you know you need GOOD GRADES to get into college, and you need COLLEGE to be able to leave this dump of a town? I can't take care of you forever. Get your head out of your ass, Hannah Marie." Their mother had pressed her fingers down on the test on the table, tapping the red circled letter a few times, and said simply, "I want more for you, Hannah." She'd pointed to her PJ Whelihan's uniform, her name tag. "You are better than me. Don't do this." And then a crash from upstairs sent her scurrying up to Wes, who had fallen in the bathroom. His forehead spurted blood on the white linoleum while Hannah stood in the doorway, stunned at both the bright red against the dingy white floor and the idea that her mother could move *so fast*. She remembered wondering, in that moment, if her mother loved her stepfather or just felt obligated to keep him from killing himself.

Which was why when Wyatt kissed Hannah against the back of the concession stand in her new pink bikini, the lifted wood of the weathered boards digging into her bare back, the straps of her bathing suit snagging on the splinters, and he pulled her against him until their midsections met and she felt his skin against hers, a feeling wholly new and terrifying and exhilarating, and it took her breath away to feel the dampness of his sweat mixing with hers in the hot August sun, she vowed to never, ever live without *this*. Without the dizzying breathlessness of world-rocking lust. That if she was going to clean up blood from the bathroom floor, it was going to be for someone who made her vision swim, who made her feel like the earth was tilted, ever so slightly, off its axis and only they could feel it, wrong footed and off balance with love. She'd never do that for Wes, whom she'd never seen her mother look at with anything other than disgust.

Years later, when she met Huck, when she called the number on the business card, he made her laugh. They went to a chain restaurant for their first date (practical, quick, and *no, not PJ Whelihan's*). He made her feel like an adult. She'd been looking for a job in marketing, a real job, not a bartending or waitressing job, and striking out. She had felt despair at falling behind, at having no real income, no career, while all her friends pursued advanced degrees, coveted externships. Huck offered a glimpse of adulthood—with a side of kindness, laughter. Later, after they moved in together (practical, like a trial marriage!), they talked about money, shared goals, starting a family. They talked about whether the carpeting in the living room needed to be replaced and whether the water heater had another year. He never made her dizzy with lust. He was a proper *grown-up* in the way men almost never were. After all, Hannah and Julia had a biological father they'd never met, a stepfather who was nothing but a drain. Huck felt like a relief. She'd never have to clean the mess from a gushing forehead off the bathroom floor. *He* looked out for *her*, a comfort she'd never known. Or hadn't known in seventeen years.

Wyatt had the power to upend everything. If the remains in the woods were Julia, what did that mean? If Aunt Fae's accident hadn't been an accident at all but a deliberate act, what would that do to her life, her future? And who would do such a thing?

And now her worlds were colliding: her safety, her desires, her buried secrets threatening to spill over into her real life, threatening to topple her carefully constructed facade of a young woman who had her shit together. She had a career she liked, a fiancé she loved, a house they were renting to own, aligned visions for the future that included joint vacation accounts and 401Ks.

Hannah didn't trust her own feelings around Wyatt. The way, even now, when she'd opened the door and he'd stood there, unexpected, looking the same as he did at eighteen, her heart had hammered in a startlingly different way. She couldn't help but remember the summers, the rush of freedom, a free-flying happiness she hadn't known before or since and had spent the last seventeen years pretending she never wanted back.

Hannah now stood rooted to her bedroom floor, watching from the turret window as the two men retreated, figures growing distant down the forest path, Huck's hands in his pockets, Wyatt's gesturing, Huck nodding, and all she could do was squeeze her eyes tight and think fervently, like a wish, *Please, please leave us alone.*

CHAPTER EIGHTEEN

Now

Aunt Fae's memorial service was tomorrow. She'd been cremated, and Hannah was going to spread half her ashes in the courtyard garden; the other half she'd bury in a plot that Fae would share with Uncle Stuart when the time came. Hannah had never heard of burying ashes before. The lawyer was specific: they were to be together. Hannah thought it was rather nice to want to be tied in death that way.

The business of death was dry, almost callous. Meetings with lawyers, phone calls where Hannah sat on hold for an hour waiting to talk to Uncle Stuart's insurance company, discussion with funeral homes that centered around whether the urn would be moisture tolerant or moisture proof and what the difference was. The payment for grave opening and closing. It was all so clinical, which was jarring but also felt like a relief.

She planned the service for a nondenominational church down in Rockwell. The Websters weren't religious and apparently had never attended church, but Hannah finally found a pastor in town willing to give Aunt Fae a memorial that didn't focus on Bible verses. She'd sat with him the previous day and talked to him about Aunt Fae, the way Hannah remembered her: kind, giving, reserved and perhaps a bit nervous, but warmhearted. The man—Pastor Jim, he'd said to call him—had listened and asked questions, taken notes, and promised to deliver a eulogy befitting Hannah's aunt. She wondered, briefly, who in town would come. Whether Aunt Fae had died with friends or not. Conspicuously, no one had come to Brackenhill, and there had been no flower deliveries.

Alice would come. And then a name floated into her consciousness: Jinny Fekete. *Oh my God, Jinny.* Hannah closed her eyes and remembered the wild black hair, the purple glasses hanging off a chain around her neck. The arms stacked with Bakelite: tones of red, amber, and gold. The hats! Pillboxes and wool shell caps with bowknots, Juliet caps and berets, and sometimes one oversize white straw hat. Jinny Fekete was Aunt Fae's best friend, her only friend as far as Hannah knew. She'd only met her a handful of times; she rarely came to Brackenhill. She smelled like sage and something smoky, like she'd just come from a bonfire. Sometimes she smoked from a cigarette holder. Hannah had forgotten all about Jinny and had no idea if she was even alive.

She was puttering around the kitchen, putting away breakfast dishes, killing time until she had to go to the funeral home for one last meeting. Waiting to find out the outcome of the excavation that was still going on outside. Huck had taken Rink out for a walk, this time toward the greenhouse, down the path that eventually led to town.

"Hey." Wyatt's entrance had been soundless, and Hannah startled, let out a small yelp. He laughed. "Sorry about that." She was relieved to see he came alone this time. Reggie made her uneasy, more on edge than she already was.

"You scared me half to death."

"I'm sorry." Wyatt's voice was low, bemused. But his eyebrows creased in concern. "I just wanted to let you know we found the rest of the remains. It's a fairly complete skeleton, buried about ten feet from the embankment."

Hannah's hand went to her throat, and she found she couldn't speak, couldn't react. "Is it . . . ?" She couldn't finish the thought, the sentence. She felt the tears welling, her throat closing up, and held a fist to her mouth to physically stop herself from crying out. It all felt too raw, on top of last night's dream and probable bout of sleepwalking (Huck said it was normal under stress), but the whole day had felt surreal.

"We don't know, Han." Wyatt's voice cracked. All the emotion she'd been holding at bay came rushing up. The night of the fight, the night Julia had run away. Hannah's anger at Julia, her fury at Wyatt, her hurt—she'd felt like a caged animal, lashing out. Wyatt misjudged the look on her face and said, "I never got to apologize, Han. For the way everything ended. I never thought I'd see you again."

"Did you ever look? The internet exists now." Hannah felt rage like a spark off a flint: capable of growing to a full-blown inferno. She didn't want to talk about this now but couldn't let it just drop, not if Wyatt was going to press his thumb right to the burn—and it felt like a burn: open and exposed, raw.

"I did, yeah. But it affected me too. You know? Julia running out and just disappearing? And then when they found her purse. Everyone just said she died." He looked around the room, at a loss for words, and finally settled his gaze back on her. When their eyes met, she felt the pain right under her sternum. He continued, his voice a whisper, "I was only eighteen. I was a kid too."

Hannah closed her eyes, shook her head, held up her hand. She didn't want to do this now, with the *remains* looming over them. With the possibility that her sister would finally be found, put to rest. Finally, she said, "How will we know. If it's Julia?" Her mouth stuck over Julia's name, and she was embarrassed by how close she felt to crying.

He cleared his throat. "Well, if you knew the name of your dentist in Plymouth, that would help a lot. In 2002, we would have taken her DNA off a toothbrush or hairbrush, I think. At least I'd hope. But dental identification is still the fastest. DNA might take a week; dental records could take a day or two. Even with teeth missing—"

"Okay, enough, please." Hannah, eyes still closed, held up a hand.

"I'm sorry." Then, softer, "I am really sorry, Hannah."

"I can get you the name in a bit. I'd have to do a quick internet search—I haven't been back to Plymouth in years. I know they were on Washburn Street." Hannah straightened her back, squared her shoulders, and took a deep, shaky breath. She was going for businesslike when she said, "I hope that works for you."

He considered her. His mouth opened and closed before he finally said, "You look beautiful, Hannah."

Hannah felt her insides slide together, felt her body go boneless. Aunt Fae, Uncle Stuart, the dream, the bones, the excavation, Wyatt, Huck. It was all too much, and she didn't know she'd broken down until Wyatt had his arms around her and she realized she was sobbing, and she covered her face with her hands and just let herself weep, in a way she hadn't wept since she was a child. Wyatt smelled the same, and suddenly she was fourteen again, against the concession stand, the splinters in her back, the relentless pulse between her legs, and she stretched up on her bare toes and clung to him, her arms around his neck, his body foreign and familiar, and her vision blurred from the tears, and her body felt alive with sensation, all the synapses in her brain firing at once, her nerve endings on fire. She felt like she was falling apart and being put back together all at the same time. Wyatt's hand stroked her back, and he pulled her tighter, and she wondered if she was having the same effect on him, if his body felt charged, like his skin alone was burning.

She couldn't stop crying.

She broke out of Wyatt's embrace, aware suddenly that the air between them had changed. She stepped back, pushed the heels of her hands into her eyes, trying to stem the flow, but tears kept leaking out anyway. It was frustrating to not have control of one's own body.

"God, I'm so sorry," she blubbered, stepping back even farther, away from Wyatt, who looked shocked and pained and something undefinable.

"Please don't be sorry, Han. Please." His voice was throaty, hoarse.

Hannah leaned forward against the countertop, hands bracing her weight at the sink, her head down, breathing deep. She felt Wyatt's eyes on her. He strode across the room, plucked the tissue box from the counter, and brought it to her. She wiped her face, her nose.

"It just . . . hit me all at once," she offered lamely, and Wyatt stopped her.

"It's understandable, honestly. I see people fall apart all the time for less, okay?"

He stood patiently a safe three feet from her and waited for her to collect herself. The back door opened, and Huck appeared, took one look at Hannah's face, and crossed the large room in four easy steps. He hugged her and asked, "Are you okay?"

"I'm fine. It was just the initial shock," she explained and met Wyatt's eyes over Huck's shoulder. Wyatt looked away, out the window, to watch as his team carried equipment and evidence bags through the courtyard and the garden and past the kitchen window to the gravel driveway, where their dark-blue vans sat waiting, the state police logo embossed on each side.

Huck let her go. "I know it's been hard. What can I do?" He gazed at her, earnest and concerned, and Hannah felt her nerves bristle.

She waved at both of them, impatient. "Nothing. Nothing! I just want to know how long until we know. If it's really her."

"We don't have a forensic unit in the county. Too small. Our oversight is the state police. So it might take a few days to a few weeks to get a positive ID." Wyatt cleared his throat, spoke directly to Huck, avoiding eye contact with Hannah. "Unless of course you can get me that dentist. That'll be faster. I'll call either of you when I hear anything."

"What's your cell phone number?" Hannah asked Wyatt, and he cocked his head, questioning. She explained, "I'll text you when I have the dentist's name. It might take some digging, and I'll call them to see if they still have my records to make sure I've got the right one. It's been over seventeen years."

"Right." Wyatt rattled it off, and then, with a small wave and a thin smile, he left, followed his team to the vans.

"Are you sure you're okay?" Huck asked. "This must be impossible for you."

"I'm fine. It's fine." Hannah thought of her cascade of tears and how all Huck said he wanted from her was her whole self, vulnerable and honest, and she couldn't help but think of how he would have felt if he had been the one to receive her emotional meltdown. As long as it was temporary, one time, he'd be delighted, she cuttingly thought. What would he do if she suddenly needed him, not just once? Swooping in to save someone once makes you a hero. Saving someone repeatedly is work.

It was a lightning-quick thought: Wyatt was the keeper of her feelings. It was a pathetic realization. She'd been fifteen; had she really not matured? Weren't emotional intelligence and development supposed to come with age?

She repeated it again, set to convince them both. "I'm fine."

CHAPTER NINETEEN

Then

Fall 2001

That initial summer of Wyatt passed in a blur of flirting, kissing, talking. Of feeling like Hannah was taking a first step toward something grown up. Did she have a boyfriend? She longed to ask him. But it felt like pressing a fingertip to an old bruise: it hurt all over again and accomplished nothing. She was fourteen, a number that weirded Wyatt out, even as he kissed her, played with her hair, gently bit her earlobe, a move that made her gasp. She hadn't known anyone could feel this way about a *boy*. The boys at home were sweaty and pawing and copped a feel in the movie theater and had no desire to make her gasp. Or at least if they had the desire, they didn't have the knowledge.

The day Trina came back to get them, that fourth summer, rattling up the driveway in the old Buick, Hannah didn't think she'd ever eat again. Her stomach felt perpetually twisted, filled up with longing for a boy she wouldn't see for over nine months—*nine months*—and in the car when Julia said, "What's your problem?" Hannah could only wave her away. She'd kept Wyatt a secret all summer, even when she was bursting to talk. Julia and Hannah had both made friends, spent their summer half-apart, half-together. It was amazing how little Julia asked her. If Hannah hadn't known better, she'd have thought her sister didn't care. What did she think she'd done all summer?

Hannah wondered if she'd ever feel that kind of love again. She missed Wyatt with every last cell in her body, sometimes felt like she was going to shrivel up, become a husk of herself.

They exchanged emails. Long newsy letters and sometimes just I miss you. It had been on the tip of her tongue to tell Julia, but she didn't want to let Wyatt down. Couldn't let him down.

She didn't tell Tracy and Beth either. Just kept him to herself like her own delicious secret.

She turned fifteen on June 1, and she was counting down the months. Fifteen sounded so much better than fourteen. Surely they'd go public then?

She had a cell phone, a cheap flip phone, and he'd call her late at night.

"I got my license," he whispered. She'd closed her bedroom door and was curled under the blankets in her bed, listening to his voice. Her mother was working, Wes was passed out on the sofa, and Julia was watching television in her room, the volume turned up loud. Hannah was blessedly alone. She remembered this exact scenario in the spring, before she'd met Wyatt. Everyone had scattered like dandelion seeds, and she'd felt hopelessly lonely. Then, "Let me come see you." His voice was hoarse.

"Really? Why?"

"I just want to kiss you again. I can't wait nine months. Just one time, sneak me in."

"It's a three-hour drive," Hannah protested, the danger pulsing under her breastbone. What if Wes let himself into her room and found Wyatt? He'd only done that once all winter and spring. Then Wyatt would know about what he had done. What would he possibly think of her?

"So what? I'll bring my dad's car. The off-season is hard on him. He sleeps a lot."

They planned it, talking every night until the day of. She bought a hook-and-eye lock for her door at the hardware store and installed it herself. She'd always been afraid to install a lock. That her mother would question her or, the biggest fear, that Wes would punish her mother for it. But for one night, she could risk it to keep Wyatt safe.

Hannah could hardly concentrate in school, could hardly pay attention to Beth and Tracy until they waved a hand in front of her face: "Yoo-hoo, is anyone home?" She raced home, changed her clothes, bra, and underwear no less than three times, and sat on her bed and just waited.

At nine, Trina left for the bar, and Wes snored softly on the sofa. Julia had gone out with a friend—to the library, she'd said, but Hannah knew that was bullshit. Her sister was filled to the brim with secrets too.

Hannah's cell phone rang once, twice, then stopped. His signal. She crept downstairs to the front door and flicked the porch light.

When she opened the front door, his smile took her breath away. He kissed her right there on the porch, so eager their teeth clashed together, and they both laughed. She shut the door softly and tiptoed right past Wes, who hadn't moved, his eyes still closed, *The X-Files* playing on mute in the background.

She hadn't thought ahead to this part: to Wyatt seeing Wes, her little dump of a half-double house in Plymouth. Wes, his gross mouth open and the stink of his feet on her ratty plaid couch. Wyatt didn't even flinch, just nudged her and grinned shyly. It made her blood rush.

In her bedroom, Hannah jumped on Wyatt, her body suddenly, virulently on fire, a pulse between her legs, her hands running along his back, his backside, his legs. Hannah had never wanted so much in her life. He laughed at her, sweetly, his fingertips skimming her cheek, the nape of her neck. Innocent places that frustrated Hannah. Their kisses grew from giggly to deep to frantic.

"I didn't come here to get laid," he gasped into her neck. Hannah didn't even feel like she could talk. No one had ever done anything like this for her. Three hours in, three hours back, just for her? Trina complained she had to do it twice a summer. The simple kindness made her hormonal. Crazy for him. What she was doing to his body made her crazy for him. "Han, I don't even have a condom." He had taken her wrists in one hand and held them down, bent over to take a few calming breaths.

"I can get one," she said automatically. She knew her mother kept them in her bedside table. She couldn't think about her mother that way—especially with Wes—but she'd seen them in there before.

She jerked her hands out of his grip and, with a coy smile, pressed her palms against the bulge in his jeans, worked it through the fabric. He groaned, "Jesus, Hannah," before kissing her again, tongue skimming her lips. "Okay, yes. Go."

In the hallway she scooted past Julia's empty room, her footsteps silent. The door to her mother's room was wide open, and the bedside table was closest to the door. She inched open the drawer and saw the foil squares, four in a strip. She eased out the whole strip—why not?—and slowly pushed the drawer back in.

"What the fuck?" The voice came from the doorway. Hannah jumped back, her heartbeat wild. Wes stood in front of her, shirtless, barefoot, and Hannah looked down at his toenails, long and yellow. "Look at me. Are you stealing condoms from me?"

"No. I was . . ." She couldn't think. Wes barely spoke to either Hannah or Julia, rarely yelled at them. In fact, he scarcely acknowledged their existence, aside from his bedroom visits. Behind him in the hall, she saw Wyatt, eyes wide with fear.

"You're what? Sixteen?" She realized then that he was too drunk to know which sister she was. He covered the gap between them in a second and stood over her. He was taller than she remembered, probably over six feet. Hannah straightened her spine, met his gaze. "You're a whore like your mother."

He said it quietly, which was why it came as a shock when he backhanded her in the face.

Her jaw cracked, and she saw bursts of light. She dropped the strip of condoms and collapsed on the floor, on her knees. She heard a noise, a low keening that she realized was her own voice.

Wyatt rushed at Wes, landed a right hook to his cheek. Wes stumbled once, his body cracked against the railing of the steps, and he fell to the ground unconscious.

The rest of the night passed in a blur: Wyatt made her call Trina at work, who came home within the hour, mumbling about being docked pay, but stared at Wes's limp form in the hall with a sneered lip. He hadn't woken up.

Wyatt had retreated to her bedroom, and Hannah claimed the punch. She even held her hand a bit for effect. It would help no one to have Wyatt discovered, Hannah reasoned to herself. Trina had enough on her plate. She doubted Wes would remember anything, and if he did and insisted that an unknown boy had hit him, Hannah would just play dumb. It wouldn't be hard to make Wes look delusional. It would piss him off, though. Hannah bit her thumbnail.

"What were you doing?" Trina asked Hannah, her eyes narrowed. By this time Julia had come home, and she watched the whole exchange with incredulity and horror.

"I was looking for nail clippers." The lie came out smooth and easy. Julia held ice to her sister's cheek and let the tears fall down her own cheeks without wiping them away.

"I should have been here," Julia whispered. Hannah almost told her then. Almost confessed. To everything. Wes and his nighttime visits. Wyatt hiding in the bedroom.

Wyatt wouldn't leave until he was sure Hannah was okay. Hannah made every excuse she could think of to try to leave. She took ibuprofen.

Let Julia fuss over her, blotting up the blood from her nose with a pile of tissues. Finally she pretended to be falling asleep on Julia's bed, and Julia let her go.

She found Wyatt in her bed, waiting for her. He held the ice to her face and brushed the hair from her eyes. She could barely look him in the eyes, she was so horribly embarrassed. She just wanted him to leave her alone. Leave this stupid, trashy little house. She wondered if he'd tell anyone where they lived. Wondered if they'd go back to Rockwell in June a laughingstock.

"What will you tell your mom and sister when he wakes up?" Wyatt whispered.

"It won't matter. He never remembers anything. He's falling-down drunk and knocked unconscious." Hannah was immediately mortified at this obviously regular occurrence.

She dozed off and on, waking only to apologize for the disaster that was her life. Wes hadn't usually hit them—his anger was mostly aimed at Trina. Sometimes, though, he misdirected.

"Hannah, I'm not leaving you," he whispered. His arms came around her, and finally, she slept soundly in the circle of his body.

When she woke up the next morning, he had gone.

CHAPTER TWENTY
Now

"I think they found Julia in the woods." Hannah sat next to Uncle Stuart, who remained unmoving. "I think they found her bones." She stroked his hand and remembered the scar near his ring finger, visible when he was younger but now hidden among paper-thin creases in his skin. The scar had come about the day he'd built them a tree house. It was more like a platform, not a full house, per se, in a maple fifty feet down the path that he and Hannah had picked together. He'd used a chain saw to cut a few larger branches to make room for the platform but reached for his trusty hacksaw to trim a few smaller offshoots. Julia had found them just as he started sawing, exclaimed, "Oh my God, don't fall!" as Uncle Stuart balanced, a foot on each remaining bough. He turned his head, startled, and slipped, slicing his hand from second knuckle to wrist.

Aunt Fae ran out, summoned by Julia, and met them in the court-yard, bandages and gauze in hand, barely batting an eyelash at the gushing blood. Hannah was reminded of Wes, the wound on his forehead pulsing red on the bathroom floor, and their mother, verging on hysterics, blotting his eyebrow with a red-soaked paper towel. Aunt Fae was impassive, clinical. She sent him back down the path with a bandaged hand and asked that he "please be more careful with a hacksaw, or you'll chop your fingers clean off." She'd retreated back into the castle, shaking her head.

Hannah retold the whole story to Uncle Stuart, fingers seeking the scar, that raised red ridge, and finding nothing. She paused, let the hiss of his oxygen fill the silence. Then, "Today is Aunt Fae's memorial. Do you know that? Can you hear me?" She studied his face. His skin was translucent, his eyelids fluttering. "Remember how I told you she passed away in a car accident?"

His eyes opened, the whites milky, the blue almost gray, clouded with cataracts maybe. He wasn't terribly old, but he looked skeletal. Hannah felt her breath catch, and her hand flew to her mouth. "Uncle Stuart, can you hear me?" she asked, louder. "It's Hannah. Your niece?"

Slowly his eyes met hers above the translucent green of the oxygen mask, and he nodded. Hannah reached out and squeezed his hand, and he almost imperceptibly squeezed back.

"I'm sorry I stayed away so long," Hannah apologized, but she wasn't sure what for. She'd been a child. If anything, her aunt and uncle should have tried to call her, contact her. She'd still been a child. At least for a while.

But Uncle Stuart was dying and had spent his whole life being deferential to his beloved Fae. It seemed likely their estrangement from Hannah had been Aunt Fae's doing. But why? What could Hannah have done to drive her away, at only fifteen? She barely remembered the days between Julia disappearing, all the police combing the property, and Wes behind the wheel of the rattly Buick, coming up the driveway, stones kicking out from underneath the tires. Her mother conspicuously absent, and later, the Rockwell police making the trip to interview Trina and Hannah for the second (third?) time.

It wasn't until she was an adult that she'd asked herself why Trina wouldn't have come to Brackenhill. She'd always grumbled about the drive—it couldn't have been that, could it? Her mother rarely left the Plymouth city limits, aside from two yearly trips to Rockwell. She'd asked Wes, in the car, where her mother was, and he simply grunted, "She's too sick to come." Sick how? With grief?

In the immediate aftermath, Trina refused to leave her bedroom. Then later, it seemed like she sometimes believed the narrative that emerged from Rockwell: Aunt Fae had killed Julia, but no one could prove it. The police never outright alleged it, but people talked: Fae, always eccentric and insular, had lost her mind in that stone castle and killed her niece. It seemed that Trina believed that story, too, no matter what Hannah said: "She ran away. She got scared of something; I don't know what." Hannah never saw anything in Aunt Fae that would lead her to believe she'd kill. Especially her niece. It never made sense. No, Julia left them. For reasons Hannah would never know. She'd long since accepted it.

She'd stayed away initially out of deference—she thought it was what they wanted. Then after she went to college, moved away from her mother, it was out of rebellion. She'd turned angry at the long silence. After college she lived her life the way everyone does in their twenties: selfishly. Bouncing from job to job, apartment to apartment. Figuring out how to pay bills and make doctor appointments and keep plants and fish alive. Then she'd met Huck, started what felt like her real life, and thought, fleetingly, about calling them. Visiting. It always seemed like she had time to figure out her relationship with her past. It was muddled in her confusion over Julia, if she'd loved Hannah the way Hannah had loved her. There seemed to be so much to work out, so much fog to break through, that it had seemed insurmountable. And now it was silly how possible it would have been. One day, make the drive. A lifetime of questions answered.

She should have come.

Uncle Stuart shook his head, held up his right hand, bobbing it in the air. Hannah gently pulled the mask from his mouth so he could speak.

"You," he said. "You."

She thought at first it was an accusation, his index finger still bobbing.

"Me, what?" she prodded gently.

"You have nothing . . . to be sorry for." He wheezed, his eyes fluttering. "We were so . . . very . . . sorry. It was . . . Ruby. Too much." He fumbled with the mask, and Hannah replaced it, moved it over his mouth.

Who was Ruby?

His eyes fluttered shut, and she felt the loss suddenly. Intensely. An emptiness blooming in her chest. Uncle Stuart had given her a key piece to the puzzle she'd never solve now, with him barely able to utter a sentence and Aunt Fae dead. Who was Ruby? There was so much that stayed just out of reach, so many secrets to this castle, her family, her sister, her past.

"Who's Ruby, Uncle Stuart?"

"She was a child. Just ten . . . an accident." His voice garbled through the plastic.

"Ruby was ten, Uncle Stuart? What happened to Ruby?"

"She never got over what she did." Uncle Stuart's voice rumbled, barely audible, and his eyes were drooping shut. "She loved all of you so much."

Then he smiled.

CHAPTER
TWENTY-ONE
Now

Hannah had no idea what flowers you bought for an estranged and now deceased aunt. There wasn't a stargazer lily specifically to say, *I'm sorry everyone thinks you're a killer, but I don't. Not really, but maybe we should have talked about that.*

She stood in the florist's shop—Pam's Blossoms—the only one in town, with a clerk Hannah could only assume was Pam herself, and stared at the prearranged baskets. So many purple and pink carnations. Aunt Fae could do a better job herself. Hannah obviously should have done this earlier, but she'd never been in charge of a funeral before.

Hannah checked her watch, an idea taking hold. Could she make it up the mountain and back down in time? Maybe. A bouquet from Fae's own garden might be perfect if Hannah could pull it off.

She left the shop, breathless, and ran directly into a wall of a man. "Whoa, slow down there. Where you rushing off to?"

Reggie. His face broke out into a slow smile.

"Hi, Reggie," Hannah said, keeping her tone light. He was in black dress pants and a white button-down. A bead of sweat worked its way down his neck, behind his ear.

"I'm glad I ran into you." He gave a mirthless laugh. "Or you ran into me. I was hoping to get you alone for a minute."

"Oh? Why's that?" Hannah checked her watch. She only had an hour before the service, and Huck was waiting for her back at Brackenhill. She cursed her own lack of forethought. She could have done this yesterday. The days seemed to be blending together.

Reggie leaned forward, his shoulder touching hers. His breath smelled like mint and cigarettes. "I've thought about you a lot over the years, you know? The mysterious Brackenhill sisters."

"You don't act like a cop," Hannah said, her voice reedy, betraying her own nerves. Reggie always set her teeth on edge. His hooded eyes felt like they were dissecting her and finding her lacking. His permanently curved lips felt like mockery, except when his gaze got caught on her mouth. Hannah could never tell if he was trying to flirt with her or scare her. Perhaps with Reggie, the line between was too thin.

"Well, I'm on your aunt's case with Detective McCarran. Sorry, *Wyatt*." His voice took on a sarcastic edge.

Hannah put some distance between them until her back was flush with a lamppost, and she realized too late she was cornered. Reggie took a step forward, closing the gap.

"There's a lot I never understood about that summer. Wyatt is a steel trap about all of it."

Good, Hannah wanted to say but didn't.

Reggie ran his index finger down Hannah's bare arm, bringing gooseflesh to the surface. He didn't seem inclined to let her go anytime soon.

"What did you want to know?" Hannah closed her eyes. If she told him what he wanted to know, would he let her leave? Why did Rockwell and all the people in it seem so intent on holding her captive?

"For starters, were you and Wyatt really a thing? I always thought you made that up. A little girl with a crush."

"I was fifteen. Hardly a little girl." Hannah hated the defensive edge in her tone, playing into Reggie's mind games.

"Then what your sister did was pretty low, even for her."

"What does that mean?" Hannah's nostrils flared. The anger felt like a fist on her throat.

"Well, it was no secret she was a bitch." Reggie leaned against her, his lips to her ear. Much too close, too intimate. "But to kiss her sister's boyfriend?"

"She didn't know. No one knew," Hannah said, her voice tight and garbled. She felt paralyzed by Reggie, his bulk, his smell, her innate fear of him. She gently pushed him back with her fingertips, and he took her hint. Stepped out of her space, pushed his hands into his pockets, and cocked his head. And too late, she added softly, "He wasn't my boyfriend, anyway."

"Right. And Wyatt didn't tell anyone. Which is kind of . . ." He let his voice trail off. "Shitty, right?"

"I don't know, Reggie. It was seventeen years ago. I think I'm over it by now." Hannah faked a laugh, trying to bring some levity into the conversation. She looked at her watch pointedly.

"I wouldn't be. I mean, how mad must you have been?" He smiled at her again, and she couldn't help but notice how white his teeth were, how *pretty* he was. Like a movie star. She wondered if women still fawned over him the way all the girls had. His skin had kept the sheen of his youth. His eyes were bright green, his hair still thick and blond, his cheeks still ruddy.

"I was mad at the time, Reggie, sure. But we were sisters." Hannah shrugged as if saying, *That's what happens.*

"I wonder, though," he said amiably, quietly, "were you mad enough to kill her?"

Hannah recoiled in horror, turned her head away from him, the tears springing to her eyes hot and quick.

"Is that what people think?" Hannah choked out.

"I don't know what everyone else thinks. People seem to buy into the theory that your aunt went crazy. Maybe she tried to run away, and your aunt found her and snapped." Reggie's voice was still lazy and slow. "People snap all the time for different reasons. We see it a lot."

"No one snapped."

"Are you sure? I mean, who could blame you." Reggie stepped back, letting her go, finally. He removed a toothpick from his pocket and stuck it between his teeth. "I'll see you at the service, I assume?"

Hannah edged sideways, keeping Reggie in her peripheral view. Afraid to turn her back to him. Her car was parked right up the street. She could make out the back end, the curved taillights of her older Honda.

Did people really think she'd killed her own sister? No. This was just Reggie, screwing with her mind. Scrambling her thoughts. Trying to scare her because scaring women turned him on. He got off on the power of it. She remembered the Rockwell Fish Fry in the park. That awful, awful festival in town. Even now, when she saw fireworks, she felt vaguely sick. Reggie's voice hot in her ear, calling her pretty. The way he'd made her feel: like one of them, but in a bad way. She needed to get away from him. Now there was nothing but repulsion. And fear.

"Oh, hey, one more thing." He jogged up to her, keeping even with her pace, which had quickened. He reached out, grabbed her forearm. Not hard, but enough to stop her from moving. She turned to him, unease certainly written all over her face. "I'm sorry about your aunt."

"Really? It doesn't seem like it." She jerked her arm away, unsure of what to do with her anger. Unsure where it came from or even if it was misdirected. Maybe she'd misread the whole exchange. Maybe Reggie was just doing his job. How could Wyatt stand him?

"A lot of strange happenings up in that castle on the hill, you know? All them missing girls years ago. Then your aunt and uncle move in, and there are more missing girls."

"Julia ran away," Hannah answered quickly, defensively. She said it rotely, automatically. She felt like she'd said it a million times since she'd come to Rockwell. Everyone questioning, even when they didn't verbalize it. Wyatt, Alice, Reggie, even Huck.

"Uh-huh. I know. I've heard." Reggie nodded, seemingly agreeable, his shoulders rising and falling like it was no big thing to him. Was he being Reggie the cop now? Or Reggie, the creep of a kid she used to know? "What about Ellie?"

"What about Ellie? You guys told me she ran away. Back when we were kids at the fish fry." The words popped out of her mouth before she had time to think about it. She'd spent so much time training her mind away from that night that now, when she was an adult, whole portions of the evening were missing. Blank chunks of time. How had they gotten home? She didn't remember.

The night Julia had run away.

"I'm just saying. In 2001, Ellie ran away. In 2002, Julia ran away. And now, seventeen years later, your aunt was running away and got herself killed." Reggie coughed, starting to walk backward, away from Hannah, toward his truck. "You gotta wonder, that's all. What's everybody running from?"

CHAPTER
TWENTY-TWO
Then

June 2, 2002

The first day back in Rockwell was always the best day. Even that last summer, the first day felt thick with promise. The lick of anticipation sweet on their tongues, unsoured by reality. Misunderstandings had yet to happen; arguments had not yet been imagined. The impending summer loomed bright with possibilities. The idea that they had three whole months together, the pool, the castle, the grounds, the woods, the river, and now: the boys. The taste of last summer fresh on their lips like blackberries, fading fast, layered with new memories the way Uncle Stuart laid bricks.

Julia waved wildly as the big Buick rolled back down the driveway, Trina's hand thrust out the window in an uncharacteristic burst of emotion. Aunt Fae and Uncle Stuart waved back from the driveway, stoic and reserved, before disappearing back inside. Julia squealed, up on her tiptoes, hands clapping silently, and she took Hannah's hands in her own and danced them in a little circle.

"This is going to be the best year yet," she gushed, her cheeks pinked and eyes gleaming. Later, she pulled Hannah to the shed and extracted the bikes.

Already? thought Hannah. It was fine; her heart skipped at the thought of Wyatt. She wanted to make up for that awful, awful night in Plymouth. Her thighs quivered (she hated that word, but that was what they did) at the thought.

She was fifteen now. Old enough for them to come out with their relationship. She had to convince him. She knew he couldn't wait to see her again. He had sent her endless emails over the winter, and she had written back. Were they boyfriend and girlfriend? They hadn't said so. Hannah didn't think Tracy and Beth even believed he existed. She still hadn't said a word to Julia. She just couldn't.

Why all the secrecy? she'd asked Wyatt time and time again, and he'd replied, *You're fourteen.* Could a seventeen-year-old get in trouble for dating a fourteen-year-old, even if there wasn't sex (there hadn't been sex, not yet, just almost sex that one awful night)? She didn't know. Had no one to ask.

But now she was back. She was fifteen. She'd thought about that Plymouth night countless times, the feel of him under her palm, his sharp intake of breath, the knowledge that *she'd* done that. Made him *hard.* She could hardly even think the word, much less say it out loud.

She followed Julia down the path, shouting to Aunt Fae and Uncle Stuart that they'd be back by dinnertime. Julia's long curls trailed behind her; her windbreaker, tied to her waist, flapped in the wind.

They paid their entrance fee at the pool, and Hannah broke from Julia almost immediately. She didn't care what her sister thought, if she saw them or not; she just ran right for the concession window.

There he was, his red hair curled against his forehead, his eyes crinkling as he laughed at something a girl at the window said. Hannah felt a brief stab of jealousy, but then he met her gaze, and his whole face changed. She could see him go from shock to happiness. Delight. He closed his eyes, smiled, like she was a dream standing before him.

He put a finger to his lips. She shook her head playfully. She was tired of being quiet. Tired of being told to sit still, just wait, be patient. Tired of being too much for her mother, too loud for her stepfather, too wild for Julia, too, too, too. She wanted to burst wide open at the seams—to be allowed to simply let herself spill out would be the greatest gift.

He held up his index finger and then cocked his head to the back of the building, splaying all five fingers. *Meet me in five.*

It felt like an hour before he burst out of the back door and crushed her against the concrete. His mouth on her mouth, stealing her breath, making her gasp.

"I missed you," he growled into her neck.

"I'm sure you had other girls to keep you company," Hannah demurred, then hated that her first words to him were jealous, petty.

"Not like you." He rested his forehead against hers and kissed her nose. "I don't drive three hours for anyone."

"This is going to be the best summer," Hannah breathed, her legs shaking and her hands shaking and her heart pounding so wildly she was sure he could feel it. She jumped up and wrapped her legs around his waist and he twirled her around and kissed her hair and his hands gripped her waist and they both talked at the same time and it was everything Hannah had hoped their reunion would be.

Later, she tried to talk to him about telling the others. He was adamant. "No one will understand. One more year, okay? I'll be nineteen; you'll be sixteen. That's fine. Maybe by the end of summer. Please?" He traced the line of her jaw with his fingertip, sending a thousand volts of electricity right down the middle of her body. So they stayed silent.

They met up with Julia and Dana and Yolanda and Reggie, with his movie-star good looks, tan like a lifeguard, skin smooth and glistening. He smiled at her, and she felt the small hitch in her breathing. Knew he did, too, gave her a sly smile like a cat with a bird trapped in its paws. She looked away.

"I didn't know the girls from Brackenhill were such little hotties." He guffawed at his own cleverness, and Dana and Yolanda and Julia giggled behind their palms.

"Shut up, man." Wyatt punched him in the stomach, playful, but he laughed too. The whole scene made Hannah's insides flip, her legs clench. Wyatt stayed on the other side of the group, his eyes following her every move. He winked at her every few minutes. And when no one was looking, his fingertips tickled the back of her neck, once cupped her ass.

She was his. Even if no one knew it. He was her sun, shining bright, blinding, in the center of her universe.

CHAPTER
TWENTY-THREE
Now

The small stone church in Rockwell held around thirty people by the time Pastor Jim was ready to start his eulogy for Aunt Fae. Hannah wondered who everyone was as she slid into place next to Alice, who greeted Hannah and Huck with a single stern nod. Huck made a face at Hannah, his chin pulled back into his chest and his mouth stretching out: *Eesh, what's gotten into her?* Hannah covered her mouth with a palm and hoped people thought she was muffling a sob. Huck elbowed her, a teasing admonishment.

The urn was blue, swirled in whites and greens around a yellow eye, reminding her of a hurricane. It felt fitting with Hannah's childhood, everything she remembered or loved about Aunt Fae. She had been the calm in the storm of Hannah's life; the one stabilizing force had become her summers away from Plymouth. The urn sat on the altar between two taper candles in plain pewter candleholders. So different from her memories of Catholic mass: all gild and incense and ceremony.

She turned in the pew and scanned the crowd. Wyatt sat in the back next to Reggie in a navy-blue suit that contrasted sharply with his reddish hair, his skin glowing a healthy summer bronze. Hannah looked away before they could make eye contact.

The first few pews also held a handful of people, but beyond that the church was empty. Hannah felt a rush of sadness. She didn't recognize anyone from her summers in Rockwell.

Pastor Jim talked about Aunt Fae in the way Hannah remembered her, but he also must have collected stories from others in town. He told a funny story about when she'd had chickens, her battles with the wildlife, hawks and foxes mostly, eliciting chuckles from the congregation. He told a story about when she'd worked for a literacy project in town as an advocate for children. These were things Hannah hadn't known. Glimpses into her aunt's recent life, as insular as it seemed.

The service lasted forty-five minutes, much of it ceremonial. She caught sidelong glances from Alice during the service. Hannah self-consciously wondered if anyone expected her to speak. What would she have talked about? Her aunt seventeen years ago? Still, it seemed noteworthy to live a life such that no one felt compelled, or even morally obligated, to speak at your funeral. The thought depressed her. What kind of circumscribed life had her aunt led for the past seventeen years? At least when Hannah had known her, she'd been reserved, quiet, but her *life* had seemed full: she had gardens and Jinny, and she'd sometimes ventured into town, into the Sunday farmers' market, and returned with armloads of locally grown vegetables and homemade breads. She chattered on about who she'd seen, who was selling what. She wasn't free with her laughter or even her words, but she radiated a quiet strength and warmth that Hannah hadn't ever known before.

Hannah hosted no catered lunch after the service. She didn't stand in a receiving line. She simply waited in her pew for everyone to file out after the memorial. She scanned the crowd in the back, telling herself that she was absolutely not looking for Wyatt. Huck's hand was warm on her back, and she leaned into him.

"Hannah Maloney." The voice came from the back of the church, thin, wobbly, but direct.

"Jinny Fekete." Hannah felt a flush of happiness. Her aunt's only friend and another adult who had known Julia. There was no one else left.

Jinny was tinier than Hannah remembered, probably less than five feet tall and thin, childlike. Her hair was still dyed black but had gone white at the roots. She wore a pillbox, with a film of netting over the top half of her face. Shiny black feathers sprouted from the top. She rushed at Hannah like a furious seagull. The hug was ferocious.

"I knew it was you. I *knew it*. I knew it from the back of your head, all that thick dark hair. Not curly like your sister's, God rest her soul, but that beautiful shine. I'd kill for that hair. HOW ARE YOU?" She waved both hands in the air, fists pumping, the Bakelite on both arms clacking together. Hannah sneaked a glance at Huck, who looked utterly baffled. Jinny's dress was black but with a lace overlay, and it was pretty, more understated than Hannah would have predicted.

"I'm good, Jinny. How are you?" Hannah turned to Huck. "This is my fiancé, Huck."

Jinny hugged him, her tiny arms around his waist like a child's. Hannah covered her mouth with one hand and tried not to giggle out loud. Jinny turned to Hannah. "This is one adorable man you have there. I remember all you teenagers running around town—you were a skinny little thing, hardly a wisp. Your sister, God rest her soul, was the pretty one. You were both so smart, too smart for your own good."

The sheer number of words gave Hannah a twitch in her eye.

"We're going to lunch," Jinny announced suddenly, loudly, her voice echoing in the cavernous, now-empty church. "You, me, Buck. We're all going to lunch. Let's go." She took Hannah's arm. "You'll have to hold tight. My balance isn't what it used to be. I get the vertigo now. See, age is a bitch. Don't get older. The alternative is dead. Fae, God rest her soul, would tell you to get older, you know. But if you can figure out how to keep your youth, you'd make a mint."

They walked out of the dark church and into the bright day. The parking lot had cleared, and again Hannah felt a heaviness pass through her. Did no one care about her aunt's life? They'd fled like cockroaches in sunlight. Jinny pointed one shaky finger down the street to the diner.

"Jinny," Hannah began as they walked, arms linked. Huck ambled behind, observing the town, the dwindling storefronts, the crumbling sidewalks. "There was no one there. No one to speak for her. Why? What's happened in the last seventeen years?" She asked the question baldly, without self-recrimination. Jinny was the least judgmental person Hannah had ever met.

"Oh, child. Your aunt had a hard time in life. Julia nearly destroyed her. But truthfully, I think it started with Ruby."

Hannah jolted. Uncle Stuart had said that name to her earlier. "Ruby was too much," he'd said.

Inside the diner, they took a booth in the corner. The waitress approached the table and poured them all a cup of coffee. They ordered their brunch, and she eyed them suspiciously. Two newcomers and Jinny Fekete—Hannah was sure the curiosity was killing her.

"Jinny," Hannah said after the waitress departed. "Who was Ruby? Stuart said something to me today—"

"He spoke? I didn't think he spoke anymore. The last time I ever heard of him talking was months ago!" She clapped her small hands together. She looked up toward the ceiling. "They'll be together soon. Don't you think it's a shame? We don't do this kind of thing to our pets. He just lies up there, waiting to die."

"Who was Ruby?" Hannah pressed, trying to redirect Jinny's wild thoughts.

"You didn't know? Fae and Stuart had a child." Jinny shook her head, lowered her voice. "She died when she was five."

"She died?" Hannah's stomach dropped. It seemed impossibly young. Oh, her poor aunt. Hannah felt a deep stab of despair. Under the table, Huck squeezed her knee. "When? How?"

"It must have been . . . oh, now, almost twenty-five years ago. Let's see, she was born in 1991, I think. I think she died in '95 or '96."

"How did she die?" Hannah's voice cracked. Hannah and Julia had been alive, preschoolers, but they'd been born when Aunt Fae had a baby. How had she not known? Hannah remembered the few times Trina talked about her sister. Had she told them about a cousin? Had she mentioned a cousin who died? Surely not—that would be entirely too troublesome for small children in Trina's mind.

Hannah had a vision then—Aunt Fae crying for seemingly no reason, her pervasive, unshakable melancholy, the rooms in the castle that had remained closed. One in particular that had been locked—the turret room that faced Valley Road. The way Aunt Fae seemed so surprised when Hannah and Julia had made her laugh: like she'd forgotten that she could. And then a darker memory. Julia knew about Ruby. She'd broken into a locked room, and she and Fae fought about it. There had been a shouting match; Hannah had forgotten all about it. *If I find you in that room again, I'll send you both home!*

"I simply cannot believe that no one has told you this." Jinny slapped her hand against the Formica table, and even Huck startled. A few feathers from her hat came fluttering down to rest between them.

"Jinny, I came to stay with Fae when I was eleven. Who would tell an eleven-year-old about the death of a child?" Hannah was exasperated. "How did she die?"

"That ridiculous castle she lived in. Over a hundred and fifty years old. No safety measures at all." Jinny reached out, gripped Hannah's hands, her long plum nails digging into Hannah's wrists. "The poor girl fell out a second-story window."

CHAPTER
TWENTY-FOUR
Now

The night after Aunt Fae's memorial, Hannah had another dream. This time, Julia appeared in her doorway, mostly silent again, her hair pulled back in a tight chignon, her skin seeming to glow in the darkened room. Julia led Hannah to the locked turret room, and they tried in vain to open it. Julia pulled bobby pins from her bun and wiggled the lock with no luck. The doorknob appeared stuck. In the dream Hannah kept saying, "This door isn't green; are you sure it's the right one?" She awoke standing in the hallway in front of Uncle Stuart's door, listening to the rasp of the oxygen tank, the rhythmic beep of his heart monitor. She crept back to bed and woke in the morning before Huck, exhausted. At least this time she hadn't ended up in the woods; she checked her feet and the hem of her nightgown to be sure.

Hannah hadn't sleepwalked since she was a child, and now, suddenly, it was becoming a regular occurrence. When she googled it, she found correlations with stress and PTSD. She wondered if she was experiencing a small amount of latent trauma just from staying in Brackenhill. While she still felt uneasy in Rockwell, she was surprisingly comforted by the house, the memories of her aunt and uncle, even the memories of her sister. It hadn't felt as traumatic as she would have expected. She felt more at home here than she ever had at her mother's house, with the thin, mildewed carpeting and peeling wallpaper.

After breakfast, Huck took Rink back out in the woods. He'd been quiet at breakfast, his conversation surface and polite. She'd asked him, "Are you okay?" and he'd said yes, but quietly, his smile pasted on.

"You want to go." She'd said it like a statement, but it was a question, and she held her breath.

"Whatever you need to do," Huck said.

"I just have to find a place for Uncle Stuart, okay?"

He'd nodded and escaped outside. She resisted asking again, tugging his arm—*No, really, are you okay?*—because that had always seemed pathetic to her: begging to be seen. She should have told him about the sleepwalking. But he'd been oddly quiet since yesterday. Jinny's bombshell about Ruby hadn't helped. She'd brought it up on the truck ride back to Brackenhill.

"What do you think it means?" she'd pressed.

"It's sad that their daughter died, Han. But it doesn't change your childhood. Your life with Fae and Stuart. Your memories."

It was so like Huck to paint over everything with a sunny brush. To make light of dark things. It used to be Hannah's favorite thing about him. But here, when she needed a partner, someone to bounce ideas off, his optimism felt like a slap. It didn't feel like support; it felt like a rebuke.

"It changes everything," she'd snapped. Later, she'd apologized, and he'd hugged her. His mouth landed somewhere between her cheek and her ear in a distracted kiss before he disappeared outside again. He didn't have the tolerance for this kind of thing: digging through dusty bedrooms, old secrets. His life was ordered, measured, line itemed.

When he was gone, she listened for a moment to make sure he wouldn't return. She crept to the end of the hall, the turret room at the other end of her hallway, facing Valley Road. She tried the doorknob and found it locked, as she'd expected. The door was antique, and the lock would have been locked with a skeleton key, but despite a cursory search around the kitchen, Hannah couldn't locate one. She found a small rusty screwdriver in the kitchen drawer, though, the wooden handle chipped and broken, and went up to jiggle it in the keyhole, pressing the tip of the screwdriver against the pin. The lock popped fairly easily, and the door swung open, banging against the wall before she caught it.

She felt immediately like she was doing something wrong. Like she needed to avoid getting caught. By whom? Alice, perhaps? Alice seemed to slip in and out of the castle soundlessly, appearing suddenly, without warning at the most unexpected moments. Well, so what? This wasn't Alice's house. It was Stuart's now.

Behind the door was a child's room, painted in bright periwinkle blue. The walls coated in a swirl of plaster, like clouds, the ceiling painted to mimic a bright summer sky. The bed had a canopy, white chenille coverlet, lacy curtains, and giant pillows with ornate ruffles. The bed held a throng of stuffed animals: bears and rabbits and puppies in shades of brown and gray. A purple plush blanket was folded neatly across a large cedar chest.

Hannah cracked the lid on the cedar chest a few inches and peered inside. Stacks of clothing and blankets. She moved to the dresser and armoire and opened the drawers: jeans and dresses and shirts and sweaters. Winter mixed with summer clothes. Small socks and little-girl panties. The armoire held the same—winter coats and bathing suits and sandals and boots. The room smelled musty, and everything was coated in a thin layer of dust. Not twenty-five years of dust—clearly Aunt Fae had cleaned the room periodically.

The dresser held a music box. A small ballerina twirled when she opened it, and she heard the opening notes of "Clair de Lune." In the top drawer, Hannah found a small leotard, tights, ballet flats. Little Ruby had been a ballerina. The bookcase contained children's books: Dr. Seuss and Berenstain Bears and Roald Dahl. An easel sat in the corner, untouched paints and dusty paper, a collection of paintbrushes in a pristine, seemingly unused mason jar.

Hannah didn't know what she was looking for, exactly. She wanted to understand why she'd lived in this house for five summers after Aunt Fae and Uncle Stuart's daughter had died and had no idea this room was here, no idea that Ruby had even existed. Aunt Fae had always been secretive, private, but Hannah's room had shared a wall with a child's room, and she hadn't even known it. She could have read these books, painted on this easel. She chastised her own selfishness, but still, a strange feeling of abandonment persisted.

Hannah went to the window and looked out, wondering if Ruby had fallen out her own bedroom window. The window opened outward, joined in the center by an antique latch. She tried to turn the latch, but it seemed to have been either painted shut or cemented together with moisture and age. The windows were old: single pane, drafty. She gazed down at the cement patio below that led into the garden and tried to imagine a child falling. She couldn't—didn't want to—envision it. How had it happened? Had Fae been with her? Had she lived with guilt as well as grief?

The ballerina stopped twirling, the music stopped, and Hannah moved to the dresser to shut the music box. From underneath the ribbon-tabbed lid of a jewelry compartment, a corner of yellow stuck out. Hannah lifted the lid. A folded piece of paper. She opened it. A birth certificate.

Ruby Anne Webster, born February 2, 1991, to Fae Summer Turnbull (mother) and Stuart G. Webster (father).

Turnbull? Had Fae and Stuart not been married at the time of Ruby's birth? Also, Fae and Trina were sisters; they shared a maiden name, and it wasn't Turnbull. It was Yost.

There was only one explanation. Fae had been married to someone else.

Hannah left Ruby's room as she had found it, closing the door softly behind her. She tiptoed down the second hall, the one facing the forest, and paused in front of the room next to Uncle Stuart's. It had been Aunt Fae and Uncle Stuart's study, with floor-to-ceiling bookcases and a stately mahogany desk. A rolltop secretary stood along the wall, and Hannah lifted the slatted door to find the desk stuffed with paperwork. She didn't know what she was looking for, but she pulled the stack out and sat on the old oriental rug and started sifting through. Bills, tax paperwork, piles and piles of medical records, all jumbled together. She sifted them into piles, pulled a new pile down, and began the same process. When the desk was emptied, she had seven piles—categories of paperwork—organized loosely by date. Nothing jumped out at her. Nothing on Ruby, everything labeled Fae Webster.

Hannah didn't even know why she was bothering to do this. What did this have to do with Julia? The body in the woods? Aunt Fae's crash? Probably nothing. But there were so many secrets accumulated over the years, jumbled together like the papers in Aunt Fae's desk. Hannah took a deep breath.

She'd spent the last decade and a half avoiding any thoughts of Brackenhill. Existing with her mother at surface level. Even with Huck, she tried to stay even, easy, happy. She buried any longing to know about her past because it seemed difficult, even tragic. Life was easier lived without tragedy. She also carried guilt—for that last fight with Julia. For not knowing if her sister had truly come back to her room that night, pale white in the doorway. For not chasing her down, helping her, stopping her. For not remembering the end, for not coming back to Rockwell sooner. Everything she'd done in the past seventeen years felt wrong, like she should have done the complete opposite. She should have called Aunt Fae.

Hannah's instinct now was to turn around, close the door. She'd avoided the study, kept herself busy with Aunt Fae's lawyers, Alice, Wyatt, the remains found in the forest. Something about a life boiled down to paperwork, grinding it down to the pulp, felt too exposed. More intimacy than Hannah deserved.

But now, Aunt Fae was gone. Uncle Stuart was almost gone. Brackenhill was her responsibility, or at least it would be soon. The problem with living superficially was that the truth always lived in the deep. Truth lived in the mess. If she closed the door, walked away, she'd be passing a legacy of secrets down to her children, should she choose to ever have them. Normal people got married, like she was planning. Normal people even had children! She couldn't imagine wading into motherhood with Brackenhill an albatross around her neck. No, she had to at least attempt to sort through it all, piece together her own history, where she came from, if she ever wanted to move forward. Figure out what had happened to Julia, Fae, Brackenhill. Ruby. Put all the pieces together and start her life, fresh and shiny and new.

In frustration, she jerked open the closet door. A small bookcase was pushed up against the back, and on the second-to-bottom shelf was a fireproof box, the key dangling from the lock. She retrieved the box, about the size of a large boot shoebox, and set it on the mahogany desk in the center of the room.

Hannah lifted the lid and saw folded squares of paper. Resting on top of the papers was a long brass key. The top contained a fleur-de-lis, and the key end was rectangular, notched. Hannah stood and traced her steps back to Ruby's room. Inserting the key, she tried to relock the door. No luck. The key was for something else, but what? She pocketed it and returned to the study, sitting cross-legged once again on the floor.

She began unfolding the papers, running her index finger along each crease to flatten it. There were a handful of documents: passports, bank statements, a copy of the castle deed, Fae's and Stuart's birth certificates. No surprises.

But then:

Certificate of Surname Change: Fae Summer Turnbull to Fae Summer Webster

Date: April 17, 1991
Reason: Estrangement, psychological distress
Petition: Granted

And the second document of interest, a folded square of yellowed paper:

New York State Certificate of Vehicle Title
Year: 1989
Make: Dodge
Model: Ram
Name and Address of Owner: Warren Turnbull, 1442 West St, Rockwell, NY

Turnbull?

There was no marriage certificate. Hannah had two questions. Why had Aunt Fae and Uncle Stuart not legally married?

Who the hell was Warren Turnbull?

CHAPTER
TWENTY-FIVE
Then

June 14, 2002

She met Wyatt every night after the pool closed, skimming her bike down the path away from Brackenhill toward town. She'd gotten bolder. Julia was off alone, whereabouts unknown, and Hannah refused to wait for her. Refused to kowtow to her sister, seek her out, beg her for company.

Besides, she had Wyatt. Wyatt with his quick smile, his teasing, the way he called her *ghost girl*, because she lived in the haunted mansion and he'd so desperately wanted to be invited up the mountain.

She waited for him to close up the snack stand, for the last of the pool goers to leave, corralling kids to cars as dusk settled around them, the light of day fading to purple, the air cooling just enough to make it easier to breathe.

"It's the ghost girl." Reggie came up behind her. Hannah had been sitting at the picnic table, waiting for Wyatt. They'd wander back to his father's house for an hour or so before Hannah would bike furiously up the mountain, racing the clock for Aunt Fae's dinner at eight p.m.

Summer dinners were later, after the sun had started to set and the yard tools and wheelbarrows and tractors had been put away.

All the girls giggled around Reggie and Wyatt. Wyatt with his teasing charm and Reggie with his boyish face, cheeks ruddy from the sun, and white, straight smile. Reggie made Hannah uncomfortable; his gaze was so intense, like he was trying to see *into* her, and his smile looked like he was perpetually mocking. Hannah didn't know how to respond to him, how to take him.

Ghost Girl was Wyatt's nickname for her, not Reggie's, and Hannah batted away a flash of annoyance. She gave him a quick smile.

"Waiting for your summer boy?" he asked and sat next to her, too close, his breath warm on her cheek.

"What are you doing here, man?" Wyatt emerged from the side door, carrying a garbage bag. He grinned at Reggie, but his eyes glinted.

"We're going to Pinker's," Reggie said easily. The bar in town, notorious for not checking IDs, letting teenagers hang in the back room with the pool tables long after they should have been asked to leave. Sometimes, if the boys charmed the waitresses well enough, they'd snag a beer or two. "You in? I'll wait."

"Nah, I'm tired. Go on without me tonight."

Reggie's gaze flicked from Wyatt to Hannah and back. "You hanging out with Ghost Girl tonight?" His voice had an edge, something mean to it.

"I'm just waiting for Julia," Hannah rushed to fill in, and Wyatt nodded once, small and approvingly.

"Ah, the two ghost girls." Reggie stood, smacked his lips together, the silence awkward. "You can both come," he said like he'd just thought of it.

"We have to get back. Our aunt makes dinner," Hannah said.

"You know, if you're looking for Julia, I think I saw her at Jinny's." Reggie took a step backward, flippant, like he was going to leave. "She's into that stuff, I heard. It's like devil worship. Witchery."

Hannah hadn't known, but it made sense. Jinny, Aunt Fae's old friend, the town eccentric with the psychic shop. A place to buy oils and herbs and hopes and dreams for a bright future provided by Jinny with her stacks of jewelry and smell of patchouli. Hannah affected a look of boredom.

"It's hardly devil worship. It's just a hobby," she said flatly, picking at the skin around her thumbnail.

"Pretty strange hobby for a ghost girl." Reggie grinned again, his eyes hard. "Anyway, you two have fun. Whatever you're up to."

"We're not up to anything, Plume," Wyatt sighed, leaning over to wipe off the picnic table with a wet rag.

"Yeah, sure. I think Ghost Girl here has a crush."

Hannah's cheeks flamed hot, and Wyatt shrugged, his face a mask. "She's just a kid, Reggie. I'm keeping an eye on her until her sister gets here."

Like he was babysitting!

Hannah's blood pressure spiked; she could feel the thrum in her temples. It was one thing to keep their relationship—whatever it was—under wraps. It was another to act so dismissive, like she was *nothing*.

"Ah, okay." Reggie nodded, a flip of his hand: *See ya later*. He flicked his soda can into the closest wastebasket and whistled his way out of the gate.

Hannah sat stiffly, unsure of what to say next. "I should head back up." She gestured toward the mountain and stood, her arms hanging at her sides heavily, unsure of what to do next.

Wyatt looked over at Hannah, his eyes darting. "I'm sorry. I panicked."

"Well, then it's okay, I guess," Hannah said, her teeth clenched as she gathered her bicycle and realized she did look like a child. And to think she wanted him to find her sexy! The whole thing was humiliating.

Wyatt's hand shot out and gripped her handlebars, his eyes searching hers earnestly. "Seriously, I'm sorry. Please don't leave."

She yanked the bike away and struggled to keep herself upright through hot tears.

"It's fine. I'm fine," she said. Hannah pedaled away furiously, Wyatt calling behind her.

Outside the park, in the parking lot, she picked up speed, the breeze lifting her hair, her thighs burning with the exertion. A shadow in the trees moved to under the streetlight, and she could make out the glint of Reggie's blond hair, slicked and shining. She rode away from him, glancing back once to see the orange glow of a cigarette like a heartbeat in the dark.

When she finally got home, breathless, her face red from exertion and still smarting with embarrassment, she realized Julia's bike was missing from the shed. Night had fallen at Brackenhill, and inside, the castle was warm and smelled like homemade dinner—meatloaf and mashed potatoes—and Julia was nowhere to be found.

Was she still at Jinny's? Hannah wondered. What had she been doing there in the first place?

CHAPTER
TWENTY-SIX

Now

"I'm going into town," Hannah announced to Huck, the yellowed truck title burning a hole in her back pocket. She wasn't exactly being secretive on purpose, but Huck rarely had time for things that weren't practical. She came close to telling him about Aunt Fae and Uncle Stuart not being married. About Warren Turnbull. But something inside stopped her.

Hannah tried to be patient. She knew he was getting restless rattling around this dark, cavernous castle all day while she chased down long-forgotten ghosts and a history he knew nothing about, especially when she kept it all close. She knew Huck was running out of steam to keep humoring her; he had a real life, a business. He was too kind to say so, too supportive to question her. Yet. But she knew it was coming. Soon he'd want to leave.

True, she had to stay until they could place Uncle Stuart. That could be any day. Alice had said that morning that he was on a waiting list for a hospice facility about a half hour south of Rockwell. To Hannah, this meant she had only days left.

If she could put together the pieces of this puzzle, she might be able to break it all down for Huck in a way that made sense. Her past was messy, immaterial to their future. She could see he was ready to box the whole dusty castle up and be on his way. Her insistence on following the leads around her aunt's newly discovered complicated private life would try his restraint.

"Oh, I'll come with you," he offered gamely, but there was no enthusiasm in his voice.

"Please stay here. What if Wyatt comes by?" Another pang of guilt: she'd still never told him anything about Wyatt. Huck, sweet, trusting, took everything at face value. Or she hid her emotions well. Either was possible. If he noticed her fluster, her nerves around Wyatt, he was too polite to mention it. It was almost troubling, in a way. What kind of marriage would they have if she was too cowardly to broach tough subjects and he was too polite to question her?

Oh, for goodness' sake, she had enough self-awareness to know that she was doing mental gymnastics to somehow blame Huck for her own silence.

"If you're so worried about the investigation, why don't you just call him?" Huck's voice was muffled behind his book, and Hannah couldn't tell if it was impatient.

"I have, a few times. I don't want to keep bugging them." Hannah paused. "Please, Huck." She tried to keep the edge out of her voice.

"Okay. If he calls, I'll call you, okay?" Huck was stretched out on the couch, his long legs folded at the ankle. Aunt Fae and Uncle Stuart had never had a television, which had always suited Hannah just fine, but a week in relative isolation from the rest of the world had to be making Huck restless. He was social, used to crowds and people.

Hannah paused in the doorway, turned back to Huck. "When I get back, can we talk?"

"Sure. Am I in trouble?" He dipped his book, smiled tentatively. A thaw.

"You? No. Never." She laughed then, and meant it. "There's just a lot you don't know. About my childhood here, my life before you. I feel like I can—and I should—tell you all of it now. Before, I think I was just trying to . . . I don't know, forget it, maybe? Pretend it never happened?" She was figuring out the truth as she spoke. "It was more than that, maybe. I wasn't ready to think about it." She still wasn't, not 100 percent.

Hannah tried to remember her life in Virginia. Her planned days, with their predictable rhythms.

"Sure," Huck said, a slow smile spreading. "I'd like to get to know my future wife." He pushed up on his elbows, a hank of hair falling over his forehead. Hannah wanted to reach out and brush it away but stayed rooted to one spot. His earlier mood seemed to shake off. "I'd like to talk too. Get a bottle of wine—we'll make it a date."

The drive down was slow, Hannah averting her eyes at the splintered wooden guardrail. She hadn't heard from Wyatt about the investigation into Fae's accident at all. Maybe it was like Huck had said, just a standard investigation. But Wyatt had said a few things didn't add up. She picked up her phone, almost texted him to ask, but then thought better of it. *Chase down one thread at a time,* she admonished herself. Was that what she was doing right now? Chasing down threads? Maybe. She just knew that Jinny knew everything about everyone. There was only one place to start.

Hannah parked next to the bank, fed the meter, and walked the block and a half. When she pushed open the heavy wooden door, she was met with a curtain of beads, which she moved aside.

"Jinny!" Hannah called, but the store was silent. Jinny owned a spiritual store: tarot cards and crystals, herbs for burning, plants and succulents that all had medicinal purposes, candles and beads and incense. "Jinny!" Hannah called again.

"I'm coming!" she yelled from the back, and when she emerged, she was fidgeting with a black velvet turban on her head, tied in a front knot, her hair poking out like straw. She looked electrified. Her lipstick was bright red, smeared across her top front teeth.

"HANNAH!" she shouted, her excitement contagious as Hannah laughed and hugged her. She smelled like lavender and something earthy, musky. She jingled when she moved, all her rings, the bells on the fringe of her shawl, her silver and pewter bangle bracelets. "I'm so happy you're back. Will you live here now? Fae didn't bring you around much, but when she did, you girls were always a bright spot in my day. Then you got moody and teenagery, but we all do, I suppose. Hell, I used to sneak smokes from Billy Crawler's pack, and he was at least ten years older than me. I was a bad kid, though—you guys were never bad kids. Come in; sit down. SIT DOWN!"

She pulled a chair out from the round table in the center of the store and got busy, wrapping a bundle of herbs: lavender, sage, and sweetgrass. She lit it on fire and danced gracefully around the room, her arm bowing in a swooping arc. She turned down half the lights and hummed as she worked. "Your aura is like death, child. What is so heavy? Is someone dying? Well, that's an insensitive question, I suppose, given the circumstances. We're all dying, at any rate." She stopped and peered right at Hannah, and again Hannah felt overwhelmed at the volume of chatter. "No, that's not it. You're not upset about Stuart. He's been dying for years. Waiting to die! Ridiculous. We treat animals better than humans. Who waits to die? Now he's alone. A burden. That would kill him, you know. No, it's not Stuart." She leaned closer still, scrutinizing Hannah's face. "It's not Fae either."

"I came with a question." Hannah picked at her fingernail, uncertain how it would be received. "Who was Warren Turnbull?"

Jinny stopped moving, stared at Hannah, her mouth gaping in shock. "Where the HELL did you hear that name?" She threw the bundle of herbs on the ground and stomped the embers out with her

Doc Martens (oh God, Hannah had just noticed she was wearing Doc Martens). She flung open the cabinet doors and started pulling out dried bales of green, stacking them on the checkout counter. She wrapped a new gathering and rambled as she worked: "Cedar, sage, I think. We need a smudge."

"Jinny, who was he?"

Jinny lit the end and blew gently across the embers. She began her dancing anew, slower, her eyes closed, her lips moving without sound. Hannah watched with amusement and awe, but the smoke was starting to give her a headache. Jinny carried the bundle over to a milk glass bowl and set it down, and a curl of smoke lifted, swayed toward the ceiling.

Jinny pulled the chair out opposite Hannah and sat down abruptly. "Warren Turnbull is a terrible human being." She slammed her hands flat against the table. "He's abusive and a drunk, and he's evil, pure evil. He's the worst person I've ever known, and believe me, I've known an awful lot of completely devoid human beings. People with no soul. The man has no soul. He's still alive, goddamn it, because even the Lord don't want him. He lives over in the brown house next to the old railroad station. It looks like it's made of kindling, and I do sometimes wish it would burn to the ground with him in it. I wouldn't say I pray for that, but I say my 'incantations,' we'll say." Jinny bunny eared her fingers around the word *incantations*. "You leave him alone. I don't want to hear of you going anywhere near him, y'hear?"

Hannah had trouble imagining her aunt married to a man who was "devoid of soul," and curiosity pricked her. "I understand, Jinny. I won't. But why is he so bad? What did he do?"

"He has no moral conscience. He'll do whatever it takes to get what he wants. He's a lowlife; he'll steal from you. I know he's killed people. Bar fights, he claimed, and whatnot, but you don't bring a knife to a bar unless you're itching to fight and fightin' to kill, right? Moral people don't do that. He doesn't care who he hurts. He's a bad egg. A bad apple."

"But who is he? To Fae?"

"She found out about him the hard way. I always knew, but she never wanted to listen to me, see? He used to be good lookin'; that's the problem. Your aunt always had a weak spot for those dashing men, personalities of boards, half of 'em. Well, not her Stuart—she finally found herself a good one." Jinny wagged her finger in Hannah's direction. "But if you're asking, you already know. Warren is Fae's husband."

CHAPTER
TWENTY-SEVEN
Now

Hannah left Jinny's with a promise to visit tomorrow, for a "proper reading," she called it.

"I'm just too upset now to read you. You understand, right? Any mention of Warren sends my blood pressure skyrocketing. You can't read under stress; that's not how it works. You have to be calm, ready to receive. But you have to promise to come back. I loved your sister so much. You didn't come around, but she did. You know she came in the shop, right?" Every sentence flowed into a new one, a new thought. "Well, she did. She and that little friend of hers. Sometimes nearly every day! I was teaching them how to scry and smudge. They wanted to do tarot, but I never had the patience for that. Anyway, you promise me you'll come back, you hear?"

Hannah felt drained, her legs heavy as Jinny pushed her out the door. Everything she'd thought she knew about her aunt and uncle was a lie. Was Stuart even technically her uncle? No, now that she thought about it. He was just some random man who lived with her aunt. The thought was depressing. They'd had a child, for goodness' sake!

"Jinny, why didn't Fae and Warren divorce?" Hannah stopped in the doorway, turned back to a fretting Jinny, who was muttering and flitting around the shop.

"Divorce? Oh, he wouldn't hear of it. Would never authorize anything. Fae tried to get him to sign divorce paperwork. Woulda cost her a fortune in court. He wouldn't hear of it. Wouldn't pay alimony, nothing."

"Was Uncle Stuart Ruby's father?"

"I always assumed so, but I guess no one but Fae knew for sure." Jinny tugged a lock of black hair, twirling it around her finger. She didn't seem to care who Ruby's father was. "You'll come back?"

"I promise." Hannah meant it. As she pushed open the door, she felt the vibration of a phone in her pocket. When she retrieved it and read the display, she was dismayed to realize her hands had started to shake. *Wyatt.*

"Hey," she said casually, with a slight wobble in her voice that she hoped was only detectable to her. Whether it was because there might be news about Julia or simply because it was Wyatt was impossible to tease apart.

"Hey." Wyatt's tone was brisk, businesslike. "Are you at Brackenhill? Can I swing by?"

"Why? Is it Julia?" She hadn't meant to sound so desperate, but it just tumbled out.

He was silent for a beat. "I'll come to you, okay?"

"I'm actually in Rockwell. I was visiting Jinny."

He laughed. "Did you get your fortune read?"

"Not this time—we had to burn sage and cedar for a smudge because I mentioned Warren Turnbull's name." She threw it out there to gauge a reaction.

Silence.

"Where are you, Han?"

"Standing in front of the diner. Want to meet me?" Her voice was shaky.

"Yes, stay put." He ended the call.

While she waited, she thought about Wyatt's silence at her question about Warren. Something about the name Turnbull pulled at her subconscious, but she couldn't put her finger on it.

Wyatt came around the corner, intent on something on his phone, and his face broke into a smile when he saw her. She felt warmed by it and then hated herself. He leaned in, kissed her cheek. It was meant to be a casual greeting—something she'd seen others do a thousand times, hell, something she herself had done a thousand times—but his skin against hers sent a ripple down her spine.

He motioned toward the diner door and opened it for her. "After you."

They took a seat in a back booth, next to the one where she and Huck had sat with Jinny only two days before. The memorial service seemed like ages ago. So much had happened since then.

They ordered coffee, and Wyatt ordered a grilled cheese, but Hannah's stomach felt in knots.

"So tell me everything." She knew why Wyatt had called her. He wouldn't have called if he didn't have news about the remains.

"Tell me first, why did you ask about Warren Turnbull?" He fiddled with a sugar packet and tilted his head.

Hannah found herself relaying the whole story: Uncle Stuart talking about Ruby, then Jinny mentioning the child, then the snooping through Ruby's room and the study and finding the car title with Warren Turnbull's name on it. Jinny's assertion that they were still married.

"Did you know about Fae and Warren?" Hannah pressed.

"Me? No. At least not until recently. I mean, we've been running background on your aunt and uncle as part of the new investigation, and it came up." Wyatt ran a hand through his hair. "They're still married."

"That's what Jinny said too. Are the bones Julia's?" Hannah's skin felt stretched, her legs cramping. Every muscle in her body was taut with the strain.

"No." Wyatt watched her carefully as he said it. "They're not."

She felt a swooping, dizzying relief. She'd always held the idea that Julia had run, had stayed away for seventeen years because of an unknown trauma, but would come home when she was ready. It was maybe a childish, outlandish fantasy, but she allowed it. The purse found on the riverbank was only a decoy—a way to throw them all off her scent. Julia was smart—if she wanted to stay lost, she would. Hannah had long, elaborate fantasies of their reunion. She had dreams so real they stayed with her for days. A body would end all that. Everyone talked about closure, but Hannah always felt like closure was a farce. Something people clung to not in their darkest moments but while witnessing *other people's* darkest moments. People who'd experienced real grief would never wish for such a thing.

"Do you know whose they are?" Hannah asked quietly, not sure if she wanted the answer.

"Not yet; that'll take some time. They've run the DNA through a federal database of missing persons with no luck there so far. Next, we'll pull local missing persons and compare dental records or DNA if we have it. We don't always have older DNA. It wasn't standard procedure, say, twenty years ago. It's the damnedest thing, though. They estimate they've been buried between fifteen and twenty years." Wyatt took a deep breath before continuing. "And it's a teenage female."

"So around the same time that Julia went missing, another teenage female was maybe killed and buried at Brackenhill, without anyone knowing? That seems outlandish." Hannah's thoughts spun. Who would have buried a body at Brackenhill in the first place? And how? It didn't seem possible. "Did you search the whole grounds? Maybe there was a murderer, some crazed madman, and they got Julia *and* someone else. She had friends, remember? Whatever happened to all of them?"

Wyatt covered her hand with his. She yanked it away. She didn't need him gumming up her thought processes.

"I'm serious, Wyatt. What if someone in Rockwell was a serial killer?"

"Hannah, if that were the case, the first suspects would be your aunt and uncle. It's *their* property."

Hannah stopped. He was right. He was right, and that was ridiculous.

He continued, "And of course we searched the property. We brought in dogs that day—you didn't see them? And they have a machine, kind of like a metal detector that looks for soil disturbances, although it's more useful for intact bodies with some heft to them. It can miss skeletal remains—"

"Stop." Hannah held up her hand. "Could it have been a mistake? Is there any way that it's Julia and someone just got something wrong?"

Wyatt shook his head. "No. We did a dental comparison and ran DNA. Neither was a match for Julia."

"Okay, but you have DNA; can't you just . . . figure out who it is?" She was a bit shocked to realize she didn't really know how that worked.

"No, it's not like TV. There isn't a master DNA database of everyone in the country. There's a big one, but of known missing persons, criminals, and a little from ancestry websites, but that gets complicated legally. If someone isn't in the system, we can't just . . . conjure them." He gave a laugh. "We aren't Jinny."

Hannah smiled. "So the body at Brackenhill wasn't a known missing person or a criminal."

"No."

The waitress brought the coffee and poured it into mugs, and their conversation halted while they waited. She left, and Wyatt stirred cream and sugar into his cup, while Hannah took a sip of hers, black.

"Hannah, there's more." He kept his eyes down, on his mug, his spoon slowing. "I need you to think back, okay? The years you were in Rockwell and hung out in town."

She felt a flush creep up her cheeks, immediately thinking of the stolen nights in Wyatt's bedroom, wedged into his single bed, the windows flung open, their bodies damp in the nighttime dew. She remembered the way they'd sneaked around, how secretive and intimate it had felt. How their furtiveness had felt new, sexy, grown up in a way she'd never known before. Even Julia hadn't known. Until she did.

"Not us, Hannah." He read her face, her thoughts. He leaned back against the booth, his left arm draped over the seat. She couldn't look directly at him. "I need you to think of the other girls—Julia's friends, who she hung out with. Did you hear any rumors at that time? Did you hear anything about anyone being knocked up?"

"What!" she couldn't help exclaiming. Her gaze snapped up, met Wyatt's. He motioned gently with his hand, *Keep it down.* She would have heard something about that, she thought. Then again, that summer had been such a whirlwind, passing in a breathless fever dream, ending in tragedy. Would Julia have told her?

"Whoever was buried at Brackenhill was pregnant."

CHAPTER
TWENTY-EIGHT
Now

Huck had music playing in the kitchen when Hannah returned. Something with a jazzy beat, slow and easy. He'd fished a boom box out of the trunk of his car and hooked up his phone on the Bluetooth. He was puttering around the kitchen, torn basil and tomatoes from Fae's garden on the chopping block. When Huck was restless, he cooked. He whistled, and when he saw Hannah, he twirled her around until they both laughed, and he kissed her. Gently, she nudged him back. His mood from earlier seemed to have dissipated, and Hannah chalked it up to frustration and isolation. She felt a pang of tenderness now, watching him. Out of his element and still making the best of things. For her. For them.

He resumed his chopping, his fingers long and practiced. It was Hannah's favorite thing: just to be in Huck's presence. So easy. He was almost always positive, optimistic. He always prodded her to look for silver linings, appreciate whatever she had, but not settle for anything less than she deserved. So different from Trina, whose whole life had been about settling. Keeping the status quo.

Hannah produced the wine out of a long paper bag, a cabernet from a Finger Lakes vineyard she'd never heard of. She showed Huck the label, and he nodded once, appraisingly. She turned the knob on the boom box; the sound lowered.

"It's not her," Hannah said, pouring two generous servings of wine into stemless Riedels that she found in the kitchen cabinet. The kitchen had been modernized sometime since she was a child, the cabinets white and the walls stone, but it was still more functional than beautiful. The floor was river stone, gray and smooth, while the walls were rocky, rough to the touch and stippled with white. Limestone? Hannah found herself wondering.

Huck stopped chopping. Turned to face her. "Then who is it?"

"They don't know yet. It'll be a few days."

"That seems . . . bizarre, right? Unlikely?"

She felt herself turn on him, just that quickly. Stupid, really, but she couldn't help it. "Well, unless Aunt Fae and Uncle Stuart were murderers." It came out snappy, almost rude, and she felt immediately sorry. The underlying question had been undeniable, and of course it was unlikely. She shook her head in apology.

Huck held up a hand. "Of course not, Han." Then, "How did you find out?"

"I saw Wyatt in town."

"Wyatt, then?" If Huck had noticed the way she referred to Wyatt, not Officer McCarran, he hadn't brought it up before. But now she could see it dawning on him, how personally she seemed to know him, how attached she might have been to this town and the people in it. He took a sip of wine, popped a slice of cheese from the counter into his mouth. Tilted his chin up to watch her, too carefully, she thought. "And who is Wyatt again? To you, I mean. Besides just the officer in this case. I know that's not the whole story."

Huck wasn't a dummy and wasn't jealous. There was no reason to keep their history from him, except that she already had. That was the only sin: she'd lied by omission once.

"Wyatt was my first boyfriend," Hannah said, breaking a grape from its stem, squeezing it between her thumb and forefinger, going for nonchalance.

Huck played along, giving her a teasing smile. "Intriguing, Ms. Maloney. This is the first I'm hearing of this. Although I'll be honest—I had an inkling. Y'all act like skittish mice around each other."

"Well, I was fifteen. And it was only for two summers. We didn't even keep in touch when I left." *Or was forced out,* Hannah thought but did not say. She was intent on keeping up the act: Wyatt had meant nothing to her then, meant nothing to her now. She affected a look of boredom. Changed the subject. "It'll be maybe two weeks until they can ID the body. Maybe more if they can't find a hit through dental records in missing persons."

"And then what?" Huck leaned back against the countertop, swirled his wineglass.

Now it was Hannah's turn to play along, pretend they were casually discussing the weather, the lack of rain. "I don't know. I mean, I can't imagine this girl isn't related to Julia's disappearance." Then, a quick thought: she hadn't meant to hide it. "Huck, she was pregnant. When she died."

"Really?"

"See, it's connected. I can feel it." Hannah shook her head, staring at the wineglass in her hand. "It's connected to Julia."

"How?"

She resented Huck pressing the issue. She wanted him to go along to get along, like he always had, always did with her. "What do you mean, how?" Sometimes she wondered if he was stupid. Quickly, she felt bad for thinking it. But honestly, "how"? Maybe she was just tired. She never used to be so impatient with him. She took a deep breath and a swig of wine. When she answered again, she kept her voice level. "Well, my sister goes missing. Seventeen years later they find the body of a pregnant teenage girl, killed around the same time my sister disappeared, on our family property. How can it *not* be connected, in some way? Seems like a no-brainer to me."

"Only if your aunt and uncle are involved." To Huck it was a thought exercise, a playful game; true for most things in his life.

Hannah felt another surge of anger, then tempered it. "No. You can access the castle grounds from the back, up the embankment on the west side. It leads down to a road." She pointed south. Then pivoted, pointed west, toward the courtyard, where the sun was glowing gold through the trees. "The river is there."

"So you think someone killed a teenager, then hiked her body up a steep embankment to bury her at Brackenhill. For what purpose?"

"I don't know!" Hannah exclaimed, exasperated. "If I knew, obviously we'd know who it was, right? What if . . . this is crazy, but what if *Julia* killed the girl and buried her? And she ran away to hide from the crime? Or! What if someone else killed the girl and Julia saw it, then ran away to stay safe?"

"Like witness protection?" Huck turned his back, resumed his chopping. He seemed tired of the conversation. "I mean, maybe. Sure. Hannah, there's something else we should talk about."

She didn't respond, didn't have to. Knew where he was going before he said it. At her feet, Rink whined, and she scratched his ears.

"I have to go home." He ran a hand through his hair, his back still to her. "It's coming into fall planting season. I have clients to keep. The crew's been keeping up with the maintenance clients: the mowing, hedge trimming, weeding. But there are incoming projects I have to handle."

She knew he was right—Huck did a lot of the design work, and it was his business. She thought back to the first night she'd met him, at the bar. All his friends in suits and ties, working in finance jobs in DC. They'd been harried, lined in the face, their mouths pinched in permanent fury: at traffic, pedestrians, clients, the market, their bosses, their *idiot bosses*. And then Huck, his face relaxed, his nails dirty, his eyes laughing. He'd left their world, the suits and ties and washed-out faces, to pursue his own path, to be outdoors, his own *idiot boss*. He'd been one of them, once upon a time, in finance. He'd gone to college for business administration, taken the requisite associate job working sixty hours a week right out of school. Left to "dig in the dirt," they'd mocked. Hannah had gone to dinner with the whole crew and their wives, new babies. They made twice Huck's salary now and had all looked exhausted.

"I can't leave yet," Hannah said. She had a job to return to too. They'd been patient so far, but Patrice, her boss, had left her a slightly huffy voice mail yesterday morning, asking when she thought she'd be returning.

She and Huck had a life together in Virginia. They had a couple of friends. "Stuart needs placement. He's on a waiting list. I can't leave him alone in the house, even if they could afford around-the-clock care. I just can't. And I have to see what comes of . . ." She motioned toward the courtyard, toward the embankment, the burial site.

"Right." He turned to face her, eyes sliding sideways out the window across the garden. "I am having a little trouble understanding, I guess. I mean, if it's not Julia, then why do you have to stay? Stuart I understand, but that could be wrapped up in a few days; who knows? But the body, well, that could be weeks."

"Yeah, I can't stay weeks," Hannah agreed, but she knew as soon as the words popped out that it was a lie. She'd stay as long as she could, sacrificing her job, Huck, everything if she had to. It was a lightning-quick realization: She'd been so long in the dark, the events of that summer shrouded in secrecy and jumbled together in a confusing clot of memory, never knowing what was real and what was imagined or even wished for. The days immediately afterward a blur. Her clearest image was of her aunt and uncle, their faces stricken, out the back window of the car, growing smaller and smaller until they disappeared completely, as Wes sped away down the winding hill faster than necessary, her heart in her throat, unsure, uncertain, and wholly out of control.

She would not be made to leave again. Not without the whole truth.

CHAPTER
TWENTY-NINE
Then

June 22, 2002

"I'm ready to go home," Julia announced, standing in the doorway between their bedrooms.

"What? Why?" Hannah had been lying facedown on her bed, reading *Little House on the Prairie* for the eleventh time. It was a baby book, but she loved it. She'd read the whole series last summer and left all the books in her room at Brackenhill. Her eyes were drifting shut. She hadn't been sleeping well: nightmares some nights, and others, well, she'd started sleepwalking. She was going to talk to Julia about it, except her sister already hated it here now. Hannah didn't want to give her more reasons to want to leave.

"It sucks here this summer." Julia pouted. She had a Blow Pop in her cheek and spun it so it clattered against her teeth. "Something is different. I hate it. Everything just feels wrong, and I think Aunt Fae hates us."

"That's the craziest thing you've ever said." Hannah stared at her sister, who had a flair for the dramatic, her moods changing on a whim.

Julia sat on the edge of Hannah's bed, her feet crossed daintily at the ankles. "No, it's not. She's mean, at least to me. And I can tell there's something wrong with her. I swear to God, the other day she was talking to me about school, and she opened her mouth, and a fly came out."

"Julia!" Hannah slammed the book shut.

"I'm more in tune with this kind of thing than you are. I can tell when people are *wrong*. Put together wrong." She got up, walked to the window, turned the latch, and gave the glass a push. The windows clattered outward, against the stone. "I know you think I'm crazy. You don't understand, though. I see things that you don't. It started last summer. This place is not nice."

"What do you see?" Hannah sat up, interested but not scared.

"People. Voices. I have dreams. Sometimes singing. Or laughing." Julia's voice was low, her hair lifting in the breeze. "Like children."

"You've been listening to the kids in town too much. They say it's haunted. That Aunt Fae is a witch."

"Well, what if she is?" Julia leaned back against the window frame, posed just so, as though for a portrait. Julia always acted as though she were being photographed, tilting her head to display the strong jawline, her eyes downcast, her chin jutted out. Hannah thought it must be exhausting to live in a constant state of self-awareness. Worry about how every small movement would be perceived, when it was likely that no one was paying any attention to you anyway.

Julia was poised, dainty, while Hannah was robust, loud. Her mother sometimes called her a bull in a china shop, stomping her way through life.

Hannah sighed, flipped her book back open. "Aunt Fae isn't a witch. You are not hearing children. You are listening to your dumb teenage friends, and you have an overactive imagination."

Julia shot her a glare and stormed back to her room. Hannah heard her sister leave out the back door and hurried to the window in time to see Julia take off down the front path on her bike.

Aunt Fae would kill her if she knew she rode her bike into town alone. That path grew narrow and steep in the middle, and they had to hoist their bikes up the embankment over the guardrail and ride on the road, winding and no shoulder, for a quarter mile. Aunt Fae would flip out.

Hannah pulled a towel from the hall closet and ran a bath. Submerged up to her chin, she could think. Was Julia right? If she was honest with herself, did Brackenhill feel haunted? She thought about the labyrinth, the creak of doors and floors in the middle of the night, the red pool (which Uncle Stuart had explained but was still odd).

The water suddenly felt freezing, even in the un-air-conditioned bathroom. Hannah stood, pulled the plug, dried herself off, and stopped.

"Jules?" she called into the hall. The shifting air felt like a person in the room. The hum of a fan down the hall. In the distance, Uncle Stuart's whistle: *"I Wanna Be Like You," Louis Prima,* he would have told her. Jaunty and bouncy.

She blotted at her hair, walked back into her bedroom, and let out a single piercing scream.

On her bed, neatly in the center, was a white lace-up baby shoe. It hadn't been there when she'd gone into the bathroom. In fact, she'd never seen it before in her life.

Aunt Fae rushed into the bedroom. "What on earth are you carrying on about?" she scolded, her voice impatient. "It's always something with you!"

"Where did that come from?" Hannah pointed at the shoe, and Aunt Fae's face went white.

"Where did you get that?" she demanded, her thick fingers snatching the white bootie off the bedspread and tucking it into her apron pocket.

"I didn't get it anywhere! I went to take a bath." Hannah felt indignant. Julia never got blamed for anything.

Hannah, did you break the vase?
Hannah, did you spill on the carpet?
Hannah, where is your sister?
Even when it was Julia, it was Hannah.

Aunt Fae propped her hands on her hips and glared at Hannah, her face twisted in anger. Hannah had never seen her like that, and she tucked the towel tighter around her chest, shrank back against the wall.

"I'll trust you not to play a prank like that again; do you understand me?"

"I didn't play a prank!" Hannah's voice pitched up, louder than she intended, but it was so frustrating. If anyone had played a prank, it was Julia. And anyway, it was a pretty weird prank that didn't mean anything to anyone.

Julia, who rode to town. After talking about child ghosts. A voice inside Hannah's head would not shut up.

"Hannah, please," Aunt Fae said, sighing. "Will you please just lower your voice?"

Julia, Aunt Fae, her mother. Everyone had a habit of sighing her name instead of saying it.

Aunt Fae turned and left then, her heavy footsteps in the hall and then the steps down.

"Yeah, well, Julia rode her bike into town!" Hannah called after her, which admittedly wasn't helping her "Julia left the shoe" cause.

"That's enough, Hannah!" Aunt Fae called back up to her.

It was always enough; that was the problem with Hannah.

She was so busy being angry with Julia that she never stopped to ask herself why Aunt Fae cared so damn much about the shoe in the first place.

CHAPTER THIRTY

Now

Hannah rolled the small canister of pepper spray between her thumb and forefinger and tucked it into her jeans pocket. *The brown house next to the old railroad station. Looks like kindling.*

The siding on the brown house was asbestos shakes, cracked and broken, hanging in some cases by a single tacked corner. The upstairs window was broken and covered with cardboard and duct tape. The porch, its middle sunken and uneven, creaked under Hannah's weight.

She knocked, hesitantly at first, then increasing in volume and pressure until she was pounding on the door. She was crazy to be here, at Warren Turnbull's house.

Then why was she here? She didn't know. Rattling around the house, waiting to hear from hospice centers, trying to avoid Alice, and skulking around like a living version of a Brackenhill ghost was making Hannah crazy. All Huck wanted to do was read or cook or walk in the woods, and if she spent too much time with him, he'd start asking when they could leave.

Besides, Hannah was following the next logical step in what felt like a rogue investigation into her sister's disappearance, her aunt's possible murder, and the unknown remains in the forest. The only clue she had was Warren Turnbull, so here she was. Had he and Aunt Fae kept in touch? Why wouldn't he divorce her? Huck would have told her, in no uncertain terms, that this was a bad idea. Warren was possibly violent, evil—what had Jinny called him? "Devoid of soul." Well, so what? She worked in advertising.

"You won't find Warren there, if that's who you're looking for." The voice behind her was thin, reedy, and Hannah turned, her hand at her throat.

The woman was old, maybe in her eighties, and stood on the street with her hands on her hips. The closest house was a hundred feet away, a small gray peeling saltbox down the alley. From where Hannah stood, she could see the front screen hanging open, a black-and-white cat watching them.

"Why's that?" Hannah asked, her hand dropped to her side, a throb traveling up her arm.

"He's at Pinker's down the river." The woman shook her head. "Spends all day there and has for . . ." She looked up at the sky, calculating, then back at Hannah. "Over twenty years, I'd say."

"Do you know Warren well?" Hannah took a step toward her, her eyes narrowing.

"Sure, this is Rockwell. We all know each other well. All our stories, all our tragedies. But I know Warren better than most." She eyed Hannah suspiciously, took in her jeans, her denim button-down, the thin purse slung over her shoulder. "You're not a cop or something, are ya? He hasn't done anything, has he?"

"No, I'm not a cop. I don't know if he's done anything. I wanted to talk to him about . . ." Hannah stopped, her voice fading. What exactly? Aunt Fae, sure. Ruby? Their marriage? Stupid to come without a plan, walking right into violence and rage and pure evil, according to Jinny, who could be powerfully persuasive. But also, a voice in her head whispered, a tad dramatic.

"About what?" Then realization dawned. "Fae Webster?"

It was Hannah's turn to be suspicious. "How'd you know that?"

"Rockwell, dear. Fae dies; a stranger bangs on her Warren's door a week later. I ain't always the brightest bulb—and sometimes I play dumb just to mind my own beeswax, you know—but this one was a gimme." She approached Hannah, studied her face. "You're one of those nieces, ain't ya. The one that didn't get killed."

"She ran away," Hannah replied automatically, her heart at a standstill.

"Uh-huh. We've had a million of 'em. Runaways from this town. Mostly they come back. Did your sister ever come back?"

"No." The lump in Hannah's throat grew—she felt choked by it.

"Well then." The woman nodded once as if that were settled then. "Do you want to come down for tea?"

"Tea?" Hannah repeated, dim witted and slow.

"Sure. You want to know about Warren. I'm an old biddy with nothing but time and no one who cares about all the gossip I know." She winked then. Hannah realized she was a bit younger than she'd thought, maybe seventies. She was dressed in a T-shirt and jeans. In her hands she twisted a pair of gardening gloves. "Besides, Warren is my cousin."

The saltbox was not shabby, like Hannah had first thought, but well maintained. Gray and white. The inside was dated but pleasantly clean and knickknack-free. The kitchen was bright with sunlight, the cabinets light wood and white and the Formica countertop gleaming. The house smelled like Pledge and cookies.

The woman busied herself with the teapot, and Hannah watched her buzz around the kitchen, withdrawing mugs, tea bags, sugar, milk.

"I'm Hannah," she finally said.

"Oh dear, how rude. I'm Lila Yardley. I've lived here in Rockwell all my life. This house was the house I grew up in. I know everything there is to know about everyone." She set all the fixings down on the table and poured them each a cup of tea, dunking a Lipton tea bag in each cup. "So you're the sister, then? Not the one who was killed?"

"She ran away." Hannah busied herself with milk and a spoon. "I guess to some it looks like I did too. It was too hard . . . after. And even now, it's hard."

"Well, sure. You were a child." She shook her head, tsked as she stirred.

"Do you know anything about my sister, if you know everyone and everything?" Hannah asked it tongue in cheek but found herself holding her breath anyway.

"Not a thing, darling." Lila reached out, her hand dry and warm on Hannah's. "I know the old-old stuff and the new-new stuff, but the years after Fae moved up the mountain? Nothing. I know she had a daughter who died. Tragic. She kept to herself mostly. The child hadn't started school, and Fae wasn't the mommy-and-me-class kind of mother. People in town talked, of course. Called her eccentric, witchy. Silly, stupid things. I hated all that."

"You didn't believe she was a witch? Or she was cursed?" Hannah searched her memory for what the kids had said to her all those years ago. She hadn't known why. They'd never told her about Ruby, probably assuming she and Julia had known.

"I always felt so bad for her. Fae was a child herself when she married Warren, had no idea what she was getting herself into. I thought when she got away from him, her life would get better, not worse."

"Why did she marry him?" Hannah wondered aloud. Who would marry an angry, abusive drunk? The only way was if he didn't use to be that way. If life had ruined him. Had he started drinking because of Aunt Fae? Had Aunt Fae and Uncle Stuart's affair turned Warren mean?

"Oh, well. Warren used to be a catch. Oh sure, he had tons of girlfriends from all over. Seemed to be plenty of women in love with Warren Turnbull. Some local, some from up north. I don't even know where he met 'em all." Lila pressed her index finger to her lips, thinking. "You know, before he pissed away his money, he was the only plumber in town. Every pipe in Rockwell was plumbed by Warren at one point or another. Even the hospital called him for backed-up toilets and clogged drains. He held a monopoly on the whole county, so he wasn't rich, but he made a living. He was handsome too. A little rough and tumble, but nobody seemed to mind that."

"How'd Fae and Warren meet?"

Lila looked up at the ceiling, searching her memory, her face twisted in concentration. "You know? I'm not sure. If I had to guess, I'd say a bar. Your Aunt Fae was pretty in her day. She came from Parksville, just down Route 17. In a town like Rockwell, everybody knows everybody, and your mama and your aunt Fae were just known. They were pretty girls from a respectable family. And everyone knew your grandmother. She was a county beauty, kind to boot, and real gem of a person."

Hannah knew this to be true. She knew her grandparents had lived in Jeffersonville, in a Main Street duplex. Her grandmother had been a secretary at the high school before she'd died young at sixty-five from a sudden heart attack. Hannah's grandfather had died a few years later from liver failure, his insides pickled in whiskey. He'd been a drunk but a jolly one. Functional alcoholic, they'd have said now, but back then he'd just been known as a widower, still in love with his wife, drinking to pass the time until he could see her again. He'd been a retired navy man, the owner of a local hardware store. When Mom had talked of her parents—which was infrequent—it had always been with fondness and a wistfulness that Hannah could never quite pinpoint.

"Then why did she leave him, do you know?"

"Well, Warren was abusive. He turned mean with age. Some men just do, you know? His anger became legendary. Most people stay out of his way now. All the women eventually left. Fae left; Ellie left. Everyone he loved left him."

"Ellie?" The name sent a jolt through Hannah. Ellie. *Ellie.* All that long auburn hair, wild around her face. Telling jokes in the center of the circle that first day at the pool. *Ellie,* Julia's best friend that last summer, the two of them stealing down the path toward the river, tossing glances over their shoulders. *Ellie*, in the center courtyard at midnight, her skin blue in the moonlight, her skirt and heels both high.

"So sad, that one. Such a troubled young woman. But see, she was a child too. Caught up in Fae and Warren's drama. She adored Fae. Then she'd been alone with Warren, and it was too hard. I don't blame her for leaving. Although I wish she'd get in touch. Last I'd heard, she just wanted to forget Rockwell. Who could blame her?" Lila opened and closed her mouth, like she wanted to say more, but instead pressed her palms to the tabletop, her lips together. "You know, I don't hate Warren; I'm probably his only ally around these parts. He had a horrific childhood. So now he spends all his days down at the bar. Drinking away his life, what's left of it."

Lila rambled on, but Hannah couldn't focus. Ellie had loved Aunt Fae? She'd never even seen them speak to each other. "Wait, Lila. Who is Ellie? To Warren?"

"Oh, I thought you girls were all friends once upon a time. Ellie Turnbull. With the red hair? Well, maybe you didn't know her. She left Rockwell the minute she turned sixteen. Had to be 2001?"

"We knew Ellie," Hannah whispered, her mind reeling.

"Oh, well then, see? You already know. Warren was Ellie's father."

CHAPTER
THIRTY-ONE
Now

Back in the car, Hannah concentrated on deep breathing. She'd left Lila's in a hurry, probably suspiciously quickly. She didn't care. She needed to sort through the knot of new facts, needed time alone to unwind the skein of memories, coming furiously now.

Ellie, with the red hair, tough but so beautiful. Bright-red lips, tight skirts, high heels. Mean, caustic. That last summer, Ellie and Julia tucked away in Julia's room, Hannah with her ear pressed against the door, trying to hear a whisper, a giggle, anything. Not understanding why she couldn't come in, be part of it. Why couldn't two be three? She wasn't a baby, only two years younger. She knew about boys and clothes. She could have been part of them. *Why?* she'd wanted to shout at the time. Why was she so excluded? The isolation felt sudden, as if she'd been surgically extracted from her sister's inner life. It had been whole and complete in a matter of a few weeks, and she'd been left alone in the castle night after night while her sister sequestered herself in her room with Ellie, who alternated between mean and forlorn.

Three days before her sister had gone missing, Hannah remembered finding Julia alone in the courtyard, her skin shining from the light of a bright full moon. Julia's eyes had been wild. Her hair matted on one side, like she'd been sleeping on it. What time was it? Almost midnight. What had made Hannah wake up and look out her window to the courtyard below and see Julia, ethereal and white, in her nightgown? What had made her run down the spiral staircase, through the halls, and out the kitchen door after her? She'd just been standing there. Hannah could have sworn her mouth was moving, like she'd been talking. But to whom?

"Why are you completely ignoring me this summer?" she'd asked her sister.

Julia's hand pressed against her forehead, as though staving off a headache. "It's not personal, Hannah, please. There's a lot of shit going down. You can't even know. You're fifteen. The world isn't like you think it is."

"That's so condescending. I know what the world is like, Julia, and since when does that matter to you? We're a team. Against Mom, against Wes, exploring this castle, spending our summers together. That was the deal. Now I'm alone all the time, and I'm tired of it, and I want to know why."

"I can't tell you why, okay? Trust me. I'm sorry. It's not what you think. It's not a club you're not part of. It's bigger than that. It's huge." Julia's hands went around in a circle, and Hannah huffed. Her sister had always been one for drama. Julia's voice dropped to a whisper. "You know how I see things sometimes?"

Hannah rolled her eyes. This again. Julia had read a book a year before about mystics and fortune-tellers, something about the *dark arts*, and since then she had claimed—too publicly for Hannah's liking—that she could see people's spirits. She could *sense things*. Events before they happened. People who had passed on. It was a cry for attention; anyone could see that. It was all ridiculous, and even Mom had lost her patience with it. "Yes. I know you say that," Hannah said diplomatically, not sure where Julia was going.

"Something around here is *fucked up*. I think—"

"Julia!" The voice came from the woods, the path leading from the courtyard to the river. Ellie appeared at the mouth of the trail, her hair glowing in the moonlight. Then she was by their side, standing next to Julia. Ellie reached down and slipped her hand into Julia's, so again, it was two against one. Julia offered a shrug, a helpless gesture.

Hannah cried out in frustration. "Why. Why are you always here? Always, always, always! It's midnight." Her black skirt, her red heels. Where could she be going in that get-up? Nowhere good. Ellie pulled at Julia's hand, toward the trail. "You can't go anywhere. It's the middle of the night. You're in your nightgown."

Hannah felt impotent, twisted up and tied by loyalty. If she ran to get Fae, her sister would be pushed even further away. No one liked a tattletale, a snitch. If she let her go and something terrible happened to her (she imagined them falling drunk into the river, churning thick as a milkshake from all the rain), she'd never forgive herself.

Julia let herself be pulled away by Ellie, down the path, her flip-flops catching on the fallen sticks and branches. She glanced back once, her finger to her lips, her eyes pleading.

Hannah spent the whole night lying awake with worry. Waiting for her sister to return, to hear her footsteps in the hall, creeping into her bedroom. She never heard her. She went down to breakfast, bleary and exhausted. At the table sat Julia: hair wet from a shower, dressed in shorts, the string from her bikini poking out of the neck of a bright-pink T-shirt.

"Hi!" Julia said brightly. Fae bustled in the kitchen, opening and closing cabinet doors. Julia chattered on about a book she was reading, filling the silence with dragons and battles and princesses. Stupid, childish chatter.

"Where have you been?" Hannah asked between her teeth as she sat next to her sister.

"What do you mean?" Julia blinked innocently.

"I mean I waited all night for you to come home. You didn't." At her sister's blank face, Hannah sighed frustratedly. "In the courtyard? I saw you, remember?" She didn't even care if Aunt Fae got mad anymore. Hannah was tired of Julia's secretiveness, tired of her games. "With Ellie?"

"Ellie!" Aunt Fae exclaimed, turning to them. Her face seemed to pale. "Is that true? Did you go out last night?" Her voice was fearful, cut with a skittering panic. She'd begun to question them, asking about their comings and goings when she never had before. Sneaking out of the house late at night would have made her sick with worry.

"Hannah, I don't know what you're talking about." Julia shook her head, patted her sister's hand. "You have dreams sometimes." She held Hannah's gaze then, her eyes clouded, impenetrable, almost gray with warning. "I don't know what you think you saw, but I was sleeping in my room all night."

CHAPTER
THIRTY-TWO
Now

When she came home from Lila's house, Huck and Rink were nowhere to be found. She'd missed a call while she was driving; a voice mail told her that Serenity Acres, a hospice center twenty-five miles away, had called. They had an opening.

An opening. An opening at a hospice meant that someone had died. Hannah felt a certain kind of hopelessness at that. On one hand, her uncle would have a place to go. Comfort and care and twenty-four-hour monitoring for his last days on earth. On the other, a family somewhere was mourning the loss of someone they loved. Or perhaps—and this was even sadder—they weren't.

The hiss-hum of Uncle Stuart's ventilator could be heard from the hallway. Hannah paused, listening for the patter of Alice's footsteps. When she was certain Alice wasn't in the room, she pushed the door open. Stuart was turned slightly on his side, propped by a roll pillow. She knew Alice would be back shortly—she never left him propped for long. It was mostly to keep him moving, avoid bedsores, atrophy. His arm dangled off the side of the bed, his fingers curled and pale.

Hannah pulled the desk chair up to the bed and covered Uncle Stuart's hand with her own, angling it back slightly to rest on the mattress for support. "Uncle Stuart, it's Hannah." His eyes fluttered above the breathing mask but did not open.

"I found an opening for you. I don't want to send you away. You understand, don't you? Are you mad, I wonder?" Her voice was quiet, and she rubbed the papery skin on the back of his hand. She felt her eyes tear, her throat sting. "You can't want to live like this. This isn't a life. This is . . . torture."

She looked around the room. The curtains were drawn, but through the slit in the middle, she could see the rosy glow of twilight.

"You understand, right? I can't take care of you, Uncle Stuart. I don't know how. I have to go back to work, or I'll be fired, eventually. Alice can't be here twenty-four hours." She took a deep breath. "I have regrets; do you? Why did we stop talking? Why did I think I had so much more time?" It was selfish, unforgivable.

Hiss-hum. Hiss-hum. Hiss-hum. The steady beeping of his electronically displayed heartbeat.

"Why didn't we ever know anything about Ruby? How did she really die? Did Fae spend her whole life feeling guilty about what happened?" Hannah felt emboldened by the silence; the darkness of the room felt like a tomb. She had so many questions. "Was Aunt Fae Ellie's *mother*?" The question had come so late—Hannah couldn't believe she hadn't thought about it before. She blamed lack of sleep; her thinking felt underwater. "Aunt Fae was at least Ellie's stepmother, but neither of you ever talked about her. Or to her. She came to this house! So many times. Nothing about this makes sense." She laughed shrilly, the sound echoing in the oversize room. "I feel like I'm going crazy."

And she did. Her real life, in Virginia, felt incredibly far away, like it had happened to a wholly different person. She could barely remember

Huck and their lazy weeknights, dinner at the pub down the street, walking home hand in hand, woozy from wine and stomachs full of greasy french fries and burgers. Falling into bed, the feel of Huck against her skin. Waking up with Rink's nose wet against her cheek. The texts from friends, the constant swirl of activity that filled her days. Her job: matching stock photos and fonts to elicit the exact response she wanted. All while Uncle Stuart had lain up here dying, the seeds of truth of her sister's disappearance slowly dying with him. Even if he didn't know everything, he must have known something.

She'd always assumed that if she wanted the time, she had it. It all seemed so vapid now. Stupid. Worthless.

"How did you and Fae even meet? How did you get this castle? Where did it come from?" And then the things she couldn't ask: *What do I do now?* She felt like she'd opened a Pandora's box and let all the questions out, the ones she'd held tight for so long and those she hadn't known to ask, and she'd never be able to leave until she answered them. Until she knew what had happened that summer and everything that had led up to it.

"I can't leave," Hannah said, breaking the silence across the dark bedroom. Huck had finally returned from his walk in the woods. A late night this time. He'd been grumpy, short with her. She'd made them pasta and pesto using basil from the garden. The herb garden was bursting and fragrant, the smells reminding her of Aunt Fae.

"What happened to you?" Hannah had barked when Huck had come through the kitchen door at almost nine o'clock. She'd called his cell phone, but it had gone straight to voice mail. There was never great service on the mountain.

"Rink ran away. Took me forever to find him." Huck was in a foul mood, his jeans and boots muddy.

"At least he didn't dig up any bodies this time," Hannah had quipped, and Huck had simply grunted a reply. She'd eaten the pasta alone while Huck had showered.

Brackenhill was getting to him, Hannah thought. It was isolating up here, the woods, the drafty castle. No one had been sleeping well. Rink had had everyone up the night before barking like crazy, running back and forth in the hall, and because of either lack of sleep or circumstance, Hannah had burst into tears at the whole ordeal, and Huck had snapped, "Get it together, Hannah." It was the first time he'd ever talked to her like that. But Hannah got it: Brackenhill made everyone edgy. Nervous. Hannah had taken to guzzling wine in the evening before bed to knock her out. She'd hoped to sleep deeply enough to ward off sleepwalking episodes.

"I know," Huck now replied softly. He found her hand under the covers and squeezed her fingertips. "I don't want to leave you up here alone, though."

"I won't be alone; I'll have Rink." Hannah knew it wasn't enough for Huck, but he had clients to appease. He'd been fielding relentless phone calls from his crew: he was the customer Zamboni, the one who solved the problems, smoothed everyone out. Everyone wanted to know where he was—one of his largest clients was an industrial complex on the outskirts of DC, and it was time to strip the beds and install fall plants. It was a job that took almost a week alone, and they had asked for an upgrade to the front entrance and were willing to pay, but Huck had been unavailable. His fiancée's dying uncle held precious little water.

"Rink found a shed. Do you remember a shed?" Huck asked her.

"Maybe? There were a lot of outbuildings in the woods. It's over a thousand acres. It was used as a camp of some kind in the fifties, I think." Uncle Stuart had told her that one day. She'd forgotten all about it.

But now that he mentioned it, she did remember a shed: a wide-plank door with peeling paint, a single bolted window, a steel slanted roof. She had a quick flash of memory, a sour taste in the back of her throat, and it was gone. She wanted to ask Huck if he'd gone inside, what had been in there, where it was. She wanted to go find it again. It was on the tip of her tongue to reach out, bridge the gap. She could almost imagine herself moving into the crook of his arm. Maybe it was what they needed.

Huck interrupted her thoughts. "Did you hear back from that place? Serenity something?"

A quick stab of irritation. Huck always defaulted back to logistics: who was moving when and where. Nitty-gritty, Hannah called it. In this case the nitty-gritty was a cover for *When can we leave?* He didn't exactly care what she was doing with her days. He didn't see how the remains in the woods could be tied in any way to Julia. He liked facts and figures, tangible evidence he could grip. He'd spent his days at Brackenhill reading—thick nonfiction from Uncle Stuart's library. Biographies of Johnny Cash, Philip Roth, Muhammad. She'd let him take a handful home with him.

"Serenity Acres?" Hannah made a split-second decision. "No."

She'd never lied to Huck before. She was doing it so he wouldn't worry, she thought. So he wouldn't wonder what she was doing up here, wouldn't wonder if she was slowly losing her mind. She didn't tell Huck about Warren or Lila or Ellie. She felt her life fracture into yet another piece. She had her normal life, her life in Brackenhill, and now a secret. A mystery to unravel, connections to make. She felt so close to it. It was possible, even likely, that telling Huck would have helped her. It was also just as possible that Huck would be dismissive.

Still, she stayed silent.

They lay like that, Huck gently cupping her fingertips, until she had almost fallen asleep. When he moved over her, his lips on her hair, then her mouth, his hand sliding up to her breast, her body arched to his on instinct. Her mind stayed blank, and she focused on the feel of his body, his skin beneath her fingertips, so familiar, so warm. They knew each other so well that even when everything else felt murky and lost, their bodies knew the way.

He slid inside her and she felt the pressure build, then explode, his sudden cry into her ear, his hand gripping her hip, and then it was over, that fast.

Later, she'd wonder if she dreamed that too.

"Give me a week, okay? Then if you can't come home, I'll come back. I just need to get everything back on track." Huck stood by their car, his duffel bag hanging in his right hand.

"I'll be home in a week. I will eventually lose my job. I'm using all my vacation time and sick time as it is." Hannah had communicated to her boss in text only, keeping her answers vague. She could sense the irritation in her boss's shortened replies. Oh well. She was only pretending to care for Huck's sake.

She'd started having elaborate fantasies of living at Brackenhill. Gardening like Aunt Fae, canning in the summer and the fall, tending to the grounds like Uncle Stuart, lazing in the pool under the hot August sun, spinning on the pink tube like Julia. Bringing the pool back to glory, sparkling in the sun. The feel of the cool water against freshly shaved legs.

"I'm not comfortable with this; I'm really not." Huck looked up the driveway to the castle, only the turrets visible over the small stony driveway knoll.

"That's silly. Rink is here. Alice is in and out. As soon as Stuart is placed, I'll come back. Just go hold down the fort at home, okay?" Hannah stood on her tiptoes and kissed his cheek. It was a chaste, almost platonic goodbye, and she couldn't help but remember the Huck and Hannah of a mere two weeks ago. This, if nothing else, underscored the growing distance between them, something their sleepy interlude last night had done nothing to alleviate. She knew their relationship well enough to know that late-night intimacies didn't always transfer to the light of day.

"You're going to go look for that shed the second I'm gone, aren't you?" Huck gave her a small, affectionate smile.

"No!" Hannah laughed, willing to go along with the ruse: he wasn't frustrated with her for staying, and she wasn't annoyed at him for not understanding her ties to Brackenhill. Why would he? She'd never explained it. Still, she had expected more. "Okay, maybe. I spent years exploring here. Sometimes alone. I survived. It's daylight. It'll be fine. I'll take Rink and my phone. I'll call if I fall down the embankment into the river."

"That's not even funny." Huck folded her into a hug. "Just stay safe, okay? Come home as soon as you can. We'll talk every day."

She watched his car back down the narrow pebble driveway and onto Valley Road. When he got to the bottom and turned right, she waved both arms above her head. He honked the horn and was gone.

CHAPTER
THIRTY-THREE
Now

Hannah snapped on Rink's leash and checked her watch. It was seven o'clock in the morning. She had the whole day ahead of her. Alice would come at nine, and she could talk to her about Serenity Acres, about the process for getting Stuart admitted. She had said she worked closely with the hospice centers in the area and she'd be able to help when the time came.

Hannah needed the walk to clear her head. Make mental lists of all the things she didn't understand or didn't know. All the questions that had poured out of her at Uncle Stuart's bedside the day before came back to her. But the one that nagged at her the most: Was Aunt Fae Ellie's mother if Warren Turnbull was her father? She tried to remember the curves of Ellie's face but couldn't clearly recall anything aside from red lipstick. Red hair. Aunt Fae had been brunette. Wispy. Mild mannered. Ellie was redheaded and sturdy. Brash. Hannah couldn't imagine it or perhaps didn't want to. That would make her and Ellie . . . cousins. No.

Rink stopped walking and spun in a circle, barked at the air. Hannah tugged on his leash, pulled him forward, back onto the path she'd walked a hundred times as a kid. Away from the courtyard in the opposite direction of the river. If she kept walking, she'd eventually meet up with Valley Road, not too far from where Aunt Fae's car had crashed. Still, that was at least three miles. She had no intention of walking that far.

But Rink would not move. She snapped his leash. "Come *on*, Rink," she said firmly. He acquiesced but whined while following her, his head bent low, his ears folded.

The shed came into view, the door slightly ajar. Hannah felt a stab of annoyance at Huck. Why wouldn't he leave it how he'd found it? Uncle Stuart would have locked it back up; he never left anything unlocked. Too many kids broke into the grounds of Brackenhill, just to explore or drink or party.

Next to her Rink whined.

Hannah pushed the door open all the way. The inside of the shed was illuminated by a swath of tree-dappled sunlight. Dust swirled up, clouding the air and settling. The shed looked unremarkable. A row of gardening tools hung on the left, shovels and trowels and rakes all lined up according to size. The space was large for a shed, fifteen by fifteen, but everything had a place. Uncle Stuart was—had been—a fastidious gardener. So odd to think of him in the past tense, especially as he lay breathing only a few hundred yards away. Hannah still couldn't reconcile the man she'd seen earlier with the one she'd once known.

A tractor sat in the middle of the shed, small by tractor standards but dwarfing the room. Hannah edged around it, eyeing the shelves along the back, lined with stacked pots in bright cobalt, fiery red, and muted clay colors. Another shelf contained bags of potting soil, fertilizers, gloves, and hats. Hannah found herself picking each item up, examining it, and replacing it.

Why had she come here? No idea. She had things to do, calls to make, a day to commence. And yet.

She picked up an old straw hat, frayed on the edges, and turned it over in her hands. Held it to her face and inhaled, looking for some remnant of life: a tang of sweat, the sweet fragrance of fresh-cut grass, a hint of Uncle Stuart's Irish Spring. Instead she smelled only must and age, generic. It could have belonged to anyone.

The metal roof sloped asymmetrically, the back of the shed a foot shorter than the front. In the corner, along the back wall, sat a stack of blankets, topped with a white pillow. How odd that it contained very little dust, as though it had been placed there recently.

Hannah searched for a spark of memory, closed her eyes and tried to intuit a sensation, something that would make her think this building was significant. That it held any piece of the puzzle. She came up empty.

They'd played here as kids; that was all she remembered. Hide-and-seek in the woods, knocking a shovel off its hook, sending it clattering to the wooden floor. Julia flinging open the door with an *aha!*

Hannah turned to leave, frustrated but unable to articulate why. What had she expected? Her foot kicked at something—a stone perhaps—and sent it skittering across the floor. The stone glinted in the sunlight, winking from the corner.

Hannah crossed the room, bent to pick it up. It was a ring. A flat black stone and a dirty gold wire tied with a jeweler's knot on either side. It looked homemade. The stone was large—the size of a dime— and even with a layer of dust, Hannah could almost see her own reflection. She brushed the stone off, polished it with the edge of her T-shirt until it shone in the dim light.

It slid onto her right ring finger effortlessly and looked an odd counterpart to the simple, silver-set one-carat diamond on the other hand.

Had it been Fae's? Fae had never worn jewelry in her life that Hannah could remember. She was plain, preferred dirt and sweat to perfume and makeup. Could it have been Julia's? Ellie's? Hannah had never seen it before, had she?

Then a sudden memory, quick as lighting: Julia gathering flowers with Aunt Fae in the garden, Hannah sulking behind her. That last summer, when everything had been off kilter. Aunt Fae talking about the incoming storm, the wind whipping around the garden, making everything look green, the sulfuric smell of electricity. Julia handing her a large glass vase, barely glancing at her, her eyes skimming off Hannah's shoulder, the top of her head, anything but her face. Hannah took the vase from her sister and saw the ring, gleaming like a new penny on her index finger. She'd opened her mouth to ask, but Julia spoke first. "I'm riding my bike into town later." No invitation to tag along. No question if Hannah wanted to go. In the past she would have phrased it differently: *Do you want to* or *What if I* or *What if we*. Julia had been gone all morning, and Hannah hadn't known where she went. And then she was leaving again.

Now with the memory sitting in her chest like a boulder, Hannah had a ridiculously childish thought: Had Wyatt given her the ring? Julia hadn't had it before; Hannah knew that for a fact. Before that last summer, Hannah had known everything there was to know about Julia and vice versa. She'd known every item of clothing in her closet, every pair of shoes, every hair barrette. So many of those items had been shared, the doors between their rooms open and belongings exchanged like currency. At any given time, each room contained half Julia's and half Hannah's things: clothes and books and shoes and tchotchkes strewed evenly between them.

Until that last summer, when Julia began to shut the door between the bedrooms. So Hannah had shut hers too. Hannah had envisioned Julia's secrets piling up, filling in the narrow space between their doors, until one day Hannah just stopped opening her own. She stopped hoping.

How had the ring gotten into the shed? Hannah felt the first prick of a headache, tired of trying to make sense of so many questions. Tired of not having any answers. Of not being able to get the right information out of everyone she talked to because she didn't know what to ask. She threw the latch on the shed door and started off back down the path, Rink in tow.

Hannah twirled the ring around her finger as she walked back toward the castle. Lost in thought about Stuart, Alice, a list of questions, the ring, Julia, Aunt Fae. She came into the garden, the wind picking up, and for a moment, she was disoriented. It felt like that summer afternoon, the one with the vase and the ring, all over again. The storm coming in, the clouds rolling, the sky a greenish gray, the smell of lightning just before it cracked.

And Wyatt standing in the arch to the driveway, his car parked behind him, a hand to his eyes. He raised his other hand in greeting, halting and unsure.

In the distance, thunder rumbled like a portent.

CHAPTER
THIRTY-FOUR
Now

Wyatt ducked his head as Hannah approached, suddenly shy. His hair, looking more brown than red in the gray morning light, his fists in his pockets, clenching and unclenching.

"Do you and Huck have a minute?" he asked, all business.

"Huck left. It's just me now. But yes, come in."

Hannah avoided looking at his face, not wanting to see anything resembling relief or hope. Not sure how to proceed now that Huck wasn't there to buffer them. The diner had been different. Public.

Hannah led Wyatt in through the kitchen door and motioned for him to sit at the island. She busied herself with the coffeepot, realized only after a moment that her hands trembled. She flexed her fingers to get the tremor out and turned brightly, smile pasted on.

"So what's today's breaking news?" She placed a cup in front of him, steam curling. Set a bowl of fruit she had cut earlier on the table.

"Why did Huck leave?" Wyatt had the infuriating habit of answering a question with a question.

"Work called. He owns a landscaping company. Most of his clients are businesses in town. It's fall planting season." She shrugged.

"So he left you up here alone?" Wyatt raised his eyebrows.

"I'm a grown, capable adult, Wyatt." Hannah felt the spark of annoyance. She didn't need his misplaced sense of chivalry. "I'm not some fragile thing in need of being cared for."

He laughed then, reached across the island and plucked a strawberry out of the fruit bowl and popped off the greens. He cocked his head, gave her a meaningful look. "Well, but aren't we all?" He sat forward, tapped her hand once across the island, the touch making her skin burn. "I just meant there's a lot going on. Your uncle dying, your aunt recently passed . . . you haven't been back here in what, seventeen years? Dealing with Julia—we found a body, for God's sake. It's a lot; that's all I meant. I never meant to imply that you weren't . . . capable."

He was dressed down: jeans and a short-sleeved button-up shirt. He looked like he was on the way to a backyard barbecue. She felt her heart betray her, a syncopated beat against her rib cage. She couldn't help but notice the flush on the back of his neck, the line of his jaw as he spoke, his perfect straight teeth when he smiled, his hair in need of a haircut, a reddish-brown curl at his collar. A brief image of running her hands through it. She hated his compassion, his ability to tune in. So opposite Huck's steady pluck.

"So what is going on, by the way? Do you have any more information on Aunt Fae's accident? Or the remains in the woods?" Hannah cocked her head to match his.

He laughed, then turned somber. "I have nothing on the accident. We have evidence in queue at the state labs, but I can't comment on anything else." He cleared his throat. "I wanted to ask you about Ellie Turnbull."

"Everyone's favorite topic of conversation lately." Hannah felt her edges go sharp, the dislike of that girl so close to the surface even now, after all this time. Suspicious of the coincidence. First Lila had brought her up, and now Wyatt.

"What does that mean?"

Hannah waved her hand around. "Forget it. What did you want to ask?"

"Eh, call it a hunch. I can't prove it, not yet. I haven't talked to Warren. So this conversation is . . . casual. I'm not on duty right now. It's off the record, okay?" He studied his coffee, and Hannah was reminded of Jinny staring at the dregs of tea in the bottom of her reading cup.

"I'm not keeping a record, Wyatt."

A chuckle. "Can we talk about that last summer?"

"Maybe. What parts?" Hannah felt brazen but tired. Tired of dancing around half truths and innuendos.

Wyatt paused, studied her face. His eyes, flecked with gold, so close to hers. They were separated by the island, but Hannah had been leaning on it. She straightened up.

"I'm sorry for everything. For hurting you, you know." His voice was soft, but he looked surprised. He hadn't planned that part, she gathered.

"For the part where you took my virginity? Or later, when you kissed my sister?" Hannah felt the rage zing through her, a surge under her skin.

"All of it. I was a stupid kid. A young, horny, stupid teenager. You know that, right? Both of you had me in a state that summer."

"I loved you," Hannah blurted, and she felt the shock of saying that for the first time out loud. She felt bolstered by the invisible presence of Huck. His existence proof that she didn't still love Wyatt, couldn't possibly, and she could have pointed to it as tangible evidence: *See, I've moved on from you. You meant nothing to me. You still mean nothing to me.*

"I know." Wyatt winced and then looked at her earnestly. "I didn't use you. You have to know that . . . that I was in love with you. Julia . . ." He took a breath. Then another. "It was complicated, Hannah. She was more my age. Listen, no eighteen-year-old with two beautiful girls vying for their attention would handle it one hundred percent correctly, okay? It's not just an excuse."

"Sure it is," Hannah insisted and felt her breathing hitch. She suddenly couldn't take a deep breath. She remembered this Wyatt. The one who spoke plainly, with an earnestness reserved for lovers and confidants. The one who made every encounter feel intimate. The one who made her do the same. Except she was a different Hannah now: she'd learned how to build walls, cordoned herself off. How easily he'd come back into her life, in whatever aspect, and how quickly she'd given up her feelings, resorted to her teenage self, free with her own emotions. *I loved you.* Who said that? She was engaged. Huck didn't deserve this: her racing heart, her inability to breathe properly. No good could come from this. She suddenly felt furious with herself.

"Wyatt." Hannah held up her hand. "I'm fine, okay? You don't owe me anything. Young love"—she stumbled over the word, now when it mattered so much less—"is always fraught and messy. It's how we all learn, how we form real relationships later." She didn't say it to wound him, even if that was how it came out. She had no idea if she hit the mark.

Wyatt said nothing.

"Are you married now?" Hannah asked, realizing she didn't know. Knew so little about him now. Maybe had known so little about him back then.

"Divorced." He gave her a rueful smile. "So maybe I didn't learn enough."

"I'm sorry."

"Don't be. I was a decent father but a shit husband."

Hannah felt her head snap up at this. "You have a child?" She could easily imagine this with his moral compass and what she knew of him as a teenager: playful, fun, insightful, emotionally available.

"I do. Her name is Nina. She's ten. Knows everything about life and is trying to teach me. And mostly failing." Wyatt half stood and reached into his back pocket; his shoulders strained against the fabric of his shirt. Hannah looked away. He produced a wallet, snapped it open to reveal a photograph. A child with dark hair, laughing in a field in a gingham dress. Holding a daisy. "My wife—ex-wife—does portraits every year. This was this past spring." His voice lowered. "She's amazing. Parenthood is amazing."

A pang right under her breastbone. Hannah could see it that quickly: Wyatt as a dad, a little ringleted girl on his shoulders, pointing out shapes in clouds, pushing her on the swings, never tiring of it.

"And your ex?" Hannah prodded, then instantly regretted it. It was none of her business.

"Liza? She's great." He shrugged. "I didn't take marriage seriously. Probably didn't take her seriously. We married too young, maybe."

Liza Rendell. Hannah vaguely recalled her from the kids in town. Pretty. Dark hair. Tall and gangly. Quiet. Kind. "You married local?" she teased.

"Yeah." Wyatt smirked at her. God, his smile was so nice. "Well, you didn't stay. I didn't have a choice."

The joke fell flat. Hannah wanted to say, *I didn't have a choice either.* Instead, she picked a piece of honeydew melon from the bowl, studied it. Let the silence do its job.

"Back to Ellie," Wyatt finally said.

"What about her?" Hannah turned her back to him, poured herself another cup of coffee, added half-and-half, a dash of sugar, all very deliberate and slow.

"When do you remember seeing her last?"

An easy one. "The summer Julia disappeared. Left. She was around all summer, off and on." Hannah thought of Ellie in the garden at midnight. Hovering. Pulling Julia down the path.

"That was . . . 2001?" Wyatt clarified.

"2002," Hannah corrected.

"Are you sure?"

"I think I'd know the summer my sister disappeared. Besides, it's easily verifiable." Hannah felt impatient.

"Yeah, sure. I remember too." His voice lowered. Hannah wasn't falling for it again, the trip down memory lane, the husky voice, the implicit intimacy of mutual regret.

She straightened her back, leveled her gaze at him. "But?"

"Well, the thing is . . ." He coughed. "Warren filed a missing persons report on Ellie in 2001. There was an investigation, but all signs pointed to a runaway. She was on camera at the bus station buying a ticket with a thick wad of cash. The missing persons case was closed after that. No one reported seeing her again. No one but you, anyway."

Hannah straightened her back, indignant. "Well, I know what I saw. The summer my sister disappeared, she was with Ellie all summer. I was angry about it. Ellie was always here. I was left out and ignored." She gestured across the island. "You remember some of it; you must. I talked to you at the time."

Had she talked to him? She searched her memory.

Hannah remembered the smell of his neck, damp with tears and summer sweat, as she sat curled against him on the swing of his front porch. He'd comforted her, but she hadn't told him specifics about why she was upset. All the words she could come up with had been childish, juvenile. *My sister likes Ellie better than me.* Hannah, so aware of their age gap, so conscious of her perceived immaturity, had instead spoken in generalizations. *She's such a bitch lately.* She'd called her secretive. Maybe even slutty. Thinking back, she remembered his surprise at that comment. It hadn't registered at the time.

She wondered if he was thinking about that moment too. Or was he thinking of later, when she'd kissed him, straddled his lap, let her hands inch up his bare chest, fingertips pressed against the ridges of his shoulders, as she marveled about his body, the first boy body she'd ever seen, so wholly different from her own that she thought there should be different words for their parts: *shoulder, chest, muscle, skin.*

But all Wyatt said was, "I don't remember you talking about Ellie specifically." And then, "We'll need to come back."

"What?"

"We need to do another search of the property."

"You think the skeleton is Ellie?" Her voice pitched up several octaves. Until that moment she hadn't fully thought that Ellie could be dead. In Hannah's mind, Ellie was just another runaway teenage girl from Rockwell.

"I don't know. Like I said, it's a hunch, based on what I remember. Based on interviews with other people who were kids with us at the time."

Hannah frowned. She knew what she'd seen, and she remembered it as though it had been that day. "Could Ellie have been living on Brackenhill property somewhere?" She thought of all the outbuildings: sheds and storm shelters, a small barn, the tower with a turret roof that was always empty. If Ellie was buried at Brackenhill, then who had buried her? *Who killed her?*

"I don't know. The winters here aren't mild. She disappeared fall of 2001. She would have had to find shelter, food, without anyone seeing her. More likely that she stayed with someone who is either lying for her or is no longer around." The implication was obvious, and Hannah felt the creeping dread up her spine. Would Julia have hidden Ellie in the castle? For a year? Nothing about that made sense. They'd gone back to Plymouth in August.

Wyatt stood to go. Opened and closed his mouth like he wanted to say more. Finally, "We'll be back in a few days. I just need to assemble the right team. I'll text you a time, okay?"

He didn't hug her goodbye, and when his car backed out of the driveway, she felt disoriented, restless. Unsettled by the feelings Wyatt had stirred up, wishing Huck hadn't left. She texted Huck but received no reply. He was probably still driving. It seemed impossible that he'd left only that morning. She thought about calling him, asking him to come back. Everything Wyatt had said had been true: her aunt and uncle, her sister, the body in the woods. It was a lot to process. Wyatt didn't even know about the dreams, the sleepwalking.

For the first time, Hannah felt afraid and unsure. Huck had always had such confidence in her, an easy belief that she'd be fine. That he'd always be fine; they'd be fine. Vulnerability was a weakness; needing others meant you were failing yourself. It explained why he loved her. She'd been closed up and shut down. It was easy to love someone with no baggage. That part of her life, the needy, vulnerable childhood part, had been packed away in a dusty corner of her brain for so long that she hardly recognized herself now. She'd spent the last seventeen years moving forward, making her life.

Then why now, for the first time in as long as she could remember, when she was careening backward in time with Wyatt blowing the dust off her memories, did she suddenly feel alive?

CHAPTER THIRTY-FIVE

Then

July 13, 2002

The river was high, thick with rain, and brown, rushing and loud. It swirled in yellow-white foam around her thighs, her nightgown pushed up to her waist. Floating, pillowing around her.

She woke up freezing.

The faint moonlight bounced off the water, the sky inky black and huge.

She hadn't even been dreaming, but she woke up in the river. The river rushed around her, cold, gripping, and she felt frozen with fear.

She was going to die.

Hannah inched her feet along the bottom, felt the sand and pebbles shift under her heels. She could hardly see her hand in front of her face. The moon, waxing crescent, barely gave her enough light to get back to the beach, where she fell forward on her hands and knees. She was soaked and freezing, trembling with fear and exhaustion.

It wasn't the first time she'd sleepwalked. It had started about a month ago, maybe more. Time was distorted at Brackenhill: a week seemed like a year, a month like a blink. It didn't always make sense.

Last time she'd woken up in the basement. On the steps, in particular. She was facing the kitchen door and ascending. She had no memory of going down to the basement. She and Julia hadn't gone downstairs since that second summer with the index cards and the moving doors. They'd been too skittish about it. After Uncle Stuart had to rescue them from the center, Aunt Fae forbade it. Said they'd "carried on too much about it."

Hannah pushed her way up the embankment and through the woods. She had no idea if she was on the path back to the house or not—she had no flashlight, and under the canopy of the forest, she could barely see her hand in front of her face.

She was so tired. She hiccuped and realized she'd been crying. Sobbing, really. In the courtyard she sat on a bench to catch her breath. She hadn't told anyone—not Julia, not Aunt Fae—about the sleepwalking for fear they'd send her to Plymouth to see a doctor or, worse, send her home for good. Julia had already been going on about Brackenhill being evil and wanting to go home. She had an overactive imagination. Did she really believe the nonsense she spewed about seeing things? About Aunt Fae? Hannah couldn't leave. What waited for her at home? The creaking open of her bedroom door, even more fitful sleep, cold hands inching up her thighs. *No.* It was out of the question.

Still, she was tired in her bones. She stood, wanting to get back to bed. The warmth of her comforter. It had to be two a.m.

A shadowy figure at the mouth of the path caught her attention, fear instant and sharp in her chest. A blur of red shirt, black skirt, a cloud of hair. Ellie. Julia's friend. The girl with the bright-red hair. Slowly, the girl raised her hand in a cautious wave. Hannah waved back. What was she doing here?

"Hey!" Hannah called out, but Ellie turned and ran away, down the path, toward the river.

She was gone.

CHAPTER
THIRTY-SIX
Now

"That's a scrying ring," Jinny said matter-of-factly. She was busy reorganizing a spice cabinet behind the counter, jars and bottles and tubes and shakers all scattered next to the cash register. Her long black-and-white hair was piled on top of her head and held in place with chopsticks. She had a ring on each finger. Most notable was an obsidian oval on her index finger set in a knotted wire. A twin for the ring Hannah wore on her middle finger, the one found in the corner of the toolshed. Hannah had recognized it as being similar to jewelry Jinny owned and thought perhaps she could point to its origin.

"What's a scrying ring?" Hannah asked warily.

Jinny stopped wiping shelves and shut the cabinet doors. "Sit at the table."

Hannah pulled out one of the two chairs at the round table in the center of the room. The table held a lazy Susan of props: a glass gazing ball, a tea strainer, paper towels, tissues, handkerchiefs, and several rings similar to the one Hannah now wore, in both black and gold.

Jinny sat opposite Hannah and splayed her hands. "You don't believe in this hoopla. You've said so. Correct?"

Hannah shifted in her seat. It wasn't that she didn't believe, necessarily. It was that she had little use for things that remained unproven. It seemed like a waste of time. She would never have the heart to say this to Jinny.

Instead Jinny continued, "Or maybe you're apathetic. You don't so much think it's beneath you as you don't care enough about it." And that was much more on the nose. Hannah winced, shrugged, but nodded. Jinny placed both hands on the gazing ball and set it in front of Hannah. "Scrying is just a meditation of sorts. If you relax your consciousness, let your own vision blur into the ball or the ring or sometimes a bowl of water, perhaps a polished crystal, you can access a plane of knowledge that most people on this earth have no idea exists. This is called the Akashic record. The Akashic record is a collection of all events, thoughts, words, emotions, everything that has ever happened to every person or ever will. It's emotion. It's spirituality. It's facts and perception and truth and falsehoods. It's overwhelming to think about. But allows us to understand our own existence and our loved ones more than we otherwise would. Do you understand?"

Absolutely not. Hannah thought it sounded like insane babbling. She nodded anyway.

"Don't lie to me." Jinny held up her hand, her voice firm. She stood, removed the tray, and set it down across the room. The table contained only the gazing ball, held on a pewter stand. "A crystal ball. Corny, yes?"

"A little," Hannah admitted.

"Clichéd, maybe. But useful. Nostradamus used a bowl of water. I like the predictability of the gazing ball. It's a classic."

"My sister used a crystal ball?" Hannah asked, incredulous.

"No. She felt like it was too much. She liked the flat ring, how small it was. She could wear it, use it whenever she wanted. She became quite quick those last two summers."

Hannah tried to remember something, anything, her sister gazing into a ring and murmuring. But nothing came back. Julia had not been herself, for sure, but Hannah would have noticed a clear exit off the rails like that.

"Let your eyes relax." Jinny stood, turned down all the lights. Behind her, Hannah heard a click, and the candelabra that lined the shelves on either wall flared to electric life. Jinny motioned toward the small lights. "I stopped using real candles after the third fire. Dried herbs and old books burn like hell, you know."

Hannah felt a chill up her spine and shivered. She didn't believe in spirits and ghosts the same way Julia had, and certainly not like Jinny did, but the room suddenly felt cavernous. She could only make out a bit beyond the table; the windows to the front of the store had long been blacked out.

"Jinny, this seems unnecessary, truly."

"Do you want to know what your sister was doing? What she could do? Try it. Here's the thing. I don't believe that second sight is only available to certain people. Everyone has it inside them to believe in infinite possibilities. I believe that certain personalities allow for the ability to access what could be available to all of us. You don't know all the rules of the universe, my dear. None of us do. Some of us go to church or pray to deal with that. Others scry and read tarot and burn herbs and talk to spirits—only in the loosest sense of the word."

Hannah jolted. "Can you talk to Julia?"

"Ah, now you're suddenly a believer. Most are when confronted with something personal. A possibility." Jinny stood behind Hannah, resting her hands on her shoulders. She smelled of oil, something richly organic. Her voice dropped to a whisper as she pressed her palms into Hannah's shoulders. "Watch the light in the ball, and let your eyes unfocus. Start with something simple: a blue dot, the size of a marble. Visualize it in the center; truly see it. Don't just imagine it. Imagine it looks like the earth, swirls of white clouds and oceans and green mountains."

Hannah's vision went blurry, the tears behind her eyelids sudden and unexpected. She wondered how many times Julia had sat in this chair. Could she see the blue dot? Had she laughed at Jinny, shooed her hands away? No. She'd believed in magic in ways Hannah never had.

"Bring your mind back to the present; place your hands on the table. Feel the tablecloth beneath your palms. The table is tangible. Your mind is not. Close your eyes and slowly open them. Take a deep breath."

Hannah tried to conjure a blue dot. She imagined a marble, swirled with green and white, like Jinny had asked of her. She placed the marble inside the gazing ball in her mind, turning it one way, then the other, until she felt as though it were possible that she was actually viewing a marble, not just imagining it. The marble moved from one side of the gazing ball to the other and then winked just out of view and back. In a blink, the marble had become real, trapped inside the shining glass of the gazing ball, which was once so clear but now almost black in the darkened room. Hannah felt the breath in her lungs, the blood in her veins, the table beneath her fingertips, the floor against the balls of her feet in her sneakers.

And then. Julia. Not in the ball itself but suddenly filling the room, Jinny gone, the table and the floor vanished. Julia sat in the corner, against a wooden wall, her hair tangled, her knees bloodied, wearing a yellow bathing suit cover-up that Hannah remembered. She looked up and saw Hannah, opened her mouth to speak, but Hannah could hear nothing. Julia held up her hands to show her sister: blood running from her fingertips to her wrists and pooling on the floor around her, and she turned, pounded and pounded on what Hannah had believed to be a wall and saw now was a door, a rusty iron bar secured across the wood. Julia swung her legs around and, with incredible force, kicked the door with both feet. The door moved with every thrust but made no sound. It was as though Hannah were watching a silent film, a horror movie on mute. Julia looked seventeen, but her long hair was stringy and greasy. Other things Hannah noticed: Julia's sunken cheekbones, a missing tooth, a gash across her protruding collarbone. She looked like she was starving. Injured. Hannah felt her heart constrict, and without volition her feet moved her toward the apparition. Her stomach lurched, and for a moment, she felt like she might vomit. She covered her ears, squeezed her eyes shut, and heard the moan of pain before she recognized it as her own: *Stop!* Her sister turned then, as though she heard Hannah. Julia met her eyes, stared right at Hannah, her mouth forming what could only be one word.

Help.

CHAPTER
THIRTY-SEVEN
Now

Hannah had stumbled home from Jinny's with a blinding headache and gone straight to bed. Jinny said it was common for divinations to bring on migraines. Hannah had never had a migraine in her life, and what she'd seen was hardly a divination. It was an overactive imagination brought on by fatigue. Stress. Emotional burnout.

Julia's word came back to her: *Help*. Over and over and over again. She tried to reconcile the vision—it was, simply, a vision. An apparition. Hannah had never been particularly susceptible to suggestion, but Jinny was persuasive. She was taken in by Jinny's store, her reasoning, her voice, the candles, the incense, the room. What was starting to feel like desperation clawing under the surface. All her random digging the past few weeks. She'd almost forgotten what home felt like, what normalcy felt like. She wanted to find Julia. She wanted, for the first time since she was fifteen, a sense of closure. She wanted Huck and her life and her job back, but this time with no tether to the past. No shadowy, unknown parts of her, just a clear understanding of what had happened that last summer, what happened to her sister. She'd go to therapy if she had to. She could do that. Huck deserved an emotionally balanced wife, and right now, she was anything but. Her insides felt wild all the time, her mind careening like a roller coaster.

Sleep was elusive. Hannah had started going to bed early right after Huck left—three days ago, or was it four?—sometimes around nine o'clock, her body exhausted. She woke up several times a night, her heart pounding, blood running fast in her veins. Visceral dreams—not nightmares but something more real. Waking up all over the house, the yard. The other night she came to in the basement, the overhead fluorescents buzzing and flickering like a strobe. She stood in the center of the maze of small rooms, unsure how to get back upstairs. She made her way through a series of small doorways, only to realize that she was heading toward the back of the house, not the stairwell, and had to pivot and return the way she'd come. She felt fluttered fingertips against her neck, a chorus of whispers chasing behind her. When she'd finally stumbled up the stairs, heart in her throat, she'd slammed the basement door and stood in the kitchen, sweating. It had been four in the morning.

Hannah was afraid that one day soon she'd come to consciousness standing thigh deep in the Beaverkill. If she drowned, who would know? Who would find her, call the police? If she told Huck, he'd make her come home. She felt like she was making progress—more than Wyatt, perhaps, at least concerning her sister. She wasn't quite ready to leave it behind and . . . what? Return to Virginia no better off than when she'd left? No.

But today she woke up here, in Uncle Stuart's room.

"Do you know?" she was asking when she came into consciousness, her voice disconnected, floating, wholly unlike her own. Hannah was sitting next to his bed, her fingertips rubbing the lace trim of her nightgown. On this chair. Seemingly in the middle of a sentence. Now what?

She absently touched her hair, flying away in all directions. A brief panic, a time slip. The sense that she'd been sitting in this room for hours, not minutes, curtains drawn. Like waking up from a nap and looking at a clock in a darkened room: Was it night or day? Had she missed work? Except here, at Brackenhill, there was no work.

Uncle Stuart opened his eyes, blinked furiously, and nodded his head. He was last conscious two weeks ago. Right after she arrived. So she waited here in this impending-death waiting room. The transfer to hospice could kill him, Alice had warned. They had until Monday to decide. The facility had agreed to hold the room for a week. Today was Thursday. Friday, maybe. The days were running together. Would he die first? This was the order of the day. Yesterday Alice said his breathing was becoming labored.

He had an infection now. Probably starting from an abscessed tooth. Seemingly minor inconveniences to healthy people were fast-track death sentences to hospice patients. The day before had doctors in and out. They'd talked about transferring him to a hospital. He was on IV antibiotics, Alice reported later.

Uncle Stuart grunted, his hand lifted, and he pointed toward the closet. What had she asked him? Whatever it was, he knew the answer. He was awake. And not unconscious with his eyes open but actually awake.

Hannah sucked in a breath, her palms slick from nerves. "Hi," she said.

He blinked at her, the ventilator hissing. His face was white in the early-morning light, with a shock of greasy gray flattened against his crown. The veins in his neck, his hands, twitched with life, even while he appeared skeletal. Hannah resisted the urge to hug him, pepper him with questions, never knowing the day he'd be conscious for the last time.

Hannah made her way to the closet door and opened it. Fae's clothing, dresses and blouses and slacks. Not many but enough that Hannah wondered where she would have worn all this stuff. She'd never, as far as Hannah knew, held a job.

The bottom of the closet held a lockbox. She picked it up, turned, held it up for Uncle Stuart to see. He wagged his finger, like a nod, in her direction, and she brought the lockbox back to his bed. The lockbox wasn't, in fact, locked, and a simple twist of the handle resulted in a click as the lid sprang open.

Where did Brackenhill come from?

That had been the question she'd asked him, only half-awake. It came back to her now. The memory of walking into Uncle Stuart's room, sitting in the chair, and holding his hand came back in full, like she'd been conscious.

The lockbox contained only one document. It was folded in thirds, yellowed on the edges, and protected in a plastic sleeve. She extracted it carefully, pinching the brittle paper between her thumb and forefinger, before unfolding it on the desk, running her thumb along each crease to flatten it.

Title Deed across the top in ornate calligraphy.

This mortgage, made the sixth of May one thousand nine hundred and twenty-two, to Randall Foster Yost in consideration for the sum of five thousand dollars . . .

Yost. Not Webster.

Yost was her mother's maiden name. And Fae's. Brackenhill wasn't Stuart's; it was Fae's.

Which could only mean one thing: unless Fae's will said otherwise, Brackenhill belonged to Hannah.

CHAPTER
THIRTY-EIGHT
Now

Get a grip.

Hannah folded the deed and shoved it back in the lockbox. She stored the box back in the closet and turned to see Alice standing in the center of the room. Where had she come from? What time was it?

Hannah said it out loud: "What time is it?"

Alice paused. "Six thirty. I couldn't sleep, so I thought I'd start PT early," she said.

Six thirty in the morning, then? Hannah felt the room tilt; her vision swam.

"Are we still doing PT?" Hannah cleared her throat, trying to get her bearings. Did they do physical therapy on a man who had days left to live?

Had Alice seen her rummaging through the closet? Did it even matter? It was Hannah's house, not Alice's.

Alice stared at her disapprovingly. "Well, death is unpredictable. Keeping him moving keeps him comfortable, in the long run. If there is a long run."

Alice set her bag down, smoothed the front of her shirt. She wore scrubs: this time, they were pink with white bunnies. Her nursing clogs were bright white, new looking. Her face pinched, severe. Hannah realized she'd never seen her smile, not once.

Hannah took a deep breath. Then another. She was still in her nightgown. "Why don't you meet me in the kitchen in ten minutes? I'll get dressed. Let's have coffee."

Alice blanched. Recovered. Gave a quick nod. "Of course, Miss Maloney."

"Alice, really. Please call me Hannah."

In the kitchen, in jeans and a T-shirt, Hannah busied herself making coffee. Scoured the refrigerator for fruit and came up with croissants, three days stale. She needed normalcy, a conversation with another adult who wasn't Jinny, speaking in cryptic riddles, or Uncle Stuart, not speaking at all, Huck, trying to tell her that all her hunches and suspicions weren't rational or based in fact. Or Wyatt, making her stomach clench and her breathing hitch. Alice was a nice, neutral normal. *N-N-N.*

Hannah felt a giggle bubble up. God, she was cracking up.

"Something funny?" Alice said behind her, and Hannah whirled. Alice's head was cocked to the side, her expression thoughtful.

"No. Maybe. Yes." Hannah closed her eyes, then opened them. "I'm thinking of leaving soon. Not immediately, but you know, I have a life to return to."

Alice smiled for the first time, revealing a browning canine. How old was she? Sixty? Hannah guessed. No. Fifty at the most. "Of course you do."

"I don't know what to do here," Hannah confessed, arranging the croissants on a plate on the island. "Alice, how long have you been here? Helping Stuart?"

"Well, I've been helping Fae since Stuart took a turn for the worse, which was about a year ago last January. So eighteen months or so."

That January Hannah had been promoted. She'd been newly in love with Huck. They'd moved in together in February, so they would have been consumed with plans. Her life, a few hundred miles away, and Fae had been hiring a nurse, feeding her husband baby food. Changing diapers? Who knew. Hannah's stomach lurched.

"Fae was kind, gave me a chance. I had been down on my luck," Alice said. "Looking for a new start. You know what that's like." Her tone was quiet, light even, but Hannah shifted uncomfortably.

"Well, yes, she could be generous," Hannah said blithely. She remembered Fae from her childhood: stern but loving, giving with her time and patience, laughing more freely than her mother ever had, but with that certain tinge of sadness.

"Oh, for sure. The most generous person I know. But . . . people in Rockwell, well. They never got over what happened to your sister. To this day, there are people who believe Fae had something to do with it." Alice shook her head, her mouth set in a line. "This town is a cancer. Everyone has too much time on their hands, their lives too miserable."

"Do you think that?"

"Of course not." Alice's reply was quick, too quick.

Hannah looked out the window, to the courtyard: the blooming flowers, the climbing morning glories taking over a small trellis in the center, their vines curling and wild. "What do you believe happened?"

"Well, it was before my time here. I guess I assumed she ran away. I don't know. There were rumors of abuse . . . at home." Meaning in Plymouth, Hannah thought. "I stay out of Rockwell. Too much gossip. I live a few towns away."

"There was no abuse," Hannah offered, but it felt thin. There was Wes. Had he come into Julia's room at night? She'd never said. Then again, Hannah hadn't asked. There was neglect. That was the same thing, wasn't it? The memory surfaced, unbidden: Julia tucking them in at night, an empty box of chocolate chip cookies lying on the floor, their mouths grainy, coated with sugar. Their mother had been at work. Wes asleep—or what Hannah later figured was passed out—on the couch. It hadn't been an unusual memory. That was what struck her, that it had been so ordinary. Julia, eleven, telling Hannah that it was ten o'clock and too late to be awake if they had school tomorrow. Children parenting children.

A change in subject. Hannah said, "So what do I do now?"

Alice paused. Then, "Well, you're next of kin. When Stuart dies, you'd just have to come back."

"When will that be?" Hannah asked, her voice growing urgent. She touched her forehead. "I just have to . . . I think Brackenhill is making me batty. It's so isolated up here. I'm not used to it. I haven't had a bout of sleepwalking in years."

"You sleepwalk?" Alice looked up, her eyes wide.

"I used to as a child. I haven't in a long time. Until now."

"And you think this is because of Brackenhill?" Alice's voice was skeptical. Hannah felt a rise of defensiveness.

"I assume it's stress related. The house, the bones, Uncle Stuart, my sister . . ." Her voice trailing.

"Ah yes. Any progress on that front?"

"Some. Maybe? Detective McCarran keeps me informed. The bones were not . . . Julia. My sister."

Alice looked thoughtful, studied her hands. "What do you think?"

What *did* she think? She had no idea. She had snippets, gut instincts, moments that felt like real discovery, then . . . nothing. The vision of Julia at Jinny's, bloodied and helpless. Ellie running away, and now, according to Wyatt, possibly buried on the grounds, pregnant? She had a scrying ring. A deed to a house that might or might not be hers. She had a whole host of memories that haunted her at night. A longing for a man who was not her fiancé that was keeping her awake, her nerve endings electric. She had pieces; that was all. Tiny little pieces of a mystery that wasn't hers to begin with.

"I think I have to leave, Alice. I have to go back to my life. This is not my life. This is . . . an interruption." She'd been at Brackenhill for fourteen days, and she was no closer to finding out what had happened to Julia. Aunt Fae's accident investigation had been quiet. Even the remains in the woods could be identified without her help. Uncle Stuart was still alive, if barely; Aunt Fae was not. She was sleep deprived, growing more isolated and delirious by the day. Alice felt like a refuge, a friend.

"Then why don't you?" Alice questioned, not unkindly.

"I've been avoiding Brackenhill for so long. I feel like I have one chance to get to the truth. One chance to get closure, and justice for Julia. And I'm squandering it because I'm tired and falling apart." It was the truth, and the frustration of it felt like a basketball in her gut. The coffee mug slipped from Hannah's hands, shattered on the slate kitchen floor. Hannah jumped, let out a little scream, and then felt ridiculous. Alice immediately bent down to clean up the mess.

Hannah bent to help her, sighing.

"You know, there is always more than one chance. Always," Alice said softly, slices of porcelain cupped in her hands. She held Hannah's gaze, steady and intense, and Hannah had no idea if that was true. She'd certainly never been given second, third, fourth chances. Not from Julia, who'd run away the moment their bond had irreparably fractured. Or from Trina, who'd fumbled through her days, bleary eyed, with barely an air-kiss to the top of her head as they'd passed in the hallway on Hannah's way to school. Or from Fae, who'd never reached out. Never tried to call, write, contact Hannah in any way after Julia had left. Or even now, from Huck, who'd left for home when things had gotten tough. Hannah felt steeped in self-pity and pathetic.

She almost said as much to Alice but stopped herself. Alice stood, her palm resting on Hannah's head, her face unreadable. She gazed out the window to the garden, or perhaps the trail beyond that led to the rushing Beaverkill. Finally, she said, "I think you should go home."

"What?"

"You have to take care of yourself, you know. I can call when Stuart passes." When she turned and met Hannah's gaze, her eyes seemed black, obsidian like Julia's stone. "I think you know this. But it's just no good for you here."

CHAPTER
THIRTY-NINE
Now

The idea that she was leaving had wormed its way into Hannah's brain since yesterday, and suddenly she was clearheaded. She could sleep, think, plan.

It was Saturday. She'd take the day, pack and clean. Wrap up loose ends, say goodbye to Jinny. Maybe Wyatt. Leave tomorrow and be home in time for Labor Day. Picnics and barbecues with their friends.

She tried to call Huck a few times. Sent a text: I'm coming home tomorrow. Can we do something fun? Maybe call the Wallers? The Wallers were their neighbors, slightly older than them and a bit further in life: They'd married. Patty Waller was pregnant. Nice, normal people to spend the last weekend of summer with.

But by noon, Hannah found herself standing in front of Pinker's Bar, the Beaverkill a rushing echo far behind it. She hadn't made the choice to come; it seemed to have happened subconsciously. An instinct. She had nothing left to lose here, now that she'd decided to leave. Why had she come? What did she hope to gain? A lone Bud Light sign buzzed and flickered in one window, the other blacked out with a taut shade.

The answer was complicated. On one hand, if she left everything open, without trying to connect all the dots, she'd return to the same half-hearted life in Virginia that she'd left behind. The lies in her past still lies. The secrets untold. But if she did all she could, if she put forth the effort, she could return with a clear conscience, a feeling she'd done all she could but sometimes the truth stayed buried. That was that. Lies and secrets would still exist, but she'd have done her part to ferret out the truth. She could proceed with Huck, free. Nothing tethering her here to Rockwell. And besides, no one would expect her to stay on with Stuart indefinitely. No one expected anything of her at all.

Inside, the bar smelled like wood and liquor. A haze of smoke sat heavy in the air, making it hard to see and breathe. Two men hovered against the wood, faces drawn, nearly identical. One had an angry red scar that switchbacked across his cheek. He'd been cut with something blunt—the scar was jagged. This, Hannah suspected, was Warren.

She bellied up to the bar next to him, leaned half-sitting, half-standing, against the chair to his right. She folded in on herself, scrunching her shoulders, careful not to touch him.

"I know who you are," he said without looking up at her. "Everyone does."

His voice had surprising clarity. No garble, no drunken slur. Hannah noticed his drink, brown and thin, the ice cubes the size of pebbles. He'd been there awhile, nursing the same bourbon.

"I heard you came round my house," Warren said.

"I did." Hannah felt stupid. She'd come without a plan. Again. She'd expected him to be drunk and therefore easy to talk to. She was good at selling herself and could be disarming. She'd relied too much on her charm this time. Hannah cleared her throat. "I just wanted to talk to you. I'm trying to figure out what happened to my sister. And maybe my aunt." Hannah almost added, *and your daughter,* but held her tongue.

"Why would I know anything about that?"

"I don't know. I can't ask Fae or Stuart. I've already talked to Jinny. Everyone else I know in Rockwell was a kid at the time. You're Ellie's father. Fae's husband. What do you remember?"

If Warren was surprised by what Hannah knew, he didn't show it. "Maybe she ran away, same as Ellie." He shrugged, and Hannah noticed a tremor in his wrist.

"Did they run away together?" Hannah asked.

"No. A year apart, they tell me."

I heard. They tell me. "You don't think so?" Hannah sat back in the barstool, wrapping her ankle around the chair leg.

Warren laughed. "You really think I'm gonna tell you what I think? Why, so you can run and tell your little boyfriend?" He still hadn't looked at her. "Do you know what they did to me when Ellie ran away? Thought I killed her. My own daughter."

Hannah had been fourteen and back at Plymouth High School when Ellie had supposedly run away. She'd had no idea what "they" had done to Warren, of course.

"But you didn't?" She said it to get a rise out of him, but the speed he turned his eyes on her made her heart hammer.

"Fuck you." He spat it at her, violent. White gathered at the corners of his mouth, his lips chapped and cracked. Up close, Warren was ugly, the scar almost pulsing purple. His eyebrows knitted together, his dark hair long and wild, growing down his face into an unruly, patchy beard. His nose was an eagle's beak, hooked at the end with a crook in the center, broken in too many bar fights.

"I'm sorry," she said softly. She'd been a fool to think that his anger would help her. Maybe. He kept his gaze on her face, a small smile forming.

"You're a pretty girl to be digging into such an ugly story," Warren said quietly, his eyes settling on her lips.

Hannah shifted on her stool, fiddled with her purse strap. "Yeah, well. It's my sister. I thought you'd have known something. Everyone in Rockwell knows you. I thought maybe you'd know things that no one wants to talk about."

"What do you want to know about? What happened to Ellie? Or your sister?"

"Both."

"You don't get to hear both. Pick one." Warren held up a single index finger, the nail yellow and jagged, stained with nicotine.

"My aunt, Fae Webster."

He looked up; his mouth opened. She'd surprised him. "What the fuck you want to know about her?"

"You were married? How long?" Hannah was on thin ice, reckless, her hands shaking.

"Five years. But technically, still married." He took a long drink.

"Why wouldn't you give her a divorce?"

"None of your goddamn business." His anger flashed again, then settled. The bartender glanced up, and Hannah made eye contact with him. He was vaguely familiar. "You wanna hear about that? How she fucked her teacher? She decided to go back to college, and I was stupid enough at the time to be proud of her. She got a scholarship. Something about architecture and history. Wanted to learn about old buildings or some shit like that. Inherited that fucking mansion and told me nothing about it."

"Who did she inherit it from?"

"Her aunt. Apparently, the woman went crazy, ended up in a sanatorium. Willed everything to Fae, nothing to her sister when she died." Realization dawned in his eyes. "That's your mama, in't it? Things'd turn out a bit differently if your mama had gotten that big old mansion, don't you think? Don't it piss you off?" Warren's face twisted into a grim smile. "Pissed me off for sure. Working like a dog on plumbing, for fuck's sake. Basically, shit pipes, and she's sitting on a golden egg, just rotting up there on the hill."

Hannah felt the full throttle of childhood memories click into place: her mother's bitterness at her sister, her aversion to Brackenhill overridden only by her desire to send her kids somewhere nice for the summer. Maybe get them away from her awful husband? Hannah didn't know. It was a lot to take in, and her thoughts spun.

"Is that why she left you? Because of Brackenhill?" Hannah placed her palm flat on the bar top to steady herself.

"She went back to college, met that shithead of a child-molester husband—he got fired for it, you know." Warren shook the ice in his now-empty glass, his voice conversational, the anger temporarily abated.

"Stuart? A child molester?" Hannah almost laughed, it seemed so ludicrous.

"Sure. He had a problem sleeping with his students." Warren motioned to the bartender, pointing to his glass. Getting warmed up now.

"Okay, but he was a college professor. His students were all over eighteen. I mean, I'm not saying it's ethical, but they weren't children."

"Well, he was fired for it, so what's that tell ya. Anyway, she fucked him, and they moved to that goddamn castle, looking down on everybody in Rockwell, and I sat down here like a chump, cleaning shit outa people's toilets."

"What about Ruby?" Hannah ventured.

"Not mine."

Hannah put the timeline together in her head. Took a leap. "Ruby was five when she died in 1996. Fae left you in 1991. Or at least that's when she changed her name. Which means she had Ruby before she left."

"She was sleeping with that pervert long before she left." Warren's voice was getting louder. "That girl looked just like him. All them freckles and that blonde hair."

Hannah studied Warren, realizing with a start that she hadn't seen a picture of Ruby. Warren's hair was dark, almost black, slicked back and oily. Fae's had been salt and pepper when Hannah knew her but dark when she'd been younger. Stuart's had been blond, shining in the sun. It had silvered early, Hannah remembered. She hadn't looked for pictures, only documents.

"Who was Ellie's mother, then?" Hannah whispered.

"Not your aunt. Ellie's mother was, and is, a druggie. Last I heard, she was in jail. You leave her out of this." He didn't look at Hannah when he said it, his lip curled.

"What's her name, if it's not Fae?" Hannah still wasn't sure what she was getting at, but she was getting more information from Warren when she pissed him off than when she played nice. Warren fixed his gaze on her, his eyes widening with anger. Hannah felt his growing rage across the small space between them and regretted this line of questioning, this intrusion, but she was so close. Too close. He wasn't going to answer her. Hannah took a breath and pressed on. "Ellie was what, eleven when Ruby died? But for the first year of Ruby's life, she lived with you and Ellie. Didn't Ellie miss her?"

"She was ten." Warren turned his gaze back to his now-full glass, stirring the ice with two dirty fingers.

Ten.

Hannah felt the click of another piece of the puzzle. Stuart's nonsense mumbling: *She was ten . . . it was an accident.* The realization sudden and lurching. "Warren." What if she was wrong? She had nothing to lose. "Ellie was there, wasn't she? The day Ruby died."

Warren stood up so fast the barstool behind him crashed to the ground. His hand circled Hannah's arm roughly, enough to leave a bruise, his breath smelling like liquor and cigarettes and decay. "Ellie had nothing to do with that little girl's death, and your bitch of an aunt saying so for twenty years never amounted to anything either. You need to go the fuck home. Before you end up in the ravine too." Hannah's heart hammered, but she squared her shoulders, held his gaze.

He shoved her. Hannah stumbled but didn't fall. A man at the far end of the bar stood up, called, "Hey!" But Warren would have easily towered over him, and he only took one half-hearted step in their direction. The few patrons scattered along the bar stopped to look at the commotion.

Warren leaned into her face. He was over six feet tall, and she'd greatly underestimated his strength. He walked her back against the bar, the wood rough against her palms. His face inches from hers, his eyes manic.

"Get out," he said, his voice low and menacing. "Don't ever come back here spouting that bullshit. Don't ever come back at all, you hear me? I'll give you one warning. I see your ass in Rockwell again, asking questions like this, I'll kill you myself."

"Bull." The warning from across the room came from the bartender, and it took Hannah a moment to realize it was a nickname: *bull. Bull.* Warren stood fully upright, sat back in his barstool.

Hannah left, her legs wobbling. She kept her back straight as she walked through the door and into the sunlight. She would not look afraid.

She might be terrified, but Julia had taught her that. *Even if you are shaking on the inside, you are a goddamn rock on the outside.*

CHAPTER FORTY

Then

July 25, 2002

Julia had always been formidable. People didn't want to cross her. No one wanted to piss her off, feel that cool chill that came off her like a stench when she was mad.

And yet somehow, without trying, Hannah felt like all she did was piss her sister off lately. She tried to talk to her about the ghosts Julia claimed to see or feel. About the baby-shoe prank. About riding into town alone. But Julia would just shrug.

Then she'd take her bike and ride into town alone.

Hannah didn't know whether or not to tell Aunt Fae. On one hand, it seemed to be the only thing keeping her sister from calling their mother and demanding they come home. On the other, if Julia got herself killed, they'd definitely have to go home.

Hannah had been spending so much of her time in the library. The ceiling-high shelves stocked with old, musty books that she had never even heard of: *Pride and Prejudice, Anna Karenina, Love in the Time of Cholera.* She'd tried to read some of them, but mostly she'd fall asleep. She still wasn't sleeping well, and she wasn't having nightmares, exactly, just dreams of wandering the halls of the castle. She woke up this morning standing in the kitchen. This never happened at home, and it was unsettling. Scary, even. And it was even more frightening that she couldn't talk to Julia about it.

Hannah hated to admit it, but Julia was right. Aunt Fae and Uncle Stuart *were* different this summer. They were quieter, more solemn. Uncle Stuart hadn't even pulled a quarter out of her ear yet. He didn't always come to dinner, sometimes staying in his greenhouse long after sunset, potting herbs under the bright fluorescent lights.

Without warning, there was screaming coming from the hallway. Julia and Aunt Fae. Fighting!

Hannah bolted upright, crept quickly to the doorway, but stayed back, out of view.

"You cannot break into rooms that are locked! That is not allowed. If I find you in that room again, I'll send you both home!" Aunt Fae was madder than Hannah had ever heard her.

"What secrets are you keeping from us?" Julia shouted back, her voice loud. Righteous.

"You are a child. I'm an adult. I can keep anything from you that I want. You are a guest in my house. This is *my house*." Aunt Fae's voice lowered, menacing.

"What if I don't want to stay here . . . with a liar?" A pause. Then, quieter, "Or worse?"

"What does that mean, child?"

"Oh, like you don't know what I'm talking about. I know what you've done."

There was some kind of movement in the hall—a whisper, a scuffle. Hannah couldn't make it out.

Then Aunt Fae's voice. "You will obey *my rules*. You don't know half of what you think you do."

Julia slammed her bedroom door so hard a book in the library fell off the top shelf. Hannah shrank back against the bookcase, her heart in her throat. What had all that meant?

Hannah slunk back down the hall to her own bedroom. She eased open the doors between their rooms, and her sister lay faceup on her bed, her arms folded behind her head, fat tears stuck on plump cheeks.

"What was that about?" Hannah prodded, without waiting for her sister to acknowledge her.

"I tried to tell you I want to go home. You don't care. There is evil here. A death. Something. It's enough to drive a person crazy. Jinny says—"

"You talk to Jinny? Does Aunt Fae know?"

"No. She's helping me."

"With what?"

Julia turned her head to look at Hannah, her nose running, and Hannah *almost* hugged her. But couldn't bring herself to do it. Her sister's need for attention—to take it far enough to anger their aunt *this much*—felt vulgar.

Julia sensed the hesitation in Hannah. "Never mind."

Hannah paused. "What did you find?"

Julia stared at Hannah for a long while before answering. "Nothing. I found nothing."

CHAPTER
FORTY-ONE
Now

"He said he would fucking kill you himself?" Wyatt asked.

"Yes, and that I'd end up in the ravine too." Hannah stood in Wyatt's house. She'd called him from her locked car in the parking lot of Pinker's, and he'd given her his address. He lived outside of town in a rustic A-frame with a slate roof nestled a half mile back a dirt road in the woods. A wall of windows faced north, and the view looked out onto shale cliffs and, just beyond that, the glittering gray stripe of the Beaverkill. The house was beautiful, and it was everything about Wyatt that Hannah remembered: warm, welcoming, charming. The great room had been outfitted with large skylights, and the whole house felt like an extension of the forest around it. "This is a gorgeous home, Wyatt." She said it softly, almost regretfully. "How did you find something like this?"

"I built it."

Hannah made a sound of surprise, but it died in her throat. Of course he had. She closed her eyes.

"What if Warren is connected to this? He got so violent so fast. All I did was want to talk to him." She waved her hand around at the vague "this," feeling ridiculous for not fully knowing which "this" she was referring to. Her sister? Ellie? Ruby? She opened her eyes and studied Wyatt, who had turned his back to look out at the river.

"Warren isn't a good guy. You can't just charge around and accuse people of being involved in criminal activity. This is what the police do, but with actual evidence and paperwork." Wyatt pinched the bridge of his nose and then gave her a small smile. "Please sit, Hannah."

She sat on an oversize leather couch dotted with chunky white knitted pillows. Wyatt perched next to her, reached out, and squeezed her knee.

"Did you decorate the place? Or was that Liza?" Hannah pulled one of the knitted pillows onto her lap, hugging it.

Wyatt seemed to startle at the mention of his ex-wife. "She did some of it, but honestly, the house was . . ." His voice trailed off, and he looked around, bereft. "One of the things that did us in. She didn't want to stay in Rockwell at all. I couldn't imagine living anywhere else."

"Why didn't she want to stay?"

"She was a transplant. Remember when she moved here? I was born and raised here. She came to the town later. We got married; I assumed we'd always just stay here. She . . . well, we should have talked more, that's all. About everything." Wyatt gave her a rueful smile, the wrinkles around his eyes the only sign of age. He still had a great smile, all teeth. His auburn hair had grown out in the weeks she'd been in town, and it curled adorably on his forehead. He brushed it back with his palm. "Anyway."

"I know you can't talk about open investigations, but what if Warren had something to do with my sister, or even Ellie? I feel like the two disappearances are connected, even though everyone said Ellie ran away and Warren was abusive. What if he killed Ellie, and Julia found out, so she ran away to protect herself?" Huck had laughed at her when she'd floated this theory. *Witness protection?* Hannah cringed. Then sat up straight and snapped her fingers. "And actually, in there, somewhere, before all this, Ruby died. It's an awful lot of death for a very small town."

"Slow down there. Ruby?" Wyatt knitted his eyebrows, leaned back in his chair. He folded a long leg, resting his ankle on his knee. Hannah turned away. Something about the sight of Wyatt in sweatpants and socks—it was all too intimate, the dark patch of leg hair on his ankle. His T-shirt was rumpled, and she wondered if he'd worked late. If he slept in that and maybe had just woken up? Oh God, she felt her cheeks warm.

"Fae's daughter. She died when she was five. It would have been 1996 according to Jinny." She focused on the mental math.

"Okay, Hannah, just think about what you're saying. You're talking about three deaths in ten years that are only loosely connected. Even for a small town, that's a negligible number. And Ruby was an accident, correct? She fell out of the second-story window. Ellie ran away; we have some old evidence. A bus ticket, security footage of her buying it." He continued, "Your sister is the only real unsolved here."

"What about the skeleton! At Brackenhill!" Hannah would not be made to feel like she was crazy. She would not be gaslighted.

"Of course that's being investigated. I know I floated the idea of it being Ellie, and that could still be true, but officially, on the books, Ellie is a closed-case runaway. We don't have an identity, because frankly, these things take time. Even if we had DNA, which we don't yet, like I said, there's no giant DNA database where everyone is logged and accounted for. She'd only be in the system if she committed a crime after 1997. But to blanketly just say *Warren is connected* and *these deaths are connected* would be irresponsible of *me*; that's all I'm saying."

"Fine, you're not saying it. I'm saying it." Hannah huffed.

"I'm not saying they're unrelated. You get that, right? I'm just saying we don't know that."

"Why else would Warren get so mad? Why would he threaten me?"

"I have no idea what you said to him. If you brought up Ruby and Ellie and Fae, maybe you just pissed him off. He's not known to be warm and fuzzy. And that's a whole lifetime of pain. He's at a bar. In the middle of the day. People do that to drown out hurt."

Hannah deflated. He was right, maybe. She spun the scrying ring around her finger. Wyatt reached out and gently pulled her hand to him, his touch sending jolts through her arm, down her spine.

"Where did you get this?" he asked, his eyes suddenly intense, his voice low and rumbling. Almost suspicious. Hannah focused on the feeling of her hand in his.

"I—I found it. In the shed." Hannah felt a stab of guilt, like she was hiding something. Which, of course, she wasn't, but something about the way Wyatt looked at her made her feel on edge. Like she should keep whatever secrets she had buried. But the truth leaked out to him anyway.

"At Brackenhill?" Wyatt examined it, turned her hand one way, then the other. He leaned toward her to get a better look. He smelled like laundry detergent and pine and trees and earth and dirt.

"Yes. Why?" Hannah moved to pull her hand away, but Wyatt wouldn't let her.

"Can I see it? Can you remove it?" he asked softly, and she complied. He pulled out his phone, shined the flashlight on the ring, and studied it. After a few moments, he sighed.

"What's the issue with the ring, Wyatt?" Hannah asked nervously.

"Don't freak out, okay? But look." He unlocked his phone and turned it to show her. It was an evidence baggie on a plain white dry-erase background. The number 72 was scrawled next to it. Inside the baggie was a ring, a twin to her own: obsidian stone, flat with a hand-made band.

"Where did you find it?" Hannah whispered, but she knew the answer before he said it.

"On the finger of the woman buried at Brackenhill."

CHAPTER
FORTY-TWO
Now

The bottom dropped out of Hannah's stomach. "And you're absolutely sure the remains aren't Julia?" she asked again.

"We are one hundred percent sure."

"But Wyatt, don't you think this proves that Julia's disappearance and this body, whoever it is, are linked? They both had scrying rings. I'm wearing Julia's."

"It's possible." He was maddeningly calm. "Listen, this doesn't actually prove anything. Jinny sold those at her shop for five bucks, and every teenage girl in Rockwell had one. They changed with your mood. You could see the future. Conjure spirits. Some crap like that. We already know the remains are a teenage girl. I'm not sure it's the smoking gun you think it is." He looked impatient, his mouth set in a line.

Hannah shrugged, acquiescing, if only a little. She let the subject drop, but only for now.

Wyatt led her into the kitchen and insisted on making her dinner. She sat at the breakfast bar, watched him move around his small but functional kitchen.

"I like to cook, and it's not like I do it for more than one person with any kind of regularity," he offered as a reason.

Stainless steel appliances, a gas stovetop, a large copper sink, and cast-iron accents completed the cabin feel, but with more sophistication than she would have expected from a born and bred country boy. He had changed into jeans and kept the rumpled T-shirt with *Hollins Ferry* scrawled across the front in seventies cursive. She couldn't bat away the sensation that this felt like a date.

"So no dates, then?" Hannah poured a glass of white from the chilled bottle and felt herself unspooling. Maybe Wyatt was right. Maybe the rings didn't mean anything. Then again, perhaps they did, and she'd figure it out tomorrow. Either way, her stomach grumbled, and she was suddenly eager to relax. Forget rings and bodies and Warren and visions.

"Some." Wyatt dipped his head as he seasoned the steak. She could see his small smile, perhaps at the fleeting memory. "I do okay for having such a small pool out here."

Hannah was sure that was true. "Girlfriend?" she pressed, before taking a sip. She picked up her phone and saw a missed text from Huck. Sorry I've been MIA. It's been a real mess to clean up here. Literally. Around tonight? I'll call at 9-ish. Xo

Hannah muted the ringer.

"Not at the moment. I dated a woman for about a year. She was an emergency room nurse." He picked up his phone and tapped into it. The room filled with music, some folk-rock mix she'd never heard. Mellow. A quiet rain pattered at the windows.

"ER nurses and cops make strange bedfellows. Was your pillow talk all crime and death?" Hannah mused, standing up. The kitchen was connected to the great room with only the breakfast bar between them. She could roam the entire downstairs, taking in the views, the art on the walls. Several framed album posters from seventies rock bands, an original watercolor of the exact view Hannah saw when she gazed out the north-facing wall of windows: a swirl of color, greens and blues and the gray ripple of the river, the sweeping orange sky of sunset. "Did you paint this?"

"Ah, no. That would be the ER nurse. She was—is—an extraordinary painter." Wyatt looked up, met her eyes, and smiled ruefully. The way he said things—"extraordinary painter"—touched a buried spot deep inside her. Everything he said was saturated with passion—not for Hannah or the ER nurse, just for life, simple things like cooking and music and art. Things Huck never talked about. She hated comparing them, hated that she was even thinking that way.

"The nurse was a painter?" Seemed like different sides of the brain to Hannah.

"Sure. Don't you have a hobby?"

Hannah thought of their nights, after work. Dinner and drinks at the pub, then back to their condo, where she and Huck would sit on opposite ends of the couch and watch nineties sitcom reruns with their own laptops flipped open on their laps. Hannah would spend the night getting the art and text positioned just so on whatever project she happened to be working on. Tweaking the copy, trying to reduce the word count to enlarge the font. Huck would be preparing invoices. The picture it evoked felt comforting to Hannah, but she knew out loud it would sound pathetic. "Just work," was all she said instead. She loved her job, she thought. That was her hobby. But did she? persisted the small voice inside. Had she thought about it? Missed it at all in the two weeks she'd been at Brackenhill?

"Your hobby, then, is collecting obscure seventies band posters?" And her eyes settled on a guitar resting on a tripod stand in the corner: golden wood and gleaming black neck. "You play!" she exclaimed.

He laughed as he chopped an onion. "Yes, I play. Have since before we knew each other. You didn't know?"

Hannah tried to remember a guitar in his old room at his dad's house and could only conjure his bed, the darkness of his room, his bed seemingly halo lit. The feel of his mouth. She felt herself flush; the room spun quickly and righted itself. It must have been the wine. She wasn't used to such a heady cabernet. At home, they drank pinot grigio. Cheap, light, readily available.

Hannah returned to the breakfast bar, and they sat in comfortable silence, Wyatt humming softly along with the radio. The windows were open, the cool air smelling of summer rain. Hannah finally spoke. "Do you believe in that kind of thing? Scrying? Fortune-telling, seeing the future, or even connecting with the spiritual world? All the stuff that Jinny peddles?"

Wyatt paused in his chopping. "Not all of it. Some of it, maybe. I mean, don't you ever think about how ridiculous every technological advancement must have seemed before it came to fruition? When Galileo announced that the planets rotated around the sun, not Earth, he was ostracized and called a fool. Advisers to Tony Blair in the nineties insisted that email would never catch on. As a society, we're insanely bad at predicting what the future will later prove to be fact. I'm always so hesitant to say anything unproven is . . . hogwash." He had put the knife down and was gesturing with both hands as he talked. "Also, you've had some pretty unexplainable things happen." He raised his eyebrows at Hannah. He meant Brackenhill. Things he knew about: the basement, the creak of doors, maybe the red pool—she couldn't remember if she'd ever told him that. When they were young, he'd been infatuated with all things related to Brackenhill. Then a memory she'd long forgotten: Their first summer together, the light pebbling of rocks at her window. She'd looked out and seen him below, his bike gleaming in the moonlight. How had he ridden his bike up the mountain in the dark? She opened the window and yelled out, "That's dangerous! You're crazy!"

"Come to the courtyard," he said, his voice urgent, his eyes, even from two stories above, glittering. Hannah flew down the steps and through the castle on tiptoe, her insides flipping and her smile so wide it hurt. When she got to the garden, he was nowhere to be found. She walked all around the castle grounds, whisper-calling his name, until finally, she sat on the concrete bench next to the fountain and waited. She woke up in the morning curled on the concrete, her nightgown damp with dew. Later, she pedaled furiously to town, confronted him behind the pool snack stand, her hands in fists against his chest. He'd laughed at her. "Hannah, are you out of your mind? It had to be a dream. I didn't come to Brackenhill last night." It never felt like a dream.

Hannah shook loose the memory. The wine, the rain, and the music were making her sleepy and happy. She didn't want to unearth an old, silly fight. She felt like turning off reality. Shutting real life down like her laptop: control, alt, delete. She glanced over at her phone, lying facedown on the counter, but she did not touch it.

Wyatt served dinner: Perfectly seasoned and broiled sirloin, sliced thin on a bias, red and warm in the center. Fresh pasta with red wine sauce, tomatoes from Wyatt's garden. Caramelized onions and fennel. While they ate, she talked about her work. He talked about his daughter, Nina. He saw her three times a week and overnight every other weekend. They didn't keep to a formal schedule, and his ex-wife gave him carte blanche to see her whenever he wanted, as long as he called first. When he spoke about her, his cheeks took on a rosy glow. He laughed easily.

As they cleaned up, they got back to talking about Brackenhill. The mysterious history. Her childhood—but only the happy memories. She talked about Aunt Fae building faerie houses and planting bright, bursting annuals along the garden's borders. How she and Julia had found the storm shelter, a secret room in the middle of the forest; was there anything more enchanting than that? How they had never gotten the chance to explore it. The basement, a labyrinth of rooms that had held so much promise when she was a child—how she had known, with certainty, that they were mystical. The rooms had moved on her, reconfigured as they ran through them, getting lost, panicking and laughing and gleeful and terrified and all things at once.

Hannah felt her insides grow warm, slippery. Her heart seemed to expand in her chest, her fingertips buzzing. The basement had been terrifying, but it had been *theirs*. Hers and Julia's. Hannah had never permitted herself to remember the magic of Brackenhill, just the tragedy, and certainly never out loud. Wyatt sat at the breakfast bar, transfixed, as she cleaned up and talked—she had insisted, as it was the least she could do for the delicious dinner.

"I've never heard you talk so much at once," he murmured, his voice thick in the small kitchen. "It's like you've . . . come alive."

And it was how she felt. Aggressively alive. Vibrating with life, in fact. Every skin cell and every nerve ending seemed to pulse.

She stood in front of Wyatt, and from his barstool, he gazed up at her. He was so beautiful, thought Hannah, and the guilt pierced her heart.

"I should go," she said regretfully. The sun had long set, the stars outside the windows brighter than in any night sky she'd ever seen.

He nodded and stood, his face inches from hers.

She couldn't breathe. Couldn't think. Couldn't concentrate on anything but his mouth, his eyes, so dark they seemed black. His breathing, fast and uneven, like he was trying to steady himself.

"What if . . . I didn't," Hannah said, holding his gaze, not asking a question exactly. Posing it as a statement. What would happen if she didn't leave?

She lifted up on her toes and kissed him. She reached out, her hands on his hips, the slightly soft pad where his jeans met his skin, her fingertips grazing under his T-shirt. He groaned softly at her touch and seemed to battle himself, his fists clenched by his sides, fingertips flexing, as Hannah trailed kisses down the side of his face, his neck, his skin warm and smooth and smelling like shaving cream—he had shaved for her. Before finally bringing his arms around her, crushing her against him. She remembered everything. Every muscle, every line and curve of his body, held the glint of memory, the same but different. No longer boyish, clumsy, and eager. Confident, adult—the disarming patience of a deliberate man.

His hand came to the side of her face, cupping her cheek, deepening the kiss, his tongue seeking hers, and she felt like her blood might actually be on fire. She wrapped her legs around his waist, and he carried her through the house to another darkened room, and she was overcome by déjà vu: this man, his bedroom, his smell, and his touch. It all came together in a paint swirl of memory, bursting with color like the sunset behind the mountains, too bright to look at directly, so instead she closed her eyes, felt his fingertips skimming her hips, his lips on her stomach, her breasts, a gentle kiss in the hollow of her throat that sent shock waves down her spine and her legs, turning her liquid. His hands slowly patching her back together. Making her feel whole, not for the first time.

CHAPTER
FORTY-THREE
Then

August 1, 2002

It was a terrible cliché that the worst fight of Hannah and Julia's relationship would be their last one.

"There's a picnic in town." Julia stood in the doorway between their rooms, wearing a white, gauzy off-the-shoulder dress and red wide-brimmed hat, looking like a model. Her hair was shining, ringlets cascading down her back. So different from Hannah's floaty wave. "For the Rockwell Fish Fry."

Rockwell was a fishermen's town. The Beaverkill was the most popular trout stream in the country, and Rockwell's entire identity came from fly-fishing. The downtown contained fly shops and bed-and-breakfasts that catered to out-of-town fishermen. At the end of every summer, the town held a fish fry.

Hannah had been lying on her bed, reading, and she looked up, startled at her sister's sudden appearance. It used to be their normal, but lately, an unspoken wall had been erected. The doors between their rooms remained firmly shut. She didn't know when the divide had happened. The first week of June had been joyful, pancake break-fasts with whipped cream and strawberries from the garden and quiet games of checkers in the evening, and then slowly, Julia had changed. By the third week in July, they'd barely been speaking. Hannah could never figure it out (and she tried plenty). Julia had turned sullen, quiet, moody. She was either gone, destination undeclared; hunched over a little brown journal; or secluded up in her room.

Julia hadn't asked Hannah to come to town with her in weeks. She ducked out after breakfast, leaving Hannah behind. Slipping back in right before dinner. Shrugging off any questions. Rolling her eyes. Acting in general like Hannah was a pest, which she'd never done before.

"Okay," Hannah replied cautiously, licking her lips.

"Are you going?" Julia inspected her nails, painted bright red and gleaming. Manicures were things that they used to do together but that now Julia did alone and Hannah had no knowledge of. She'd always worn pale pinks, sometimes purples or blues, making her hands look like a corpse's, and Hannah would make fun of her. Now, red. So many differences in such a short time.

"Do you want me to go?" Hannah's voice was small, wheedling, and she felt sick of herself. No wonder Julia preferred her friend Ellie, with the wild red hair and skimpy bikinis, or even Dana Renwick, another girl in their group, with a short blonde asymmetrical bob and fuchsia lipstick: bold and confident, with a loud mouth and brash laugh.

"Of course," Julia said, like nothing had changed. Hannah thought of Wyatt. He'd kissed her, fingertips grazing the skin under her T-shirt, soft moans into her mouth, her back against the concrete of the pool snack stand in the early evening after closing. She'd been riding there for weeks, helping him clean the fryers, keeping up a steady stream of chatter. When they kissed, they both smelled like old grease.

He found everything she said interesting, sometimes even asking her days later to retell a story, something about Trina or Julia, or that Tracy or Beth had said, or about boys at school (they all seemed so childish now). She told him about going out on Beth's dad's boat and catching a trout once. Beth's dad showed Hannah how to hit it on the head with a pipe, and she was so horrified she cried, and Beth's brother laughed so hard he fell off the boat. They ate the fish later, and Hannah couldn't even take a bite, and Beth's gross, acne-riddled brother chased her around their backyard campfire with a square of flaky trout wobbling on the end of a fork, held together with blackened silvery skin, laughing meanly, his voice cracking.

Wyatt was riveted the whole time.

She followed him home, curled up in his bed at his father's little white cape cod a block off Main Street. They taught each other about skin and touch and warmth and want and, yes, sex, too, but other things that Wyatt had never known of and Hannah had only read books about. She wondered if Julia had done this yet, felt a man's naked legs between her thighs, the downy coating of hair on his backside. If she'd ever known how powerful it sometimes felt just to be a woman. Because that was what she was now, not a child.

She was drunk on love and lust.

What Julia had vacated, Wyatt filled. She didn't even miss her sister during the long crystallized silences in the castle as Fae and Stuart worked outside and Julia was off wherever on her bike now. Hannah had spent much of June and July roaming the halls during the day, exploring the unlocked but empty rooms, looking under beds, finding old books with illegible scribble in the margins, smelling like mildew and rot. Feeling abandoned and sorry for herself but also, conversely, free. Julia wouldn't want to dig through boxes in the attic, finding old photo albums of people Hannah didn't know. She would have called it "pointless."

But now she was suddenly back, present, asking to be with her, and Hannah forgot about Wyatt, his kiss, his fingertips on her skin, his shared horror at the fish story.

"Okay." Hannah said it again, like talking to a stranger.

"Okay," Julia said, softer now, and then turned back to her bedroom. They rode into town in silence, Julia leading the way and Hannah watching her sister's bike tires spin faster and faster as they took the switchback turns too quickly, gravel kicking out under their tires. Hannah felt the burst of fear in her chest, followed by joy. Maybe whatever had plagued Julia all summer had passed.

The park was decorated with red, white, and blue bunting left over from the Fourth of July, and the amphitheater stage held a band covering Bruce Springsteen and Neil Diamond and all the songs Uncle Stuart listened to on transistor radio in the greenhouse. Hannah hummed along, then stopped because she suspected that it wasn't cool to know all this music, *classic rock.* The air was thick with the smell of frying fish: deep fryers and pan fries on grills behind fish stands. People sat around on lawn chairs listening to the band, eating fish, drinking beer, lamenting the end of summer.

Wyatt stood with Reggie, who flashed her a white smile. They stood apart from the group of kids, laughing and joking, until one girl reached over and swatted him on the arm. Hannah recognized Dana, the cigarette dangling between her fingertips.

Wyatt raised his eyebrows when he saw Hannah. Their relationship had existed in a vacuum, and now here it was, thrust into the open. Would he finally acknowledge it? Did she still want him to? She hadn't pushed him again since that first night back in June. She liked the bubble they'd lived in—no friends or sisters to mess it up. She bit her lip, gave Wyatt a nervous smile.

Wyatt came over with cheeseburgers, and Hannah ate greedily, hungrily, with two hands. She was starving. Julia picked at her bun and put the plate down next to her folding chair. She held a red Solo cup that another girl—Yolanda something, maybe—kept pouring something into. Hannah realized too late, like a dumb little girl, that it was beer. The Coke can in her hand felt clunky and idiotic.

They had a secret, though, Wyatt and Hannah, and that alone made Hannah feel above them all. She could tell they idolized Wyatt, all turning to him after they told a story or a joke to get his reaction. If he laughed, the girls preened, sharing smug smiles.

Dana hardly acknowledged Hannah. The other girl, Yolanda, with black spiral curls down her back, studied her interestedly, like she was a new pet. Julia ignored Hannah altogether.

Reggie caught Hannah staring more than once before he flexed for her, making his biceps jump and move, and Hannah looked away, her face on fire.

She suddenly felt stupid—were they all laughing at her? Was Wyatt? He paid her less and less attention as the afternoon wore on. She had agreed to go along with the secret, but now, she wanted to barge onstage and grab the microphone, announce that Wyatt was her boyfriend, that they were together now. What would Dana or Yolanda say to that? She wondered if Wyatt ever touched these girls, licked their lips, finger-tips making damp circles on their bare bellies as their bodies pressed together against the rough brick of the snack stand.

Dana, Yolanda, and Julia sat as a threesome, talking softly and giggling on the rock wall at the edge of the park. Hannah sat apart, the concrete scratching at her bare thighs.

"Where's Ellie?" Hannah asked the group suddenly, and they all stopped. The band took a break between songs, and it seemed like the whole park stopped talking, the silence between them thin and crackling.

"Who the fuck knows," said another boy Hannah didn't know, hadn't been introduced to. The boys laughed, even Wyatt, which surprised Hannah.

Reggie slung his arm around Julia's shoulders and whispered something in her ear, and she curled into him, her mouth curved into a red-lipped smile that Hannah had never seen. Julia and Reggie? Was he her boyfriend? *Don't be stupid, Hannah.* She could practically hear Julia's sneering.

Why had Julia asked her to come if no one was going to talk to her?

And then, without warning, Reggie was right next to Hannah, with his arm around her waist, his voice like silk in her ear. "I didn't know Julia's sister was *so* pretty." His breath smelled like beer and salty grease. "She said you were a kid."

Wyatt watched them keenly, saying nothing. Why did he say nothing?

"I am a kid." Hannah wanted him to go away. His nose was straight, his eyes bright. He looked like something from a teen movie: too pretty to be real, his skin smooth as cream, cheeks pink and shining. Out of the corner of her eye, Hannah watched Wyatt, who looked away.

Hannah squirmed under the weight of Reggie's arm, but he leaned closer, his breath on her cheek. "You're no kid." And his hand cupped her breast over her shirt. He smelled like sweat and cigarettes and reminded her of Wes; her mouth turned to sawdust.

Hannah pushed him off, harder this time, her breath coming in puffs. Her heart raced under his palm. She bit down hard on her own lip, bringing tears to her eyes. She wanted to go home, suddenly, urgently. She wanted Wyatt. Hannah craned her neck but could not see him.

It had grown dark. The band played something old and slow that Hannah vaguely recognized. Some people by the stage started to dance, coupled up, swaying in the damp heat.

Hannah stood. How were they going to ride their bikes back up the hill in the dark?

She couldn't see Wyatt anymore, could barely make any of them out, only silhouettes against the white spotlights shining onstage. Reggie's arm tugged around her waist, fingertips sliding against the waistband of her shorts.

She broke away, her hand slipping from Reggie's, feeling sick. She wanted to find Julia. And Wyatt. "You girls from Brackenhill are all teases," she heard Reggie mutter.

"Where's Julia?" Hannah asked Dana, who was lying flat on the concrete divider, eyes closed, head moving to the music. She looked up at Hannah like she'd never seen her before.

"Dunno," she said, her eyes glazed, a hand waving in the air toward the tree line behind them. They were all drunk, Hannah realized too late. How would they get home on their bikes if they were all drunk? Hannah felt like the older one, more responsible, having to care for the children.

Hannah hiked off in the direction of the trees at the edge of the park. Mosquitoes nipped at her ankles; she'd have bites there tomorrow, the itching fierce. There was a couple sitting on the grass, underneath the largest oak.

She made out the shimmer of Julia's blonde in the passing of a headlight. The copper streak of Wyatt's. Their heads too close for whispering, talking. Hannah stood still, her legs gone dead and heavy. One of Julia's hands came up, those bright-red shimmery nails curling into the hair at the base of Wyatt's scalp. His face in the sliver of light: eyes closed, mouth parted, euphoric.

Like all his dreams were coming true.

"Oh my God." Hannah said it out loud, even though she hadn't meant to. Dana and Yolanda turned to look, something finally interesting happening. They followed her gaze to the tree line and smirked.

"'Bout time," Dana said, her voice caustic. "She's been chasing him all summer."

"They're perfect together," Yolanda sighed, a happy little drunk.

"Julia!" Hannah shrieked. Her insides felt wild. In this whole summer of being ignored, the only good thing had been Wyatt, and now

Julia was taking that away too. She took away Brackenhill; she took away the magic; she took away everything she touched. And the worst part was Hannah had no idea why. She had no idea why her sister had changed, why they couldn't stay kids at Brackenhill forever. They had forests and basements and passageways and secret doors to explore, and now she was alone, and if Julia took Wyatt, Hannah was *really* alone, just like at home in Plymouth, and she put her fist in her mouth and screamed into it, not caring who saw her or heard her and not caring that Dana and Yolanda watched with glee, sitting at attention, feet swinging against the concrete. She didn't care about any of it anymore. She hated them all. She wanted to go home.

Julia broke out of Wyatt's embrace—Wyatt's embrace! *Oh my GOD!*—and turned to her sister, bewildered. Only Wyatt knew, and his face was unreadable. He did look sorry. He looked a little confused. And something else unknown to Hannah.

"Hannah, wait!" he said but then stopped, not knowing what to say next. Not knowing where to go, how to make things better.

Julia ran across the green between them, closing the short distance in a few seconds, and stood before Hannah, who was shaking with rage. Her thoughts were a jumbled mess; she knew she was careening, likely making a fool of herself, and couldn't stop. She felt like everything was so *wrong* that it would never be right again.

"Why! Why do you have to ruin everything! Why!" Hannah shoved Julia's shoulders, and Julia stumbled, her mouth open in shock. They'd never touched each other like that before—not in anger. Never, not even as children. They protected each other—from Wes when he was drunk and raging, from Trina's neglect—but they did *not* hit each other.

"Hannah! What's wrong with you?" Julia gripped Hannah's wrists and held them out so their faces were inches apart and Hannah couldn't hit or push her again.

"I hate you! Wyatt was the only good thing I had." Hannah felt the tears in her eyes, dramatic and childish, and knew she was ruining it for herself at this point but was unable to stop. "He was the only thing in my life that I *liked*. You've ruined everything."

"Hannah." Julia's voice was gentle, placating, and Hannah fought against her sister's strength, tried to hit her again, but Julia stopped her. "Hannah. Please, honey, stop."

"Shut up! Just shut up!" Hannah sagged back, losing the strength, and stole a glance at Wyatt, who stood, paralyzed, ten feet away, watching the scuffle with his hands fisted in his pockets and his face blank with shock.

"Hannah," Julia said gently, "why do you think you had Wyatt?" She lowered her voice, the way you talked to someone unhinged, and Hannah realized that was what she was: unhinged.

"Because we've been . . . together all summer." Hannah faltered and in the background heard Dana and Yolanda laughing.

"Hannah." Julia looked around helplessly. "You can't think that, can you?"

Hannah looked over at Dana and Yolanda, back to Wyatt, even to Reggie, whose mouth curled in a curious smirk, and realized they all thought she was making it up. A delusional child. A foolish idiot.

Her face burned, and she stepped back, away from Julia, who truly had no idea what she'd been doing all summer. Only Wyatt could set the record straight now.

Hannah looked at Wyatt, her hands splayed outward for help.

Wyatt turned his head, exposing the white of his neck, the neck Hannah had kissed so many times. He extended his hand, the hand that had caressed her hair, her back, all summer.

"Hannah," he said. She wished everyone would stop saying her name like that. His face was pained, his eyes clouded.

He wasn't going to save her.

CHAPTER FORTY-FOUR

Now

She'd escaped Wyatt's on Sunday morning in a flurry of guilt and sickness—some from the wine but mostly with herself. She'd left him sleeping and sneaked out the front door. He'd called three times and texted even more; she'd lost count. Nothing harassing, just wondering if she was okay, and could they talk? She hadn't answered yet. Her mind swung wildly between guilt—Huck—and snatches of the night: Wyatt's hands on her hips, his breath on her stomach, a light, feathery tickle. The feeling of him curled against her as they slept, the way she fit in the hook of his body, perfectly. And disloyally, how she and Huck had never done this. She'd thought she liked to sleep alone, the feel of sheets beneath her palms, the cool distance of his biological furnace. She could breathe freely. She'd thought she wanted that. But with Wyatt, she hadn't felt suffocated.

She was unable to reach Huck. They were missing each other—talking to each other's voice mails, texts going unanswered for hours. Almost as if he knew what she'd done. She sent him periodic missives: How are you? Hope you're not too crazy there. But she acknowledged that if she hadn't stayed at Wyatt's, she would have been out of her mind trying to reach Huck. What must he think of her? It didn't matter; she deserved all of it.

She spent the day sick with herself. Packing up a suitcase, preparing to leave. She had to get home to Huck. Had to figure her life out. She literally felt like she was losing control of everything. She took Rink for a long hike, down to the Beaverkill, and followed the river trail halfway into town and back. He'd been stuck inside during the night while she was at Wyatt's, adding to her guilt.

That night she slept deeply and startled awake in the morning, crying out when she realized she was in Ruby's room. The locked room. She sat on the floor, legs folded, surrounded by pictures. A photo box next to her was tilted on its side, glossy images strewed out and around her.

The smell of death permeated the air, stuck inside her mouth and nose. The gentle image of dirt sifting over a shovel. The remnants of the dream.

She shoved the pictures back into the box and put the lid on. Then stood helplessly in Ruby's room holding the box. Her sleeping self had found it. Her conscious self had no idea where it had come from.

Her head felt foggy, and her eyes burned. The nauseous pit in her stomach was made worse, not better, by the appearance of Alice in the doorway.

"Why are you in here? No one is supposed to come in here," Alice said, and Hannah offered a feeble "I don't know" before Alice turned and brusquely headed down the hallway to Stuart's room, where Hannah followed her. She'd left the box on Ruby's bed.

"We can't move him. You realize that by now?" Alice's voice was sharp, and Hannah found herself feeling chastised. No. She hadn't realized that. She'd thought they were waiting a few days but would be making the decision—the one she'd assumed would be yes—and Uncle Stuart would move to the facility. She would go home. This was the plan.

And yet she was still here.

"He has hours. Days. Possibly a week," Alice whispered in a hiss, held up his catheter bag. The liquid inside had turned a deep brown. "Kidneys are shutting down. His heart rate is erratic, fifty, then ninety."

Hannah took her seat next to her uncle's bed and again picked up his hand. His skin looked blotchy and blue; fifty thumbprint bruises dotted his arm like islands.

So she would stay. See this through. Organize another funeral, another luncheon. This time without Huck. Would he come back? She couldn't even bear to ask him to. No, this was hers to do alone. She'd made a mess of everything, even if Huck didn't know it yet. She'd tell him, eventually, about everything. Right now was about priorities. First Stuart. Then Wyatt. She had to close the door on him, on them. She knew she owed him a conversation. Then, home and Huck and whatever the future held for her. Would Huck stay? She didn't know.

Alice busied herself changing saline, the catheter bag, then the blankets, snapping fresh, clean linens in the air while Hannah sat silent. The woman's silence seemed almost antagonizing.

"Is there treatment for sleepwalking? Medicine?" Hannah asked her softly, partly to make conversation, partly because it hadn't occurred to her to ask until this moment. Alice was a nurse. She might know.

"Is that why you were in Ruby's room?" Alice stopped snapping the sheets and stared at Hannah. Hannah felt like a moth pinned to wax.

"Yes. I think so? I wake up in different rooms here. This didn't happen at home." Hannah didn't say that at home she had six rooms in her whole condo.

"Klonopin," Alice finally answered. A heavy-duty antianxiety medicine.

The front bell clanged, echoing through the house, and Hannah cried out, startled. Alice looked at her strangely—Hannah was so on edge. Hannah stood, letting Stuart's hand fall by his side, and made her way to the front door.

She looked through the small window. Wyatt.

What did he want? She could refuse to answer, but if it was about the case, her sister, Ellie, Ruby, or Warren, then she wanted to know.

She opened the door, and his face was unreadable. She was still in her nightgown, no bra, and she folded her arms across her chest. Stupidly self-conscious.

"Hannah, are you okay?" he asked, his face the picture of concern. His voice low.

"I'm fine. Why are you here?" Hannah's voice was sharper than she'd intended.

"I have . . . a development." He stammered over his words, reaching his arm out to touch her elbow, but she stepped away. "Can I come in?"

She opened the door wide for him, and he brushed past her. He smelled like soap and *Wyatt*, and she instinctually wanted to hug him. Feel him against her again. She noticed how well his dark button-up shirt fit his frame, tucked into jeans, with a black belt. How long his legs looked. She closed her eyes and tipped her head up to the ceiling.

In the sitting room, she sat on a velvet armchair, letting Wyatt take the love seat alone. Her emotions were too wild, her impulses too unpredictable with Stuart upstairs and Huck radio silent, to trust herself. Physical barriers felt necessary.

"So what's up?" Hannah finally asked when the silence grew.

"Hannah, you just left. The other day. How are you? Are you okay? Can we talk?" Wyatt leaned forward, his elbows resting on his knees. "I'm not sorry it happened. But I am sorry if it upset you."

"Stuart is dying. Probably today," she blurted, and his eyes softened, his face slack. "So I'm staying awhile." She gripped her elbows with the opposite hands, her arms tucked tight against her waist.

"I'm sorry, Han. I really am. It's a lot for a person to take." Wyatt motioned around the sitting room. "All of this."

"Yes. Well. Did you have news?" Hannah clapped her hands, oddly, and Wyatt looked alarmed.

"I do," he said slowly. "But you don't seem yourself. You seem like you're . . . cracking."

"Just tell me the news. I'm fine. You said there was a case development." Hannah's heart picked up speed and slowed down, like Alice had said Stuart's was doing, and she wondered if she was channeling his death, or maybe she was dying too. Maybe her heart would stop right here in this velvet sitting room, on this green velvet chair, and she could just go to sleep—real sleep, instead of waking up all over the house.

"It's about Fae."

Hannah's head snapped up. Fae? She'd expected Julia or even Ruby. Warren. What could possibly be advancing in Fae's case?

"We now officially have reason to believe her accident was likely not an accident."

"What else would it be?" It had been a week since Wyatt had mentioned Aunt Fae's accident. Hannah had assumed they'd closed the case.

"Well, there was some paint transfer. Which by itself isn't indicative of anything. Someone could have bumped her in the parking lot of the Fresh N Save. But we looked closer at the scene because of it, and there are no skid marks."

"What does that mean?" Hannah was tired of asking for the truth. Tired of chasing it. She just wanted something to be simple and easy and plain.

"It means she didn't brake. If you were losing control of your car, you'd brake. Unless . . ." Wyatt cleared his throat, then reached out and took her hand. "Unless you were surprised. Unless someone clipped you on the left corner of your truck, leaving paint transfer and sending your vehicle into the ravine, right?"

"I mean, maybe?"

"The truck was far into the ravine, indicating a pretty steep trajectory. If she was trying to gain control of her truck for a few seconds because she'd been going too fast or whatever, she would have slowed down quite a bit before breaking into the guardrail."

Hannah closed her eyes, felt Wyatt's hand grip hers, and let him. "So someone killed her?"

"It seems possible, yes."

CHAPTER
FORTY-FIVE
Now

"Now do you believe me?" Hannah demanded, anger finally rising to the surface. For weeks she'd been wandering around, aimless, feeling hollowed out. Now she seemed to be filling up with rage, bubbling over, and she felt helpless to stop it. Wyatt rubbed his jaw like he did when he was thinking, nervous. They both stood. He made a move toward her, and she held her hand up.

"It's not that simple, Hannah. We can't just connect dots simply because they all exist. Yes, we are obviously exploring all avenues, and that means that maybe an old crime connects to a new crime. That's Investigation 101. But it could also be a drunk who had a little too much at Pinker's, tried to pass her, and misjudged. Do you understand?"

"No, I really don't. You haven't talked to Warren. Did you talk to Lila? Warren's neighbor?" Hannah pressed, closing in on Wyatt, so close she could see the stubble on his chin, the spray of dark curls at his neckline.

"I know who Lila is, Hannah." Wyatt's voice was measured, and his jaw worked. He was getting angry, having his job questioned. Too bad.

"I just can't leave here until I know something. And all you keep doing is showing up with new questions. The girl in the woods"— Hannah pointed toward the backyard—"was pregnant. She's not Julia. Aunt Fae was murdered." And then things she didn't say. Ruby had fallen out a window. Ellie was Warren's daughter. So many pieces—but all to different puzzles. Or maybe if she could find the center, it would all connect, like a key. Somehow.

Then a thought. "Am I allowed to go home yet?"

"I can't make you stay. I can and will ask you to until we close the investigation."

"That could be months."

"We'd let you leave before then." He shoved his hands in his pockets. "You're all we have, that's all. Alice has been around for a while, but no one in town knows Fae anymore. If we have a question about her history, her life, you're all we've got."

"I don't know anything about her life. I haven't spoken to her in seventeen years."

"But she's your family. You know more than you think you do. Just give me a week, if you could?"

Hannah had to stay anyway for Uncle Stuart. She had to sort out the house, the estate; there would be lawyers. Who would clean the house out? She'd have to sell it. Who would buy an almost two-hundred-year-old castle? She couldn't imagine bringing the plumbing and electrical up to code. The very idea of it made Hannah tired.

Unless she lived here. The thought popped in again, and she quickly extinguished it. Ridiculous. Hannah took a step back, putting some air between them. He followed her, closed the gap.

His hand went to her waist, like he was going to hug her, but stopped. The heat of his palm through her nightshirt had its own current. His head dipped, his voice low, he said, "Can we talk about the other night?"

"No." The answer was automatic, and then Hannah wilted. "Yes. Of course. I'm acting like a child; I know that. I just . . . I can't."

"I know."

"I'm engaged."

"I know." Wyatt drew a breath that sounded, to her ears, ragged. He took a step back then and released her. "You're it for me, though, Han. Kind of always have been."

"I don't know what that means, Wyatt." But of course she did. She'd be an idiot not to.

There was a sound, a throat clearing, perhaps, and Alice stood in the doorway between the hall and the living room. They jumped apart as though they'd been kissing. Hannah's cheeks grew hot. Alice was a hospice nurse, nothing more. Hannah didn't owe her an explanation about her life, and yet Alice stared at the two of them, her jaw tight and eyes narrowed.

"What's the issue, Detective McCarran?" Alice asked, her voice crisp.

"We think there may be another car involved in Ms. Webster's accident. We found paint transfer on her bumper, and the road marks suggest she was surprised to find herself out of control."

"Would have had to be a bigger truck to take that risk then, yes?" Alice asked. "To run her off the road? You wouldn't attempt that in a small car."

"Yes, ma'am. We're looking into who owns trucks in Rockwell. It's almost everyone, unfortunately. Even you own a truck."

"I do." Alice's eyes narrowed. "Would you like to look at it?" She gestured toward the driveway.

"I might on my way out, thank you." Wyatt seemed unfazed by Alice's sudden change in demeanor. But Hannah avoided her eyes, keenly aware of her judgment.

"Why would anyone want to kill Fae?" Alice asked, her hands splayed out before she let them fall to her sides.

Hannah knew why. The town had turned on Fae years ago; she was a witch. She and Jinny together, practicing devil worship. Somehow Jinny had escaped the widespread scorn. Fae had lived in a castle. She'd aged before their eyes and committed the ultimate sin of not caring. Her hair had grown long and gray like she'd deliberately fed into the gossip. She'd secured herself up on the hill, saying nothing, ignoring the chatter in town that called her a curse, a witch. That called the house a curse and, Hannah now realized, her family crazy. Hannah had always thought the people of Rockwell had blamed Fae for Julia without cause. But there had been a reason, even if Hannah had been unaware of it. If everyone but her had known that Ruby had existed and died, it shed new light on the way they'd viewed her. Everyone but Hannah had known that Fae's family had inherited Brackenhill. That they had crazy in their bones. That girls went missing from Brackenhill as a regular pattern: Ruby, Ellie, Julia.

She hadn't just killed Julia in their eyes. She was a serial murderer. *A sick woman.*

Who would kill someone like that? Well, just about anybody.

CHAPTER
FORTY-SIX
Now

The parking lot of Pinker's was packed with mostly trucks. Ford F-150s and Chevy Silverados and smaller, older Toyotas with various letters missing (*Toyta, Toota, Toyot*) from the liftgate. Fae's truck had been an old, rattling Ford Lightning from the late nineties. She'd rarely driven it into town, preferring to take their Volkswagen when she needed to go somewhere.

Hannah walked carefully around the lot. It was dusk, the sky lighting up with streaks of velvet purple. With her cell phone flashlight, she examined the front bumper of each and every truck in Pinker's lot. Not a trace of paint on any of them. You'd think one of these drunks would periodically hit a fence on the way home.

"What you looking for now, sugar?" The words were drawn out, and Warren stood ten feet away from her, swaying slightly on his feet, arms folded across his chest. In his left hand, he flicked a cigarette.

Hannah stepped back out of his reach, and her heart picked up speed. He stood at least eight inches over her and could have leveled her with one meaty punch.

In his younger years, he would have been good looking. Now he looked worn, with an old flannel shirt rolled up to his elbows, his hair a mix of gray and black, greasy and slick. But she saw the handsome hiding under there. She tried to see what Fae had seen.

Wyatt would kill her if he knew she was here. Warren might kill her now. She remembered his menace, his hatred of her, evident in his face, the spit at the corners of his mouth, a visceral violence.

This time, he smiled. He looked her up and down, an exaggerated leer. She realized the parking lot, while full of cars, was deserted. Pinker's pulsed with loud classic rock music; no one would hear her scream. Hannah palmed a small can of pepper spray and steadied her breathing.

"How did you and Fae meet?" she asked, and Warren raised his eyebrows, surprised. He didn't seem drunk.

"In town. Went to different high schools, but our mothers knew each other. Saw her for the first time at the community center, sitting on a picnic table with her friends. She was a beauty. Like you." He paused, smiled. "Like your sister too."

Hannah felt the chill up her spine. What was she doing here?

"Did you kill Fae?"

The question was bold. Unformed in her mind before it was out of her mouth.

Instead of flying off into a rage, Warren tipped his head appraisingly. His voice was quiet, almost gleeful. "Well, I'll be. You and McCarran a thing now, ain't ya?"

Hannah felt her neck flush red. "No, of course not."

"See, because he's asked me that same question five times or so. Keeps at it, hoping if he hits me hard and long enough, something will shake out. I'll fuck it all up. Warren the drunk, I guess. Can't remember what he tells people, changes his story." He walked into her space; Hannah could feel his breath on her cheek. "I got no reason to talk to you, but see, I was here. Thing about being the town drunk? Perfect alibi for every crime. Can't pin it on me!" He threw his head back and laughed. He raised his arms to the sky and stumbled once before yelling, "Ask Pinker! I was here. All night. Every night, baby. Every fucking night of my life."

He was still laughing as he climbed into the truck in front of her. The truck she'd been studying when Warren had caught her was his own. He started the engine, peeled away. Hannah watched the truck fishtail in the gravel and called Wyatt, left a message. "Warren just gunned it out of Pinker's, probably drunk. Might want to get a guy on that."

Inside the bar, the dance floor glowed red. The music switched, something twangy and new country with a steady beat, and a few bodies pulsed to the rhythm, pressed together. Some kissing. At the bar, the man from the other day was filling mugs on tap. Simple, straightforward beer: Miller, Bud, Coors. Someone down the bar top asked for an IPA, and the man barked out a curt no without looking up.

Hannah sat in the corner and waited for business to die down. The man she assumed was Pinker was younger than she'd thought he'd be. Maybe her age. With a mop of curly blond hair and biceps bursting out of his T-shirt. His mouth moved to the song coming from the jukebox, and someone across the bar from him said something that made him laugh. His smile was disarming.

"Can I help you?" He appeared in front of her holding a rag, his eyes skipping around the room.

"Are you Pinker? Do you own the place?" Hannah asked, a smile coyly playing on her lips. More flies with honey and all that jazz. It was much easier to flirt with Pinker than Warren.

"Depends on who's asking." He laughed and filled another mug before setting it down in front of an older woman to Hannah's left. "Are you the IRS?"

"No. I'm Fae Webster's niece?" Goddamn it, that had come out like a question. She hated that.

He stopped moving and gaped at her. "I thought she was dead."

"The other one. Her sister." And then because Hannah couldn't help it: "She's not dead."

He studied her, his brown eyes searching her face. "Ah yes. I always forget she had a sister."

"Everyone does." Hannah let it hang there untouched for a moment. She was always the *other one*, at least since she'd been back in Rockwell. Then she cleared her throat. "Was Warren in here the night Fae died?"

"All night. Already checked those records for McCarran." Pinker didn't make a move to wait on anyone else, despite the clamor at the other end of the bar.

"Why would Officer McCarran think that Warren killed Fae?"

"You'd have to ask him." Pinker shrugged and made a move to walk away, but Hannah called him back. He gave her a look and said, "Besides, why would you?"

"Because he's the meanest guy in town. And he had a history with my aunt."

"*History* is one word for it, yeah. They hated each other, loved each other, then hated each other for the past forty years."

"Okay, but I'm no detective. Obviously."

"Obviously. Listen, is that all, or do you want to order something?"

Hannah looked around; the place was starting to empty out. It was ten o'clock on a Tuesday. Summer or not, some of these folks had to work. "Miller Lite," she said. From a tray on the bar, she picked up a matchbook emblazoned with *Pinker's* on the outside and a phone number. She stuck it in her jeans pocket.

Hannah nursed the beer for a half hour. Alternating between checking her phone and watching the door. She didn't want to be around if Warren stumbled back in—or worse yet, Wyatt.

Pinker made his way back to her end and gestured to her glass. She shook her head.

"What's your real name?"

"Joel Pinkerton. Pinker's was my dad's; I took it over after his stroke." He had started to clean up, pushing each glass down over the wash spigot and setting them on a clean towel next to the sink.

"Sorry about your dad." She tapped a credit card on the glass, and he took it from her, ran it through the machine. "I'm Hannah Maloney."

"I know who you are. Bull's been ranting and raving about you for a week now."

"Me? Why?"

"Poking around his life, he says." Joel stopped washing glasses and put both hands facing down on the bar, leaning toward her. "He's not a good guy, you know. You'd be wise to stay out of his way. He and your family are entwined, and you don't live here. He's a hothead."

"I know. I can handle myself." Hannah straightened her spine, felt her jaw square.

"I'm sure. But you're getting yourself wrapped up in shit you don't understand. It's ancient history, but not to Bull."

"What's ancient history? His marriage to Fae?" Hannah spun her glass, her fingertips tapping in the condensation puddles on the wood.

He knitted his brows, studied her face. "Is it possible you really have no idea? I thought you were putting on an act."

"I assure you, I cannot act. Have no idea about what?" Hannah did her best to meet his gaze, opening her own eyes a little wider. *Another flirt trick from Julia.* She'd forgotten most of them, but somehow lately, she could hear Julia's voice. Remember her sisterly advice—even the ridiculous kind.

"Ellie. Warren. Fae." Joel circled his hand around like, *You know.* She did not know.

"Ellie is Warren's daughter. Fae was her stepmother until she was ten. Warren and Fae were married. That's all I know." Hannah splayed her hands out like, *See?*

"Damn, you're not playing me." Joel ran a hand through his thick hair. "Okay, listen, but you didn't hear all this from me. The night Ellie ran away—and she truly ran away, she had a bus ticket, the cops have her on camera at the station—Warren swears on his life he saw her up at Brackenhill. He's been spouting nonsense about it ever since. I mean, he's been a drunk for twenty years or more; it's not credible, but . . . he did get McCarran to reopen the investigation."

"Wait, spouting nonsense about what? What investigation?"

"Into what happened to Ellie. Warren saw Ellie at Brackenhill; he followed her up there after an argument, he says. Then she disappeared into the woods, and he *says* Fae followed her. He tried to chase them down, but it's thick back there, and he got turned around. Look, he was probably drunk as a skunk." Joel's voice was low, and Hannah had to lean forward to hear him.

"I don't understand, though. If she ran away, what could he possibly be saying? What are the police investigating?"

"That night he saw them? Warren is convinced that Fae killed Ellie."

CHAPTER FORTY-SEVEN

Now

Huck had left eight days ago. Hannah spoke to him once briefly on the phone. He hollered in the background to someone else: a worker, perhaps. "Sorry, hon, that's just Dave." Like she should have known who Dave was. Hannah played along ("Oh, right, Dave! Tell him I said hello"). When they hung up, she felt no more connected to him than she'd felt before the call. They might as well have not even spoken. The exchange was perfunctory, transactional.

They'd always been a tiny bit transactional. *Can you pick up Rink's meds? Sure. Sushi tonight? Yes, the place on Circle Drive.* Hannah assumed most relationships fell into this pattern. She'd always felt a streak of pride in it: *Look how functional we are!* Trina had done everything; Wes contributed nothing. After Wes left, after Julia disappeared, Trina fell into a state of disrepair, and Hannah filled in the gaps. Her teenage years were benchmarked by dysfunction. There was something satisfying about her and Huck's partnership—they were a well-oiled machine. No messy emotional glitches, no meltdowns on the bathroom floor, no shattered glasses against the walls. They didn't even squabble about housework. What she couldn't get to Huck would do, and vice versa.

If she put laundry in, he'd hear the buzzer and deftly switch it. She'd come home from grocery shopping to find him folding her shirts the exact way she liked them—which was slightly different from how he liked them, but he complied.

They would have been perfect parents.

Would have been?

The thought jarred her. The engagement ring still glinting on her finger. The scrying ring on the other hand. The wedding date not set, the wedding itself rarely discussed in detail. The idea of a wedding so attractive to both of them—she assumed, anyway—but perhaps not the actual mess of it. He'd asked her once, "How many people on your side?" And that was all it took. She'd never brought the wedding up again. He had a list. He'd made it one night over wine. Aunts and uncles, cousins and childhood neighbors turned Thanksgiving table-mates. Some of them Hannah had met, but mostly not, and Huck regaled her with stories about drunk uncles at Saint Patrick's Day parties and an older aunt who wrapped up half-used beauty supplies at Christmas: shampoo and blue clamshell bath soaps with dried bubbles still on them (once even the curl of a black hair, and Huck and his brothers had howled for years at the "pube-soap Christmas"). Hannah sat next to him looking at bouquets on her iPad, something innocently impersonal, and laughed hollowly at Huck's stories and wondered if she'd feel this kind of joy once his family became her family.

And yet he didn't ask. He didn't ask how Stuart was or any details of the investigation. She should have told him the latest: that Wyatt thought that Fae's accident hadn't been an accident. It should have come out unprompted. That Warren thought that Aunt Fae had killed Ellie.

He'd talked about his work, how sorry he was that he'd had to leave. How he missed her. How he wished he could have stayed. He asked if there had been any word on the bones. She said no. He asked when she was coming home, and she said she didn't know.

Then Dave interrupted, and Huck had to go, and that was the end of it.

Hannah snapped the leash on Rink, and he skittered to the back door, impatient. He hadn't been walked for days. Hannah had let him out once to run, but afraid he would come back with another bone, she'd whistled him back after ten minutes, limp with relief when he'd returned empty mouthed.

She dragged Rink away from the courtyard, toward town. Away from the path that led to the river, away from the castle. A path on the north side of the castle had been overgrown. She remembered it well; it had been her preference as a child. One path led to the river, well traversed and visible from the castle windows. This one, hidden in the back, led nowhere.

What if Warren was right? What if Fae had killed Ellie? Wouldn't that give Warren motive to do something to Julia? Or even Fae herself? But why almost twenty years later? What was the point of driving Fae off the road now?

As she pushed into a clearing, the greenhouse came into view. Hannah exhaled, remembering Stuart in there, surrounded by glass, the windows fogged and the top of his head only partially visible. She used to love to sit on a stool inside the greenhouse and watch him. The summer sun would beat down, the slanted roof that faced east gathering the morning and midday light, beaming onto her uncle's head, making him bead up with sweat while he worked. A classic rock radio station would play on the transistor, and Stuart would sing softly to himself and to her.

"This is the Who," he'd tell her. "Everyone knows 'Pinball Wizard' and 'My Generation,' but do you know 'Tattoo' or 'Disguises'?" He'd wipe sweat from his brow, leaving a thick streak of dirt from forehead to ear.

The greenhouse now was a ghost town. Pots half-filled with dirt crowded the benches, the skeletal remains of brittle sticks shooting up from the soil. The floor was covered in a film of grit, a few clay pots upturned or broken. Animals, maybe. Not Stuart; he'd been meticulous.

By the time Hannah arrived in June, Stuart would be ready to move his starter plants to the garden bed: tomatoes and peppers and cucumbers all started from seed, sometimes while there was still a smattering of snow on the ground. By August, the greenhouse would be largely unused, holding some heat-tolerant herbs but mostly waiting for his winter planting: turnips and swiss chard. All his starter plants had been labeled with Popsicle sticks in his jagged handwriting with half-uppercase, half-lowercase lettering.

At one time, Hannah loved learning about the plants: their growth patterns and needs, which vegetables were drought resistant, which fruits needed acidic soil (blueberry bushes, blackberries, rhubarb—which was actually a vegetable), and which vegetables needed to stay dry (broccoli, asparagus). It all seemed complicated and yet reliable. Blueberries needed acidic soil, full sun, good drainage. That never changed. If they needed that when she was eleven, they would need that when she was thirteen. Fifteen. To Hannah at the time, it had seemed solid to invest in plants. Their needs were predictable and well documented. People could change like quicksilver. Julia was proof.

Julia, on the other hand, could never be bothered. She didn't understand the appeal. The greenhouse was hot and dirty, and Uncle Stuart's taste in music was terrible, she said.

Out the back door, a path wound down the mountain and eventually led into town. There was a short unpaved driveway that intersected with Valley Road. The north-facing wall of the greenhouse was wood, not glass, with one small round window above the sink. Rink jumped up, his paws on the sink, to lap at water that had puddled on the counter. Hannah shooed him off and peered out the round window.

A mint-green truck was parked in the driveway. She'd forgotten Uncle Stuart's old utility truck. Rarely used on the road. She'd only been in it once. He'd sometimes used it to transport flowers from the greenhouse to the courtyard. The path between them was wide, and at one point it had been well traveled. It was easier, he said, than making twenty trips on foot.

Hannah tugged on Rink's leash and let the wooden door bang behind her. The truck had rust along the front grille and running board. She opened the driver's-side door with a creak; the inside stank like hot vinyl and sweet antifreeze. She opened the glove box and pulled out the owner's manual. The truck was a 1989 Dodge Ram. Hannah closed her eyes, her mind reeling.

1989 Dodge.

In front of the truck, she bent down and studied the passenger-side fender.

A dent. She followed it with her fingertip all the way down to the bumper. A streak of black. She scraped it with her fingernail, and it curled up easily. New. Paint transfer.

She studied the ground. Two oil stains: one large, one small, mere inches away from each other. In a few days or weeks, the two spills might have pooled together, forming one indistinguishable puddle.

She pulled out her phone and took a picture.

"Hannah!" Wyatt loped toward her, and Hannah stood. His gait was urgent, his hand motioning her toward him. Hannah stood rooted to the ground, her legs frozen. Her mouth went dry. She could tell by the look on his face that it was something big. They'd found Julia, perhaps.

"Alice thought you may have come out this way." Wyatt stopped when he reached the driveway, the truck between them. He'd half jogged there and was breathless. "They ID'd the skeleton. We know who it is."

She knew it before he said it.

"We were right. It's Ellie Turnbull."

CHAPTER
FORTY-EIGHT

Now

"It's all connected, isn't it? Aunt Fae, Ellie, probably even Julia," Hannah repeated, a broken record, a parrot.

"Maybe, yes. You have to be careful," he said softly. "Can you please back off the amateur investigation now?"

"I'm fine." Hannah's response was rote; she'd been so used to saying this for so long she wondered what it even meant anymore. She was fine. *Fine* could mean any number of things: she was alive, at least. Was that fine? "How did it happen?"

"Blunt-force trauma to the back of the skull. She was hit with something."

"Was it Warren?"

"We don't know. Would he have dragged her body up the hill behind the river? Or the mile and a half from town up this trail?" Wyatt indicated the trail behind her. "It doesn't make sense."

"That's true for everyone but—" She stopped. It seemed unimaginable to her that Aunt Fae would have killed Ellie. And if she'd killed Ellie, could she have also done something to Julia? Nothing about this felt real or true. The Aunt Fae she remembered would have never killed another person, much less her own niece.

"Fae and Stuart, yes." Wyatt's eyes were clouded, unreadable.

"Are they your only suspects?"

Wyatt paused, rocked back on his heels. "I shouldn't talk about an open investigation, Hannah. You know this."

"You can tell me if they are on your list and if there are others."

He held her gaze before saying, "Yes. And yes."

"So everyone in town thinks my aunt Fae is a murdering lunatic, and now the police do too."

"That's not what I said. It's not an unreasonable path of investigation, that's all." Wyatt stepped toward her, placed his hands on the hood of the truck.

"He's been saying for twenty years that he followed Ellie up to Brackenhill that night she left," Hannah persisted. "He could have followed her, hit her here, buried her."

"Hannah, we know." Wyatt was gently reminding her that they had it under control. That anything she thought of would have already occurred to the police. To Wyatt. She was being treated like a petulant child. Hannah's impatience flared.

"We should talk—" Wyatt started to say, his neck flushed.

"This truck belongs to Warren. I have the title back at the house," Hannah said at the same time, remembering what she'd found only moments before and cutting Wyatt off. If he wanted to "talk," Hannah did not. "It also has black paint transfer." She gestured behind her. "And it's been recently moved." She hadn't meant to cut him off, but now that it was out there, Wyatt's eyes sparked in interest.

He cocked his head, seemingly impressed. "How can you tell?"

Hannah showed him the photo of the oil stains under the truck. One large, one small. Currently two distinct stains, but not for long. He whistled.

"How did Warren's truck end up here?"

"I think Fae just took it when she left him. As far back as I can remember, they've had this truck. But I'm not sure. It might mean something . . . or nothing. Either way, Warren knows it's here."

"Who else had access to it?"

"Well, Warren, obviously. But the keys are in the visor, so theoretically anyone."

"Who would know the keys are in the visor?" Wyatt murmured, more to himself.

"Everyone in Rockwell does that," Hannah said, her voice tinged with bitterness. Small-town mentalities and habits she'd shed long ago. She tried to envision her neighbors in Virginia, or Huck, leaving the car unlocked, never mind the keys inside. Ridiculous. They locked the car doors in their own driveway, their house doors when they were home. They had doorstep cameras. She lived a more deliberate, less carefree life. Arguably more considered. Did that equal happier? It should have.

"We'll get it tested. I'll get it towed today," Wyatt said decisively. "It's fairly simple to figure out if the paint matches Fae's truck. From there, we can process the interior: DNA, fingerprints, that kind of thing."

Wyatt retrieved his cell phone and called the state police, asking for a forensic team and a tow truck. He turned away from her, and she could only hear snatches, irritated bursts of the conversation.

"They can't come out until tomorrow. Downside of small towns: we're at the mercy of the state police. The state lab is busy; this is a lower-priority case. Unfortunately."

"Why is it lower priority?" Hannah asked.

"The possible crime is several weeks old. Could be a hit-and-run. It's not a blatant murder. Missing persons are the highest on the list—it's a ticking clock. It makes sense, but still . . ." Wyatt splayed his hands helplessly.

"I just don't understand why it's taking so long to determine if it was an accident or if someone did this to her." Hannah balled her fists, frustrated.

"It's not that simple. They had to do a full investigation on her truck, which was demolished. Make sure, as much as possible, that everything was working properly at the time of the crash—brake lines weren't cut and whatnot—collect and test paint transfer, and it wasn't until the results started coming back that we thought it might be something other than an accident. You have no idea where your aunt was going? We think she was going pretty fast."

Hannah shook her head. Wyatt had been keeping after her for weeks now—*Are you sure you haven't spoken to your aunt and uncle recently?* Did he think she was lying?

"Well, it sucks," Hannah finished for him, and he nodded in agreement.

Wyatt shifted, his reluctance to leave a clue. His fisted hands were shoved into his jeans pockets, and he scanned the horizon behind her, his eyes unfocused.

There was something else, Hannah realized. Another fact to relay, another bomb to drop. He'd done it enough times in the past few weeks—hell, the past few minutes—for her to know what it looked like when he was stalling. Looking for the words.

"Remember how you thought you saw Ellie in 2002? The year that Julia disappeared?"

"I didn't *think* I saw her; I'm sure I saw her—all summer long. The night Julia went missing, in fact. I'm not crazy, Wyatt." She took a deep breath. "You saw her too."

"I didn't, Hannah, and I don't think you're crazy. Just hear me out." He sighed. "She was definitely pregnant at the time of death. Pretty far along, at least over thirty weeks. Have you ever heard of the term *coffin birth*?"

Hannah shook her head. A wave of nausea swept over her.

"It's pretty gruesome, I know. But when a pregnant woman dies, sometimes the baby is expelled after death. We found fetal bones in Ellie's grave. Some were inside the pelvic region, some outside the body. Which suggests a partial coffin birth. She was not buried with a small child; she was definitively pregnant when she was buried. You can also tell by the pelvic bones if she'd given birth alive. She hadn't."

Hannah must have looked horrified, because Wyatt touched her arm. "I'm telling you this for two reasons. First, Reggie is on leave. We were able to run DNA on the fetal bones. Reggie was the father."

Hannah's hand flew to her mouth. Reggie and Ellie? Well, what did she really know, anyway? So much must have happened between September and June that Hannah knew nothing about. Just a regular reminder that the summers that had meant so much to her had been so transient and fleeting to all the others. Including Wyatt? She didn't know.

She did know that Reggie had been a creep of a teenager, and it seemed like he'd taken that into adulthood. "Is he a suspect?"

"I can't tell you that," Wyatt said evenly. "But even if he isn't, he's too close to this case, and finding out his child . . . well, there is some expected trauma, that's all. Plus he has his own family now."

Wyatt rocked back on his heels, letting her absorb the information. He took a deep breath and continued. "But more important to *you* specifically, once we identified the remains as Ellie, we were able to subpoena prenatal records. She'd been to see a doctor. She was pretty far along."

"Okay," Hannah said.

"The records were from August 2001. Do you understand?" he asked.

She did. Ellie was pregnant in 2001 and killed while pregnant. That meant she'd incontrovertibly died in 2001. It didn't change the fact that Hannah saw Ellie a whole year later, all that summer and on August

1, 2002, the night Julia disappeared. That she saw them leave together and never come back.

Hannah had never allowed herself to consider that any of the mysticism she'd experienced at Brackenhill was real. She'd pushed away the instinct, the creak, click of the doors at Brackenhill, the basement maze shifting rooms almost in front of her eyes, the feeling of being watched, of never being alone. Hannah had rationalized waking up all over the grounds: in the woods, the basement, Ruby's room, the river. She'd brushed aside that the hair on the back of her neck stood up or the way Ellie had made her feel all those years ago: vulnerable and afraid. She'd scoffed at Jinny with her potions and her crystal balls and her smudges. Even when Hannah saw Julia in the vision, she'd made excuses for it. She was tired. She was stressed. The vision hadn't been real; her sister hadn't been in pain. Her sister hadn't been pounding on a door, blood on her fists. Her sister hadn't died in horror. And yet.

Ellie had worn a black skirt and red flutter top and high heels. It was the same outfit as the night in the courtyard. The same outfit she'd seen her in that whole last summer—how could Hannah not have noticed?

But Ellie had been real, at least to Julia and now to Hannah. Ellie had been as real as earth and soil and river and stone.

It was possible that she just hadn't been alive.

CHAPTER
FORTY-NINE

Then

August 2, 2002, 12:30 a.m.

It sounded like rain on her window. Faint, pebbly, but lacking the rhythm of a summer storm. Hannah's eyes opened, blurry, then focused on the ceiling, the intricate medallion that encircled the chandelier, visible only by the moonlight streaming through her bedroom windows.

Pat-pat-pat-pat-pat, sounding like a spray from a hose. Or pebbles. Pebbles.

Hannah rushed to the window, pushed the heavy wood casement out, and stuck her head outside into the humid night air.

Wyatt.

"What are you doing?" she snapped. His hair curled on his forehead, and he wore a rumpled T-shirt and mesh shorts.

"I'm sorry. I'm a jerk. Can we just talk?" he stage-whispered.

"Go away, Wyatt. You've done enough." Hannah felt the ache in her chest. The vision of Julia's red nails curled around Wyatt's hair flashed in her mind, and she felt sick, her throat constricted. She pulled the window in and had started to latch it shut when she saw Julia, her blonde head appearing below.

"Hannah, wait!" Julia called, and Hannah paused. "Just come down and talk to him. I didn't know, okay?"

"Whatever. You guys can have each other."

"Please just come down? I want to talk to you too."

"Why, so you can both act like I'm a child? A crazy kid with a puppy-dog crush? No thanks, both of you." Hannah pulled the window shut, latched it tight, and crawled back into bed, pulling the coverlet to her chin. Below, she heard the faint murmuring of voices and felt sick. Would they just pick up where they'd left off?

She imagined them below, kissing, Wyatt caressing Julia's face and her back the way he used to touch Hannah. She pulled her legs up to her chin and moaned. Why did they call it heartbreak? She felt like her whole body was breaking.

A creak on the staircase, and suddenly Julia stood there, between their rooms. Looking uncertain. Beautiful. Hannah hated her. She wanted to claw at her sister's face. Imagined leaving a scratch with her nails, deep and red, that would later turn to a purple scar. She wouldn't be the beautiful one; she'd be the ruined one.

"Hannah." Her voice floated through the darkness, and Hannah's stomach coiled. "I have to go to the police, okay?"

Hannah sat up, narrowed her eyes. "What? Why?"

"There's so much you don't know, but I need you to trust me."

Hannah let out a laugh. "What?"

"I know. I can't ask for it. I can barely bring myself to say it. But on this, I have to. Things are . . . unraveling. Something's happened, and I'm afraid for us." Pause. "It's Fae."

This time Hannah laughed for real. "That's ridiculous."

Julia stepped into the room, her face visible in the full moonlight. Stricken. Pale. Terrified.

Hannah *almost* felt something for her. Almost.

"I know it seems that way to you. Aunt Fae killed someone. I can't explain it all right now, but I know it's true. I confronted her, and she flipped out and screamed at me. We aren't safe here. I have to tell someone. I have to tell the police." She took a deep breath and continued, her voice small. "Will you come with me?"

"What? No."

Her sister was a liar. There was no way Hannah was getting involved in going to the police over something her sister had invented. Besides, Julia had spent the whole summer ignoring Hannah. Why should Hannah do anything for her?

"I'm going with or without you. I'm telling the police everything I know."

Hannah felt a stab of fear. "Then what will happen?" she whispered.

"They'll come arrest Aunt Fae and maybe Uncle Stuart. They aren't good people, Hannah. You have to know that."

"Then what happens to *us*?" Hannah pressed, her voice pitching higher.

"We'll go home, I'm sure."

"Home. Like to Plymouth."

In the moonlight, Julia nodded. "I'm sorry," she whispered. "I know you love it here, but you don't know everything."

"That's because you haven't spoken to me all fucking summer!" Hannah let it loose. Her blood rushed in her veins, and her temples throbbed. Her sister was going to ruin everything.

"I'm sorry, Han. I love you." Her voice was desperate, pleading, her cheeks pinked and shiny.

Her sister had ruined Wyatt.

Her sister was going to ruin Brackenhill.

Her sister was going to ruin Fae and Stuart.

Hannah would not be made to leave. She would not go back to Plymouth a minute early. What waited for her there? The creak of a bedroom door. A cold hand on her thigh. The smell of cigarettes and beer.

When Hannah said nothing, Julia sighed. She turned to leave and paused at the door. "I have to go. I hope you understand."

And she was gone.

August 2, 2002, 4:42 a.m.

Hannah woke up in the courtyard. She was in her nightgown, but she wore sneakers. The hem of her nightgown was soaking wet. She'd been crying.

In the dream she'd followed Julia down the path, a sick pulse in her head. A rage she hadn't known existed had seemed to burn her from the inside out. Her hands had clenched in fists.

The sky was inky blue, a streak of purple dawn along the horizon.

She missed her sister. The sister of summers past, when they'd been partners. Best friends. Confidantes. Her shoulders racked with sobs, tears and snot on her face, as she stumbled inside and up the stairs and crawled back into her bed.

She was just so goddamn tired.

Later she'd remember Julia standing between their bedroom doors, her hair tangled. Dirt and tears streaked tracks down her face, her mouth open like she was a trout from the Beaverkill, eyes wide and glassy.

"Hannah, please," she'd said.

When Hannah blinked, she was gone.

CHAPTER FIFTY

Now

Wyatt left Hannah in the greenhouse with a promise to come back later for the truck. "I need a forensic team. Again." He sighed when he said it, and Hannah felt the need to apologize.

Back at the house, Hannah rattled around, restless. She opened and closed the kitchen drawers, looking for what, she didn't know. Just looking. In the drawer under the sink she found the fleur-de-lis key. Huck must have put it back before he'd left. She tucked it into her sweatshirt pocket. There had to be a door it opened somewhere, right?

She pulled out a cutting board and began peeling carrots for dinner, tossing pieces to Rink on the floor. He loved carrots. Hannah wanted to make soup. Something to warm her from the inside. She didn't know what she was doing anymore. She thought of Huck back at their condo in Virginia. The white, clean kitchen. Stainless steel appliances. Hardwood floors. Cream and neutral throw rugs. Everything modern and styled and bright and functional. It seemed like another life, belonging to another person. The shape of her had changed—she no longer fit in that house. She imagined herself there, dirty as a chimney sweep. Here felt better, like home. Damp and musty and dark.

Alice appeared in the doorway between the dining room and the kitchen. She had a peculiar look on her face, questioning.

"Was that Detective McCarran again?" she asked, her voice strangled and reedy.

"Alice," Hannah asked warily. "What do you know about Stuart's truck?"

"What about it?"

"Who had access to it? Have you seen anyone drive it?" And then, even though she knew the answer, "Who it belonged to?"

"Fae told me once it belonged to her ex-husband," Alice said, her bird nose starting to twitch. "And no, I have no idea who has driven it. I wouldn't think it's been moved since he got sick. I never saw Fae drive it. Why are you asking?"

"Her ex-husband," Hannah repeated dumbly. "You mean Warren."

"Is that his name?"

"You know it is, Alice. Do you know Warren?"

"I—I don't." Alice's hand encircled her throat, fingers pulsing at the neck.

"I think that's the truck that ran Fae off the road," Hannah said, sliding the blade under the carrot slices and pushing them into a pot on the stove with her fingertip.

"Someone ran Fae off the road?" Alice asked in a pitchy tone. She moved her hand to the back of her head, pulled her hair off her neck, twisted it before letting it unwind like a serpent. The gesture felt familiar, and Hannah stopped chopping, watched her, interested.

Finally, Hannah shrugged. "They aren't sure. I think so. Wyatt isn't positive."

"Wyatt? You mean Detective McCarran."

Hannah met Alice's eyes. Saw something hard flicker there. "Yes. That's what I mean."

In the dream, Hannah smelled the fire. It became part of the sequence—first she was running through the woods, away from the blaze, and then she was running toward it, the heft of a child on her hip. She couldn't see the child's face, just a blonde curl, a wisp that kept blowing across Hannah's cheek. The girl's shoes were patent leather, white. She squealed in Hannah's ear.

Hannah sat up, her heart pounding, and for a moment, she was relieved to wake up in the same place she'd gone to sleep. Not in the forest or in the courtyard or thigh high in the Beaverkill. She thought, for a moment, she was still in bed.

Then the smoke.

She didn't ask herself until later how or why she could smell the smoke before she felt the heat of the blaze, before she saw the flames lick from the bottom of the room to the top.

She just knew she was in the greenhouse, and now the greenhouse was on fire.

She pushed against the door, but the door seemed to be stuck or locked, the metal frame red hot to touch. The smoke was starting to fill the small space, crowd out the oxygen in her lungs, make her feel light headed, and sting her eyes. The upper windows, usually slanted open, had been shut.

Hannah slapped her pockets and blessedly found her cell phone in the pocket of her hooded sweatshirt. She dialed 911 before she remembered that Rockwell had no 911, and then she just gave up and called Wyatt. When he answered in a husky, sleepy voice, she coughed into the phone that she was stuck in the blazing greenhouse. She realized then that the east-facing wall of windows was not burning. The wooden frame was blackened and crackling but not engulfed.

Though the window, backlit by moonlight, was Alice. Her normally slicked-back hair was wild around her face; her eyes seemed to glow from the firelight.

"Help!" Hannah screamed it through the window, but Alice didn't flinch. Didn't move.

Hannah picked up a large galvanized watering can and swung it hard against the glass, splintering it into pieces. She was barefoot, she realized, but she'd have to take her chances. She used the bottom of the aluminum watering can to clear the jagged edges from the frame as much as possible, then launched herself out the window.

Hannah landed on the broken glass, but her feet felt no pain. It wasn't until later that she'd even notice the blood. She ran to the clearing between the greenhouse and the castle and turned around to watch the fire. The structure burned brightly in its entirety like a round, glowing fireball. Like it had been set all at once, burning in uniformity. Even the glass was starting to buckle and crack.

Parked next to the greenhouse was Stuart's truck, entirely engulfed in flames.

Hannah looked around wildly, but Alice was gone. Had she been there at all?

Hannah knew then that the fire had been set deliberately and was meant as a warning. Perhaps even to kill her. Wyatt would tell her later she couldn't know that. That maybe she'd followed the smoke in her sleep. "You've been sleepwalking. Were you dreaming about starting a fire?"

In other words, had she set the fire herself?

Hannah would insist that Alice had been there.

"She lives in Tempe. Alice is at home," Wyatt would say gently. Soothingly. The way he'd spoken to her that night at the fish fry, in that pacifying tone. Tempe was ten miles away.

Later, the fireman would tell her about the backdraft. When she'd broken the window, she'd created a rush of air. "Almost as powerful as a bomb," he'd say. It was a miracle she'd made it out alive, really.

She stood alone in the clearing, first watching it burn, then listening to the crack as the rickety roof finally caved in on itself, and the wood beams seemed to give way all at once with barely a groan, just the folding of boards like dominoes down to the soft, wet earth, the glass popping.

By the time the firemen (all three of them) and Wyatt had shown up, with trucks and sirens, huffing down the path like drunken bears, the whole building had burned, taking with it the green truck, blackened and burned out. They found Hannah sitting on an old, rotted tree stump with her arms around her knees, her feet filthy, and her sweatshirt stuck to her skin with sweat.

Her head was bent low, and later, Wyatt would tell her he thought she was crying. Something wild and keening that cut Wyatt to the bone because it was wholly unchecked. It wasn't until he tried to comfort her that he realized she wasn't crying at all.

Hannah was laughing.

CHAPTER
FIFTY-ONE
Now

"I need your help," Hannah blurted to Jinny, who sat opposite her, the crystal ball between them. Hannah was distracted by it, the silliness, the Hollywood of it. Jinny huffed impatiently and stood up, placed the ball into a cabinet, and shut the door.

"Hannah, you need medical attention." Jinny pointed at Hannah's bandaged hand, fallout from the greenhouse fire: shards of glass lodged in her palm.

"I had medical attention. I just left the hospital. Checked myself out. I'm fine. Everything is fine."

Everything would be fine if she could just figure out what had happened to her aunt, her sister, Ellie, maybe Ruby; whether Warren wanted to kill her; and why Alice hated her so much. It was a lot to figure out, but she had to get back to Virginia. To Huck. She had to get away from Wyatt before she ruined her life. Before Brackenhill ruined her life.

Hannah took a breath. "I need your help."

"You don't. Anyway, I can't help you. I don't know who burned the greenhouse down. I don't know what happened to Julia, or even Ellie, for that matter." Jinny's voice was impatient, almost petulant. "You don't understand how this works. I don't know everything. I can't see everything. I can see *some* things, but even then I can't control what I see. And I can't command certain facts. Do you understand?"

Hannah didn't, and she didn't care. "Talk to me about Fae."

Jinny paused, her nails clicking on the tabletop. "To be honest, my dear, we drifted apart the past few years. There isn't much I can tell you that you don't already know."

"Why?"

"Some of it was her life. Caretaking is so stressful. Hard on everyone. Some of it was me. Before Stuart got sick—again—I'd wanted her to be more social. Come down from the hill, visit with friends. I know they see me as a kook, but I'm harmless. They might even think I'm the village idiot." Jinny fluffed her black hair with her fingertips; a ringlet caught on a bracelet, and she wiggled it free. "I'm not. I know that. But I know how they all see me. Everyone likes me, though. Your aunt, however . . ." Jinny cocked her head, twisted her bright-coral lips. "Not so much. I knew better; I tried to tell people—especially those bingo biddies down at the Rockwell firehouse—Fae was a good person who had a tough life. Friendship is good for the soul. You can't make a life out of plants and one man."

"What about Alice?"

"Oh. Well, Alice." Jinny rolled her eyes. "Yes, well, there was Alice."

"You don't like Alice?"

"I don't know her!" Jinny threw her hands up, her rings and bracelets clattering. "I invited them both to the firehouse. They had poker, bingo, spaghetti dinners, what have you. Poker was my thing. Anyway, they always said no. Alice practically lived there. She loved your aunt; I'll give her that. They were strange birds of a feather, together. And the three of them up there, secluded on that hill? People in town thought it was straight-up weird. And that's coming from me!"

"How did Aunt Fae meet Alice?"

"No one knows. She showed up one day—'from the agency,' she said. Before you knew it, they're inseparable, and I'm nothing to Fae. She hardly came to see me anymore, never called. She had Alice; that's it."

"Why do you think she became so reclusive?"

"She never stopped flogging herself for Ruby. And then Julia." Jinny sighed, her eyes teary. *And likely Ellie?* thought Hannah. Jinny continued, "Even if people in town could understand—and I do think they could, at least the Ruby part. Accidents happen!—Fae would never let herself be forgiven. But people see it differently. If she didn't kill anyone, then why hide? Why seclude yourself if you're not guilty?"

"So when she needed you the most, you abandoned her?" Hannah asked, and it came out sharper than she intended. It was a barbed question, and Jinny flinched.

"No. *No.* You can't make people need you. Your aunt sequestered herself. That life sentence was her own making. You can't help someone who doesn't want to be helped, Hannah."

This Hannah knew to be true. She thought of Wes, Trina, even Julia toward the end of that summer. Scattered, lashing out, impatient, mean. All the things she'd never been before. Even to Aunt Fae; especially to Aunt Fae. *Oh, like you don't know what I'm talking about.*

Hannah had only heard that part of the fight, Aunt Fae's voice too quiet, too circumspect, to be heard from the library, where she spent so much of her time. Julia's had been clear as a bell, loud and angry. What had it been about? She'd forgotten it entirely in the years since. It had seemed fleeting, inconsequential.

"Did you blame her for Julia?" Hannah asked.

Jinny's eyes slid sideways, and she adjusted her earring. A tell. "No. Of course not."

A lie.

"I don't believe you." Hannah felt her face flush. Why would Jinny lie to her? Who was there to protect? Everyone was dead.

"Well, I don't know why. I've no reason to lie to you. I don't believe your aunt had anything to do with Julia's disappearance. And the only thing I think she had to do with Ruby's death was folding laundry while her child played in a room with an unsecured window."

Hannah had been asking the wrong question. "What about Ellie?"

"I don't know who killed Ellie."

"You have a theory. A suspicion."

"I don't. Even if I did, I wouldn't share it. I have no proof of anything." Jinny was starting to look like a trapped animal, eyes darting one way, then the other.

"I heard that Fae said Ellie was there. The day Ruby died," Hannah pressed, leaning closer. She could smell Jinny's perfume, cloying and organic.

"Fae said a lot of things. That didn't make them true."

"But she was there, wasn't she?" Hannah reached out, gripped Jinny's skinny wrist.

Jinny nodded.

"Did Ellie kill Ruby? On purpose?"

"I don't know!" Jinny said finally. She stood up abruptly and scurried to the back room through a beaded partition. She reemerged with a yellowed envelope, folded in half and resealed with masking tape, careful and precise.

"What's this?" Hannah asked as Jinny handed it to her.

"It's a letter. The night before Fae died, she came to see me. She hadn't come to town in months. She wanted me to have this; she said she was preparing for Uncle Stuart's death and needed someone to guard her secrets."

"What secrets?" Hannah pressed, and Jinny's face crumpled.

"I don't know! She asked me not to read it, just keep it. She said I could read it when she was gone."

"Gone where?" Hannah's voice was sharp.

"She meant dead." Jinny's chin wobbled, and she took a breath. "She wasn't going to kill herself. I think she thought that without Stuart . . . she had no one to protect her."

"From who?"

"I didn't know! I was so thrown by her being in my shop. By how she looked—skinny and pale and her hair long and gray. I was consumed with my own guilt that I let her wither away up on that mountain."

"Why wouldn't you give this to police?" Hannah asked.

"Why would I? I don't know what's in it. I promised to protect my friend." Jinny straightened her spine; her jaw jutted outward. "I wouldn't let myself read it."

"Did Fae kill Ellie because Ellie killed Ruby?"

"Hannah, hand to God, I have no idea. You have to believe that," Jinny pleaded. Tears fell down her cheeks.

"You don't believe in God," Hannah said before she stood up.

She left Jinny at the table, crying.

On the street, she looked one way, then the other. She unfolded the envelope. It was addressed to Fae Webster at Brackenhill. No postage. No return address. The blue ink on the front was young and bubbly but faded.

In the distance, a shining black truck rumbled toward her. Wyatt. Hannah didn't want to see him, talk to him. She didn't want to relate what Jinny had told her or think about Jinny hiding Fae's secrets for seventeen years. She tucked the envelope into her back jeans pocket and ducked into an alleyway a few buildings down. Hannah watched Wyatt as he parked the truck in front of the diner.

She expected him to enter. Sit down, have a cup of coffee. She didn't expect him to furtively glance up and down the street and, when he was certain no one saw him, open the door to Jinny's shop and disappear inside.

CHAPTER
FIFTY-TWO

To Fae, from Ellie

September 2001

Dear Fae,
    I'm leaving Rockwell soon. I wanted to tell you that I was so sorry. I've thought of Ruby every single day for five years. You are the only mother I've ever really known. The only woman—person—who encouraged me, took care of me. But did you love me?
    I was jealous of Ruby. It wasn't fair that she got you, and Stuart, and also got to be beautiful. When you would parade Ruby around town like she was a show horse, people would constantly remark on her strawberry-blonde soup-can curls, soft and shiny. The spots of pink on her cheeks and her full red lips. Mrs. Jinny asked once if Ruby was wearing lipstick. For God's sake, she was five.
    I loved that you would pick me up at the little brown house and take me shopping. When Ruby was old enough

to go, she would slide a little hand into mine and her skin felt squishy, like a puffy marshmallow. You'd introduce us as "Ellie and my daughter, Ruby." I didn't have a title.

I'd pretend to be your daughter, but everyone knew the truth. I was no one's child. I was motherless. My own mama was a ghost—I'd only met her a few times. Daddy said she was on drugs. Whenever I saw her, her breath smelled sour like garbage. She had stringy hair and skinny arms and a brown tooth on the side. You were warm and smelled like cookies.

Mama hadn't been back for a long time. Most of the time I couldn't remember her face.

I tried so hard not to love you, in case you didn't love me back. I knew you didn't have to. I tried to do all the right things. You called me a "mother's helper," and I liked to make you happy. I liked to wash dishes, fold laundry, play with Ruby. A mother's helper seemed like a better title than nothing.

For a while, I pretended Ruby and I were sisters. She was cute and funny. And I felt lucky to spend every weekend in a magical castle. I know I begged you to let me sleep over. I could tell that you didn't want to say yes as much as you did. Maybe I was too loud or too hard or something else? I don't know. I saw how you looked at Stuart and then would say my name, Ellie, like a little sigh.

You put me in the room next to Ruby's. There was a door between our rooms. I could sneak in there at night and we could play or talk. It felt like I had a real family, sometimes. Except on Sunday night, I would go back to the little brown house and Daddy would be passed out on the sofa and sometimes the lights wouldn't work and

I had to make myself butter sandwiches in the dark and I knew the castle was warm and there would be music and maybe cookies and spaghetti. I would just get so mad! I'm sorry.

I wanted to move to the castle with you and Stuart in the worst way. But you had Ruby now and you were a family. You left me in the little brown house.

I saw the bed on TV first. A commercial for Kmart. It was a canopy—pink and purple swirls of flowing fabric all around the bed like for a princess. I showed Daddy and he laughed. My mattress was on the floor, he said. Where would he hang that? I hated him so much! I asked for the bed for Christmas, even writing Santa letters (I was ten, I knew Santa wasn't real). On Christmas morning, nothing was there. Daddy bought me a sweater.

In the spring, after the snow melted, you came down to the little brown house and picked me up again. It was just you and we had the whole car ride back up the mountain together. You asked about school and soccer and my friends and we talked the whole time. I felt like I had a week's worth of news just bursting out of me. You laughed in all the right places and I never wanted to leave the truck.

We pulled in the windy driveway and the castle was lit up from the inside and I knew it would smell like spaghetti and there would be music playing on the radio and Stuart would pull a quarter out of my ear and we would laugh and maybe play Rummikub later.

Inside, there was nothing on the stove and nothing playing on the transistor radio in the kitchen.

"Come on!" you said excitedly, motioning for me to follow. "I want to show you what Stuart built Ruby."

I always felt a little stabbing pain right in my heart when you talked about Ruby. Your eyes would go all shiny and sparkly. I knew if I wasn't nice to Ruby, I wouldn't be invited back. I tried to make my own smile big and excited like yours.

You hop-skipped up all the winding steps to the second floor and led me down the long hallway to Ruby's room and when you flung open the door, Stuart stood in the middle, his face cracked open from smiling, holding his toolbox in one hand and a hammer in the other.

Inside the room stood the most beautiful bed I had ever seen. It had a beautiful ring of pink and yellow flowers above it and hanging from the ring was a white canopy that went all the way to the floor and puddled at your feet. It was just like the bed from television. The material was see through but still silky and made for a princess.

Everything inside me hurt and I thought I was going to cry and I absolutely did not want to do that so I said the only thing I could think of.

"I think it's ugly."

And you closed your eyes and sighed my name, Ellie, and you and Stuart left and went downstairs talking softly, probably about me, and I was so mad I started to cry. I knew I disappointed you and you would never, ever, ever love me. Not now, not in the future. That maybe you felt sorry for me, the way I feel sorry for stray cats and homeless people but I don't love them.

You didn't love me.

You didn't love me.

I don't remember what I did, I just remember how I felt. How it pulsed like a drumbeat in my head. How I wanted to rip the whole thing down from the ceiling and

*feel the tug of the material in my hands as it came apart.
I don't remember doing it, I swear.*

    *I remember Ruby screaming at me. "I hate you!
What are you doing? Mommy!"*

    *I wanted her to shut up. I knew I'd done something
awful.*

    I didn't think, didn't plan it.

    *The windows in the castle were tall—almost to the
floor—with glass panes that opened outward like a story-
book mansion. It had been warm for April, so they were
opened to let in the soft evening breeze.*

    *Later, I would say Ruby got tangled in the net. That I
tried to catch her and that's why it was ripped. No matter
how hard I try, I can't remember exactly how it happened.*

    *One second, Ruby was screaming. The next, she was
gone.*

CHAPTER
FIFTY-THREE
Now

Hannah sat in Aunt Fae's Volkswagen on Main Street, debating where to go next. On one hand, if she went back up to Brackenhill, she had the whole night ahead of her. She could go sit at Pinker's. She could go to Wyatt's.

Her thoughts zinged around like Ping-Pong balls. She cruised Main Street twice. The teenagers would start coming out, walking up and down the main drag. Visiting Jinny just to say hi.

Buck, who owned the hardware store, and Bo, who lived upstairs, had already set up lawn chairs on the front stoop, and Buck flipped the store sign to closed, as they'd done every summer night since Hannah was a kid. Hannah could hear the hiss-pop of a Bud Light from across the street. She turned off Main Street and headed down toward West.

Hannah rubbed the letter between her index finger and thumb. She felt drawn to the little brown house, to Warren. To see where Ellie had grown up, the misery she'd lived in. What had compelled her to push a child? Hannah felt sick.

Warren would probably be at Pinker's, and she knew she had to stay far away from there. Three visits in a week might get her killed. She edged the Volkswagen down Henley Avenue, which ran perpendicular to West Street, and could see Warren's truck parked in front of the house. What was he doing home? Hannah's pulse picked up, a staccato beat.

Hannah cut back and came up to the left of the house, past Lila's, up the alley. She pulled behind the small shed in back of Lila's and threw the car in park.

It was reckless. And probably stupid. If he found her, who knew what he'd do. She thought, briefly, about showing him the letter. What would he say? What would he think? Did he know it existed? It seemed unlikely.

Hannah eased out of the Volkswagen, shutting the door quietly behind her. She looked around—it was probable that someone was watching her from behind parted curtains. In Rockwell, watching the street was a pastime.

In back of Warren's, on the corner of the property, sat an old outhouse. Hannah stood behind it, catching her breath, trying to organize her thoughts.

What exactly did she hope to find here? She wasn't sure, but it felt safer, more comforting, to be standing behind an old shit house in Warren's backyard than to go back to Brackenhill, alone, again.

The back screen door creaked open and shut. Hannah's throat constricted, and she squeezed her eyes shut, willing herself to become invisible. She pressed her back flush against the splintered wood. A woman's voice. And Warren.

Not yelling, but not friendly either.

She couldn't be sure, but it sounded like "fucked too."

If Lila came outside, even to simply take out the trash, she'd be screwed. If whoever was on Warren's back step took ten steps to the left or right, she'd see Hannah immediately.

Instead, the woman beelined straight for the alley, and instead of turning right, toward the outhouse, she turned left, toward the street. Hannah breathed a sigh of relief, counted to ten, and leaned forward to get a clear look at who it was.

Alice.

The nurse paused and looked left, then right, before darting across West Street and turning right on Henley. From half a block away in the Rockwell quiet, Hannah could just make out the sound of a truck engine turning over.

Hannah's heart thrummed in her throat, and she doubled back to Fae's car, hopped in the driver's seat, and threw the gearshift into drive. She followed the truck back up the winding road to Brackenhill, too late in the day to be tending to Stuart, staying far enough back that she dropped out of sight of the truck's rearview around every turn.

Alice's truck eased into the driveway before she cut the headlights. Hannah parked on the edge of the property and made the reckless decision to follow her on foot. Why had Alice come back? She never came back at night. Maybe she'd forgotten a med? But then why cut her headlights?

Midway up the driveway stood a little tower. As a child Hannah had always played in it, throwing notes and pebbles up and down with Julia. The tower contained nothing but a winding concrete staircase and a small, empty room on the second floor.

Alice glided the truck behind the tower and slowly crept out of the driver's seat. Hannah watched her from behind a thick oak as she switched on a lantern and followed a well-worn path from the tower.

Hannah knew at once where it would lead and followed silently. She felt the creep of dread up her spine.

When the shed came into view, she ducked behind an old tractor. Alice would have the advantage of a lantern. Hannah, the idiot, hadn't even brought a flashlight with her. However, she had the element of surprise on her side.

Something else clicked into place, then. A brown tooth.

You leave her out of this, Warren had said.

Alice slipped into the shed, and through the single two-by-two window, Hannah could see the soft lantern glow.

Hannah placed her hand on the door and slid it open.

CHAPTER
FIFTY-FOUR

Now

Alice was spreading a blanket when she was caught by surprise.

"Hannah!" Alice startled, her tone shrill. "I can explain. I was evicted yesterday. I just need a place to stay for a few days."

"Why wouldn't you ask to stay inside?" Hannah's voice sounded strange, even to her own ears. Strangled.

"I didn't want to bother you." She lifted up her hair, twined it around her fist, and dropped it. Her long ponytail grazed her back, and Hannah could see the roots: a bright-auburn stripe around her crown.

The gesture felt intimate. She'd studied it as a newly minted teenager, thinking at the time that it was hopelessly sensual, exposing that raw curve of neck, the glimpse of pale skin.

Alice turned her head, and in the lamplight it was so obvious Hannah couldn't believe she'd never seen it. That no one else saw it.

"You're Ellie's mother."

Alice's head whipped around; her eyes narrowed. She didn't deny it. Her face transformed, hardening and taking on a wholly new shape: revenge personified. She dropped the blankets and from her bag extracted a hunting knife.

Hannah's heart hammered, but her thoughts were too slow. She was too sleep deprived, too detached to assemble it all quickly in her mind. Hannah didn't have anything to defend herself with—she hadn't known she'd need it.

She had to buy time.

"If you're Ellie's mother, there's only one reason you're here." Nothing about Alice being at Brackenhill was coincidental. She'd purposefully taken a job as Stuart's nurse. Was she even a nurse? "You killed Fae." It all seemed so glaringly obvious now. "You killed Fae because you think Fae killed Ellie."

"Fae did kill Ellie. I heard her confess to Stuart the night she drove away." Alice's face contorted. "Unburdening herself. Crying about it! Ha."

"You followed her."

"I confronted her." Alice's voice boomed now. She was yelling, angry, her hair slipping from the tidy ponytail. "I heard her tell that vegetable of a husband how sorry she was for what they did. How she ruined his life and their lives. What about *my life*? She killed Ellie just as I was getting sober. I was ready to form a relationship with my daughter. Do you know where Ellie was going the night she ran away? The night she came here first?"

Hannah felt the answer flow through her like water.

"To meet me. She was taking the bus to Tempe from Rockwell. Then we were both going to New York City. Figured we'd both waitress, get a studio apartment, start over in a place no one knew us. I didn't have a car. We'd been talking on the phone. Writing letters. Warren had no idea, but he was an abusive, alcoholic drunk. I was trying to finally make things right for my daughter." Alice dropped her head to her chest, caught her breath. "When she didn't show up, I took a cab to Warren's house. He drove up here to find her because *I told him to.* He was drunk, I wouldn't get in the car with him, but it was the only chance I had. He came back with *nothing.* All he told me was he saw her run into the woods, and he saw that bitch Fae chase her." Alice sliced the air with the knife, the serrated edge glinting in the dim light. "She never loved Ellie."

"How did you get this job?" Hannah felt breathless, almost paralyzed with fear, her legs shaking.

"God, it was so stupidly easy. I just showed up. Warren told me Stuart was sick. It was his idea. He said you can pretend to be a nurse. Years ago, I was an orderly in a hospital. I knew enough to get by. You can research anything on the internet. I didn't need to actually help him; I just had to be believable. I had Fae order his medicine through his doctor. I said I was from the hospice agency. She never bothered to check. I didn't collect a paycheck, so it's near impossible to get caught. If I had tried to collect money, it would be a different story. He did have other home help: therapists mainly. But the hospice system is such a mess it was easy to lose me. Every time I came close to getting found out, I'd invent a paperwork glitch."

"Why? Why now? Eighteen years later? What were you trying to do?" Hannah asked, her voice quiet, hands still.

Alice sighed, the knife making a zigzag in the air. "I spent a long time after Ellie disappeared on drugs. Anything I could get my hands on. Pills and coke. Whatever was cheapest. Booze and weed. When I sobered up, I wanted the truth. Warren heard that Fae was looking for in-home help, and he called me. Nobody in Rockwell knew who I was. If Warren tried to even set one foot on Brackenhill, McCarran would be called up here so fast. But me? I never lived a day in my life in this dump of a town. Nobody knew who I was."

"What was your plan?" Hannah was appalled but fascinated. Alice had dropped all the pretense of an educated woman. Her mountain accent was getting thicker by the second. While Alice talked, Hannah tried to corral her thoughts. Why was Alice telling her all this? It must be a relief, to finally be free. She'd been carrying the burden of hate around for eighteen years.

"I thought if I got close to Fae, I could get her to confess. I stupidly thought she'd confess to me. She never did, no matter how I prodded her." Alice kept sagging, her voice quieting, and then straightening up, squaring her shoulders, staring at Hannah defiantly. She stabbed the air when she said "never did," and Hannah backed away quickly. "I started coming back at night. It's easy to hide in a castle. Fae ignored every little noise anyway. I didn't even have to be that careful."

How many of the noises in the night had been Alice? At least since Hannah had been back? Hannah pressed her palm to her forehead.

This was crazy. Alice was crazy. The lantern flickered, the batteries waning. Hannah was starting to not feel so sane herself. Truth be told, she hadn't felt sane in weeks.

"You confronted Fae, and she fled down Valley Road, and you chased her off into the ravine?"

Alice stopped, studied Hannah's face. "What would you do, if it were your daughter?"

A tough question to answer. Hannah couldn't imagine having a daughter. Truthfully, she'd never been able to imagine it.

"I don't know," Hannah whispered.

"That's right. No one knows." Alice seemed to notice the knife in her hand for the first time. She stepped closer, and Hannah swallowed back a knot of fear in her throat. "I was waiting to make sure the remains were Ellie. Then I was going to leave town. Start over somewhere new. I did what I had to do to get peace for my baby girl." Her voice lowered, patient and slow. She smiled. "But the thing is . . . you found me out here. Maybe . . . you went a little crazy; you know how you get. Everyone's worried about you, you know. Detective McCarran—I'm sorry, *Wyatt*. You're running all over town, confronting Warren, talking to his neighbors and family. Harassing Jinny, making her cry. See, Warren and I are partners in this thing now, so I know everything." She grinned wildly. "You found me out here, went a little wild. Tried to hit me . . ." Alice stopped, looked around, grabbed a shovel off the wall. "Maybe with this. I mean, fitting, don't you think?"

Hannah didn't have an answer. She couldn't think a step ahead of Alice, her mind moving underwater. She had to *think*, but every breath felt shaky. Every racing thought edged out the one before it, and she couldn't focus on any of it. Alice was going to kill her. *Think, think, Hannah!*

Alice continued, "I was just defending myself. I plead self-defense, I get to walk away. That's how it works. If you try to kill me and I accidentally kill you, I'm free to go. Start my life over, like I wanted to all those years ago. Without the drugs, knowing my baby girl will rest in peace."

Hannah took a step back toward the door, adrenaline surging under her skin. "You should do that. Go and start over."

"Well, I can't now, see? You know everything." *Swipe, slice* went the knife.

Hannah's hand fumbled behind her back for the latch. In seconds she was outside, running down the path, away from the shed.

Behind her, she heard the thump, thump, thump of Alice's nursing clogs.

CHAPTER
FIFTY-FIVE
Now

Hannah had one advantage over Alice. Alice may have been staying at Brackenhill for a year and a half, but Hannah knew the forest. She knew the trails and the paths, the rocks and trees. She took off down the path that led from the shed back to the driveway, crossed over the driveway, and veered left on the trail that paralleled Valley Road. This path was steep and in some places dark where the towering pines and ash trees formed a jungle canopy overhead, blocking out the bright full moon.

Hannah ducked under boughs and kept her eyes on the ground, trying as best she could to make out the roots and rocks. Breaking a leg or even rolling an ankle might cost her her life.

But still.

When the embankment came into view, she didn't think it or plan it. She just zipped to the left and tucked herself into the hillside between Valley Road and the path in a small gully swollen with rotting leaves and stagnant rainwater. Something scurried over her left foot, either a large spider or a small vole, and Hannah bit the inside of her cheek to keep from screaming.

She could make herself small. She'd spent her whole life practicing.

Alice thundered by—grace wasn't her strong suit. Her thick rubber soles slapped the ground, the wet leaves sliding.

Hannah knew that fifty feet or so past the embankment, the trail tapered into a narrow edge, thin as a blade and slicked with a mushroom bed. Especially treacherous in the summer, when the temperature dipped and a heavy rain pounded down, spreading spores.

To the left of the narrow trail was a steep incline up to Valley Road, not completely impassable but not easily traversed without hiking boots and equipment. To the right was a gully, deep and wide, the bottom of which contained a tributary.

An accidental slide into the gully could easily break a leg.

When she and Julia had ridden their bikes into town, they'd avoided that stretch of ground and instead cut to the left before the embankment entirely, walking their bikes on the shoulder of Valley Road until the path evened out, widened, and became safer than the road.

Hannah doubled back and felt her way along the embankment, making sure to keep herself flush with the foliage. If Alice looked back, she wouldn't be able to make out the shape of Hannah against the shadows of the trees.

Hannah's hand hit something hard. A metal knob. Her fingertips reached out, spread along the expanse of greenery, and found only splintered wood.

The storm shelter. Underneath her palm, the old wood seemed to buzz with life. If she'd had a light, she knew she would have seen the door was painted green, peeling and flaking.

Find the green door.

The key in Hannah's sweatshirt pocket hummed. She'd forgotten about it. She'd taken to wearing the same hooded sweatshirt every day now, not wanting to venture to the basement to do laundry.

Her fingertips found the doorknob again and then the lock. She slid the fleur-de-lis key into the lock, and underneath her palm she felt the click of tumblers sliding into place, a sick swelling in her chest, her

breath coming in gulps. Something about the storm shelter felt dangerous, hidden. The knob turned in her hand, and she was able to slide
into the narrow stairwell and ease the door closed in front of her. She
could only hope the vines fell back in front of the door, the way she'd
found them. Or that Alice wouldn't double back and look closely with
her lantern. Or that she'd fall into the gully.

If Alice found Hannah here, she'd kill her.

Hannah ran her hands along the walls on either side. The stairwell
was narrow, with dirt walls and only (she counted) four steps into what
felt like a larger room. She could hear her breathing hollow in her ears,
her pulse loud as a full drum line at a football game. She didn't have
Alice's battery lantern or even a flashlight.

Too bad she wasn't in the greenhouse. Uncle Stuart always kept
small portable propane lanterns in the greenhouse. Mostly because he
said the batteries didn't make it through the weather changes, and he
wanted to make sure he had them for emergencies if he had to get back.

The matches! From Pinker's! She'd swiped them so she'd have easy
access to the phone number, address, manager's name. She lit the first
match.

The room was tiny, maybe ten by ten. There were shelves on the
walls. Flour sacks on the floor.

A pulse of familiarity. She'd never been here before; they'd never
been able to find a key.

But wait. That wasn't right. She'd been inside, hadn't she?

On the first shelf to her left sat three of Uncle Stuart's propane lanterns. She hadn't even known he'd ever used this room. He must have
stored them and not remembered? He was always prepared. Behind
the lanterns were stacked cans of vegetables—corn and carrots—and
a carton of preserved eggs coated in an oily sheen. Two decades old,
rotting, inedible.

She lit another match to see what she was doing and turned the
knob on the bottom of the lantern. A gentle hiss told her the tank was

full. She touched the flame to the filament, and the room lit up with a muted glow.

It was the room from her vision at Jinny's.

Hannah felt the breath leave her lungs, her heart constrict.

A woman stood in the center, her face in shadow, her hair long and loose around her shoulders, shining even in the dim light. She moved, and the swish of a yellow sundress swirled around her legs.

"Julia," Hannah said, her voice a croak, her throat closing, her vision starting to pinhole. Her hand went to her mouth in a silent scream.

"Hello, Hannah," said her sister. She stepped closer, the lantern light bouncing off the walls, creating shadows and pockets of light and dark. She smiled then, at once familiar and foreign and beautiful, after all this time.

And then, "You came back."

CHAPTER
FIFTY-SIX
Now

Hannah cried out, her voice strangled. Julia! Here!

What was real? It didn't seem real. She reached out, touched her sister's soft skin, her hand as warm as her own. Hannah hugged her fiercely, her vision blurred with tears.

"How are you here?" Hannah asked, her thoughts tumbling. "I knew you'd come back."

"I've been here the whole time," Julia said slowly. She held Hannah out at arm's length and studied her face. "I'm still here."

"That's . . . not possible. How?" Hannah looked around. There was no food, no water. Just the small enclosure of the storm shelter, lined with shelves containing old canned vegetables; even the oiled eggs would be rotten. A dirt floor. In the corner a burlap blanket. On the far back wall, a second door, seemingly secured.

Nothing about any of this seemed real or possible. But then again, with Brackenhill, nothing ever had.

"Hannah, look at me," Julia said softly, her voice almost soothing, and Hannah felt herself lulled into the spell: the small dark room, her sister—alive!—who had come back for her, as she'd known she would.

"I knew you'd come back," Hannah said again, repeating herself and knowing it and not caring.

"Look at me," Julia repeated, her voice softer still, and finally Hannah did. Her sister's face didn't look a day over seventeen: pink, plump cheeks, her lips full despite the years, her eyes still shining, sparkling.

"You haven't aged a bit," Hannah said, pressing her palms together. "You look incredible. I'm just so happy." And she was so happy her chest felt tight with joy. She forgot about Wyatt and Huck and Stuart and Brackenhill and Fae. Her whole world felt bright again, like Julia could open up parts of her heart that had been sewn shut forever.

"Remember how excited we were when we found this place?" The memory came rushing back, the two of them finding the little door in the side of the hill. And trying every which way to open it and failing, the lock rusted shut. Wait, that wasn't right. It hadn't been rusted shut. What was it? Hannah couldn't remember.

"Why haven't I aged, Hannah?"

Why did Julia keep saying her name like that? Like the night in the park, the way everyone had treated her like she was crazy. She hadn't been crazy. She'd been angry; there was a difference.

"You've always been the beautiful one," Hannah said finally, her voice faltering.

Click, click. The turning of a key. Thump, thump.

Why couldn't she get that out of her head? She'd always done that—hyperfocused on things. Dwelling, her mother had said. She was a dweller. *Click, click. Thump, thump.*

"Hannah, listen to me. I didn't run away. You know that, right?"

"Of course you did. Everyone said Aunt Fae killed you, but I knew that wasn't possible. That wasn't possible, right?"

Julia tilted her head, shaking it, and studied Hannah. She took a breath. "Hannah, I need you to think for a moment, okay?"

Hannah nodded. How easily she fell back into it, her sister the leader, the teacher, the mother. She the faithful student, the child.

Oh, there was so much she had to tell her. Wyatt and Huck and Aunt Fae. Aunt Fae! Oh, poor Julia. "Aunt Fae is dead, Julia. She died in a car accident—"

"Hannah, STOP." Julia's voice was loud and firm in the tiny room, and Hannah's thoughts stilled. Her sister always did this, though. If Hannah got too excitable, Julia tempered it. Hannah had been too much for Julia. Too much for Trina. Too much for everyone.

"I didn't run away. I need you to think. I need you to remember. You need to remember." Julia's voice edged higher. She took Hannah's hands in her own, and now they felt cold. "Think, Hannah. I can't make you remember. Only you can do that."

"It was starting to rain. You packed a bag. The path was slippery. I hurt my ankle." Hannah spoke slowly, the images coming in bursts.

"Did you really hurt your ankle?"

Yes. No. "We would be sent back to Plymouth. I just wanted to stop you from going to the police."

"But then what?"

"I just wanted to stop you. I just wanted to stay here," Hannah whispered.

"Then what, Hannah?" Julia pleaded with her, her face wet with tears.

Hannah shook her head, closed her eyes. Her sister's face in her memory, white in the blue light of the moon. *Fae killed Ellie. I have proof. We aren't safe here.*

You ruin everything. You ruined Wyatt. You ruined Brackenhill. We were so happy, before. I can't go back to Plymouth.

"You ruin everything. You're still doing it," Hannah moaned, the dirt hard beneath her knees when she sank down, resting her forehead against her forearms. Julia held tight to Hannah's hands, swaying slightly. "Stop. Just stop ruining everything."

Click, click. The snap of an old lock. Not rusted.

The key in her fingertips. A fleur-de-lis.

Oh my God.

Hannah wanted to crawl inside the dirt, bury herself. Make it stop, the pain, the emptiness, the *missing*.

She'd been so angry. Furious. She remembered everything suddenly, like a flash. The fury, the hurt. She'd been so tired.

What had she done?

CHAPTER
FIFTY-SEVEN
Then

August 2, 2002

"Julia, wait!" Hannah's voice cut across the courtyard. The moon was bright, but Hannah had grabbed one of Stuart's battery-powered lanterns from the kitchen. Julia turned, her duffel bag slung over her shoulder, and studied her sister.

Hannah was so tired. Her body was screaming for sleep, her legs heavy and back aching. And yet her heart raced and stuttered. Couldn't find a rhythm.

"Where are you going?" she called after her. Julia turned away then, hefted her bag higher, and took off down the path toward town, legs pumping.

Hannah raced after her.

Julia, who had everything: Wyatt. Josh Fink. Secrets. Friends. Trina. She was going to ruin everything. For what? Because she wanted to? Everything Julia did was because she wanted to. Because she didn't care who she hurt. How could she have not seen it before? Julia didn't love

Hannah. Julia loved Julia. She didn't care who she stepped on as long as she got what she wanted. She wanted to leave Brackenhill? She'd make sure it happened. By going to the police? About what? What lies would she make up now?

Hannah was destined to live in her big sister's shadow, forever falling short. The uglier one. The dumber one. The one that was ignored by her mother and preyed upon by her stepfather. She couldn't go home to Plymouth. She would not be made to leave Brackenhill again.

Julia picked up speed.

Hannah had never been to this part of the forest at night. The path to town was steep and narrow, pebbled with rocks, and Hannah's ankle rolled, her hip hitting a painful root. She leaned forward to massage it, her fingertips finding the tender spot below the bone. Her sister's blonde hair in the distance was growing fainter; she could barely make her out. In a few seconds she'd be gone.

Hannah looked around and saw with astonishment that she'd tumbled right outside the embankment. From the path the embankment looked nondescript, the side crawling with dead blackberry vines, spindly and broken. Hannah knew what lay underneath the vines.

A door.

Slowly, as if in a trance, she touched the fleur-de-lis key in her pocket. And then *she knew*. She'd tried every door in Brackenhill but this one.

She stood, tentatively putting weight on her ankle. It seemed fine. She faked a limp.

"Julia!" she called after her sister, her voice breaking with the effort. The night was still. Bright. Clear. In the far distance, she heard the rush of the river, so faint, like the inside of a conch shell.

Julia stopped, turned. "Leave me alone, Hannah!" she yelled back, and Hannah felt the burn of fury in her gut. *That bitch.*

"I'm hurt!"

She retracted the key from her pocket and pulled the blackberry vines away from the opening. Just as she'd thought: a rough wooden door, once painted but now splintered and weathered.

The key fit perfectly in the old padlock. When the door swung open, she saw nothing but concrete steps down into blackness.

"Julia!" Hannah called again, the lantern casting dark shadows into the cavern.

So strange, thought Hannah, *that I'm not afraid.*

Hannah descended the steps, careful with her ankle, holding on to the wall. Julia's face appeared above her from the opening, moon bright and shining.

"Hannah, what are you doing?"

"I'm hurt. I fell." Hannah felt the half lie in her mouth, sweet and full. Would her sister worry? She might pretend to worry.

"Hannah, please."

Hannah, please. Oh, a refrain from her childhood. *Please go away. Please leave me alone. Please be quiet. Please stop talking. Please make yourself smaller. No, smaller. There, now you are invisible.*

"I got the door open," Hannah said from the center of the room. She swung the lantern out before setting it down in the middle of the floor: shelves, flour sacks, canning jars—some filled with brown liquid, most empty. A pile of burlap in the center of the room. A few glass jugs filled with water.

"Hannah, it's not the right time for this. Please, I have to go." Julia's voice was quick, panicky.

"You don't have to go. You *choose* to go."

"You don't understand anything!" Julia screamed, her face red with rage. "I just need you to leave me alone for five minutes. You don't! You're always after me. Do you know there are bigger things happening than *you* this summer?"

"Why would I know anything? You don't talk to me. You haven't talked to me in months."

Julia panted, trying to catch her breath. She descended the concrete stairs, stepping carefully into the beam from Hannah's lantern. Finally, she said, calmer, "Hannah, listen to me. She killed Ellie. Aunt Fae *killed someone*. Maybe more than one. We are not safe here. We are not safe with her."

"That's bullshit. Aunt Fae couldn't kill anyone!"

Did Julia's selfishness know no bounds? She'd accuse Aunt Fae of murder?

"You take everything from me." Hannah covered her face, willed the tears to come, but her eyes stayed dry. She felt nothing: not fear, not sadness, just a blank emptiness deep inside where feelings should have been. Like she'd been flayed open, all her insides out for the world to see, and now she had nothing left.

Hannah didn't recognize the girl in front of her: the tangled blonde hair, the flush of her cheeks, the sour smell of her. "I can't go back to Plymouth. Do you understand? Do you know what he does to me?" Her voice cracked, the tip of an unpleasant feeling surfacing. Despair. Hannah tamped it down, stamped it out. "Did he do it to you?"

It was a big gun, Hannah knew. Her sister wilted, her face transformed, and Hannah had her answer. *Not anymore.* Julia didn't have to say it.

Julia's old silence was Hannah's new burden.

Fuck that.

Julia took two steps forward and folded her sister in her arms. Hannah didn't return the embrace, just waited. Counted to five. Breathed in and out. Bubbles of anger rising up, her throat on fire with it, her skin burning where Julia touched her. Julia, who had always sworn she'd protect her.

Hannah slipped out of the hug and bounded up the concrete steps two at a time.

"Hannah!" Julia yelped.

Outside, the air felt cooler. A breeze was blowing a storm in. The air hummed with energy.

Hannah slammed the door shut.

Clicked the padlock closed. Click, click.

Julia's footfalls hit the concrete steps on the other side. Then: thump, thump.

"What are you doing, Hannah? Let me out!"

Then, "Hannah, please." And softer, again.

Thump, thump. The weight of her sister's fists on the other side of the door.

Hannah on the outside. Combing the vines—just so—with her fingertips over the wood. Until the hillside looked like a hillside, nothing more or less.

The muffled sound of her voice. "Hannah, please."

If she took three steps back, onto the path, Hannah couldn't hear it anymore. Tamped down by earth and dirt and the quiet sound of rain and the rumble of thunder.

Like no one had ever been there.

CHAPTER FIFTY-EIGHT
Now

How long had she been there?

What time was it?

Thump, thump. Hannah, please.

Thump, thump. Hannah, please.

Thump, thump. Hannah, please.

And then, "Hannah, get up." A woman's voice.

Hannah lifted her head off the dirt floor. Expected to see Julia, face pinched with anger at what she'd done. But no, Julia was dead. She was gone. That was Hannah's fault. She felt the beginnings of the truth of that: the dull body ache, something sharp in her chest, making it hard to breathe.

Instead Alice stood above her, the hunting knife glinting in her hand. Hannah sucked in air. Julia was gone.

"How did you . . . get in here?"

"You were moaning. I could hear it from the path. Screaming, really." Alice shook her head, her eyebrows knitted sympathetically. "I have to say I wasn't expecting this. I thought you were long gone." She smiled, all lips, no teeth. "You killed your sister?"

"Where is Julia?" Hannah asked. "What have you done to her?"

"Julia? Hannah, dear. You aren't well, are you?" Alice tipped her head to the side, scrutinized Hannah's face. "Have you been sleeping poorly?" Her voice took on a sympathetic tone. "Did you take the Klonopin like I told you?"

"Detective McCarran will be looking for me." Hannah's voice shook when she said it. An empty threat, and they both knew it.

"Oh dear, I'm afraid he won't. *Wyatt*, as you affectionately call him, has no idea you're here. See, there's no service underground. There's no cell service in this forest."

Hannah struggled to stand but felt weighted—heavy and broken—and her mind slogged through the possibilities. The door behind Hannah, where did it lead? She had no idea. Underground, she assumed. Alice blocked her exit to the forest.

"Where's my sister?"

"Your sister is dead because you killed her," Alice snapped.

She had no idea what to trust—what tricks her mind was playing on her. She'd spent the past two weeks walking through Brackenhill in a dream state: half-asleep, half-awake. She had no idea if this was any different. Had Julia been here? No. Because that was not possible. What Alice had said made sense.

Hannah had killed Julia. She'd left her in the storm shelter to die.

Her mind handed her images then, things she'd long forgotten. The day after, she and Uncle Stuart had combed the forest, calling for Julia. Circling past the storm shelter, down to the shed, through the courtyard, and down the river. Over and over again. Each pass of the storm shelter, Hannah would call her sister, wait a beat and listen, but hear nothing back. She remembered the feeling of relief then, a sagging, heart-pounding, thrumming relief.

No. Hannah had loved Julia. Hadn't she? Oh God. Hannah was a monster. A killer.

Ellie had pushed Ruby, the impulse of a child. Fae had killed Ellie, blinded by grief and rage. Hannah had killed Julia (she could hardly believe it still) out of fear. Alice had killed Fae for revenge. A tragic, violent daisy chain. Brackenhill hadn't killed anyone: they'd all done it to themselves, consumed and isolated.

Oh God. Hannah was one of them now. Had been the whole time.

Alice stepped forward, her hair wild, her breath coming in gasps, the hunting knife flashing. A graze off Hannah's shoulder and a slicing pain.

Hannah turned and took two large steps to the door in the back of the storm shelter. She said a silent prayer that the door would be unlocked and pushed with her whole body weight. The door flew open, almost sending her spinning into a dark hallway. The lantern swung wildly in her hand, and she kicked the door shut behind her. In the hallway before her lay a stack of cut wood.

She wedged the first two-by-four between the walls of the hallway, in front of the door. From the other side the door opened violently against the aging beam. She stacked five beams, one on top of the other, wedging them between the walls of the door, just to keep it closed.

The banging against the interior door stopped, and Hannah realized what Alice must have already known: the door to the forest remained unlocked. Alice was free. The beams just bought Hannah time.

How much?

That depended on where she was.

She swung the lantern out in front of her. The tunnel stretched as far as she could see, narrow, the sides packed dirt and shored with rough-hewn beams every few yards. She understood now that the beams she'd used to bar the shelter door had been used in the construction of the original tunnel. By whom?

Hannah took off running, the lantern shaking in her hand and her breath coming in panicked gasps. The tunnel seemed to get smaller and more cramped, until she was hunched over. If she stood, the top of her head touched the dirt. When she passed the wooden braces, she had to duck. Where would she end up? The castle? What was above her? The courtyard? Would she eventually hit the Beaverkill? Would she come out in a manhole in Rockwell?

She had a momentary panic. A sudden flood of water would kill her. There was nowhere to go. It was too far to run back, and she had no idea of her destination.

Hannah pressed forward, the lantern flickering, lasting longer than it probably should have. Who knew how old the propane tank was or when it had been put there?

The tunnel wound around a curve, and Hannah slowed as she followed the sharp right bend.

And came abruptly to yet another wooden door.

Hannah took several calming breaths and pushed on this door the way she had the one at the storm shelter. It didn't open. She tried the knob—turning one way, then the other. Locked.

Hannah removed the key from her pocket. It was a perfect fit for the lock, and the door clicked open easily. Her hand shook as she pushed it open.

She was in the labyrinth.

Oh God. The basement.

CHAPTER
FIFTY-NINE
Now

The basement was dark; the lights had long ago burned out and the light bulbs not been replaced. Who would have replaced them? Stuart? There was nothing of Fae's or Stuart's in the basement anyway, save for the first small room. The rest, well, the rest was for them. For Julia and Hannah.

Hannah's skin prickled, and blood rushed in her ears. She hadn't been down in the basement since she was twelve. She remembered dropping cards one after the other. She remembered being stuck in the center room, the walls closing in literally and figuratively, Julia's breath hot on her cheek, suffocating her, making her feel short on oxygen. They'd screamed until Stuart had come to rescue them, the door popping open easily, and he'd shaken his head, grumbling about their "wild imaginations."

They followed him out of the maze of rooms, and the cards were numbered in order. Julia poked at one with her toe: *Look!* Ten, nine, eight, seven, six, five, four, three, two, one. In order. Unreal. They weren't crazy; the rooms, the index cards, had shifted when they were alone. They'd both witnessed it. There were still two or more doors in every room, but Uncle Stuart walked purposefully, in a straight line, and in a heartbeat they'd been climbing the steps back to the kitchen.

Now Hannah hesitated. She hadn't then, when they were kids, but now she stopped. The first door she came to was ajar, only slightly. She paused with her hand on the doorknob, not knowing what she'd find. The lantern sent strange shadows racing along the walls, and Hannah closed her eyes.

She was an adult now. This nonsense about shifting rooms was just that: nonsense. The first room was dark, empty. Cobwebs gathered in the corners, and strange shapes darted around the walls, thrown off by the swinging lantern and Hannah's shaky hand. Hannah tried to remember the path, then work backward. When she and Julia had come down as children, they had made sequential rights and ended up at the center. She assumed if she made lefts, she would eventually end up back at the kitchen stairs.

She couldn't remember the number of rooms, but as she looked around, she noticed a white card on the floor. She flipped it with her toe.

#11

Immediately Hannah's eyes welled. Tangible evidence of a Brackenhill adventure with Julia. She bent down and picked it up. Instinctively she held it to her nose, hoping for . . .what? Julia's perfume? Silly.

It should have been yellowed with age, dirty, curled at the edges, but it wasn't. The card was bright white, seemingly untouched by time, the edges crisp, the writing still sharp. She ran a finger over the ink, half expecting it to bleed onto her skin. Hannah replaced the card on the floor instead of keeping it.

The second door, straight through, was closed tight. Hannah had to jiggle the handle, the doorjamb swollen with humidity. The door finally gave. The second room, too, was empty except for cobwebs. She studied the floor: dirt, no discernible footprints. Had no one been down here at all since she and Julia? Seemed impossible.

A second index card. She flipped it over. Blinked.

#2

Hannah sucked in a breath. Closed her eyes. Visualized the walk back with Stuart leading the way, watching those little handwritten index cards count down in perfect order their foolishness.

Now here was proof.

She was an adult; this was ridiculous.

The house seemed to sigh, something from deep within like bellows, the walls themselves exhaling, and the air shifted. Smelled different: stale and ripe now. Like a living thing.

Or. Something like death.

Hannah pushed through the third door, searching immediately for the white index card.

#5

Then the next:

#8

She pushed through door after door, straight from one side to the other, never using the doors on either side, just kept on in a straight line like Uncle Stuart had done on the way back out. And yet the cards were all out of order.

A simple, grown-up explanation: someone had been down in the basement and moved the cards in the past seventeen years. Plausible. But who would do that and why?

A test occurred to her. She exited number eight and entered number one.

Closed both doors and waited a moment. She heard it—or perhaps felt it—the moving of air, like the house was *breathing*.

With her eyes closed, Hannah pushed open the door she'd just come through. She opened her eyes and searched the floor, seeking the white square card.

Saw it lying on the floor: *#11*

She was back at the beginning. Or the end.

No. It was impossible. She turned and pushed open the opposite door, which should have led to number ten.

#2

Then the next room:

#8

She somehow had started over. Hannah tried to remember the initial order—eleven, two, five, eight. Her head swam, and she felt panic settle in her bones. Oh God, how was she going to get *out?*

Her synapses were misfiring, making her thoughts ping around like pinballs. She was desperate to get out. She didn't care about anything: Julia, Wyatt, Huck, Virginia. She only cared about getting to the end, finding the end. Getting out of the castle, leaving Brackenhill behind, and then what?

She'd left Julia to die. Her life was never going to be the same.

How long had she been in the basement? It felt like hours. Days.

Hannah took a breath. In. Out. In. Out. If she ran from one side of the maze to the other, maybe she'd make it. She rushed through the doors, one after each other in a straight line, leaving them swinging open. Ran, her feet pounding on dirt, leaving footprints in the dust. The fifth room made an L shape; she turned the corner easily and pushed through the doors one after the other. Not bothering to look at the cards, just *11, 10, 9, 8, 7, 6, 5, 4, 3, 2.*

The trick was to keep the doors open.

Finally, the #1 card fluttered at her feet. She looked up the steps to the door into the kitchen.

She should just let Alice kill her. Then at least Huck would think his fiancée was a good, moral person.

Maybe, just maybe, it was this fucking house.

She who lives here goes insane. Aunt Fae's aunt. Aunt Fae. Hannah. Alice.

She belonged here now. There was no "after" for her anymore. Alice couldn't kill Hannah, and she couldn't go back to Virginia. She didn't belong anywhere but Brackenhill. Not anymore.

As sure as the Beaverkill flowed southwest, you should never prune Juliet roses in the summer, and Brackenhill was haunted by ghosts—living and dead.

CHAPTER SIXTY
Now

The kitchen was dark. Brackenhill was dark.

Hannah crept upstairs. If she could hide and text Wyatt, maybe he would come arrest Alice. She didn't dare make a phone call. Alice could be anywhere.

It was likely that Alice knew the storm-shelter tunnel led to the basement. She could be lying in wait. Hannah ascended the curved concrete steps. A nice thing about concrete: it was silent, her feet barely making a sound.

In the hallway, Hannah turned down the lantern and listened.

Hiss, hum from Uncle Stuart's room.

Creak, click from somewhere in the belly of the house.

Please come BH, Hannah texted Wyatt.

Inching along the wall, Hannah ducked into the first room in the hall that wasn't Uncle Stuart's. It was Ruby's.

The netting floated over the bed, ethereal and beautiful.

In the moonlight, the room seemed to glow. A rustle behind her, and Hannah spun one way, then the other.

A whisper.

A giggle.

The room seemed to echo with the spirits of little girls. The purple walls, the pink bedding. Tiny, quick footsteps across the plush carpeting.

The music box on the dresser spontaneously played a sluggish version of "Clair de Lune," the ballerina spinning slowly, drunkenly.

And then, "Hannah." And Alice stood in the middle of Ruby's room, her face contorted. She didn't even look like herself anymore. Her hair was wild, her hands steady, her face steel. She was slight but powerful, and Hannah found herself truly afraid.

Alice lunged, the hunting knife at shoulder level, aiming for Hannah's neck. Hannah ducked to the left, and Alice crashed hard into the window, the force of a full-body blow breaking the painted seal. Hannah watched in horror as it cracked outward, the glass splintering, the latch giving way, and the windows swinging wide for the first time in over twenty years.

The knife fell to the courtyard below, clattering against the concrete. Alice's hand shot out, gripped the window frame, her balance failing.

Hannah could have saved her. Reached toward her, grabbed her hand, pulled her to safety. Alice let out a scream. It reverberated through the mountains.

Hannah reached her arms out, not to save her but to push her.

One second, Alice was screaming. The next, she was gone.

CHAPTER
SIXTY-ONE
Now

1:13 a.m.

Hannah's mind was blank. She sat on the floor of Ruby's room, not looking out the window at the courtyard below. She didn't know how much time passed before she felt a hand on her shoulder. She turned her head.

Huck.

Hannah stared at his face. She knew it as well as her own but felt like she was seeing it for the first time. The long, straight nose. The heavy-lidded eyes. His eyebrows creased with worry. His jaw ticcing.

"I called the police," he said, indicating the window. "What happened?" A task man as always. Taking care of the business of the moment.

Hannah closed her eyes, sank her cheek back to her knee, and said nothing. Didn't know how to answer the question. Since when? Since 2002?

"I'm sorry I left," he continued, squatting down next to her. Rubbing his palm on her back. She leaned into his warmth. "I've been calling you for days. I finally couldn't take it anymore and drove up here right after work."

"I texted you," Hannah said, her voice floating.

"I didn't get any texts," Huck replied softly.

She believed him; she didn't have a reason not to. She just wanted him to carry her away from Brackenhill, away from Rockwell. She wanted him to take care of everything for her, like he always had. She wanted the life she'd had before: before she'd known what she'd done to her sister, before she'd known that Fae had killed Ellie. She thought of Alice gasping her last breaths on the concrete below.

"Alice killed Fae," Hannah said to Huck. "So I killed Alice."

And there it was. She couldn't just leave it all behind because she belonged here. Could murder be genetic? She was one of them. A killer, continuing the Brackenhill tradition. In fact, she was the worst offender. She'd killed Julia; then she'd killed Alice.

Self-pity had never been her style, but maybe it was time to wallow a bit. Or at least self-sequester.

"Hannah," Huck said, uncertain what to make of her admission.

"Hannah," said a voice from the doorway.

Wyatt.

CHAPTER
SIXTY-TWO
Now

"Hannah, are you okay?" Wyatt said softly. "I've been calling you all day. Your phone is never off for this long. I got worried."

"At one a.m.?" Huck asked amiably, his head cocked.

"I'm fine," Hannah said, tired of repeating herself. So tired of everything. She wanted to lie down on the plush carpet and go to sleep. "Alice is out there. I pushed her."

Wyatt held up a hand. "Hannah, slow down. What happened?"

"She had a knife. She killed Fae. I followed her to the shed. She's been sleeping in there. I confronted her about Fae, and she tried to kill me. I . . ." Hannah didn't know how to explain the rest. The chase through the woods. The storm shelter. Julia. She closed her eyes. Skipped over it. "She chased me here. Tried to stab me. I pushed her out the window."

He knelt next to her, replacing Huck. Touched her shoulder, pulled away a bloody finger.

"You should be seen at the hospital," Wyatt said quietly.

"Why aren't you surprised?" Hannah asked him. He stood up.

"We put it together today," Wyatt admitted. "Actually, Jinny tipped us off. She's the one who told me that Alice was Ellie's mother. From there, it was easy. She's not registered as a nurse. We were going to arrest Alice tomorrow. For Fae's death."

"I killed my sister," Hannah said. "I killed Julia." She felt removed from herself, distant, watching the scene unfold like an outsider. She'd expected the words to be harder to say. She'd expected Wyatt to immediately arrest her.

"Hannah." Wyatt and Huck exchanged a look. They were saying her name like that again: like the day at the fish fry when they were kids, like Julia had in the tunnel.

"I know what I did. I remember it. I didn't for a long time, but I do now." The sob crept up her throat, bubbled out.

"Hannah, you're not thinking clearly. Let's not worry about . . . Julia now," Wyatt said.

"She's down there somewhere." Hannah indicated the basement. "I'm sure of it."

"How do you know?"

"I saw it. I saw her. She told me." Had it been her mind or her sister's spirit? At Brackenhill, you could never really tell. Huck ran a palm across his forehead, then through his hair. He didn't believe her. Why would he? Why would anyone?

"We'll find her, okay?" Wyatt put his arm across Hannah's shoulders, and she let him. She looked over Wyatt's head at Huck, who stood a few feet away, his hands in his pockets. He looked from Hannah to Wyatt and back.

He knew.

Hannah was an adulterer and a murderer. And Huck knew.

Maybe he'd leave her now. The thought was a relief. He could find someone with less baggage. He didn't do baggage. She could stop pretending to be fine, to be whole. She could be one half again, the way it had felt for the last seventeen years, only this time openly.

She was so tired of pretending.

CHAPTER
SIXTY-THREE

Five Months Later

Hannah wiped the countertop down in the kitchen, washed her single plate and fork. She gazed out the small window above the sink, sipping her coffee.

The courtyard was no longer bursting with flowers, because February in the Catskills was brutal and killed all living things all the time.

Hannah found that she quite liked the *deadening*, as she'd come to think of it. Alone in the castle she could hear herself think. The snow was thick and blanketed the grounds such that she could stand outside for an hour and not hear one single sound.

She hadn't visited Uncle Stuart during the last few days of his life. He'd died alone. With the woman who'd killed his wife. While Hannah chased some version of the truth, slept with her childhood boyfriend, and cheated on her fiancé, Stuart had died. Alice knew he had died and left him in the bedroom to follow Hannah. Had she at least been in the room when Stuart took his last breath? Hannah didn't know and never would. Some questions haunted forever; that much Hannah had learned.

Huck went back to Virginia alone, with his vague disappointment that she wasn't who he'd thought she was. She wasn't stable, reliable, put together. Huck didn't do anger or rage. Hannah got to keep Rink, who ran around in the snow in the woods around Brackenhill. At Brackenhill, Hannah didn't have a real job. She was home all day, and Rink could run miles if he wanted. Better for him than to be cooped up in a condo all day while Huck worked. Sometimes Huck texted her, just to check in.

She said nothing to Huck about Julia. She didn't revisit the topic. She just let him believe whatever he wanted about that night in Ruby's room. Let him believe her confession was born of delusion. Trauma from the night with Alice. What harm would that do?

"Did you sleep with him?" Huck asked her once and only once. His voice had been subdued, not angry. He didn't do fiery shows of emotion.

She'd spent much of her relationship with Huck pretending to be easy. Happy. Free. But the truth was she was tethered here, to a life she'd fled long ago, without any right to do so. And now, more than ever, she owed Julia—and Brackenhill—her time.

"No," Hannah lied. Why tell him the truth to only hurt him? She didn't expect or seek forgiveness. Why give him those images, those intrusive middle-of-the-night thoughts?

She needed something Huck could never give her: closure. She still hadn't found it. No one had found it. Not dogs or metal detectors or sonar devices checking for soil disturbances or forensics teams or police. Wyatt said, simply, *You didn't do what you think you did.*

But she knew, down to her marrow, who she was. Who she'd been for seventeen years. What she was capable of. She *remembered* closing the door on her sister. It hadn't been a vision or a dream. It had come back to her, full force.

The days after, though. They remained blank. The castle growing smaller and smaller out the back window of the Buick, four days after Julia went missing. What had happened in those four days?

Some questions haunted forever; that much Hannah had learned. Sometimes crimes weren't mistakes at all.

I'll pick you up around 5, the text from Wyatt pinged. Hannah glanced at her watch. It was just after noon. Good, she had plenty of time. He tried with her—really he did. When she had told him that she and Huck had split up, his eyes brightened. When he touched her, she still felt something, a reverberation up her spine. But it wasn't enough. She had to stay focused. Only after she found what she was looking for would she be free of Brackenhill. She had to break the cycle somehow.

Another text: Do you mind if I bring Nina?

Wyatt's daughter, Nina, loved Brackenhill. She loved the forest, the river, the courtyard bursting with color. Hannah tried to dissuade her, tried to tell Wyatt once, "It's not safe for her here." Hannah, better than anyone, understood the lure of it. The magic. Having Nina in the house was exhausting. Hannah watched her every move. Nina, with her glossy dark hair, her eyes bright with curiosity. It was like holding a mirror up to her eleven-year-old self, seeing Brackenhill for the first time.

Hannah still sleepwalked. She was getting used to it, that coherent dreaming. Knowing where she was and what she was doing while semiconscious. Floating around the castle in a nightgown, her very own ghost. She was growing into the role. The new eccentric who had taken up residence.

"Come on, Rink." Hannah motioned Rink to the basement door. He followed eagerly, happy to have a cameo in Hannah's newfound purpose.

Hannah ambled through the basement labyrinth. Never again had the rooms shifted. She'd long ago collected all the cards and stacked them up on one of the boxes. It could have been stress. Anxiety scrambled your thoughts, played tricks on the eyes. She no longer believed in magic, not the way she used to anyway.

She believed in stress. She believed in the fallibility of the human mind. The ability of the mind to box up certain events and file them away in a locked cabinet. Throw away the key. She believed in the effects of sleep deprivation and emotional trauma. She believed in temporary psychosis. She'd spent the last six months reading psychology articles online. Wandering the grounds of Brackenhill, willing a memory to come rushing back. Furious and clenching when she could not.

Despite Wyatt's protestations, Hannah knew what she'd done.

Sometimes when you push people, they break.

Julia knew Hannah better than Hannah knew herself.

Perhaps Hannah had confessed to her crime knowing Wyatt wouldn't believe her.

Julia hadn't broken out of the storm shelter, run away, and lived happily ever after in some tropical paradise. There was only one outcome that made sense.

Hannah had buried her.

Hannah had slices of memory. It had always been there, but without context she'd always believed it to be a dream vignette.

A shovel full of sandy dirt.

The permeating smell of death, days old.

How had Julia's purse ended up in the Beaverkill? Again, there was only one answer. Hannah couldn't remember the rushing water, the purse sailing through the air, the gentle swish as the current swept it away. She would have been the one to do it, but she had no memory of it.

She had no memory of any of it.

Hannah must have gone back. She had to have returned at some point and found Julia dead. She'd turned it over so many times in her mind and always came to the same conclusion. She'd returned to maybe let her sister out, and Julia had been dead. It was the only possible scenario.

Wes came to retrieve Hannah four days after Julia went missing. She had no clear memories of those four days. Jumbled snapshots. Like photos that fell out of an album, mixed up and out of order.

Four days wasn't enough time to die of hunger or even of dehydration necessarily (although it was possible, according to Hannah's research). As much as Hannah could figure, Julia had died trying to get out of the storm shelter. Perhaps something had fallen on her. Perhaps she'd cut herself trying to break down the door.

She asked Wyatt. "There would have been remains, Hannah. You didn't do what you think you did."

Hannah said nothing.

Instead, she spent hours in the storm shelter, trying to shake something loose. Any memory remained locked up tight. Just one image: dirt sifting over the curve of a spade with a red handle.

You might never find her. Wyatt's voice was gentle when he said it, but the words always felt like a slap. She knew what he thought: that she was broken and maybe even crazy. He encouraged her to see someone. Talk to someone. Hannah admitted he was right about that. And yet if she confessed, even to a therapist, would she go to prison? Then who would find her sister?

She'd tried to make sense of the after: She'd gone back to Plymouth. Her mother had stayed in her room, prayed for Julia's return, and barely spoken to Hannah. Her stepfather never again came into her room, never laid another finger on her. She went back to start her sophomore year of high school. Did she just pick up where she'd left off?

No.

She shunned her friendships. Tracy and Beth had been confused, then distraught, then later, after months, indifferent. She'd been the girl whose sister disappeared. Died. Hannah remembered floating through the rest of high school. Probably failing but getting a pass for being so wrapped up in tragedy.

Her sister should have graduated. Hannah had one sharp memory, one moment where she might have held tight to the memory of what she'd done. The guidance counselor had called her down to her office and presented her with her sister's graduation cap. "You should have this," she said. She meant it to be kind.

Hannah had cried. "It's my fault."

Everyone thought she meant it to be dramatic. Maybe metaphorically. Maybe because they'd fought. The guidance counselor had clucked sympathetically and placed her hand on Hannah's head. "Darling girl," she'd said.

She saw a therapist only once: a young twentysomething blonde woman in a bright office who clicked her pen relentlessly. She looked astonishingly like Julia. The same blonde curls. The same graceful flit of her hand. Hannah never went back.

Hannah pushed through the green door and followed the tunnel that wound approximately a hundred yards. The length of a football field. A few months ago, she'd strung up heavy-duty construction lights. With the flick of a button, the tunnel illuminated, bright as a snowy Catskill morning.

As far as she could see, she'd dug wide holes—trenches, really. The floor of the storm shelter itself had already been completely unearthed, the newly turned dirt a raw reddish-brown color. She'd dug a perfectly measured four feet down.

It had taken her months. If she didn't find what she was looking for in the tunnel now, she'd go back to the beginning, back to the shelter in the little hill, and dig another four feet down. If she had to.

She'd do it forever. She owed it to her sister.

She owed Julia that much.

CHAPTER
SIXTY-FOUR
Nina

Spring 2020

Nina loved the sounds of the forest. There was a bird in the distance that called every afternoon. It sounded like a bike horn that Mom had gotten her for her tenth birthday. Hannah said it was a crane.

Nina sat on the forest floor in a clearing she'd found last weekend. Everything felt different. New and fresh and alive and magical. Like anything was possible here. She could forget about school, about Quinn Palumbo and her band of mean girls that stole the key chains off her backpack when she wasn't looking. She could forget about her best friend, Abigail, who was sometimes nice and fun and happy and sometimes not. Dad said her parents were divorcing, so Nina should have patience with her.

Nina understood divorce. But now Dad lived here, with Hannah, who was her third-favorite person, and then on weekends, she sometimes got to live here, at Brackenhill, which had quickly become her absolute favorite place. Her bedroom had a princess bed with a canopy and everything.

At Brackenhill, she just got to be alone. She got to be herself.

Sometimes the girl would find her. She lived "down the hill," the girl told her.

Today the girl found Nina lying in the middle of the clearing. Her eyes were closed, and she was waiting for the crane. Hannah had told her cranes were creatures of habit—they lived in the same places every year. Fed in the same streams and rivers. This crane felt like hers. She hadn't seen it yet; she'd only heard it.

The girl lay next to Nina in the grass. They both listened for the crane, and when they finally heard its call, ehrrrrret-a-ret-ret, *they gasped and laughed. Nina stood, brushing the dirt from her legs. She had to get back. Hannah would be making dinner. Hannah worried about her roaming the forest by herself.*

She couldn't explain how much she loved it. How alive she felt, for the first time, in the woods. How her skin prickled and the hair on the back of her neck stood up and the woods seemed to come alive along with her, breathing and laughing and whispering secrets that only Nina could hear. Secrets about other lives and magic and love, the air sparkling with mysteries.

She loved the girl too. The girl was older, at least sixteen. Nina didn't dare ask her. She was thoughtful and listened to Nina blather on about school and Quinn or Abigail.

Nina was a little afraid of the girl too. She rarely spoke, just smiled. She followed Nina around the forest as they chased butterflies, shadows, and glints of light. As they ran along the riverbank watching a trout twist out of the winding water, a fly trapped in its mouth. As they hunted for morels (You'll find them when the oak leaves are the size of a mouse's ear, *said* Hannah) *among the hickory and ash trees.*

The girl had long, delicate fingers, and her voice was whispery. She painted Nina's nails with polish Nina borrowed from her mother. The girl told her about the forest, the stories of the castle, the missing girls. It was supposed to be scary, but Nina never felt scared. She just felt welcomed. Happy. Home.

Sometimes Nina would brush the girl's hair, braid it elaborately in a way her mother had taught her, winding it around her head like a princess crown.

She had the most beautiful red hair Nina had ever seen.

ACKNOWLEDGMENTS

First and foremost, thanks to Jessica Tribble for seeing the potential in my story and taking me under her wing at Thomas & Mercer. In its infancy, Brackenhill was a much shallower version of a "ghost book" (although a soft ghost, ha), and she never stopped reminding me to focus on the relationships and the real characters on the page. A particular thanks to Tiffany Yates-Martin, who had an inordinate amount of confidence in my capabilities and said, "What if we did the craziest thing ever?" and then we actually did it. I would not have had the courage for this book on my own. Thanks to the whole T&M team, including (but not limited to) Sarah Shaw, Laura Barrett, Jessica Tribble. As always, thank you to Mark Gottlieb, who works tirelessly on my behalf.

I'm forever indebted to readers, bloggers, Instagrammers, book clubs, Facebook reading groups, Goodreads reading groups, friends, sorority sisters near and far, who continue to read my books, support my work, invite me in, invite me back, tell their friends, show up at my events. I couldn't begin to name all of you for fear of forgetting someone, but I wouldn't still be doing this crazy gig if it weren't for you. Your messages and emails and social media comments and beautiful faces in the crowd lift me up and keep me going.

A particular debt of gratitude to those authors who've talked me off a ledge and/or helped me celebrate with champagne (there is no in-between) this year: Kimberly Belle, Emily Carpenter, Ann Garvin,

Sonja Yoerg, Kim Giarratano, Heather Webb, Elizabeth Diskin, Amy Impellizzeri, Kelly Simmons, and the whole Tall Poppy crew. The ever-expanding lady squad of Bouchercon and Thrillerfest, I love you all to death. I have a true tribe of amazing, kick-ass women behind me, and I'm so incredibly grateful to all of you. Thanks to a few authors who offered timely advice and gave me the courage to tackle my first-ever ghost story simply because it wouldn't leave me alone: Cate Holahan, Jennifer McMahon, Todd Ritter, Wendy Walker. I mean, what's the point if we're not having fun?

And finally, my family. Mom, Dad, Meg, your support and enthusiasm is as great with book seven as it was with book one. Part of my crew of first readers: Becky, Aunt Mary Jo, Molly, and of course, the world's loudest publicist, Unk. It amazes me that you're all not sick to death of me. To Chip, the whole reason I can do any of this is because of you. I only hope I can give you a fraction of the love and support you've shown me. To my girls: the day is soon coming when you'll read my books. The idea of it terrifies me to my very soul. Your mother is fine, I promise. Although, I am very sorry about that time I almost got us killed in the name of researching this book. The trespassing, in retrospect, was probably a bad idea. But if you learned nothing else from me, remember: every terrible adventure is worth having if you end up with a good story to tell later.

ABOUT THE AUTHOR

Photo © 2016 Pooja Dhar

Kate Moretti is the *New York Times* bestselling author of six novels and a novella. Her first novel, *Thought I Knew You,* was a *New York Times* bestseller. *The Vanishing Year* was a nominee in the Goodreads Choice Awards mystery/thriller category for 2016 and was called "chillingly satisfying" (*Publishers Weekly*) with "superb" closing twists (*New York Times Book Review*).

Moretti has worked in the pharmaceutical industry for twenty years as a scientist and enjoys traveling and cooking. She lives in Pennsylvania in an old farmhouse with her husband, two children, and no known ghosts. Her lifelong dream is to find a secret passageway.